That Was Very Nearly Awe

By J.R. Hamantaschen

SOME SORT OF INTRODUCTION

I always tell myself that I should get one of my more popular or more respected peers to write my introductions. Yet it'd be hard for me to criticize the hyperbolic "this young author will blow your mind and probably cure cancer" type of introductions that are so common in the small press world if I succumb to the temptation myself. Also, there's nothing that readies the pitchforks of critical approbation like an introduction that overpromises and underdelivers, so like my mother told me growing up, keep expectations about yourself low and people likely won't be as disappointed.

This is my third collection of short horror fiction. It will likely be my last for the foreseeable future, as I move onto longer works. For fans of mine, I view this collection as a fitting end point and an encapsulation of the themes and motifs I've explored in my short fiction (particularly with the last story in this collection: hopefully that's enough of an impetus to get you to read the whole book!), and a showcase of the styles that worked best in my previous two collections. Like always, I prefer that you read the stories in order. But it's best to say as little as possible and just hope you enjoy what is to come.

As always, I can be reached at Jrtaschen@gmail.com. In addition to my previous two collections, "You Shall Never Know Security" and "With a Voice that is Often Still Confused But is Becoming Ever Louder and Clearer," I also host a weekly podcast called The Horror of Nachos and Hamantaschen, where I bloviate about horror movies, horror fiction, and general horror "culture" with my trusty co-host Derek Sotak. I live in Queens, New York, and if you ever find yourself in New York City, I'm often available to grab a coffee (or a hamantaschen, naturally) and talk horror / ceaseless psychological torments. Over the years I've met several readers for coffee or at conventions, and you've never read any heinous news stories about any of these meetings, right? Right! That's really all the commendation I can give to keep expectations correspondingly low.

Sincerely,
J.R. Hamantaschen
Jrtaschen@gmail.com

PRAISE FOR MY FIRST COLLECTION "YOU SHALL NEVER KNOW SECURITY"

What, did you think I subsist on my own sense of self-worth?

"A twisted, uneasy, satisfying book." - Kirkus Reviews

"A cross between Lovecraft and Chuck Palahniuk, this book of short stories is as memorable as it is terrifying ... we haven't been this horrified by a collection of short stories since Chuck's own 'Haunted' ... 'You Shall Never Know Security' is a wonderful collection of short stories from a dark and original genre voice. That title - it's a promise." - Starburst Magazine

"J.R.'s debut anthology kicks open the doors of the traditional horror fiction genre and takes the reader to a far darker place ... Hamantaschen handles some deep topics ... [t]his is fiction for readers that like to think, that like to be challenged, that like to squirm." - The Drabblecast

"Hamantaschen's stories are beautifully written and quite brilliant in making the reader feel uncomfortable, sympathetic, and horrified all at the same time. There isn't a bad story in the bunch. I thoroughly enjoyed 'You Shall Never Know Security' and its play on human weakness and emotions. Highly recommended." - The Monster Librarian

"In J.R. Hamantaschen's 'You Shall Never Know Security' ... dark fiction is back to what it was meant to be: a bloodcurdling jump into the gloomiest and most sinister corners of the human psyche...[the] stories are the kind that tend to stick with readers after the reading is over." - HP Lovecraft eZine

"J.R. has crushing debts, and the book is pretty cheap now, so why not help him out?" - Paraphrasing the moral from J.R.'s credit card statements

"I have never read anything like this, and I don't know if I ever will. A very high recommendation." - 30 Second Sci-Fi Book Review

"J.R. Hamantaschen's 'You Shall Never Know Security' is one of the best dark fiction collections ever published. It contains fascinating, disturbing and beautifully written stories that range all the way from dark fantasy to horror." - Rising Shadow Magazine

"In all of the above, the author delivers powerful, ugly images, using a battery of verbal pyrotechnics that make the stories demand to be read carefully. Buried in the razzle-dazzle language are clues to the intended meaning. If horror is your poison of choice, these will definitely fill the bill." - Innsmouth Free Press

"J.R. Hamantaschen's 'You Shall Never Know Security' hit me almost immediately with that frisson; the first few pages, the first few stories, crackling with a kind of morbid energy ... the reader will know from the first page whether this collection will enrapture or repel, those in the former camp having found something they have no doubt been starved of and scavenging after for some time." - Ginger Nuts of Horror

"Jesus Fucking Christ I'm essentially groveling to convince you to buy a book that's like 2 dollars on Kindle." - Reality

"Many regard [this book] as a gem of horror lit. We're inclined to agree." - Space Squid

"J.R. Hamantaschen won't be underground for long." - HorrorWorld (this review gets more and more bittersweet with the passage of time)

"I would urge you to keep on writing. You clearly have a nucleus of talent." - S.T. Joshi, in an email after he said he had mixed feelings about two of my stories. I consider this high praise.

PRAISE FOR MY SECOND COLLECTION "WITH A VOICE THAT IS OFTEN STILL CONFUSED BUT IS BECOMING EVER LOUDER AND CLEARER"

Shouldn't J.R. be commended for choosing such an off-putting, overlong title, encasing the book in a doom-laden all-black cover, and refusing to put the title on the front cover? If the sales are any indication, the answer is a resounding "fuck no!"

"A brilliant and vital addition to the landscape of dark fiction…It's not often a collection of this caliber comes around." - HellNotes

"Perturbing, anomalous stories that will bore into readers' minds." - Kirkus

"True, great horror. I love this book." - Chris Lackey, HP Lovecraft Literary Podcast

"9 out of 10 ... there are nine tales in this collection, each of satisfying length and immediately striking, from first page to last… stories that will grip you for their humanity and soul." - Starburst Magazine

"Hamantaschen has a knack for crafting what seems to be an unwieldy tale, but plies it with enough realism and logic to make it work. The ridiculous even seems at home next to the cynical and down-to-earth. His tales are peopled by real and richly crafted characters." - Shock Totem Magazine

"An excellent follow-up to the author's debut collection ... It's one of the most impressive dark fiction collections of the year, because it's fascinatingly different from other collections and contains beautifully written stories ... an exceptionally good and original dark fiction collection that deserves to be read by fans of the darker side of speculative fiction. It's a perfect marriage of literary fiction and dark fiction." - Rising Shadow Magazine

“4 out of 5 stars ... Overall, I enjoyed this collection of short stories ... [t]he stories certainly stayed with me for a few days after reading it.” - Literary Titan (pretty lukewarm-sounding for 4 out of 5 stars but whatever).

“4 out of 5 stars.” - Scream Magazine

"Eclectic, poignant, thought provoking ... too awesome to pass up." - HorrorTalk

"Those who an artistic approach, psychological depth and small details are going to read through this collection and remember it for days to come." - HorrorPalace

“This book is filled with many horrors and some pretty deep and disturbing stories. It may not be for everyone, as any book may or may not, but I found it intriguing and enjoyable.” - The Scary Reviews

"Resonating, delectably weird and spooky collection, thoroughly enjoyable." - IndieReader (received Official IndieReader Stamp of Approval)

“Readers would benefit greatly by taking a gander at Hamantaschen’s mix of stories that lead from one cold dank corner to another.” - HorrorNews Network

“No amount of praise will instill a sense of meaning or purpose or accomplishment. Why don’t you volunteer at a park and plant some fucking trees for children or something.” - Me (until I remember I dislike children)

A Deep Horror That Was Very Nearly Awe

By J.R Hamantaschen

These are works of fiction (but are they really?), and each of the characters, entities, locations, and events portrayed in this work are either products of the author's imagination or are used fictitiously and, let's be honest, a bit facetiously (Isn't this what they want you to think?). Any resemblance to actual persons, living or dead, business establishments, events or locales is entirely coincidental and not intended by the author, with the exception of characters obviously based on people I know, I just want you to know that you will be getting everything coming to you in time, in time, yes, in time, let this serve as a warning dear God I can almost taste it....

All previously published stories contained in this collection remain the sole and exclusive copyright of J.R. Hamantaschen, even if he sometime misspells his own name, including stories published in the collections "CTHULHU, CTHULHU, CTHULHU, CTHULHU!!!: New Approaches to Lovecraft (i.e. Don't Expect Any Cthulhu)"; "LOVECRAFT'S DISCIPLES (P.S. don't be alarmed the introduction will explain that despite that title we actually hate Lovecraft as a person don't worry)"; and "IA! CTHULHU, DAGON, and the INFERNAL QUEST TO JUKE AMAZON'S ALGORITHMS."

A DEEP HORROR THAT WAS VERY NEARLY AWE

transmitted, they shall be transmitted without words, without thoughts, and without consent, appearing in the mind as if they've always been there, just waiting to be unearthed; and to the extent these stories shall be distributed, they shall be distributed surreptitiously and with some degree of shame, a hushed secret, an ignoble pact.

CONTENTS

Rococo Veins and Lurid Stains

I WALK TO the window, as swiftly as I can without drawing attention to myself. I don't want to alert my parents to what is going on. There's no point. Scaring my family needlessly won't do anything. No one would know what happened. I could tell them now what might happen, but why? Who would believe me? I would just die, in my sleep, I guess, and that'd be it.

Kristen killed herself, they'd say, and in a way, they wouldn't be wrong. It's what I'd wanted. I hope that's what my father and mother and brother would eventually settle on. I should write a note, tell them that I chose to kill myself, that it wasn't their fault, that I know they tried their best. It's the best I could really do for them.

I wanted to die but I never wanted to make my family suffer. They didn't do anything wrong, or at least they didn't do anything uniquely wrong, nothing any more wrong than all human beings can't help but do. Sure, they were selfish and entitled and ignorant and oblivious but no more than any other middle-class, suburban family. There are millions of families like that and they don't all have defective daughters who choose death.

I look out the window and I see Aaron. At least that's what he told me his name was, although I guess he didn't have any reason to lie about his name. He still looks to be about my age, so that's consistent from the first time I met him. His black, greasy hair is arched diagonally over his eyes. His eyes are intense, lit by a dark fire. He has raccoon eyes.

I can tell this even though, by all appearances, he's all the way by the curb on the other side of the street and I'm staring out my ground floor living room window. I'm a normal girl with normal vision, 20/20 when squinting. I shouldn't be able to see him so vividly. The only reason I'm able to is because he's allowing me to, no, more like making me, see him.

Am I supposed to be intimidated?

He waves with his right hand. His long-sleeved flannel shirt is rolled up so I can see his wrists, even though it's dusk out and he appears far away. I shouldn't be able to see them so clearly. I see the lurid stain on his right wrist. The hand jerks harshly and the skin of his wrist tears back like the peel of a banana. I can hear the snap that exists only for me.

I see the sharp, multicolored brambles inside his wrist, rising steadily and spreading outward, that make me think of an accelerated time lapse of crops growing in a field. "Rococo veins." That's a term that Aaron had used to describe his exposed gore, beautiful like prickly shrubs made of bone and blood. He told me that phrase, "rococo veins," the second time I'd met him, when he was still trying to impress me with our shared morbid sense of humor. I love decadent words and expressions like that. Rococo Veins and Lurid Stains, sounds like a band I'd love unabashedly for a bit and then feel deeply embarrassed about once I went off to college and "matured" in the way people are expected to do. I didn't really even know what that word Rococo meant but his injuries were such an enticing combination of gross and sad that I just couldn't look away, like an exposed wrist full of car crashes.

Or maybe if I'm being honest I was really scared, too, both scared and fascinated. He was a pretentious dick, I now realize, but a charming dick, and I'd been too fascinated to do anything other than agree. I felt I was doing him a favor. I suppose I was. I suppose I am, still. He seems really eager, I tell myself.

Who am I fooling, he was probably a pretentious dick in real life, which makes me feel really sad and pissed. It's like giving your virginity to someone and, even though you enjoyed it, too, you wonder if that was a gift that should have been saved for someone, I don't know, more worthy?

But then again, I'm a pretentious fool, too, aren't I, so why all the hate? Stop thinking the worst of people. There's no point now.

I breathe heavily and head down for dinner with my entire family. The gang's all here, my father, mother, and brother, all looking at me funny. What else is new? They look at me with worry. Constant worry, and it'd been so satisfying to rail against them all, tell them to stop worrying about me, but they'd been right to worry about me, weren't they?

I look at my mother and am reminded of how much we look alike. We share the same mousy brown hair, same flat nose and too-large forehead. I get my large breasts from her, too, although she doesn't call them that, she refers to them when we've gone bra shopping as our "heavy build" or something like that. When you're a suburban mom you can't just acknowledge you have big tits, you have to refer to them as something else; that type of language is for kids who get in trouble.

I can look at my mother and think about what I'd look like when I get older, and I know I'll never get older and I want to cry. I want to cry and I should, I should share this one great cry with them all, but if I do that, then they'll spend the rest of their lives thinking that this was the last warning sign, that they should have done something to save me. But they can't. I'm beyond saving. It's the greatest, what is that, irony? I'd have a greater irony than any of those O. Henry stories I had to write about in English class.

I wanted to die until the very moment I agreed to do so. It was unbelievable, really.

I've tried to kill myself twice. My parents only know about the second time.

The first time was 92 days ago. Funny, I think life is valueless, yet I kept track of my attempt to end it. If life is valueless, then shouldn't my attempt to end it also be valueless? Anyway, I tried to slit my wrist. Not knowing exactly how to do it and maybe not researching it as a way to subconsciously sabotage my attempt, I made one clean slash too far up on my arm. That hurt like hell but had no chance of doing any permanent damage other than leaving a vicious scar. Really, I slashed my lower forearm rather than my wrist. I immediately got a towel and put pressure on the wound and ran down the block to Eliza's to bandage myself up. I maybe could have bled out and died, I suppose, so I count that as a suicide attempt.

Eliza wanted to die, too, and she had a mixture of concern, awe, and resentment that I'd made such an overt attempt. She thought I'd wait for her, although she's all talk. Then the funny argument that followed, about whether I cut my upper forearm or my lower forearm, had me in stitches (and yes, that was a pun we'd made and further laughed about). It all depended on your perspective: the area near the wrist is the "lower" forearm if you think your arm starts at your shoulder, it's the "upper" forearm if you think your arm begins at your hand. That stupid argument, both of us being so stubborn, Eliza maybe being ultra animated to get over her shock about the whole situation and me being ultra goofy because of my blood loss, all that kind of made me want to go on living. Just the sublime silliness of it. You live for moments like that.

We later settled the question about what constitutes the upper versus the lower forearm by looking it up on Google, and the conclusiveness of the answer kind of sapped my good mood. It made me sad, I know, so dramatic, like the availability of information is a bad thing. It felt like a closed door, just more mystery lost. The silly argument about the forearm with my equally silly friend had made me feel like a naïve child again, and that's a feeling I'm nostalgic for.

So being the pathetic baby I am and still in low spirits about Google having robbed me of the joys of ignorance, I stole, only four days after my first suicide attempt, ten sleeping pills from my mom and downed them with some swigs of purloined Jack Daniels from my parents' liquor cabinet. (Purloined, I like that word. I like words. I don't want to think about things I like anymore. Good thing we are eating chicken cutlets with mashed potatoes for dinner. I'm tired of chicken cutlets and I hate mashed potatoes, think about that, concentrate on the things you hate.) It was stupid to steal the Jack Daniels: if I hadn't taken the Jack, I'd probably be dead. It was the smell of alcohol that tipped my mom off that something was amiss. She checked on me and found me unconscious.

So I got my stomach pumped and had to endure tepid jokes from kids at school when word spread. Eliza was worried for me. Her enthusiasm for killing herself seemed to be gone, and she was in a tough position because her mom instructed her not to associate with me anymore, which of course is the most selfish thing ever. I mean, your daughter's friend is hurting and you order your daughter to shun that friend? What a horrible person. Eliza's mother was always a cunt, no wonder Eliza had the problems she had. Although like I'm one to talk. Things like that though make me want to keep on living just to correct people's terrible fucking opinions and advice. People can be such assholes.

I've been in counseling ever since the second attempt. My parents never let me out of their sight. Even my shithead brother, when he talks to me, is unfailingly nice.

But none of it worked. I don't want to live anymore. That's just the way it is. That's what I'd decided.

><><><

Aaron remembers screaming:

It hurt so badly. I remember looking at my wrists and thinking how selfish and stupid I am, how crazy am I, why am I doing this, my poor mother, my poor mother, I feel so badly for her, that's even worse than the pain somehow.

I remember thinking, "I'm dying, I'm dying, I'm dying." I'd thought before, "I'll show them," but then it was, "I'm dying, I'm dying, I'm dying." Like when you have the flu and your brain is infected with macabre thoughts, when you're dying your brain goes into manic overdrive. I saw the blood as life, I saw it gushing out of me, and I thought how fucking stupid I was. I'd thought life was pointless and worthless, and I always had a flair for the melodramatic so kept I burying myself more and more in that idea, that people are so stupid, that life is so worthless, how I'll show them, I'll get back at them, and, lacking the ambition to blow everyone up, I sat in the tub and gashed open my wrists, and as I saw that blood pour out of me I realized how wrong I was about everything. Like this was getting back at anyone, like they'd care.

Please God, I'm so sorry. I didn't mean this, I need to take it back. My wrist burns in a terrible way, in an unalterable way.

Mom. Mom. Mom. You don't deserve this. I saw her face but even that's robbed from me because as I was dying my memories of her were being distorted. I saw red behind my eyes, so her face was blindingly red, like staring directly at the rising sun, and dripping, gloopy. What did I think this would be? Did I think I'd gain some insight?

The mole on my mother's face, the thing I so cruelly associated her with, was the only thing I could see through the river of red that overtook her face. The mole is the only thing peeking above the lake of blood I saw before me. I didn't want to close my eyes but I couldn't help it — I became so hot and exhausted; it was all the blood loss.

I'm so sorry. Even in death I didn't do you justice, I made an unwitting mockery of you. Your only son and I do this. My last thought was wondering if I'd shit myself. If it'd get stuck inside me, like when you find a mouse caught in a glue trip, gnawed off limbs, clogged bowels. God, how awful. There's no tragic nobility in this.

I don't deserve you and now I've left you. Please, please, please, *please*, not like this ....

>< >< ><

I didn't want to live anymore, I decided.

I'd gotten so low that I couldn't be convinced otherwise. Of course I'd tell the counselor my parents sent me to that I was making progress, made sure to give the appearance of dips and valleys, a real erstwhile effort, but the issue had already been resolved.

I chose death.

Then they all came to me. I'd say it was a dream but it wasn't. I wasn't in bed, I wasn't sleeping. It was like, if this makes any sense, like telemarketers, almost. So many offers came, whizzed by. So much static, chatter in the air. I felt their presence but only some could, it seemed, slow down to make an impression on me.

Life is a limited resource, I learned. Life was wasted on the living, one of them said, which I found clever. I think it was Aaron. If I'd decided I really wanted to die, why not give another the gift of rebirth?

There was the college girl from Columbus who stole her father's handgun and blew her brains out. She realized that she wanted to return to kill her ex-girlfriend. I didn't want to encourage murder, so she was out.

Then there was the girl from near Cincinnati who went to a Catholic prep school who hung herself. God, how petty will this sound, but I blew her off because I didn't want to help a girl from Cincinnati. My father grew up in Cleveland and hates the Cincinnati Bengals. Yeah, I'm a girl who says fuck the world but I still want to make my daddy proud by not helping someone because she had the misfortune of killing herself in a rival football team's region. Plus, I told myself, that hanging yourself, especially inside a Catholic school, was too self-indulgently dramatic. The petty narcissism of the narcissistically suicidal. Also, I felt bad for the unknowing janitor who found her.

Then there was the boy who looked a couple years younger than me, maybe he was as young as thirteen, even. He cried and cried, he had these terrible, burnt, crusty-looking strawberry facial scars, lined with this kind of rancid-looking pus. They reminded me of exploded Strawberry Pop-Tarts, like some terrible blend of both the red insides and the dotted sugary frosting, all combined and seared on this poor kid's face. I felt terrible for him. I think he was Albanian or Polish or something; all I know is that we didn't understand each other. He was shy even in death, ashamed of his inability to communicate. I tried to ask him about his scars and meant to say "pus-y," like, "it looks like pus," but said "pussy" and I giggled and he didn't. How alienated and alone must a teenage boy be to not laugh at the word "pussy?" But he didn't catch it or understand. He seemed to be in terrible pain, but I couldn't understand him, so I, I don't know how to explain it, but I broke the connection.

I liked Aaron, though. Maybe it was like Goldilocks. The Albanian had been too young, the college girl too old, the hanged girl too much of a bitch (I thought), but Aaron, he was just right (or "right" enough). He had a flair for sophisticated drama like me and he said all the right things about his mother, about needing to go back and help his single mother who was all alone without him, because of his rash decision. He acted like he was torn: on the one hand, life wasn't worth living, but on the other, he should have made sure his mom was taken care of before parting this mortal coil. (I remember he said this "moral coil" and I found it endearing that he was trying to sound smart but fucked it up.)

He had scars on his wrists and I showed him my forearm scar and we both treated this like we were showing off earned war wounds that should come with a purple heart or something. How stupid, I know. I told him about my clumsy attempt and shared the "upper forearm" versus "lower forearm" anecdote. He'd agreed with my analysis and I liked him.

I felt like I didn't want my life anymore and I was just wasting it, so why not do a good deed and give him my life force so he could come back and make things right?

Everything was such a blur, there was so much, I don't know, clamoring in my head. It was like after I'd decided that I wanted to die I got this, like, just flood of noise and requests. I wanted that to end but it wouldn't.

Aaron got lucky when he visited me for the second time. It was perfect timing, for his purposes anyway. He visited me while I was sitting in the waiting room of that quack therapist, Ms., or Dr., Gotezman or whatever she called herself. I'm someone who tried to kill herself and that bitch is taking time out of my therapy session to correct me when I said "Miz" instead of "Dr." I mean, *hello*, I tried to kill myself here, I think we have more important things to concentrate on here! I hated her so much that I thought, I'd love to be a patient of hers and kill myself, let myself be a black mark on her record. So, as I sat listlessly in the waiting room, stewing in anger just anticipating her stupid pushy face, I agreed to forfeit my life for Aaron. It would be painless, seamless, and I agreed to forfeit myself later that night.

That was yesterday.

It's the strangest thing. Today, at school I watched the cafeteria staff, people I never really paid attention to at all, or when I'd really noticed them in the past, it was usually with mild condescension, you know? Like, these poor uneducated people, you know, like a mix of condescension and pity, making slave wages or whatever. But today I watched them serve the kids, run around in the back and grab drinks and toast bread and ... just the kind of camaraderie there, white and black and Latino people all working together, and I found it pretty beautiful, in a way. They seemed satisfied doing their tasks. I imagined the logistics of it all, imagined what it would be like if I were in charge of the cafeteria operations, and that would be something I'd enjoy, planning things out, the inventory, doing a job together with others. Making cafeteria lunch, something I never thought about before, and I now had a new perspective on it, and all the other little mundane things in the world. There was something real noble about all the world's little tasks. Now that I knew my life was ending, everything became so overwhelmingly, like, imbued with meaning.

A rush of other buzzing voices came to me today, all wanting me to sign on their dotted lines, so to speak. "No, me; no, me, I deserve it more," they said in their various ways. "No, it's really *me* who needs to come back [for whatever reason.]" They told me that Aaron lied to me. You don't come back as who you were before, for obvious reasons. You probably come back as something else and it's doubtful you'd have any real memory of who you were before. Even the Albanian kid with the gruesome, encrusted burn came back around and made impassioned gestures that I assume were about what Aaron had told me.

So, Aaron's claim he needed to come back to help his suffering mother was a lie, because he wouldn't come back as Aaron at all. Or maybe he didn't know, I told myself. Maybe he meant he'd come back as someone else and find his mother and help her without her knowing it was really her reincarnated son. I didn't believe that myself: when you are dedicated to something like coming back to life, I think you'd know the basics.

I could back out, I thought, although of course I don't really know the rules about this. Last night I didn't go to sleep, and I just filled my head with as many images of being closed off as I could: doors shutting, locked vaults, sealed manholes. I don't know, I just remember my agreement with Aaron had so much flowery-feeling language about opening myself up to him that I figured the opposite thoughts would keep him out. I don't know if it worked, but I'm still here. But I can't stay awake forever.

Now Aaron is sitting next to me, at our dinner table. So strange: this is a small table, with only room for the four of us. What chair can he be sitting on? Did he bring his own chair? Is it a ghost chair? That's the kind of person I am: I notice the telling detail. It's something I like about myself.

Strange, I don't hate myself. I wanted to die but I never hated myself. Rather, I hated other people and wanted out of this endless rat race. I wonder if my tendency to notice strange things will carry on to ... wherever I go after all this.

I see Aaron's smudged-ink raccoon eyes, his melodramatic angular hair, his flannel shirt, his alabaster skin that is now swirling with a sort of showy, angry rouge. I look down at his wrists and they are gushing blood, just insane amounts, like his wrists are angry at me and this is their version of yelling. I don't understand so much of this, why he's dressed at all, why he's looking so angrily at me? Maybe he's angry because he's afraid I gave him some kind of false hope and now I'm trying to, what's that phrase from business class, something like renege on the deal.

My family doesn't see any of this. They don't see the angry dead boy pouring curdled blood on the floor by the gallon-full. Only I can see it, which I suppose means maybe it isn't there.

Who am I fooling?

I hear a kind of howling outside my house. It has the cutting force of gusting wind but there's more to it than that, there's like a chorus of howls.

"You hear that. That's all the competition out there. If you think I'm being annoying, just imagine how bad they are going to be once they get their hands on you." And it was true, I knew. I imagined the strawberry-scarred Albanian boy out there, screaming; the Cincinnati prep school girl with her fat blue eel of a tongue sticking out all crooked, groaning at me as best she could given her circumstances; and all the other spirits out there, a whole army of dead, angry kids closing in on me. Maybe it's like a satellite, and when I told myself definitively that I wanted to die, the spirits nearest to me heard the message. Now the word has spread that I was receptive to giving my wasted life to another and the hungry herd has come to lick the plate clean.

"I know you probably think I'm an asshole. I'm not. We made a deal and if this were any other deal, I'd understand if you wanted to back out. But this is different, we made a deal and you're doing a good thing. Just let me in and it will be entirely painless, I promise. Let's just get it over with, friend." He seemed genuine, a bit like he did the first time we met.

But I detected a subtle threat underlying all that. Why all the theatrics, then? Why the pouring blood, why the rouge face, if not to intimidate me? Or maybe that's just who he was, a melodramatic look-at-me boy. I got the feeling he was enjoying the allure of success, of getting his way; it's the kids who feel the world owes them something who most abuse any newfound power.

That's real profound, isn't it? I'm just chock full of wisdom. All for nothing now, I suppose.

I don't express this but I'm afraid that somehow he'll hurt my family.

I agree to go upstairs with him and excuse myself from the dining room. I wanted to say something to my parents but couldn't without alarming them needlessly, for what could they do? I politely put my dishes away, food half-eaten, and said I just wasn't feeling very hungry. I smiled gamely at them and it was heartbreaking because the smile was genuine. I saw my mother and father and brother as damaged but ultimately good people just trying their best under the circumstances.

I loved them.

Maybe that's a type of closure.

Or maybe it's the love you feel when you know you are never going to see someone again. Love is an easy emotion, then, when it's consequence-less.

See, I can ruin everything.

As I get up and walk, I see Aaron in my peripheral vision, following me, and he's too jaunty, too self-satisfied. That hurts me the most, somehow, like he's getting something over on me. Like, even if it was something you wanted to do, the other person's insistence makes you think you are getting a raw deal. Like I'm being had. I get the terrible feeling like I'm interested in a boy and I want him to like me, so I'm agreeing to go upstairs and let him feel me up or maybe suck him off, but as I stand up I just grow to detest how smug and satisfied and excited he is about it, like he "won" and I'm the sucker. All of that was part of why I wanted to kill myself in the first place and, to think, even on the brink of death, it's the same thing.

The greatest horror of it all might be that the afterlife is full of the same frustrating terrible shit as real life.

It never ends.

I go upstairs and I don't know what to do, maybe reason with him, deep down he seems like a good guy, really, that's why I agreed to this at all, maybe I can reason with him. Or I can scream, maybe if I just draw attention to myself, it can help things, delay things. Maybe the voices outside will rush in.

I start to speak and he's disappearing inside me and I feel a fullness in my head and chest, there's too much life here, there's something inside me, it's a war in here, in my faculties, this place is too full, I'm too full, I see myself outside myself, I sense myself being carried away, and I don't feel any pain.

><><><

I awake, startled. I look at my wrists, so afraid they'd be torn open, but they look fine, of course. That woman who I dreamed was my mother, she seemed so real, so strange. I remember that woman I dreamed was my mother had a mole on her face but that's the only detail I remember upon waking. But that will fade. If I told my mother I dreamed she had a mole on her face, hah, she'd be pissed.

I'm trying to laugh off the frightening dream but layered beneath is the fear that this isn't normal, like there was too much to that nightmare for it to be something I can just shrug off. But that's just how dreams are, and I'm sensitive. I've always been extremely sensitive.

In fact, I just know there has to be more to these persistent dreams. I'd been a despondent teenage boy. Aaron, not even close to my real name, and I'd read somewhere that names or smells are almost impossible to experience or recall from a dream. I'd died somehow, this dream-Aaron. Blood pouring out of me, so hot, I remember. It's all so visceral. Guilt over a depressed middle-aged woman all alone somewhere that I need to save, that I owe something to. My mother, I dreamed.

My mother is just fine, and if there was something wrong with her I'm sure she'd be the first to tell me. Just stay positive, breathe deep, and drink some water.

I'll get over it.

No One Cares But I Tried

TUESDAY

CAROL BURPED WHILE heading back from lunch with her co-workers Maryanne and Angela. She burped softly, softly enough for her co-workers not to hear. Or if they did, they didn't say anything. Both Angela and Maryanne were senior to her, and on paper Angela had supervisory capacity over Carol, but at a company like this no one lorded seniority. It was one of those types of companies. And Carol was comfortable enough with the two of them that if they did hear her burp — even if they heard her burp gutturally, unapologetically, indulgently — they'd probably just congratulate her.

"I just burped vomit, I think," she said, between sips of iced coffee, as she scanned her employee I.D. card and passed through the turnstile, Maryanne behind her, Angela passing through the adjacent turnstile. Two men leaving through neighboring turnstiles, apparently both blessed with the auditory abilities of bats, somehow heard both her soft burp and her following comment; or maybe they were just checking her out and intuited the burp from the contortions of her mouth. One of them made a fleeting taken-aback face, at the gross words from what he perceived as the uncouth, prettyish but not too pretty light-skinned Asian girl who had the privilege to say uncouth things out loud without getting shamed or in trouble for them; the other guy snickered and looked amused at what came out of the mouth of the pretty-in-a-curious-way, little-heavy-but-still-pleasant-to-look-at half-Asian whose casual openness militated against the intimidation he'd otherwise feel in approaching a good-looking professional young woman. He worked in the building and would remember that aspect of her personality if he ever decided to talk to her.

"Lovely," Maryanne said. "Just lovely. You sound just like what my weekend will have in store for me. Do you need to be burped, too?" Maryanne, 39 and nine years Carol's senior, had two young children at home.

Carol pursed her lips and blew a tiny gust in Maryanne's direction.

"You bitchass!" Maryanne shot back excitedly, pretending to cock back her hand to strike a blow (as if she'd ever compromise her own iced coffee).

Angela's eyes widened and she yelled out in delighted shock something like, “Oh goodness,” then tittered to herself about how antiquated and out-of-fashion that phrase was.

"’Bitchass!’ I love it!" Carol said. "Is that one of your go-to insults?"

"I'm an old lady, I don't often insult people. I'm a bit rusty. Carol, you’re so perfectly young and well-kept that even after burping your breath still smells like heaven. And don't worry, you know you aren't really a bitchass." Maryanne tugged on Carol’s elbow as they all went into the elevator together.

"Thank you for confirming that I'm not a bitchass. I kind of want to be a bitchass, though. Especially a ‘Maryanne-approved bitchass.’" Carol exhaled into her hand and breathed in. "Hmmm, it doesn't smell that bad. It smells like vanilla, actually! Oh my god, I burp vanilla! I'm magic! I'm creamy, I burp condensed milk! My Vietnamese mother will be so proud!"

Maryanne and Angela laughed.

"Now I learned what your other half is without even having to ask. I'm the one who is magic." That was a nonsensical thing to say. Maryanne and Angela both knew Carol was half-Vietnamese, half-white. Carol and Maryanne were pretty close, as work friends go; if Maryanne wasn't older and living in a farther-flung suburb with a full family of her own, then they might be real friends and not just work-besties.

Carol placed her nose into the pocket of her hand again and inhaled. "Oh, it's just my hand cream I'm smelling ....”

"You two are too much." Angela was always friendly and excitable but often a sideline participant in the repartee. Carol could see that she was already itching to get back to work.

They shared the elevator with one other person, an older black lady named Bernice, who worked one floor above them. Bernice silently agreed with Angela's assessment: they were too much, especially the young bougie Asian, flighty and dumb, coasting on the excuse-making afforded by youth. *I don't want to hear this nonsense. People should have more composure.* The Asian girl's brashness was an imposition, the fact that she was drawing attention to herself while others were held as a captive audience in the elevator. *Nobody wants to hear this.*

They all worked for BBDQ, a large, reputable design and marketing firm that fortunately hadn't been hamstrung by its ungainly name. Carol joked that the first marketing job the firm ever had was selecting its own name, and on that front it had failed utterly. But maybe times were different back then: the name was actually the combined initials of its long-dead founders. Half the clients instinctively called it "BBQ" and, as homage, barbecue joints were the go-to company outing. The firm had a ton of business, and Carol, who worked on production design on media campaigns, had been consistently busy since she started working there four years ago. Carol didn't know how long Angela and Maryanne had been at the company, but she felt it had to be at least ten years for both of them.

The trio got off together on the 8th floor and walked in tandem to their respective offices. Bernice was glad to see them go. Bruce, a middle-aged manager, walked past them and gave them all a good-natured greeting, his eyes lingering a bit longer upon Carol. When Bruce caught Carol alone, he'd usually make up some pretext to chat with her for a moment or two, just to enjoy her vivacious presence, but currently she was flocked on both sides.

Jordan was walking down the hall now. Jordan was aware of Bruce's attempted flirtations with Carol, and looked down on Bruce for it. Bruce was old, and Jordan found his attempts delusional and sad. But now Jordan, see, he had a chance. Jordan believed Carol was single (true), that she liked and was charmed by him (speculative), and that there was an opening for him to pivot their friendship into something sexual (doubtful). Some aspect of his masculinity demanded that he one day make a move on her and he suspected (without corroborating evidence) that the office collectively wondered why they didn't pair off, since they worked together, were of similar age and interests and roughly equivalent desirability.

He was walking toward the trio en route to the bathroom, but abruptly diverted and made way instead for the water fountain, because he didn't want Carol to see him going to the toilet, for no real reason other than to avoid any weird associations that subconsciously develop when you see someone entering the bathroom, as if doing so preserved the option to later hit on her overtly. The art of the sexual hunt required a lot of foresight and ground work, and you had to plant seeds that would later grow into ... the metaphor didn't have a conclusion. No need to handicap himself; these minor decisions all added up in the long run.

Lydia, an older secretary, stated the obvious to the trio with, "all coming back in from lunch?" just to have something to say and create the illusion of bonhomie, even though she firmly believed (without being able to articulate it as such) that minor-key class warfare raged at BBDQ, and the reason that the trio never invited her out was because they did client work and Lydia was only support staff.

"Mhmm, I miss lunch already, can't it be lunch time forever," Maryanne responded. Angela added something more cheerful, like, "Wouldn't that be great!" and Carol put her hands on her belly and jiggled it slightly and said, "More food!" in a deep Cookie Monster voice and then, normal-voiced, "Did everyone hear that? My stomach agrees with Maryanne."

"Oh, don't you know it, wouldn't that be great, got to enjoy those breaks when you can," Lydia said to the air, and then fake-laughed and said, "Carol, you crazy," even though she hated Carol for being too demanding with work requests. Whereas Angela was always nice and Maryanne always relaxed, Carol always expected too much, with her follow-up questions and emails if things took longer to complete than she expected (which was *always*).

In reality, all three of them had complained about Lydia at various times for competence and responsiveness issues, with Angela actually being the most ruthless in her anonymous personnel reviews. Unbeknownst to Lydia, Angela had just recently been counseled about, and subsequently approved, an impending work probation for Lydia, which would result in Lydia not being given new assignments. Lydia disliked Carol the most because Carol was younger and prettier and looked wealthy and spoiled, with her stylish clothes and saloned-hair and glowy-face.

Back in her office, Carol dicked around on the Internet, extending her lunch break in spirit, as the office churned onward in the way that offices do, with most of the churning being done by certain competent taskmasters while others loafed or procrastinated or fucked up their respective assignments. The burbling of her stomach took a toxic, cutting turn. She passed gas, as silently and delicately as she could — didn't want to spook the interns — and laughed sharply and loudly about it, like how some of the dumber employees did when they surreptitiously watched a funny video at their desks and forgot that they were at work and, presumably, supposed to be working.

Her office had no windows, and she thought to call in one of her lovelorn male colleagues like Jordan and wait for him to start in with his insistent attempts at engaging her in what he intended as witty banter. Let's see if he'd act the same while marinating in her gas. He'd probably act the same, plow right through; farting Asian girls was probably a fetish of his. She laughed harmlessly to herself. Having the interns right outside her office helped divert Jordan's attention. He liked the younger women who were passably pretty but not especially so, maybe thinking they'd be more receptive to his banter than some of the older, financially secure women who worked here.

Carol left her office, didn't detect any indication from Shoshana, the intern closest to her office, that she'd heard her popping off in her office. Shoshanna looked up from her YouTube videos and said hello, but in a way that suggested more conversation was forthcoming. "Hey giiirl!" Carol responded but kept swiftly apace.

>< >< ><

When Carol was done with her business in the bathroom, she came back, chatted with Shoshana about frivolities. She was always surprised, impressed and sort of horrified to be reminded that interns were all unpaid college graduates, most commuting long distances to work here. She couldn't ever imagine having to commute such a long distance, and for no money, and for no guarantee of a job? That would've been psychological hell for her. Carol's parents had paid for all of her college expenses, had paid her rent when she was starting out, and paid the down payment on the apartment she now owned. She had an easy commute to her current office. That allowed her to save up money. Carol knew she was relatively lucky, but pretty much everyone Carol grew up with had a similar, fairly privileged story. Carol didn't tell people she came from a relatively privileged background, of course.

As soon as she returned and sat down in her office, she heard, clear-as-day: “You are a disgusting whore.”

She didn’t really hear that. It was just there, formed behind her eyes, like it bypassed her ears and took residence straight in her brain. Like the thought originated elsewhere and was implanted inside her; or her own thoughts had been tricked, commandeered.

“In addition to being a disgusting whore, you are also completely insensitive to other people. Although that isn't a surprise, we can take just one good look at you and know that you only think about yourself."

As weird as that first thought had been, she’d brushed it off as just a synapse misfire, something that maybe she hadn’t actually thought, only mistakenly thought she’d thought, if that makes any sense. But that second thought concerned her, being more complicated and appearing a few mental beats after the first. Anyone can have just an aberrant, half-formed grunt of a thought. But that second thought ... there was something more to that. She couldn’t deny that she just had a violently weird, self-lacerating, complete thought.

She ceased moving and stilled her mind. The mind-body conundrum is something far greater minds have spent far greater time considering. She was no expert on the elusive nature of consciousness, but she'd never felt so disassociated from her own mind. Because those hadn’t been her own thoughts.

She was resolute in her conclusion yet aware of the paradox. How confident could she be that those weren’t her thoughts? If those weren’t her thoughts, were these very thoughts disavowing her previous thoughts also her thoughts? How could she know when her real thoughts began and ended? Didn't all thoughts spring from the same source, and, like the tree that bears the poisoned fruit, all such thoughts would be equally contaminated? Or were there self-contained super-structures in her brain that allowed one house to function while the other burned down?

She conjured mental pictures of recent events to confirm she still had control of her mental faculties: the Mexican-style corn and radioactive-lime-green cocktail she had had with brunch over the weekend; the logo of a purple, friendly-looking dragon reading a book that a client was considering using for a new ad campaign; the name, 'Nordic Naturals,' of the fish oil pills she kept behind her computer monitor. The thoughts all came normally. She had some semblance of control. Whatever invasive wavelength she was receiving these messages from hadn't signaled a complete loss of her mental facilities.

"You are not having a panic attack," she was told. Yes, there was no one else in the room, no one else talking, but she had no doubt that she was somehow being told this by an outside force.

"I am going to make your life hell. I am going to make your life hell, do you hear me?" There was a pause of sorts, and then a more aggressive missive, but as if to overcompensate and shroud an obvious woundedness. "I'm going to make your life hell. I'm going to make your life hell at first, but I'll still be a good person — do you know what that is, being a good person? — and let you quit and be done with you. Once you quit, I'll leave you alone."

Quit. These thoughts were being directed at her from someone who worked here.

She got up with a start and opened her office door, almost tripping in the process, as her shoes weren't made for velocity. She looked out at some of the interns near her office, at the doors in the hallway, all closed or partially-opened offices, no one visible inside. As if by preternatural instinct, she made herself appear as calm as possible, just straining her neck and relaxing. She breathed deeply, as if the air in the office hallway was markedly fresher and cleaner than the air in her office.

Shoshana turned to look at her, headphones on, a video of some important-looking politician or media figure on her computer. She smiled, let the look linger as if expecting Carol to give her work, and then, seeing Carol canvass the office, returned to her video. In the office ecosystem, not hiding YouTube videos from someone meant you trusted that person.

"You look so determined," Shoshana finally said.

"Just needing to stretch."

"You are too busy, go get coffee and stretch outside!"

"You're right. From the mouth of babes."

"Who you calling babe?" Shoshana responded cheekily.

"You," Carol said back, not sure what they were doing or what they were talking about, and Shoshanna made an ironic-satisfied face and put her hands up as if saying "hell yeah." Carol, not looking to take this any further, went back in her office and closed the door.

It wasn't Shoshana, she firmly concluded, although whomever had the power to send these threatening messages by mental osmosis could presumably be a good actor. Shoshana was too bubbly to send such thoughts; she didn't seem to have an ounce of hate in her. But you could never really know someone.

She very quickly accepted that these thoughts were coming from elsewhere. Perhaps she thought this too quickly, perhaps her acceptance of this fact, in retrospect, should have suggested some flight from reality that itself explained the situation. But having experienced so many of these thoughts, so clearly and in such short succession, quickly convinced her that these thoughts were truly being directed toward her.

As in, this was really happening.

Who could it be? Bruce could be creepy with his paternal neediness; could that creepiness have graduated to the next level? Or Jordan, could his stymied eagerness have curdled into something more toxic? Or it could be some co-worker she didn't even suspect; hell, maybe someone she never even met, someone who had spied her once months ago and harbored some unfathomable secret vendetta against her ever since. She'd have to counsel with Maryanne, but carefully, of course. Just gentle inquiries about any office gossip concerning her.

She called Maryanne's extension.

"Sup?"

"In your office?"

"Uhhh, no other way I'd be picking up my phone, right?"

"Oh, right."

"Brain is on post-lunch mode I take it."

Maryanne had a brassy, cynical voice that became charming and warm when it was on your side. Hearing Maryanne made her feel like things would be okay.

"I guess so. Hey, can I swing by for a second?"

"Sure."

She left her office towards Maryanne, passing Lydia's workstation. Lydia looked up from her computer. Poor Lydia: she was just not a competent employee and was eventually going to get fired, Carol was sure of that. Could it be Lydia, just raging out at her, at anyone?

She passed Lydia's station and ran into Angela. "Carol, great, you have a second?"

No! she wanted to respond, but of course she didn't. "Sure, what's up?" She saw Angela had a slim manila folder in her hand. Her body tensed when it became obvious Angela was in fact going to require her to re-route herself for some asinine chore.

"Have you met Jamal? He sits on the other side of the office with some of the other assistants. He's one of the new assistants who is going to be working on the Brecklen account. It's being, uhhhh, moved from Lydia. Here, I'll walk over and introduce you."

Carol, eager to expeditiously knock this task out herself so she could move on to Maryanne, started to tumble over words trying to convince Angela not to bother taking the time to introduce her. Fate intervened and Angela looked down at her phone. "Oh shoot, I have a meeting with Parakh in a minute." Soneel Parakh was one of the senior bosses. You had to be on time with Parakh. Parakh was also intimidating because he demanded a lot, spoke a mile a minute and expected you to keep up, and (this last gripe was expressed only behind closed doors) retained an accent that didn't entirely aid comprehension.

"Is it okay if you go meet Jamal alone?"

"Of course, I got it."

"Great. He's a young, African-American man, glasses, very short hair, I saw him earlier, and he's in a green tie. Look for the green tie!" Angela said as both she and Carol diverged, each attending to their own separate stressors.

"Got it." Carol hurried on over to where the assistants were. Come to think of it, Lydia should have sat near the other assistants, but maybe when she was hired there wasn't space for her, so she was assigned a cubicle elsewhere and no one ever did anything to remedy that discrepancy. Without that proximity to the more experienced assistants, maybe she didn't have as much support, didn't learn enough, and that gulf in experience just kept snowballing until she just became inexorably behind in her skills and expertise. It was sad, really, just how such unexamined, seemingly innocuous decisions like that could actually have such dire ramifications.

The assistants were housed in a cluster of four cubicles. Three of the assistants were clustered in the middle, talking to one another. Jamal was one of them: a young, professional-looking, bespectacled African-American man with short hair, wearing a green tie, just as Angela had said. Ricky, the senior director of the assistants, worked at his adjacent cubicle while the other three chatted toward the center. Carol rested her elbows on the opening of the cubicle cluster.

"Hi, Jamal?"

They all kept talking.

"Jamal?"

Jamal and another assistant, Rosa, looked toward her. Rosa wore a quizzical, bothered expression.

"Hey, Jamal. Angela wanted me to give you this file for the Brecklen account. You got stuck working with me on it."

"Hey Carol," Ricky came over to her. He hobbled a bit because he'd been in a semi-serious car accident just a couple of months prior. "Who are you looking for?"

"Jamal." She pointed at the black man in the green tie. She didn't have time for this.

"Do you mean Kevin?"

"No, Jamal," her finger still absentmindedly pointed at him.

"There is no Jamal who works here. There's a Kevin ..." and he turned, body positioned like an opened door between Carol and Kevin, the young African-American man wearing the green tie. "Do you want to speak to Kevin?"

And "Jamal," with that blend of trepidation and eagerness to be a good sport so common in new hires in challenging positions, ceased conversing, hurried over to her, and extended his hand. "Hi. I'm Kevin. I don't think we've met, I just joined last week. Nice to meet you. Do you want me to take that file?"

Carol was flabbergasted. "No, I, I'm so sorry, I may, maybe I'm confused about who I was told to give this to?" And, as she sunk into existential despair, that part of her which still expected things to somehow always work out woke back to life and she comported herself as she should in a professional setting. She introduced herself to Kevin, and while she couldn't completely rid herself of her grimace, she whipped up enough corporate geniality to make it through the encounter. She felt terrible about what she'd done, wanted to apologize, but knew there was no credible way to do so.

She slumped back to her office, file in hand. Shoshana looked up at her but detected Carol was stressed and immediately returned back to her computer screen.

Good God, Carol didn't even think about what might be contained in this file. It was just a matter of luck that, in her bewildered state, it had been easier and perhaps more comforting to hold onto something rather than give it up. She opened the slim file, expecting the worst, but it contained only what appeared to be the expected materials on the designs and strategies surrounding the Brecklen marketing campaign.

"You might as well come and see me," the voice said. She concentrated on the voice sounding in her mind, to hear it in Angela's high, usually friendly voice. It didn't work. If anything, the voice was interpreted as Carol's own. But that couldn't be. It would never not be disconcerting to hear a voice inside your mind that should be your own but whose provenance could not be determined.

Carol made her way to Angela's office, the file still in her arms. The door was slightly ajar. She knocked and heard "come in," in the typical raised cadence anyone would use to make sure a knocker heard you. Carol entered and didn't know what to say or what she should do with her face. What should her expression be? It was so easy just to go into usual workplace-congeniality mode. She could even pretend like there was nothing wrong here, maybe this was all just some kind of bizarre, improbable misinterpretation? Maybe this was what a nervous breakdown was like? Carol hadn't ever really been too stressed and was generally a positive person, but who knows, mental health breakdowns are an insidious thing, right?

"Close the door behind you and take a seat."

Angela didn't look mad or vengeful. Someone who didn't know any better might even regard her appearance as placid. But Carol could see, as Angela prissily rearranged items on her desk, the precise, strategic, determined person she was dealing with.

Carol did as requested.

"So, Carol, we've had our fun. I'll make this quick and to the point. I want you to quit."

Carol didn't respond, but rather just stared straight ahead. She studied her adversary. She saw the same diligent, helpful, short, unthreatening, high-pitched Angela she'd always seen, with her fair skin, well-kept but somewhat large and frizzy deep black hair, in her unremarkable, perfectly normal, perfectly acceptable outfit, dark shawl over dark shirt, and beneath her desk, undoubtedly dark pants. Beside Angela was her turquoise handbag with an oversized circular clutch; it would look better if it didn't feature geometric shapes of flowers, a needless, basic ornamentation. If you have an ornamentation, the last thing you want it is to be basic.

Beside Angela's computer there was a framed family portrait with her husband and two young sons, one maybe three- or four-years-old, the other between six and eight. There were also individual pictures of each. Her husband's picture looked like an enlarged professional photo, as he was wearing a suit and it was zoomed in too tight on his face, like that very same photo must appear somewhere on a workplace I.D. in her husband's wallet. The individual photos of Angela's children must have been taken when they'd both been newborns. Each in that familiar new-baby pose, looking like diaper-swathed, camera-averse hairless baby moles. Carol didn't know the name of Angela's husband, or the names of her children, when those pictures had been taken, or which little mole-baby had grown up into which child in that family portrait. On the opposite wall Angela hung some accoutrements and decorations; from the periphery of her vision Carol could see a framed degree and hand-drawn pictures Carol assumed came from one of her sons.

"Angela, did I somehow do something to upset you? If so, I'm sorry."

Angela put a hand up and blinked dramatically. "Carol, please don't, I didn't call you in here to talk with you about it. I — actually —" and her gaze turned steely. "Put your phone on my desk," Carol heard in Angela's voice, although the timbre was off; the difference between a voice entering your ears and a voice germinating from within your mind.

A sheath of pressure enveloped Carol's forehead. It was like a knifehand strike of cosmic energy slid through the side of her head, and now the fingers were extending, getting her skull in its grip, now squeezing. It was a fitted baseball hat becoming tighter and tighter. She closed her eyes and the increasing pressure brought light flashes, spottiness, and a vertiginous nausea.

"It's in my bag in my office," Carol answered languorously. She didn't feel languorous, she certainly didn't want to respond as such, but it took so much energy just to stay awake, to just avoid toppling out of her chair.

"Prove it. Empty your pockets," the skull-voice ordered.

"These pants don't have pockets." And Carol patted at where pockets would be as proof. She didn't want to get up to demonstrate; she wanted to take migraine pills and sleep. It felt like shoelaces had been looped through the sockets of her eyes, up around her skull, and were ever-tightening. Now the orbital socket had been hollowed out, no pesky eyeball mucus in the way, easier for the laces to squeeze against the ridges, get all the way in ....

Carol stood, fearful she might tip over. She straightened her legs and turned around to show she had no back pockets.

Miraculously, the pain and instability vanished.

"Thank you," Angela said in the skull-voice. "I appreciate you being smart enough not to come in here and try and record me. Don't ever come in here with a phone or any recording device. If you looked at the file I gave you, I didn't put anything terrible in there. I could have, if I wanted to. I could have put any old terrible, horrible thing in that file, that would have gotten you fired, maybe even publicly shamed. But I didn't. I was lenient with you. I just want you to quit."

"Do you understand?" That last sentence was in her normal, chipper voice. That would be a recurring thing, Carol realized. The voice Angela used depended on whether it was something she would risk being overheard.

Carol realized she had never seen Angela angry before, and she still hadn't. Angela always spoke with this encouraging, 'you can do this' tone, a tone which had made her a great supervisor and workplace confidante, and that tone hadn't abandoned her. It was the most encouraging "do you understand" that, under the circumstance, could have also doubled as a threat.

"Angela, I ... I'm sorry, I—"

Pain is something that can be remembered only as a dim reflection of how it was experienced; and Carol understood, if only subconsciously, that if she'd still been under the continued duress of that vice-grip that had, just moments ago, taken control of her skull, she'd never had uttered a protest. The abeyance of pain had spoiled her. She realized this and stopped talking. There was no conversing about this, not on any terms other than of Angela's choosing, at least.

"Carol, just know this. These, whatever you want to call them of mine, I don't know, special powers, let's just say," and she laughed — that excitable, that tad unmeasured, uncool laugh, like she reacted too strongly to an unexpected joke — "they only work in a limited range. They work when I know where a certain person is, and when I am in their range. For all intents and purposes, once you no longer work in this building, you will be out of my range." She was saying this aloud so she spoke in these circumlocutions.

"So basically, as long as you work in this building, you're in my range. Once you quit, you'll be free. And don't ask me 'why' again. Life isn't fair, Carol. You have advantages yourself that I don't ask you about. Now, is it fair that I have what I have, but am only able to use it sparingly, within such a limited range? It's like owning a Corvette that you can't take out of town! But I manage, I make do, the best I can. That's all we can do, the best we can."

"Right."

"So I'll give you to until the end of the week to give your notice. I'll let you put in your full three weeks of notice. Company policy requires three weeks of notice here, if you didn't know."

"I didn't know." *Because I had no plans on quitting.*

"Well, just so you know. I don't want you to entirely burn your bridges here. I'll personally give you an excellent recommendation, if anyone asks me. I know you wouldn't think it, but you should think of putting me as a reference, because since I know the circumstances the most, I'd give you a recommendation immediately if it will help you land on your feet. We've all had those people in the past, I'm sure, who you give as a reference, but they take so long to respond that you fear it may reflect badly that you used someone as a reference that's not responsible enough to respond to requests quickly!" She smiled during that last sentence, moved her hands back-and-forth lightheartedly with the emphasis in each clause.

"Okay."

The lightheartedness, as if noticed, was routed and chased out of Angela's system. "Glad it's agreed," she ended coldly.

"Okay."

Carol sat there, her head and face burning with indignation. Angela just sat there looking at her expectantly, as if waiting for her to just get up and go back to her office, pack her things.

Angela could plant thoughts into her mind, but could she read thoughts? Carol's thoughts whooshed in a million different directions. Her thoughts weren't even known to herself, how could they be read by another with any quantum of reliability? Carol focused herself and thought terrible things, of grabbing one of Angela's sons, whichever was represented by the closest newborn picture. Carol pictured swinging the unlucky baby by the umbilical cord, swinging so hard the cord ripped, blood and mucus and belly-slime everywhere, the baby screeching as it sailed through space ... only to land on a highway, to flatten like a bloody pimple as a huge truck ran over it, compressed it into a disorderly crater of flesh and guts and blood and used diapers.

Angela's expression didn't change. No, she can't read thoughts. The difference between implanting thoughts and reading thoughts was like the difference between tossing a rock into a lake and dredging a rock from the bottom of one. Some rocks skipped on the surface, some floated just below, some were caked deep down in the muck. No, she couldn't dredge those rocks.

"That is all. Meeting adjourned."

"Okay."

And Carol got up and busily walked back to her office. She could close her office door and in the silence pretend like nothing had changed; who was here to contradict her? And that's what she did, utilizing the ubiquitous narcotic of the internet, fashion blogs, digital coupons and upcoming events. And it worked, amazingly, if only for a bit. After all, could that frightening distortion of reality really have just happened, in the same universe of Yoga in the Park and Thirsty Thursdays, buy-two-get-one-free deals?

She expected a mental message to violently disrupt her reverie any second.

She got up, went to Maryanne's office and asked to come in.

Maryanne was scooping cottage cheese, and had the disposition of someone clearly not working. "Can you see this shit, look at me, eating fucking cottage cheese. This is my health food. I had fucking celery before. I eat Goldfish crackers and feel bad so then I eat something healthy, but that's not how being healthy works. That's just eating more calories. Here's my advice: stay young."

Maryanne was half-looking at Carol, half-looking at her screen. "So what's up, kid? Oh yeah, weren't you supposed to swing by earlier?" Carol had meant to look normal, project nothing, but Maryanne diverted her attention from her computer screen in a way that just seemed like *caring* and Carol wanted to cry. Carol didn't want to leave Maryanne, or this job: sure, there were things she disliked about her job but it was *her* job to hate.

"Yeah, I'm okay." And to get Maryanne off the scent of her distress, Carol led her on an aimless, ambulatory chat, about future vacation plans, unfounded office gossip, and Maryanne family drama. Then, if almost as an afterthought addendum to what Maryanne had intimated about Advancement Communication Coordinator Judy Eisengadt's workplace political savvy, Carol probed, oh-so-delicately, about their mutual-friend Angela's workplace aspirations.

"Angie D? Beats me. That girl doesn't have a political bone in her body. I mean, don't get me wrong, she's great at what she does, and that's enough for her."

"Or maybe she's so good at politics that it just looks like she's not trying."

"*Aha!*" Maryanne finger-pointed like Carol had made a big discovery. "But, no. Not her. At least nothing that I'm aware of."

Carol leaned in, and spoke with an intentionally staccato rhythm, as to show goofy Maryanne that this was both pure business but also not to be taken too seriously.

"Maryanne."

Maryanne leaned in and mirrored Carol's faintly robotic tone: "Carol."

"I'm going to ask you something, just a stupid question, and you can't repeat it to anybody."

"Got it. Ask away,"

"Angela ever say anything to you about me?"

"Nada."

"No?"

"Nothing. Trust me, I'd love to tell you if she blew your young ass down a peg, but she didn't. I have nothing to report."

"Ok." And then: "blew my young ass?"

"I know," Maryanne grimaced. "The second that came out of my mouth ... I've lost my touch! I've lost my touch! Whatever you people are saying these days."

"You realize I'm not that much younger than you, right?"

"Oh, a few years matters, kid, it matters," and Maryanne leaned back for emphasis, able to retreat from that comment back to that savvy, I-know-things pose she liked to assume.

"Seriously, though. Did Angela ever say anything to you about me?" Carol repeated.

"Why, did something happen?" Maryanne asked as if it may have just dawned on her that there might be a connection between these questions and that sallow face Carol had when she'd first entered.

"No, no. I was just thinking aloud. There've been a lot of people who worked for Angela who just abruptly quit though, right?" There was no proof behind that question: it was just a fishing expedition based on a hunch.

"I don't think so. Demi V., Faye Leo. There was that assistant Danielle with that impossible Russian name or something, she worked with Angela and quit but she was, like, in college or something still, so that's not unusual. Those are the only three people I can think of who worked with Angela at any time who quit without another job lined up, as far as I know.

"And Katelyn ... what was that slutty girl's name? Katelyn Donnolly ... did she even work with Angela? Hmmmm ... I don't think she even worked with Angela come to think of it, but remember her, she worked here and she quit in a hurry, remember? Probably got caught fucking someone, she gets fired, the guy doesn't, you know how that is ...."

Carol remembered Katelyn Donnolly: there was nothing that

would lead someone to believe she was slutty. Maryanne used "slutty" as a metonym for 'young and felicitously proportioned.' And Danielle Klemenko, that had been that assistant's name, right? She had been young and attractive, too, got along well with others, seemed reasonably competent, and then just quit, right out of the blue. And Faye Leoso, too, now come to think of it; she'd left almost right around when Carol had started, but she'd quit abruptly, too. Faye had been youngish and pleasant-looking. Carol didn't know Demi Valentine, but knew her name because she still appeared in the Outlook mail directory. She must have been before Carol's tenure.

Carol went back to her office and looked at the picture directory for Demi Valentine and yes, as she thought, she saw the bright glow, proportional face, sultry eyes, and altogether appealing countenance of another of Angela's possible victims.

What was even worse about the whole thing? Those four women had all been younger and better-looking. Katelyn particularly had been almost outrageously attractive. If the "crime" for which they had been punished was their youth and perceived beauty, Carol thought ruefully, then Katelyn deserved the death penalty, the other three should get life imprisonment, and Carol should get maybe a week of community service.

It wasn't fair. Why was Angela forcing her out? Carol posed no threat. Hell, she'd previously entertained the idea of looking for another job, entertained idle talk with recruiters. She wasn't gunning for Angela's job or anything. And if it was an issue of competence, then this was the first she'd heard of it. She was good at her job. She got along well with others. Carol scanned again through the pictures of the four previous victims in a desperate attempt to find some invidious racial angle that could explain it all away but came away with nothing. All were white, save for Demi, who looked darker-skinned, possibly Latina or maybe South Asian. Angela was White Hispanic, if memory served, and Carol had never detected one iota of racial resentment from her. A racial animus was really grasping at straws, but then again, this was all so impossible.

Carol fumed at how inextricable her predicament appeared.

She stayed in her office the rest of the day and saw no one. She decided to leave early to avoid running into anybody at the elevator bank. She snuck out of her office at 4:15 p.m.

A yellow parakeet flew straight up from Shoshana's desk, furiously beating its wings. It came toward Carol unnaturally, in too straight of a line. Carol stared, transfixed at how fast it fluttered. The little yellow bird's head shot straight off and its wings bloodlessly detached. Carol, mesmerized, still heard the fluttering, which continued without reason, and stared slackly at what was left of the little bird, its skinny feathered body, without head or wings, still heading toward her. As it approached, it exploded with a great popping sound into a sparkling confetti of pastel, cartoonish stars.

Carol yelped in fright, and slammed her hand shut over her mouth. Fortunately, Shoshana was not at her desk to witness, and no one else was around. Carol felt a sour feeling in her stomach and, as she scurried to the elevator, was left with the phrase: "by the end of the week."

She was riddled with anxiety at home. Fortunately she had made no plans that night so she had no one to alarm with her problems. The food she ate was a bland non-entity. She thought about calling her mother and father but decided against it. She talked with them often and got along well with them and often leaned on them for support or guidance, or just to hear them talk, their voices, their existence alone some kind of soothing balm, confirmation of the world outside her head.

But not this time: she feared losing her composure and being confronted with the inescapable reality that this was a situation for which they could provide no succor, and if the situation was properly explained, they would only be left with the understandable conclusion that their daughter had suffered some kind of work-related mental breakdown. So she did nothing and kept to herself, assumed a folded spiral shape in bed like she was once again a stressed child.

WEDNESDAY

She dreaded going to work. When people spoke to her, she took an extra beat to comprehend and respond. Any added work responsibility was a particularly agonizing affront, as it became an additional obstacle to her hopeless ruminations. She rushed assignments but then again what did it matter, she wouldn't be here much longer, would she?

Clever, she thought, the effects of the situation with Angela could get her fired for cause. Wouldn't that be funny? Maybe she could then try and rationalize her incompetence, say, "No, really, it was Angela, she mentally vexed me, she cursed me!" Right.

Carol got lunch by herself and ate in her closed office. There was an unpleasant smell now; sweat, heat, and flatulence in an unventilated room.

She had to do something. She looked up each of the four other 'victims' individually on Facebook and LinkedIn, and was glad to see that, if their social media pages were any indication, they were all at least gainfully employed elsewhere. All still attractive, professional and presentable. Angela hadn't disfigured their faces in any way, Carol thought with watery optimism.

She sent them each a message, which, in sum and substance, went something like this: "Hi. I work at BBDQ and understand that you also worked there. I have a question about your time there, if you have a minute. Thanks."

Before the end of the work day, all four girls had messaged her back some version of "what's the question?" And her follow-up went something like this: "Did you work with or for someone named Angela Diego?"

Carol tidied up her office, got an energy drink from a vending machine on her floor, gave Maryanne a diluted smile and made it look like she had somewhere important to be. She responded cordially to some work emails, checking for further messages from the four girls all day, each time disappointed that the beep or gurgle of her phone was something else.

She overheard Bruce talking to some support staff.

"And I told my cousin when he started dating Mai, who he worked with, remember, and I later learned that Mai is a great girl, a fantastic woman, don't get me wrong, but when I heard my cousin was dating Mai, I told him, 'look, you just don't dip your pen in the company ink.'

"But you know, then I thought about it. And, if there's anywhere you *should* dip your pen, it's the company ink! I mean, I'm just saying, I'm only saying as an expression, 'don't dip your pen in the company ink' has to be about the worst expression ever. I mean, you have a job, you need to write things, you work at a company, why on Earth wouldn't you dip your pen in the company ink? What else is your company's ink for if not to write with?"

She heard the laughs of the support staff. One said, 'Oh you bad' and she assumed Lydia only laughed because Bruce was using his 'funny cadence.' Bruce and his Creepy Seinfeld shit. She fucking hated him and hated everyone else here. She hated this fucking job. She'd been here long enough. She was tired of the incompetent, stupid support staff; creepy and cloying Bruce; insistent Jordan; obese, depressed Judy; airhead Shoshanna; clingy Maryanne. Any job that could allow a sociopath like Angela to thrive wasn't a place she needed to be.

THURSDAY

By the time Carol awoke the next morning, none of the four previous victims had gotten back to her. Although she couldn't be sure she ever actually fell asleep, famished as she was from her anxiety-stricken inability to eat properly; drained as she was from her sour, volatile stomach that refused to retain the meager foods she ate; and terrorized as she was by the scorched, powdery, brittle wings of the butterflies that had taken root inside her stomach.

She forced herself to come to work. She didn't want to go. Her mental grogginess impelled her to stay home. Her awful sleep didn't help, so full of restless torments that she began to doubt whether Angela's mental projections were as limited as she'd promised.

All the coworkers she'd grown to love would soon be lost to her. Maryanne, her confidante; Judy, such a good writer; Jordan, always happy to see her; Bruce, cleverer than she gave him credit; Shoshanna, ebulliently bright-faced, with all the news about the fun events around town, all the cool bars; Lydia, well, Lydia tried. All the other people here who'd nurtured her talents. Maybe it was the torpor of sleepless nights and the vertigo of pounding headaches but she couldn't deal, she wanted to prostrate herself before the entire office, beg them to keep her, to protect her, *don't let Angela take me away from all of you.*

She had to do something. But what?

She went to Angela's office. She knocked, no answer. But she heard some kind of murmur in there, the intuition of a presence. She knocked again, keeping her knuckles against the door, and pressed it open.

She was blasted by freezing air, subsumed in the great roars of wind. The gusts stung her face in different spots, at different times as the wind blew over her; her nose, her cheek, her chin. Scarring cold, an almost frustrating puncturing sensation that felt malicious and frightfully random. She leaned forward, pressing ahead, face in the bends of her arms to shield from the frigid winds. She entered the office and the door slammed behind her. Like nothing, the wind ceased. She returned her arms to her sides in an instant, looked around furiously to acclimate herself to her surroundings.

Just Angela's office.

She sensed before she heard the terrible collapsing sound, a large mass breaking away and falling toward the carpeted floor. She looked up in an instant and saw a stalactite come into being, the cheap ceiling plaster telescoping into a pointed spike, straight for the top of her skull. Had she been a moment off-beat, the stalactite would have blown through her, and there'd she have stayed, pinioned to the ground, hands hanging helplessly by her side, chintzy plaster speared through her skull, down through her spine, gore-soaked with blood, brains and bowel, erupting through her legs down through the threadbare carpeting. But she saw it coming and moved, without thinking, out of the way.

When the plaster struck the carpet its momentum stopped completely. It glowed white-hot for a second before exploding outward, countless tiny, barbed fragments shooting everywhere. Carol screamed and curled her face into her body, making herself as small as possible to avoid the debris. She didn't make it unscathed. She breathed the dirt into her nostrils, exhaled harshly and saw the plaster lumps that had lodged somehow in her nose, in her mouth, felt blinding pain in her mouth and prayed what she chewed on wasn't her fractured teeth. Vicious curved shards hooked through her lips. She'd die when she saw the extent of her disfigurement.

She jolted into awareness.

She was knocking on Angela's door.

"Sorry, I couldn't help myself. I'll miss torturing you when you're gone so this won't be easy for both of us. Haha. Now if you didn't figure it out, don't come in, you idiot slut. I don't want to talk to you. I have nothing else to say to you. Tomorrow is resignation day. If you don't come in and quit tomorrow, I am going brutalize that body. You'll be more brutalized than you were after your first drunk gangbang in college."

The daymare lingered, and she took active control of her breathing. Gangbangs in college? What? Who did Angela think she was? Why did Angela say such vindictive, absurd things to her? What had Carol ever done to her? If only she could be given the chance to explain things.

But that hysterical daymare quashed any remaining hope that Carol had, somehow, after all this, just been imagining Angela's powers. And those powers extended beyond just implanting messages. They could create frightening illusions; illusions so powerful that they were essentially real while they lasted.

She couldn't risk it. If Angela wouldn't speak to her, so be it.

So Carol retired to her office. She caught her breath and did some work, as ridiculous as that was given the situation. She went to Maryanne's office and made small talk, just for the creature comforts it provided, and agreed to get coffee with her.

As they left to get coffee Maryanne went to Angela's office and knocked to see if she was interested. Carol did nothing to stop her; it happened so quickly, unfolding like an entrancing dream. There Angela sat guilelessly, that happy-to-help grin as always, politely demurring. Why, she explained, she just got coffee recently and she could only handle so much, she didn't want to fly away, and she made an exaggerated, hokey buzzy motion.

"Yeah, you're an itty-bitty, too much coffee and you'd explode," and, like nothing, Maryanne returned back to Carol and said something like "she's a character," and Carol agreed.

As they waited in line for their coffees, Carol said something about feeling a bit sick to explain her timorousness in the face of Maryanne's zeal about gossip and office politics, and Maryanne said some bromide like "yeah, there's something going around" and encouraged Carol to play hooky tomorrow. Carol smiled meekly.

After they ordered, Carol insisted on paying but Maryanne refused. "Why would you do that?" Maryanne asked with moxie.

Carol insisted again and Maryanne again refused. "You realize I have absolutely no control over you getting a raise, right? Allocate your coffee bribes better. That's something you'll learn in time."

Maryanne spoke directly to the cashier: "despite what this crazy girl is trying to do, please ring up my coffee separately."

"Aww, see now you're making her ring up two separate orders, you are making her do more work."

"She's a strong girl, she'll live."

The barista smiled and said good-naturedly. "Don't worry, I got this. I'm trained to handle more than one coffee."

"See, she's got this."

"I see."

And they walked back to work, coffees in tow. When Maryanne turned and readied her ID card in the lobby, Carol took the opportunity to delicately hug her.

"Bitch, you almost made me spill my coffee, what are you doing!"

"Just showing my appreciation, Maryanne. That's what you get for not letting me buy you coffee. You get shame-hugged in public."

"You must be sick after all. It's gone to your head, poor girl. Don't come into work tomorrow, stay home. We can't afford your sickness-induced positivity to spread."

"Trust me, I'd love to stay home. But I have to come in tomorrow. I have some nonsense I have to get done."

"Same as every other day, then."

"Yup. Something like that."

She'd forgotten that she'd told her friend Amy that she'd join her at her workplace happy hour. She texted Amy that she unfortunately wasn't feeling well and had to raincheck, but definitely next time. Amy understood and was cool about it.

So Carol went home and wondered if maybe it'd been better if she went out, distracted herself from tomorrow. No, likely not. Even if she drank moderately, alcohol would cloud her judgment, the judgment that she'd need primed for tomorrow. Better to focus. 'Focus' was a better word than 'prepare' because she had no idea what there was to prepare for, really.

So she made dinner for herself, an easy stir-fry, and watched a documentary but then turned it off halfway. It was interesting, but she needed to read something. Reading jogged her brain, connected the synapses and made her feel more lucid. Thoughts came more easily after she read. So she read a novel she'd been reading on-and-off for the last few months. Then she did a quick thirty-minute workout streaming onto her television screen, read a little more and turned the documentary on again.

As the documentary played, she searched on her phone for articles about telekinesis, expecting to find only unhelpful things. She wasn't disappointed. She watched an animated six minute how-to video online titled "Telekinesis for Beginners - Learn how to do Telekinesis (Psychokinesis)." The voiceover narration was provided either by a young, post-lobotomy woman of unknown provenance or a strangely accented female robot set to "sound human." Either way, it didn't help. Maybe she was below beginner level. Remedial-grade.

Only Danielle ever messaged her back again. "I don't have much to say about her, except just do what she says. Please don't message me again about her because I have nothing more to say and nothing that would be helpful." So that was that. They would be no help.

She hadn't done anything to look for a new job. She knew there was no way to quit her job and get unemployment insurance payouts. So she'd have to find something in the next three weeks between giving notice and leaving.

She called her parents, who were both at home. She spoke to them without becoming maudlin. It wasn't easy. She usually told her mother everything going on with her life: every date, every venture with friends, work developments, everything. But she didn't tell her much about her week because there wasn't much she felt comfortable telling her. All she said was that she was having trouble at work with a superior who didn't like her for completely irrational reasons.

Angela? But hadn't she mentioned an Angela before, gotten coffee with her before? Yes, that Angela. But something changed somehow. Her mother, being her mother, suggested that maybe Carol had offended her somehow and essentially advised rapprochement. She should apologize and try to understand this Angela's point of view. Carol said she'd tried but Angela refused to tell her what the problem was. Her mother agreed that sounded strange and unprofessional, and advised Carol to speak to another supervisor about it. Of course she would, Carol told her. Her father offered his usual well-meaning but hackneyed generalities and that was that.

It wasn't fair.

She spent the night thinking.

FRIDAY

If today was going to be her last day, then at least she'd dress nicely. She had a decently sized wardrobe and many shoes to choose from. Nothing particularly fancy, though. She wondered how Angela's opinion of her would change if she could see her wardrobe. Would she think she was a spoiled brat, with all these clothes? Most of these clothes were bought second-hand, though from upscale consignment shops. Would that change things? Would it matter? Or were Angela's entirely irrational opinions set in stone?

She wore a navy blue Perry Ellis skirt suit and her black Rockport flats. Those were comfortable, all-day shoes.

Carol got to work early. She went in for coffee at the usual spot and recognized the barista. It was the same one who had served her and Maryanne the day before. Carol ordered her coffee hot, with a little room, put some cream in it and asked for a couple cubes of ice, just to cool it down. Didn't want to burn her tongue. She had a few dates this weekend, you know how it is, she told the barista jokingly. The barista covered her mouth and laughed.

She went up to her office, took the lid off her coffee and turned her computer on. It was 8:20 a.m. Most people didn't come in until 9 a.m. at the earliest.

Jordan stopped by her open office.

"Hi C, what's going on this weekend?"

"Not much. Seeing my parents. Fun times, I know. Basically nothing, if that's what you want me to say. You caught me, I'm doing nothing this weekend." *'Hi-C'* she thought. *That's a new one.*

"Well I'm sure you can find yourself into things if you wanted. And note I said Hi-C, like that fruit soda. I'm a master of wordplay."

"Very punny."

Jordan gave an "ah hey" face and pointed at her with a handgun gesture.

"I never had Hi-C but now I want to try it," Carol responded.

"Now I know what your Secret Santa present is going to be!"

"It won't be a secret anymore. I'll see that Hi-C and I'll know it's you."

"You know what, you got me, dead to rights. Nailed me."

She made the hand-gun back at him. "Bang."

He pantomimed taking a bullet to his heart.

"See ya, C."

"See ya Jordash."

The office filled up as usual. She had work to do but didn't do it. No point. She put the lid back on her coffee and folded the lip. She did a lap around the office, to look at everyone one last time.

It was 9:30 a.m. She stopped at Angela's office, the door ajar. Shoshana was using the copy machine nearby. Angela peeked her head from her desk.

"Carol, just the person I wanted to see. Come in."

She sounded her usual self, perhaps with just a little less contrived good cheer than usual. Carol began to enter. Angela interrupted her sternly: "and please close the door." Carol pivoted away from Angela to pull the door closed, just as Shoshana passed Angela's office, copies in hand. They met eyes and Carol furrowed her brow tightly, her face a map of sickly concern. "You okay?" Shoshana silently mouthed, and Carol accelerated the process of closing the door.

She sat down, facing Angela, coffee still in hand. If a frightened rabbit could sit in a chair, it'd look like Carol.

"Just the person I want to see," Angela boasted. *She already said that*, Carol thought, and Angela looked like she realized she'd already said that too. Angela swirled a bit in her chair, said, "give me a second" as she closed some windows on her computer.

Carol put her coffee on Angela's desk.

"So, has it been done?"

"Yes."

"You gave your notice?"

"Yes."

"How much."

"I said three weeks."

"Who did you tell?"

"Parakh."

"Did you give a reason?"

"No. I just said I needed to move on. I said my father was ill, which is true, by the way, but didn't give that as an excuse to quit. But just another factor."

"Good. Did you tell anybody else?"

"No. Am I allowed to at least go around and say goodbye to everyone else?"

"Don't pout. It doesn't look good on you, despite what other people might have told you. And, yes, you can say goodbye to people. You can also come in these next three weeks. I promise I'll keep my torture to a minimum, as much as I can control. Maybe don't come in the last couple of days because I may be so gleeful I can't help myself and fill your mind with the most horrible things."

"Understood."

Angela smiled. "So, that's all there is, folks. Be well."

"Can I just ask you why? Please, can you just tell me why?"

"Carol, Carol, Carol," Angela clucked. "Explaining is for people who need to explain. I don't need to explain, so I won't. I just don't like you and that should cover it. I tolerated you for a while, then I thought to myself recently, 'You know, I don't like her. I should stand up for myself. I have the ability to get rid of her, so why not?'

"Now, I'm not hateful. Trust me, I could be killing you right now, if I really wanted to. I could be filling your head with images of you, I don't know, being gang-raped on repeat. But maybe you'd like that, I don't know."

"Angela."

Angela put her hand up as if to recognize that her comment deserved to elicit some response, but there'd be no further discussion. "Yeah, yeah, okay. Carol, don't you worry, you'll leave here and your life will be fine. You are competent and pretty and present well enough, you'll get some job elsewhere and be fine, you'll get married to some rich man who takes care of you and your two to three biracial-but-essentially-white kids and you'll be fine and dandy, okay. So spare me the sob story you had planned before

I revert back to the old me. Take this as an opportunity for self-improvement. Another fork in the road."

"But why are you acting like this!" Carol shrieked dramatically.

"Now Carol —"

"There's your coffee, it's right there. I got it for you!" Carol pointed to the coffee she'd placed on Angela's desk.

"I don't —"

"Why are you acting like —" and Carol stood up, took the coffee with her left hand, squeezing it hard enough to pop the lid. Angela stood up too, her face bemused, an aura of worry at this escalating diversion.

In quick, fluid motions, Carol extended her left arm to put the coffee in Angela's right hand, and then covered Angela's hand with her right. Angela, naturally thinking she was in some kind of struggle, grabbed Carol's wrists. Carol used all her might to launch the coffee at herself. She was hoping cool liquid would sail harmlessly over her shoulder, and while she mentally prepared for some coffee to splash her, it was still a shock to feel the viscous, cream-laden liquid coat her shoulder and contaminate her face, get in her eyes.

"Ahh!" Carol yelled exaggeratedly.

She put her left hand to her face to wipe away the coffee in her eyes.

Angela, gladdened by this hysterical display, began to speak.

Carol took out her smart phone she'd stuffed in the bottom of her shoe and hurled it as hard as she could into Angela's face. Bullseye, right into the nasal bridge. Angela fell backward, unable to smell or breathe, hands attempting to make sense of the deadening impact to her face and the fluids that flowed forthwith.

"Huhpth," Angela muttered wetly. The blood that entered her mouth when she opened her lips took her by surprise and caused her to panic. She looked down and some blood dribbled onto her shawl.

Carol said nothing, kept her head low and stared at Angela, trepidation and contempt at war with each other.

Angela's interregnum of confusion ended. She'd been hit in the face with a phone, it hurt, there was blood, but she was still conscious. And she was who she was, with the powers she had.

Angela focused on Carol and her stolid face. Angela saw pride on that face, and it inflamed her furies. That execrable insect, staring her down as if she had the upper-hand. Angela would blight her hopes and dreams, she would rend her mind into mush; she would, if she could, undo her very existence. When Angela was done with her, Carol would be a catatonic, drooling mess, sequestered somewhere in an institution to prevent her from eating insects and choking on her own spittle. Angela would visit her in that institution, say placating things to Carol's family, get Carol alone and whisper into her ear to remind her about all the things Angela had done to ruin her; and Angela, she would wait, she would sit and wait for Carol's glimpses of recognition, her tears, her realization that Angela had caused this ruinous condition. It wouldn't be enough to know that Carol suffered. Angela wanted to be there, to watch her suffer in person.

"You fucking whore!" Angela screamed, with clenched fists slamming against an invisible cage. Searing blades crisscrossed Carol's skull, her vision blurred at the edges, her bones lost their composure and she crumbled onto the ground, landing atop her right knee, which was sprawled out at a terribly acute angle. She wasn't foaming at the mouth but she felt through the pain the sensation of drowning under sparkling acidic spray.

"Carol! Oh my God! Carol!" It was Jordan in the doorway to Angela's office. This conflict had gotten so out of hand that he'd opened the door to Angela's office out of concern, both an intrusion of personal privacy and display of actual caring about the well-being of another that were both anathema to the BBDQ workspace. Behind him Carol could intuit Maryanne. And Bruce. And Shoshana. And others piled behind her. With Angela's attention diverted Carol came to.

"What the hell is going on in here?" she heard Maryanne's brassy voice. "Carol!" Maryanne put her hands to her mouth in shock. That was the first time Carol had ever seen her lose her cool. If Angela made Maryanne lose her cool, then she was done for, Carol thought, only semi-seriously.

"Please don't hit me again, please don't hit me again," Carol sulked on the floor. The wrenching of her bones had stopped, as had the blurring of her vision and the implosion inside her head. Angela's hold had ended.

"Carol, what happened?" Jordan came to her side and dramatically took a knee, positioned as if he was offering water to a dying wanderer, when the appropriate thing to do would have been to just help her up. No matter, let Jordan believe he was saving the fair damsel. Carol spoke and she knew he would be an advocate for her in the inevitable he said / she said between her and Angela; or, in this case, the she said / she said.

Angela had been acting very strangely toward me, giving me inappropriate orders, Carol explained in several written statements. *Setting me up for embarrassing situations. Treating me like a butler. Making me get her coffee. So I brought her coffee this morning, but it wasn't to her liking. Too much milk, or not hot enough, I don't remember exactly. So she screamed at me. Threw the coffee at me. Lunged at me. Struck me. I can't work in an environment like this anymore. It's just not possible. I can't be here, I can't be here.*

Angela, of course, denied everything, and claimed that Carol was acting hysterically, maybe having a mental breakdown. Or maybe the poor girl was trying to pull some kind of scam. Everyone internally agreed that Carol's story seemed incredibly bizarre, and to accuse Angela, of all people? Angela? It was absurd. Outrageous, really; I mean ... Angela!? Might as well blame a field mouse.

There were some causes for concern, though. Shoshanna said Carol looked frightened and tearful when entering Angela's office that morning, before the outburst. And Maryanne reported that Carol had seemed sullen recently, out-of-sorts the day before, and had asked her if Angela had been talking about her. And Angela's perception that Carol was having a mental breakdown conflicted with what Jordan said, about how Carol seemed pleasant and lucid that very morning. And didn't Angela say something about Carol telling her she'd given her three weeks' notice to Parakh? Carol hadn't said anything like that to Parakh, or anybody for that matter.

All in all, it was a real clusterfuck for BBDQ. Carol didn't want to press any charges. Carol didn't want to leave, but she had to, she couldn't work in an environment that employed someone like Angela. This was a sticky situation; better to handle things amicably. So, hush-hush. Carol was given an unusually, some might say extraordinarily, generous severance deal. She took the next six months off before she started working at her new job, even though, with the package BBDQ provided her, Carol easily could have gone a couple of years without working.

Angela had presented an insurmountable obstacle. Angela would have been able to mentally and, apparently, physically torture her, without redress, as long as Carol had stayed at that office. Sure, people were a little suspicious of Angela after this incident. Maybe Angela would think twice before forcing out the next employee she didn't like. Maybe there'd been a little polish off that apple, but nothing fatal. Angela was a good worker, after all, and strange things happen. People would forget about it in a year or so. Just an unusually vicious co-worker spat. Carol knew that.

But she'd done something, at least. Life could be inscrutable, it could be horrendously unfair. But you make do, as Angela said, with what you have, the best you can.

That's Just the Way Things Are These Days

"YOU KNOW, IN almost any other circumstance, this would be considered pretty hot. I mean, still is, but you know. You're free to join us, you know, I think that's pretty obvious, if Sara didn't tell you. Pretty sure she said you could. She told me to tell you."

Nathan, seventeen, maintained eye contact with Carla, his face plastered with his goofy, overly expectant smile, a parody of merriment. Carla, also seventeen, having expected Nathan to say something to that effect for some time, rolled her eyes and nodded her head wearily, but in equal good humor, to show that she'd been biding her time for just such a comment.

"Had to be said, Carla, I'd hate to let you down."

The way Carla was tolerating and even amused by his mildly sexual comment was, of course, in itself pretty sexy. Carla was Sara's best friend — Care and Sar' — and Carla was cute and fetching in her own right. Nathan had been with Sara since sixth grade, before they'd both met Carla in the ninth grade, so he'd never seen her as a prospective partner. So expressing this sexualized tweak, this little nudge, was thrilling. He'd planned on saying that to her ever since this little rendezvous had been planned.

It'd be hotter if Sara had been out here to hear him say that to Carla, see how she'd respond. Carla and Sara looked good together, aesthetically, both slender, appealing souls, brunettes both blessed with warm, brown eyes and larger-than-average mouths, fine tools to accentuate their expressive miens; Carla a bit taller, shapelier, Sara, a bit more twee and vulpine. Carla was Puerto Rican and coffee-colored, while Sara was Irish-English stock and almost pure alabaster, and he'd be lying if he didn't find something sexy about their color pairings. He'd had many dreams about sleeping with Sara, his beloved, only to have the door open up and see Carla, cheekily pursing her lips, throwing her clothes off, giggling, radiant in her eagerness to join them. He'd made many a bedsheet translucent from dreams of that sort.

"I think you can handle it yourself," she responded, thumbing through a magazine. That comment, of course, if selectively interpreted, was shot through with sexiness. Any way she responded other than punching him in the nuts could be construed as sexy (and maybe even that, too, could be so construed if the damage wasn't bad; contact with his genitalia, after all).

Carla was sitting on one of the couches in the living room that faced the little hallway that led to the bedrooms, Sara's bedroom at the end of the hall; her younger brother Jason's to the right; and their parents' "master" bedroom to the left. From where Carla was seated, she could see the closed door to Sara's bedroom.

"Just try not to listen in, okay? I mean, I'm sorry you left your X-ray glasses at home, but you know."

"Alright there, I do hope you have a good time in there, that's all you'll get from me." She spoke a bit like a Little League coach.

"All I can ask for." He thought of making another comment, but decided against it. He liked jiving with her, the playfulness letting him linger on the excitement and stall the anticipation. He said a few more words to Carla before heading to Sara's room, letting her know where certain drinks and foods were in the kitchen, as if Carla didn't know, wasn't here almost as often as he was, and telling Carla to help herself to whatever, as if she didn't already have that privilege.

"Thanks," she responded, in a way that acknowledged that they both knew she knew all this information. "Have fun in there," and that of course sent a trill of physical elation through him, and he thought maybe to say something but he didn't. Carla smirked. Cut the cord, he thought, best not ruin the moment with analysis, get in there.

He knocked lightly on Sara's bedroom door even though the house was empty except for the three of them. Sara told him to come in. He smiled inwardly; he'd been with her so long, and hung out with her so often, that he recognized all her speech patterns. That "come in" was her missing a beat and then misjudging her volume, yelling a bit louder than needed, like she did if her mom called down to them when they were downstairs immersed in a movie and hadn't heard the call at first. It was high-pitched and endearing in a classically clumsy-cute Sara-way.

"Hi."

"Hi," she responded, while lying back on her bed, reading something on her phone.

"How's it going in here?" He was speaking softly for whatever reason.

"Good," she responded, sotto voce. He walked into her room, the room he'd been in hundreds of times, almost always with the door open at her parents' request. Now, he closed the door behind him.

Sara and her uncarpeted room. He'd never been in a bedroom that didn't at least have some kind of carpeting. A younger Sara had demanded the carpeting be taken out of her room, insisting that she liked the cool, natural feel of a wood floor, a decision she defended as being "precocious" but that wasn't right. That decision was made during the initial blooming of her hippie au naturel phase, where she briefly entertained veganism and flirted with being a kind of Luddite, which ended at about the same time as her parents allowed her to get a phone. She'd been enveloped in and pecking away at the reflected-glow screens of computers, tablets, and phones ever since. The veganism was still something she aspired to but constantly cheated on. The uncarpeted room was the last vestige of that early "precociousness," but Nathan sort of liked it, gliding around the wood floors on his besocked feet.

Her room was brightly lit, with glowy streamers in comforting colors, like Dutch Sky and Tangerine Cream, wrapped around the light-bar on the ceiling that provided the primary illumination. There was endless stuff crammed in her closet and upon the shelves along the inside of the closet. He recognized all of the outfits, from the yellow-and-blue striped tight shirt he liked her to wear, to the black long-sleeved jumper with the Japanese lettering on it, and the green corduroy pants she almost never wore. All the drawers of her bedside stand were closed, though he could recreate all their interiors by memory, except maybe her underwear drawer on the top, which he had only seen opened a few random times. Last time he'd seen it open some months ago everything in there had been crumply and messy, which he'd teased her about and she'd said "stawwwp" and closed it with a jolt. All the posters on the wall he recognized, the forever-ago classic movie tributes like *Breakfast at Tiffany's* and the new ones she loved like *These Times for Now* and the ironic ones, like the free poster she got at the mall for *Infinity Stars*; all the music posters, too, and she'd probably gotten his input on all of them, including the most recent one, that she'd gotten with him last summer at the Chobo Fest in Harrisburg.

He sat next to her on the bed. He stared at her as she fiddled on her phone, and then she stared back at him, until they became locked in a game to see who would break first. He usually didn't like people looking at him dead-on; the valley between his chin and lower lip was usually coarse and flaky from flattened pimples, and now was no different. But with Sara, he doubt she saw that, or even saw him as he really was anymore, the gaunt, chicken-chested, weak boy who longed to gain weight, aswim as he was in anything but the most tight-fitting outfits. She didn't see that, just as he never really saw the "oblong-rectangle" of her face that she pointed out sometimes when she looked in the mirror, or her "razor blade" pointy chin. He just saw the person he loved, and she the same; what he looked like now, or what she looked like tomorrow, mattered not at all, as long as he was he and she was she.

He forfeited the contest and broke his stare.

"I win," and she stuck her tongue out at him and went back to her phone.

"So you did. I threw the contest, of course, but I guess you still won, sort of." He looked loosely around the room, pantomiming interest in some corner, unsure of how to proceed.

"So what's my prize?" she asked, turning the phone over.

"Me. Here I am."

"You're the prize? I had you before I won. And no bow?"

"No bow. You can tie me up though."

"Hah, well, you better have a bow."

"Hah, yeah, I have a bow of sorts I guess." He opened his wallet and showed her the gold outline of the Trojan condom wrapper.

"It's like a bow. It tightens," and she made pincer motions with her fingers.

"Are you trying to scare me off using it? Because I'll have you know that I've tried them on a few times, and when you say it tightens, you aren't lying."

"I know, I was there the first time you put it on, remember?" Indeed, she had put a condom on him a couple of weeks ago, just to make sure she knew how to do it and could do it without mangling him. "Wait, when you said you've tried on condoms, you know it needs to be a different one each time, right?"

"I figured that out after I ripped through a bunch of them. Notice that this one is still wrapped up? See, I learned."

"Doi," she said, which was a kind of guttural comment like "duh," but sounded dumber, like something a clown would say.

"Doi yourself." This wasn't really like them, this space-filling teasing. It was pageantry borne of nerves.

"You'd love to rip through condoms, you wish that story was true."

"Well, I am a guy, you know." He could have said something else, kept the jousting going, but he recognized it for what it was and wanted to move on. He was nervous, too.

"Carla's texting me," and she lifted up the phone to show him. 'All good N there?' the text read. "What a good friend, eh?"

"She's a keeper."

Sara returned to her phone, typed a message with great alacrity, and then turned the phone over and put it on her nightstand.

"What'd you say?"

"That we're good, you know. Nothing, you know, momentous yet, but we're good. Stay tuned."

"I hope you didn't really say that. Please tell me you didn't say, what was that, 'momentous?'"

"I did."

He thought of leaping over her and grabbing the phone mock-aggressively, her play-wrestling with him to keep the phone away, an interlude that could take a life of its own and further prolong their ... what, exactly? Their innocence? That put things in moral terms that neither ascribed to. Their compatibility? Maybe just that this was safe, this calm before the storm. Haha, he could imagine her reaction if he said "calm before the storm" — she'd say something like "pretty confident in yourself there if you are prepared for a 'storm'" or maybe a simple "you wish."

But it's best not to say something like that. Because maybe she'd think more about this, and then express, with words reedy and elegiac, what they'd both be thinking; or worse, not express it, and then they'd both be left alone to dissimulate, to pretend not to understand the import in the implication. To be isolated with those private fears would be a mockery of their companionship, so predicated as it was on continued affirmations of their open and boundless kinship.

"You know, Sara, if you don't want to ...."

"That took a turn there, didn't it?" She had a way of disarming awkwardness by diving headfirst through it.

"You know."

"I know, listen," and she drew in close to him and kissed him, and he kissed back. Their breaths were hot on each other's face. Nathan smooched on her shoulder, then up along the side of her neck, his nipples a bit uncomfortably hard from the soft abrasion of Sara's petite chest against his.

"I love you."

"I love you, too, Sara, you know I do."

"I know you do. Wow, you must be really trying to convince me, saying my name and everything."

She was being clever, as she was. His natural instinct was to be clever, too, but he felt compelled to be emphatic, if even leadenly emphatic, in conveying his love and tenderness. He was a man, and men in the old movies he'd watched would say anything, be disingenuous and conniving if it worked to get them laid. Times change, of course, and they both knew better, but he just ... he just wanted to let her know, seriously, that he loved her, and she should only do this with him if she truly wanted to.

As if their kinship extended to telepathy, she whispered into his ear: "I want this." That should be enticing, erotic, and in some sense it was, but he was getting nervous, fearful.

"I want this, too," he lied. No, that wasn't it. He did want this, but he wanted it to be over. He wanted them to be lying next to each other, besotted with relief and release, exhausted but ecstatic, eager to replenish themselves, to do it over and over again, until they could never remember the time when the initiation of their physical intimacy was fraught with so much trepidation.

He looked squarely at her. "We'll be forever together. I'm with you forever."

"I'm with you forever."

"I'm just, I'm just scared, you know."

"I know. I'm, I'm scared, too, you know."

"I don't want to make you scared."

"It's okay. It's okay. It's natural. It's unavoidable."

"I know, but I don't, you know, I don't want to make you

scared."

"I know, of course. Who would want to be scared?" and she giggled, and then play-bit his nose. He felt fleetingly self-conscious about how oily his nose must have tasted, but lost the thought beneath another kiss.

They tumbled around a bit in bed, both perhaps overemphasizing small moments, pausing the act to laugh or giggle, and it was a curious thought they both had, both aware they were delaying the act, but wasn't that a good thing, wasn't this an act to be savored?

Yes, it was, but only retroactively.

Countless times they'd engaged in meandering palaver; that's one of the joys of knowing someone so intimately for so long, a hallmark of a true connection, but this was one of those rare moments where he felt ashamed, somehow, using their easy rapport as a pretext to be dilatory.

They had both been accepted to Penn State. They had their dorm assignments; from the directions on the maps, they'd only be a 22-minute walk from one another. They, of course, would go through college together, just as they went through high school together. This was just one more moment, epochal as it may seem now, that would eventually form part of the interconnected skein of their shared lives. Nothing to fear, he told himself, just as she told herself, both of them employing mental tricks for relaxation, both concentrating on their breathing, on the tactile pressure of lips against lips, hot breath against dry skin; him adding to it his satisfying firmness, her concentrating on his delicate cupping of her breasts.

He knew not what images flashed behind her eyes, and he dare not ask. None, he told himself. She'd told him, none. She wanted this.

>< >< ><

Yet they were aware of the risks, however infinitesimal that might be. Sex always bore risks, didn't it, from STDs to unexpected pregnancies to all sorts of quieter lamentations, let-downs or regret. Both virgins, yet both having gotten "tested" (as vacuous as that word was nowadays), so they at least didn't have STDs to worry about. Their love was true and lasting, so regret or let-downs shouldn't be in the cards, and any poor performance could be worked on with practice (a joke he'd thought to make before, but passed upon). And, God forbid, if there just so happened to be an unwanted pregnancy on their first act of lovemaking, as remote as that possibility would be given all their preparations — the condom AND the birth control pills she had been hiding from her parents for the past three months — then that would be dealt with. And as naïve as it sounded now, he would be relieved if their post-coitus fears were so, well, typical. Fears that still had, to him, some understandable semblance to reality, situations that family and friends and professionals could be turned to for advice.

He didn't feel himself softening, but his vigor, his dedication to getting through this, was weakening. His buzzing thoughts were causing his head to hurt, his stomach to lurch. What the hell, he thought, to try and rush through this, this moment that should be so meaningful. That *was* so meaningful.

He tried to redirect his focus again, moving to her bare stomach for playful nibbles and then moving up to the flat valley between her breasts, licking around her left nipple, a full rotation, getting the desired effect from her. She pulled him toward her by his unbelted-jeans, which were still on, and, with an inexpert heave, she pulled them down, so they bunched in a knot with his boxers.

She, lovingly and graciously, put his penis into her mouth, and he closed his eyes to savor the warm sensation, the tingle, the feeling of disconnecting from his upper mind. How come this wasn't enough? How come this wasn't the test? How come he, and others, could receive blow jobs to completion, and that wasn't an indicator of sexual fitness?

Buried in these thoughts were his usual impudent ones; he hoped Carla would text her, or, better yet, call them now to check up on them and Sara would answer with a mouthful of his cock. Maybe Sara would take a selfie and send it to Carla to show that things were going well. He imagined it fleetingly, Sara's cheek extended, winking for Carla's benefit, one of those weird, exciting fantasies that blaze up out of nowhere and are almost immediately forgotten, doused by a splash of reality.

Other thoughts intruded upon him, as if encouraged by the vacuum of his extinguished fantasy. Oral sex was no indicator of sexual fitness. Everyone knew that. And then flooding right behind those thoughts were the phantasmagorical, the wretched, the horrific, the amplified hearsay he'd heard all his life.

Of course, every town had the story of the masturbating boy who loses control. The story was told so often through his childhood, through everyone's childhood, that no matter who told the story it always had the same basic elements:

A mother comes home (it's always a mother). She knocks on her son's bedroom door, or maybe, but not often, it's a downstairs computer room or some other young boy's man-cave. She hears movement inside so she knows he's in there. Headphones on, she thinks, or maybe she doesn't think and just opens the door after a few frustrated knocks. She sees him, from behind, his wrist flexing, arm pumping. Caught pleasuring himself with flagrant abandon, every young boy's nightmare. The mother closes the door immediately, mortified, for herself and even worse, for her son. She knows, too, that this is every boy's nightmare.

And then the story differs depending on the telling. Either in that brief panicked interaction she saw something so disturbing she's compelled to open the door again, too scared to consider the consequences if she's mistaken or so sure she saw what she thinks she saw that she has to intervene; or maybe the mother never actually closes the door, maybe she opens it and just stares with the idiot glare of terror, until she breaks down and relents, runs toward him; or, perhaps, she does nothing productive, just stares and screams.

For the boy's wrist was flexing, his arm was pumping, he had been doing exactly what she thought he'd been doing: except any traditional pleasures he got from the act ceased long ago. Because his dick was in his hand, that's for sure, but only the mangled part he ripped off after his mind turned, when the palliative of the turn caused all other concerns to drop away, so he sat there, doing only what he could instinctually still do, fapping away with his severed, blood-soaked, nail-gnarled gristle of a dick.

Nathan had heard the gory story so many times as a kid. Growing up, if you ever met a kid from out of town and they wanted to scare you or get your attention, that's the story they'd most likely tell. Some kids had more fun with it than others, maybe highlighting the dark visual humor, adding in elements like brightly-colored veins or viscera still stuck to the cock, fluttering like streamers; or some garish embellishment like insisting that the blood that comes out of a severed cock was actually purple ("Nuh-uh" he imagines another kid saying in protest).

Having gotten older and learning about the ailment — disease, condition, virus, whatever you wanted to call it, the curse of his generation – he was well-equipped to pinpoint all the reasons why the urban legend couldn't be true. Kids would argue passionately as to why the story couldn't be true, and in their insistence, they would miss the greater horror.

The boy wouldn't be sitting there still jerking off, severed dick in hand, like a mindless ghoul. He'd never rip off his own dick. How else would he satisfy his proverbial master? Also, if you were one of those statistically unlucky somebodies to suffer The Turn, you still have a sense of yourself. You are still rational, capable, strategic to some extent, even if you are now powered by the singular obsessions of sex and violence. You get uncovered eventually, but you can put up a rational defense for a while, try to explain yourself, retain the faculties to cozen your way out of the accusation.

There were other reasons why the urban legend seemed like bullshit. It was highly unlikely for masturbation to be enough to trigger the turn. Highly unlikely, but not impossible. As he learned early on, being able to masturbate or even receive oral sex was some indicia, but by no means conclusive, of fitness for sexual intercourse. Each of those smaller sexual acts served as successive indicia of fitness. But again, not quite there yet.

But all that being said, all those purely logical and nigh-irrefutable reasons why that urban legend just had to be bullshit, well, Google and you shall see, in a galaxy of haystacks you are bound to prick yourself upon a needle.

Sara ended the oral teasing, letting his dick fall out of her mouth on the backward bob. He was fully hard now, he could see and feel. It felt good, sustaining, his young body flexed and his heart pumped. He felt full of vigor, like he had just worked out and, strangely, felt like he was part of a greater, bestial universe.

For the past few weeks, while privately testing out condoms at home in anticipation for their much-talked-about, eventual big day, he'd been sometimes unable to get or maintain erections. It was bad enough his dick hadn't been complying when being summoned with the task. As if his dick was tired of just being defensive on its war with his self-esteem, it launched its own counter-offensive, refusing to give him his usual morning woods. That inanition made him sick with fear that his problems weren't just mental, but physical. What seventeen-year-old has ED? What else, congestive heart failure? But now, satisfied with his rising to the task, he rolled around in bed with his beloved, doing his best not to Observer Effect his dick into torpor.

>< >< ><

He remembered being ten and his father talking to him about the condition, struggling to find the words. Through the prevaricating, the main lessons he learned were these:

That he would feel certain physical urges that were normal and healthy. That he should never be ashamed of those urges. But those urges [and here the veiled language had been confusing] carried a risk. Sometimes a boy would be physical with a girl and he would just go crazy. Those exact words weren't used, but that was the gist; a man would go violent and crazy. This was called Turning.

That it only affected the younger generation. You couldn't wait it out. If a boy or young man had the condition, and waited decades to have sex, he would still turn.

That he would be hearing about all this at school, in health, science, and gym classes, endlessly, but with good reason.

That the odds of having the condition are slim-to-none, 1%, his father told him (a statistic that was on the optimistic side of close, really more like 1.5-3%, depending on the community studied).

That there was a possibility that, while a man wouldn't make a complete turn, he'd have enough of whatever caused it in his system to make his partner ill with "a really bad cold." (Why was that the only part of the conversation that he could recall an exact phrase? Later, in health class, he'd learn that the real diagnosis was something more like seizures mixed with immediate flu-like symptoms.)

That there were no tests to detect the condition, no tests whatsoever (information he later learned was unfortunately, devastatingly true).

That, while people had theories, about biological or chemical terrorism, that Hamas or one of those groups had claimed responsibility, for whatever that's worth, that at the end of the day they were all just theories, no one had an answer.

That he had to be forthright with his father and that his father would always be there for him, no matter what Nathan was feeling.

And that his father had cried. His father had cried and then muttered, basically to himself, that he couldn't believe this was real, still; that it'd been, at that point, over twenty years since the condition had been discovered and still, he couldn't believe it. What a world they lived in, a world that was only getting worse.

>< >< ><

She placed the condom on him. A couple of his pubes snagged, but other than that, not bad, swift and efficient.

"Done this more times than I thought? Should I be asking questions about how you got so good at that?"

"Shush, you. I've left a lot of satisfied bananas. I should email Ms. Howden, tell her I nailed this." Ms. Howden had been their seventh grade sexual health and home economics teacher.

"Maybe you'll get extra credit," he cooed, in an unnaturally low octave.

She looked at him. "That's not sexy at all, you know that?"

"But isn't anything I say like this ... sexy, baby?" he continued, driving the voice into knowing self-parody.

"Let me try it, baby," she said, in a low masculine register, deep and velvety. "I just grew chest hair."

"Is it bad that I'm more turned on?"

"Not at all," she said, back in her normal voice. "I love an open-minded man."

"By the way, you're lying about having grown chest hair. I can see your tits, remember?" Sayings tits aloud, her acknowledging that he was indeed seeing her tits, was additionally enticing, exciting. They continued to fool around, him doing with his fingers the things that she liked, her sounds proof of that (although he suspected she made her noises chiefly for his benefit).

He thought of saying that they can just do this, fingering-type stuff, that he would be happy just pleasing her, if she wanted. But he didn't want to disrupt the moment, lest she misinterpret.

>< >< ><

He thought of Jacob, or what his classmates had said about Jacob. Jacob had been in their grade. Last year, both Nathan and Sara had shared gym and lunch session with him. Nathan also had English with him, but he wasn't sure if Sara shared any other class with him.

One Friday last year, as Bobby told it, Jacob walked into Ms. Lebson's history class, his last class of the day. Jacob had piled into the class alongside everyone else, the kind of comedic 'this is drudgery' way, the 'I can't wait to get out of here' way that all the kids did going into their last class before the weekend. Jacob had talked about weekend plans and parties, cracked wise before the introductory bell, took his inconsistent, day-dreamy notes; basically just like any other day.

Halfway or so during the class, Bobby, who sat next to Jacob, noticed a little cut or mark or something, above Jacob's eye. Not a big deal, whatever, Bobby only tipped him off with a hand gesture, because the cut was bleeding and Bobby thought maybe it'd been a popped pimple or something and wanted to give him a heads-up.

Jacob didn't understand at first, so Bobby, a respectful kid and good student, leaned in and furtively said, "you're bleeding, dude," and when Jacob looked befuddled, Bobby repeated it with a bit more urgency, and added, "you got blood on your face, dude." Then Jacob felt at the spot, looked at the smear of blood on his hand, tilted his head up and said, matter-of-factly, "no, I don't."

Bobby, who was possessed with both a sense of humor and a love of arguing, almost took the bait, because this was a clear case he was going to win. But something in the way Jacob responded was so perplexing. It didn't give him any inkling of what was going on — how could it, really, so minor a thing – and hindsight is 20/20, but something about the way Jacob had said it convinced Bobby to decline the challenge. It'd be like trying to prove your point to someone speaking a foreign language, as Bobby later described it.

Before class, Jacob had lost his virginity with his girlfriend, Virginia, who went to a different school and was maybe a year younger. They'd apparently hung out at lunch time, maybe Jacob had drove over to her school, who knows. They'd had sex in his car, apparently, because that's where they found her. Her corpse was desecrated. That was the only way to describe it. Jacob was arrested later that day, just after history class, supposedly, as someone must have scene inside his car. Supposedly, her blood, feces, phlegm, saliva, and fluid from her vagina, brain, and eyes were all found on his penis.

That was obviously all terrifying. Jacob had fallen into that terrible 1.5-3%, with Virginia as his awful, loving, unfortunate victim. That much was horrifying in its own right. But what seemed to vex Nathan the most, what he couldn't wrap his brain around, was the fact that Jacob didn't hide the corpse, didn't try and run. He just left her body in his car, even drove back to school with her corpse still in his car, for God's sake, and attended his last class.

What murderer in that situation wouldn't just get in his car and flee? He'd had enough sense — if that was the right word — to clean himself up, even if he missed the tell-tale spot by his eye, which turned out to be a nail scratch from Virginia's vain effort to save herself. When Jacob had been confronted, he supposedly denied, obfuscated, rationalized, no more or less persuasive than he usually was. Something had, well, turned — that was it, wasn't it? What else could be said?

In this world, Nathan would be fine just never having sex. Of course, he wanted to, ached to, both for the obvious primal reasons but also to consecrate his love, for his imagined future family, for the physical blessing of the act itself.

Africans had run the risk of producing children with sickle cell syndrome. There is some Jewish genetic disorder that kills their children, after causing their children's bones to literally decompose, their bodies to seize, their eyes to stop working. There were tests for those disorders now, but for how many decades of their history would those peoples have to just take the gamble? Or when syphilis and other venereal diseases ran rampant all over Europe, causing people to lose their minds. Ben Franklin died of it, Nathan half-remembered hearing. Or consider AIDS in Africa. People all over the world, since time immemorial, have been running the risks against the rewards. Why should now be any different?

That he had to persuade himself to overcome these fears was partly why his father had cried.

>< >< ><

Carla waited outside, fiddling idly on her phone, texting with friends and keeping discreet about what she was doing at Sara's house. 'Real Gs stay silent like lasagna,' as the lyrics went to that classic, decades-old rap song. Her on guard duty, keeping mum. She was listening in, though, sort of, not really; what else could she really do?

She was just there in the extremely rare chance that something went wrong. Not really even that. She was just like a talismanic figure, like a security blanket. You heard all the stories, and if something terrible happened, she'd be here to defend Sara, call 911, something. That's what they'd said, anyway, but maybe that was pretext, an excuse to get her here, who knows. Again, what could she do?

Straining to hear the goings-on inside the bedroom was also kind of exciting. She hoped to hear the sounds of their mutual pleasures. She wanted to have sex, but was single and wasn't taking any chances. The boys at school who'd successfully had sex reaped the benefits, were able to "shoot above their weight," a gross, innuendo-laden term. But none of those boys interested her. C'est la vie.

><><><

Nathan was inside Sara, his body atop hers, his face pressed against her neck; her face returning the favor, buried, nibbling, into the recess of his collar bone. He rocked slowly, gently, doing his best not to hurt her. He kissed her ear, then her cheek, her cheekbone, and she returned the kisses. He kissed her square on the mouth, a big unsexy smooch, and she kissed back while he pushed to his full extent inside of her. She reacted, seemed to freeze, holding her breath, in an enigmatic state held between pleasure and discomfort. She released, looked up at him, smiling and nodding her head, yes, it felt good, yes, you are inside of me, yes, it hurt a little but now it doesn't, now it feels good. None of that was vocalized but she hoped she expressed it otherwise.

He lurched forward on her, felt the tips of her breasts brush against him, thought about kissing her forehead but stopped himself, that's something a grandfather would do. He laughed, which caused his body to quiver, and she felt that too.

"What's so funny," she drawled, kissing him on his neck.

"Nothing," he breathed hot at her, kissing her face, just her dewy flesh against his.

"I love you, too."

>< >< ><

Carla swore she heard the revelatory bumping of bed frame against wall. And, yup, she's sure she heard the insistent little screeching of bedsprings. Subtle, but you could hear it if you really trained yourself to listen. Bow chika wah wah. She thought about texting them, to see if they would respond and, if so, how. But she didn't. She'd adopt a knowing, 'how you doin?' look for when the love-fuzzy couple came back out after they were done, she didn't know, cleaning themselves up or whatever.

She returned to fiddling with her phone, thinking again of the right balance of saucy and innocent that would make for the best post-coitus texts. She wasn't that bold, gave that up soon, and concentrated back on her news and tabloidy websites, the distinction between the two nigh impossible to discern.

She was reading some article about a new breed of miniature poodle when she thought she heard a voice from the bedroom, low enough to be likely Nathan's. "Fuck," she thought she heard, but it was indistinct enough for her to let it slide. She paused her reading, though, and readied her eyes on the door.

She looked for another five seconds or so, the silence that greeted her inviting her eyes to shift back to her story.

"Fuck!" she heard again, and now she started standing up when she felt her phone shake. A text from Nathan.

'Call 911, get N here she's sick!'

"Oh fuck, fuck-fuck-fuck." In an instant she felt exposed, humiliated, how stupid she was, how dumb they were, placing her out here. What could she do? She thought of being in a changing room and having the curtain ripped open, naked, exposed and embarrassed. Fuck, fuck?

She ran to Sara's bedroom.

"Nathan, what's going on in there?"

"Carla!" she heard him just beyond the door. "She's, she's sick, I think I infected her, God, she's sick, she's like, seizing?"

"Can she talk?"

"No, help us! Come in here and call 911."

"Did you call?"

"No, I'm freaking out, I tried pushing on her chest, giving her mouth-to-mouth. I don't know what to do! Help, I need help!"

"Open the door!"

"It's open. Help me!"

She lifted her hand to open the door, but stopped herself. Her friend was seizing, she could die. Carla needed to help. She couldn't delay, she imagined being told at the hospital that EMS got to her friend too late, that Sara could have been saved if only Carla had responded faster, done something. Carla wouldn't be able to live with herself if that happened. She couldn't let that happen.

But still, she stopped herself.

She wanted to see Sara before she actually entered the room.

"Sara, wake up!" she heard Nathan yell, sobbing, now farther away from the door. Carla imagined him on top of her, wiping away the mucus and saliva that threatened to choke her, doing anything in his power to assist his seizing girlfriend.

"Fuck you if you won't help!" she heard Nathan yell, tear-choked. "I'm calling 911 myself," she heard him say, a bit off-kilter, as if his neck was askew to balance the phone between his head and shoulder while he continued to work to save Sara's life. "Come in here and help me. Help us, please!" she heard closer to the door.

She felt movement near the door and he opened it, about half-way. She leaned in and she saw what had to be Sara, who appeared to be on her side, her back to the door.

"Sara," Carla said breathlessly, dialing 911 with her right hand as she pushed her way through the door to get to her friend.

Nathan, behind the closed door, wondered when he'd feel the effects of this third testicle. For now, it was still just a gooey eyeball, nestled, viscous and slimy, beneath his balls. He hoped it didn't roll back and get stuck in his butthole. That'd be sort of funny and a bit ironic, given how chaste he and Sara had been. Brown-eyed Sara, seeing the ole brown eye. Gross, haha.

He closed the door, softly, still gripping Sara's beauty scissors, once stainless steel, now plenty stained, and closed the distance to Carla.

A DEEP HORROR THAT
WAS VERY NEARLY AWE

Bleecker and Bleaker; or, Gay for Muesli

"SO, IT'S LIKE this," Ken started, breaking through the lull in the conversation that took over at the gathered table. Ken paused to catch himself, noticing his thoughts were getting murky from the alcohol. He hated clichéd, rambly drunk-talk, and he wanted to make sure he sounded sharp and put-together with this next comment ....

Actually, I'm Ken so it's just easier if I tell this first-person. So ignore that first part in the third person. I'm Ken and this story is about me. Sorry for that, was going to go with an objective literary device but this is a subjective story so let's be upfront about that and keep it that way from here on in.

So, anyway, where was I? Right, sitting around the table, there was me, Tommy, Beth, Ron, Allison, and two or three other people I didn't know. Beth and Allison were identical twins, and Tommy and Ron were each dating a sister. I was friends with Tommy, who was throwing the party at his three-bedroom apartment in Greenpoint, so I guess Aaron, Tommy's roommate, and Aaron's girlfriend were around, too; maybe one of them was also sitting at the table, I'm not sure. Greenpoint is a neighborhood in the northern part of Brooklyn, by the way, that used to be heavily Polish but is now heavily — correction — oppressively, hipster-twee. I'm not trying to be pretentious in telling you that part. I understand not everyone knows about New York neighborhoods so if you already knew that information, I apologize, just bear with me.

So yeah, Tommy, you can do the math. Tommy had a three-bedroom in Greenpoint with only one roommate, so he was doing pretty well, or his Mommy and Daddy were doing well and sharing some of the largess with him, something I had no idea about but suspected. The suspicion was enough for me.

"You got it together there?" Ron started with me. "Keep it together, keep it together, you got this." That was him teasing me about slurring my words. I'd just met Ron that day but had preemptively judged him as an insufferable douchebag. That decision was final and not appealable. He was someone whose personality seemed derived from the shitty unfunny movies he'd absorbed throughout his life, and any natural pause in a conversation he used as an opportunity to make himself heard. Even that mantra, the way he repeated it — "Keep it together, you got this" — sounded like some pull-quote from some garbage television show or something, and the look he made after, searching for recognition, only lent credence to that conclusion.

As additional evidence in support of Ron's douchebaggery: he called Aaron "A.A. Ron" for reasons that escape me, but I guess it sounded funny and ironically low-class? He'd also committed one of my personal pet peeves. See, I asked him where he was from and he said "Philly." First, he called it "Philly" which is obnoxious in and of itself, but naturally I followed up with, "Oh, do you mean inside the actual city? Where in Philadelphia?" Then he said, "Like South Jersey." "What town in South Jersey?" I continued. "Cherry Hill," was the answer. So, we go from the mean streets of Philly to the manicured lawns of rich-kid USA, Cherry Hill.

So I'm sure you too have concluded that Ron is a piece of shit, and are no doubt impressed by my perceptive ability to read people. That's good — keep that in mind for later.

What Allison saw in him, who knew, she was too pretty to be with an idiot like Ron although she was an idiot herself, but a pretty female idiot has higher value on the dating market than a normal bro male idiot so who knows.

Keep in mind I was pretty drunk at this time, too.

I pressed on despite his interruption.

"What I'm saying is, what has to be interesting about dating twins is, like, the sexual attraction to your partner's sister is just, like, out there. I mean, they look identical. If you think Beth is hot, you have to think Allison is hot; so if Beth is sufficiently attractive for you to sleep with, then Allison must be also. I just think that's interesting, it's like, the quiet things people always think about but don't say: attraction to your partner's sister. But here it's like, it's so obvious, it's unavoidable. It's like the subtext with other people is like, above the surface here. The Urtext. Is that what that means?"

"Oh boy," someone said. One of the sisters said something like "Exactly, we are *exactly* the same, 100 percent," trying to be sarcastic but her delivery was shit so her point was lost. "No difference here between the two of us, exactly," the other sister tried to add as a tag to her sister's unacknowledged comment but she shared her sister's sloppy delivery, ironically undermining their shared point. I thought about pointing that out but it'd be too mean and with the cross-talking my insightful observation would likely be lost.

"I mean, it's interesting, is all I'm saying. I mean, you are identical twins. Identical, it's in the description, if you find one of you attractive, you have to basically find the other one also pretty much in the same, in the same territory, you know?

"I mean, be honest, Tommy, when you're sleeping with Beth," which elicited a bunch of ruckus and laughs, to which I defended my choice of words with: "I said 'sleeping with,' I'm being respectful and ... coy ... I didn't say 'when you're fucking Beth.' I'm a gentleman. A gentleman of proper breeding and etiquette. Anyway, as I was saying, when you're fucking with, fucking Beth, are you telling me you don't ever, ever think about Allison? Ever, *ever*? I mean just even imagining what it'd be like to have the same thing but just slightly different?"

"I'm dating Allison, you moron, you got them reversed."

"That just proves my point! My point is proven!"

He actually was dating Beth. I was right. He was fucking with me, deflecting the topic. But people laughed at his joke and I let him have his moment in the sun.

"All I'm saying, it's just, it's interesting. You don't have to answer it."

"See what he says, 'you don't have to answer it. You don't have to talk about what you think when being intimate with your girlfriend and your thoughts about her sister — you don't *have* to answer.' Thanks, inspector." See, Tommy was pretty cool, had a sense of humor about himself.

"That's what friends are for. See, I like you, we're friends, you don't have to answer."

A pause.

"I don't really like you though, Ron, so you have to answer the same question."

There was laughter at the table and more drinks. I slinked away soon after to smoke a few bowls on the porch with some acquaintances I had from the Tommy-circle of friends. Tommy was a good dude. We met because he used to live near the West Village

TechCenter where I worked and he'd stop in. We hung out a couple of times and I ingratiated myself into his circle of friends and wound up at cool parties like this. He moved to Brooklyn a couple months ago, to this nice luxury Greenpoint pad where he hung out with his hot girlfriend and her hot twin sister and friends who went to the gym and played shitty EDM music under the name TrashPatch or some dumb thing like that. And I don't know why it was that I liked Tommy but instinctively disliked his other friends and teased him a bit and gave him a bit of a hard time even though he was smarter, better-looking, more well-adjusted, and successful than me.

(You'll note that I included me saying "like" a lot in that previous little anecdote. That shows that I'm honest, because I easily could have eliminated those "likes" in the telling of this tale, and it certainly would have made me sound smarter and more eloquent if I'd done so. But I'm honest. Keep that in mind, too, when it sounds like I'm straining credibility.)

I guess he didn't like my identical twins queries, which is too bad because when we first met he kind of liked my blunt ways. My blunt ways were partly a pose, an identity I adopted; like, it came naturally to me, but I amplified it intentionally for comic effect. I guess he didn't like it when it directly involved him, though. Supposedly both Beth and Allison mentioned to him after the party that they didn't like me and thought I was creepy. I wanted to ask if they both had the exact same opinion on the matter, which would further prove my point about their identicalness. If I remember correctly, I think Tommy told me that Beth had later grilled him about his potential answer to my query, and interrogated him as to whether he'd put me up to asking it, maybe to exorcise some weird fetish? I guess she didn't believe that a sane person would be so tactless in asking just a naturally interesting question.

I mean, identical hot twins, who wouldn't think about sleeping with the other one! C'mon! *C'mon!* The conversation had gotten boring so I just asked. And people seemed to be laughing and enjoying themselves. Though, again, I was pretty drunk and high and I don't handle those things particularly well.

So anyway, as you can tell from where this is headed, Tommy and I kind of stopped talking after that. Which is too bad because if I'm being honest, Tommy was really my only friend in New York at the time. At that point I'd only moved to New York about six months prior, and he was the one person whose apartment was large enough to have people over, so a lot of weekdays I'd just go over there and watch movies and drink, and on weekends we'd go out to brunch with other people and then hang out at his apartment. So Tommy was basically the axis around which my New York social circle swung. Without Tommy, my New York friend list dropped by a perilous 100%.

So this story isn't going to be about Tommy at all. He's out from here on in. This just sets the stage for where I was at mentally when Kaz came into my life.

So I didn't mean to bait-and-switch but it just sets the sad stage. Me, in New York, essentially friendless, before I met Kaz. And I think the Tommy anecdote is kind of fun and when I talk about Kaz I get kind of bummed, although it's good to talk about it, I think.

So before I move on, let me just set the record straight and state that I was obviously remorseful about upsetting Tommy. I really didn't mean to; I was just fucking around with him. I mean I don't feel good about it at all. I was resentful toward him, with all his friends and success. But you got to move on, right? I guess I can still reach out to him one of these days.

So anyway, onward and upward. I mentioned before that I worked at VillageTech, which was like an electronics repair store in Greenwich Village, on Bleecker Street, the western part of the diagonal, nicer part of the West Village in Manhattan, where none of the streets are straight lines or follow the grid plan that Manhattan is known for. There's the east-west part of Bleecker Street that's like NYU town with the storied past and everything but is mainly now just cheap trinket stores, bars and fast food from around the world. Then there's the diagonal part of Bleecker Street that's yuppie-tourist town, of boutique cupcake shops, Moleskin stores, you know those 10 dollar artsy notebooks containing 20 pages of paper, Goorin Hat Brothers and, like, Murray's Cheese Shop and luxe-shit all around. Not a practical store in sight. You can get a thirty dollar cheese and a three hundred dollar bowler hat but don't you even think about getting a sandwich under ten bucks. It's such an odd area because it used to be very popular but the commercial rents kept going up, so now there's what's called high-end blight: a lot of fancy stores in the area, but also a ton of vacancies because it's harder and harder to find stores willing to put up with such high rents.

So anyway, that's where our shop was, for some reason. Even though I'd only been working there in New York for six months, I knew the shop wasn't long for this world. First, I mean, given the location, rent must have been astronomical. Second, these were all tourists in this area. No one flew in from Japan or Argentina to get their computers repaired. Strangely, one of our main sources of income was Brazilian tourists buying electronics to smuggle back into their country to avoid their apparently outrageous import taxes. Strange world, right?

Did I tell you how I came to work at VillageTech? It's pretty interesting, you always hear all these negative stories about the American economy, and I'm not saying those aren't true. I guess the story I'm telling ends up being a negative, sad story that takes place in America, after all. But sometimes things do kind of work out for you, at least temporarily.

Before I moved to New York, I was an assistant manager of the electronics section of a Sam's Club in Raymore, Missouri, near where I grew up. They were closing the electronics section down — I guess Raymore, Missouri just didn't have that cultural and retail cache it must have once had — and Sam's Club offered three options to its staff: an employee buy-out; an in-house transfer to a different department but with reduced pay; or an out-of-state transfer. I bet they didn't think anyone would take that out-of-state transfer. I wasn't the best employee, but I'd been there a pretty long time, five years, which is a lifetime in retail. I'd always been sufficiently unmotivated in regard to improving my lot in life, and I guess upper management interpreted my life paralysis as company loyalty. So I noticed that one of the transfer opportunities was at a place called VillageTech in New York City. Oh yeah, that's right, people think of VillageTech as this independent institution in the West Village, a neighborhood that still coasts off the fumes of supposed independent small business, but in reality Sam's Club actually bought them out years ago.

Anyway, I didn't know that, and I thought, how weird is that, like they really needed us hayseeds from Missouri to fill positions in New York City? Was that an oversight on the list? I knew so little about New York City that I didn't realize that it was in Manhattan. I saw the location, "Greenwich Village," and thought, a village in New York City? Weird, like was it Colonial Williamsburg or something. As a sidenote, I learned that most New Yorkers would prefer a Colonial Williamsburg to what the neighborhood of Williamsburg, Brooklyn, had become, but that's another story.

Anyway, so I took the transfer and found myself with a new job, a new city, and no friends, living way out in the ass-end of Brooklyn, by Coney Island. And outside the theme park, Coney Island is, mind you, a shithole. Screams of excitable kids during the day, screams of murder victims during the night. Kids passed out from cotton candy sugar-high crashes and adults passed out from heroin crashes. And when it's off-season, forget about it. These are hyperbolic but you get the point. No one wanted to trek all the way out there and Tommy had been my only real friend. And now he was out. So I was in a rough space.

So Kaz. He worked right around the corner from me, at a coffee shop, that's how we met. Yeah, Kaz, that's what he called himself. I know, right, hard to tell if that's a man or a woman's name, and I'm sure that was the point. It was his abbreviation of Casimir. I didn't think there were Venezuelans named Casimir. You know, it's not like Castro or Javier or something. When he told me his full name he had like five additional middle and last names, one was "nacho" and one was "pepper." It's not like I checked his I.D. to verify any of that, I just called him "Kaz."

So you know, I looked up the origins of the name 'Casimir' recently, and it's Polish. It's a combination of two words that separately mean "to destroy" and "the world." Like, "kaziti" or something in Polish that means "to destroy." Pretty interesting.

I'm getting ahead of myself here, anyway. Okay. So how's this for a segue: Kaz worked at the gayest coffee shop in the world, and he should have been their corporate mascot. And I mean that as a compliment. The highest compliment.

He worked at Le Bois, which is French for "The Wood" and yes I think the employees made approximately 19 million inappropriate jokes about the name. It's a mid-sized coffee spot that seemed geared more toward a high-volume, in-a-rush crowd: coffee and grab-n-go bowls of granola, fruit salads, muesli bowls and all that stuff, you know. I think everyone who worked there was a gay guy or a pretty lady.

I don't know why I didn't go there when I first began working at VillageTech, as I do love me some good coffee. Maybe because I liked to play up some folksy Midwestern roots thing even though that's not who I am at all, and I saw that frou-frou French coffee shop and said "fuck it" and went to the out-of-the-way Dunkin' Donuts instead. But I found myself in Le Bois one day at an off period although it was still fairly busy, and one thing I noticed right away is that Kaz had, like, regulars. Like, people would be in line and let others go in front of them so as to time their purchases so that Kaz would ring them up.

Kaz was a curious creature. While heavyset, he had graceful, delicate features and was surprisingly agile on his feet. He had wide, pouty Cupid-bow lips that should have been featured in the type of high-resolution black-and-white erotica-lite ads that Chanel or whoever used to sell colognes and perfumes. He also had fashy hair in a kind of pompadour swoop; by fashy hair, I mean David Beckham hair, short to the point of shaved on one side, long on the other, clean and tidy with almost a military sheen, although he added that Elvis-pomp on top that made me think of frosting on a cupcake.

But really it was his lips that I noticed first. I found it uncomfortable how I was drawn to them. They really were so almost transcendently feminine, yet connected to this soft-looking, corpulent male body that always had a slight regnant whiff, underneath his cologne, of the type of body odor that attached often to sweaty, heavy-set men. If Kaz were straight, he could easily end up as your typical, slightly smelly lumpen male. But he wasn't: his gayness came, however stereotypically, with the added features of fashion sense, smart cologne, and a kind of in-the-moment vivaciousness that I found clinically curious. Like, how can someone be so happy? He worked what seemed to be a shitty job: a barista, basically, not even in a tucked-away sacrosanct island of coffee repose where they take feted-over pictures of fluffy cappuccinos embroidered with unicorn-designs, but a highly-trafficked get-in-get-out type of place. To add to his élan, he was Venezuelan, so he peppered his talk with "papis" and bits of Spanish phrases whose meaning eluded me but often seemed just right.

And if you were thinking I was attracted to him, then you're wrong, but not completely wrong. He was such a strange blend of delicate femininity peppered with a strange aggressive machismo. It was as if he was somehow striking a blow for all the in-the-closet gay people by being so aggressively sexual at inappropriate times and with inappropriate people, but his latent, tittering femininity balanced that out so people would just find it hilarious instead of off-putting. After we became friends, he'd hug me, or if he liked the colors or design of a shirt I was wearing, he'd just touch the part that he liked, even though he knew it made me a little uncomfortable. Maybe he did it *because* it made me uncomfortable, I don't know.

Anyway, I'm not sure how we became friends, even. I think maybe the first time I was on his line I said something like, "Whoa, you're the popular one here," and he said, "Oh, thank you, honey! You're too kind — you're just saying that to cheer me up," and then called to the backroom to an unseen coworker: "You hear that, my milkshake still bringing all the boys to the yard." Such a dated reference but he completely sold it. If I'm remembering correctly, he was yelling it to that tall Spanish girl I like who works there, and she said something like "woot woot" and Kaz did this flourishy dance and she slapped his ass and he scream-laughed in high-pitched surprise and then wiggled right back at her and said "don't stop honey" and it was just kind of amazing to me.

I wanted to interview him. It was like, here was this overweight man who could just as easily be a dumpy wallflower but through some inherent spark or maybe studied perseverance had just become this life of the party. I admired him before I ever got to know him.

"This one's on the house. Have a great day, see you," he said, or something like that.

So I started going there in the mornings for my coffee, and he recognized me almost immediately. I believe the second time I went in was during a more typical early morning workday rush. There were three people behind the registers and maybe there were supposed to be three separate lines, at least that's what the people I assumed were managers would often say, something like "three separate lines, people." The whole line thing was amorphous: you know the drill, people standing ambiguously in multiple lines and then opportunistically darting to the closest available cashier.

All except the Kaz lines. Those people were rigid about line order. Those people waited for their man. And on that second time I visited, he said: "I know you. So what's your name? That will make this a whole lot easier going forward." I told him, he told me his, and added, "I know, the world's only, lonely, gay Venezuelan named Casimir."

"It's a cool name."

"Why thank you, you're sweet." And I got my order that day — a grab-n-go little plastic pot of muesli with nuts and Greek yogurt, a large iced coffee, and a cup of water — on the house.

I soon became what was known at the store as a "Kaztomer."

I basically got the same thing every time. I'd say about half the time I paid for it; other times, Kaz would give it to me for free. He said at some point, on the sly, that to reward loyal customers, the store had an unofficial policy of giving stuff away for free, part of their attempt to create a festive atmosphere. But I never caught any other employee doing it and I'm sure the policy wasn't meant to be exploited so excessively. But who was I to complain? I told him a couple of times that he didn't need to give me the stuff for free, and I always had a credit card out in case I had to pay, although that was just for optics. Truth was when he made me pay I'd think "dammit," you know? Like, every little bit helps.

He learned that I put just a splash of cream in my coffee, so he'd always give me just enough room. Even though the other employees were usually present and must have heard my orders, they never seemed to remember who I was, so whenever someone other than Kaz took my order I'd have to always re-state it. Half the time I'd get a "cup of ice" instead of a cup of ice water, or they'd neglect to give me room for cream, and I'd never get it all for free, although that last bit couldn't really be expected. But really, who would order a cup of ice!?

And when Kaz wasn't in, I swear the efficiency at that place dropped by at least 50%. They had this stupid general policy of having people order and pay at the register, then another barista behind the counter would make the drink while you waited on the side counter. This always resulted in bunching at the side of the counter and people impatiently waiting in a too-tight corner of the shop. Kaz had none of that shit, and took the order and made the drinks himself and handed them to you without relegating you to the side-corner ghetto. That's what he said: "no corner ghetto for my folks."

He was the soul of that place. I remember there was some Star Wars related thing ... actually, I think it was May 4, you know, "May the Fourth Be With You," and he came dressed up as a (still fashionable) Ewok. None of the other employees went that far.

Most times it would be too busy for any real conversation, but I'd come at off-peak hours to speak to him. At first, I felt it was partially out of obligation: I mean, this guy is giving me, what, probably like $50 worth of free food and drinks a week, I could at least learn about him. Also, again, I was curious and he made me feel good. He had a real zest for life, and somehow he inexplicably saw those same qualities in me. Nuts, I know, right? From the very beginning he often said how nice I was, and that I was always friendly and "seemed chill," and the cynical side of me thought "yeah, I seem chill because that's getting me free food," but that wasn't really true, if I'm being honest. It's like a city full of people who, at best, brush past you without giving you a second glance and, at worst, actively trample over you, and here was this guy always with a smile, who took pride in his appearance and presentation.

So anyway, on those slower times I told him a bit about me, and I learned a bit about him. He was, as mentioned, from Venezuela but was "white as snow" because his ancestors had all emigrated from Europe. I think Portugal he said, or maybe Italy? Not Spain because that'd be "too easy" for people moving to a Spanish-speaking country. He was a struggling actor and lived in East Harlem and he made some off-hand references to dates he was going on; he went on so many dates that I half-wished I was gay. You know what I'm talking about: the way Kaz described it, any gay man could step out of apartment and fuck or get fucked at will, basically. And God bless them for that.

I made references to being heterosexual. I don't remember what, exactly, don't worry, nothing as obvious as blurting out a sexualized comment about any of his pretty co-workers or saying "me like titties!" or anything. I don't know what it was, I think I mentioned a girl by name I hooked up with, like, four months ago. I know, such a master-dropper of cues I am, displaying those heterosexual credentials. But I just didn't want him to think I was interested in him sexually.

"Honey, I knew you were straight from the moment you walked in there with your little off-the-rack Levi's and Mr. Man button-ups," he'd said, or something like that, although I guess it had to be that because where else would I get "Mr. Man" from? I don't even know what that meant.

I tried to give him a tip one time, although they didn't have tip cups, oddly enough. I know, it seems like every barista has a tip cup these days, like, goddamn, now we're supposed to tip them, too? But him, I wanted to tip. He said I was sweet in his Kaz-zy way but deflected for a while, with an aggressive smack of my wrist. But I insisted and he eventually accepted some tips. Some of those tips I left were quite generous I might add, like $20. But the tips were just here and there. I was still getting way more value from a purely transactional standpoint.

So maybe two months into our little relationship of sorts, I told him I wanted to take him out for lunch. I took him out to lunch to a dosa place nearby on Bleecker, nothing fancy, but not cheap either. I think on Yelp it was a two-dollar signer, which means average price. You know, to pay him back for all the free coffee and muesli.

It was pretty funny, that first time I picked him up outside of the shop he gave me a big Kaz hug, which would become a Kaz tradition. I always hugged him back weakly, just because it is, of course, strange to hug a male friend, especially one as strangely soft as Kaz.

"I only did that because I knew it'd make you uncomfortable," he said, in that way he has of making everything charming and frivolous. What would a Kaz unrestrained by workplace etiquette be like?

>< >< ><

Our lunch date made me envious of his life. Over dosas and with a steady backbeat of classic hip-hop (which is the musical selection at every minimally- or aspiringly-hip New York eatery), he casually mentioned that his father was apparently an extremely wealthy business owner back in Caracas and owned factories that produced, like, aluminum products or something. It's weird, with a certain type of person I loved being a bit of a dickish edgelord troll.

It's my version of "afflicting the comfortable and comforting the afflicted." On the one hand, I love getting a reaction out of people; on the other, I always want people to like me. What a dilemma. Anyway, with Kaz, I thought to myself for a second about the impropriety of asking a question based on my natural reaction, which was something like, "I didn't know there were rich people left in Venezuela." But then I said it anyway.

He laughed and said Venezuela is horrible. He had no idea how long his dad could last, but his dad was connected to the powers that be down there. Kaz was sent to New York for the unstated but acknowledged reason that his family didn't approve of his homosexuality. Not like Islamic throw-you-off-a-building disapproval, he explained, more like in denial South American machismo disapproval. Like, where Kaz's brothers played with toy cars and water guns when they were little, he was adding stylish flair to the toy cars, putting flowers in the water pistols, and playing dress-up with his sister's Barbies. His family didn't know what to do with him once he got older and his homosexuality became obvious to anyone with eyes. So with the pretext of keeping him safe from the phantom even-more-homophobic other Venezuelans, his father had him educated abroad in America, set him up with a nice one-bedroom apartment, and paid him a monthly stipend.

So much for struggling actor.

"Shit, sounds like a good deal to me."

"You don't hear it spoken too much, but I'm working on making Gay Privilege a thing."

I revealed a little bit of myself to him, about my insecurities, I suppose, although those are the same insecurities I express to anyone after I've known them for, like, more than a few seconds. You know, living in poverty, being a rudderless failure slash loser. I broke out my old chestnut, how I'm glad I'm at least currently employed and housed, instead of hanging outside of Home Depots giving hand jobs to Mexican day laborers for wooden nickels.

He laughed and smiled energetically, saying something like, "well, it's always good to have a Plan B."

"Shit, doing it for wooden nickels would be an improvement. I've been doing it for so long without getting paid, I think I'm good enough to get a few shekels thrown my way."

The wooden nickels/Mexican day laborers line is one I've used before, and it often serves as a kind of coolness litmus test: if the other party laughs or, even better, plays along, then they're cool. If they look uncomfortable or swiftly change the subject, then they suck. And trust me, I've had plenty of those latter reactions, which I sort of find exhilaratingly hilarious.

But Kaz was cool. His homosexuality gave the talk of hand jobs a kind of teetering, on-the-edge thrill. It was fun to tease, hop over the line of propriety and run back and yell "just kidding, safe-no backsies!"

><><><

So I'd say from then on in we got lunch about every other week, always me paying, although he'd offer but I'd insist, you know, based on all the free food. I'd see some of the other regular Kaztomers and wonder if he went out to lunch with any of them, too, although he mentioned at some point that he didn't. I believed him, he indulged me even more than his other customers, but I'd call him a liar and a food whore. He'd say, "look who's talking, at least I'm gay for real, you're just gay for muesli."

I was also still forcing tips on him. Not much, like $10 in the weeks we didn't get lunch or something. It occurred to me that what had basically been a kind gratuity on his end had basically devolved into bribery: I was paying him and treating him to meals in return for free breakfast and coffee. I told him he didn't need to keep spoiling me with the coffees and stuff, which only made him seem to delight in really hamming it up. Like one time I came in and he walked up to me on the line, took the muesli, went behind the counter and made the iced coffee and ice water, put the muesli in a bag for me, put it to the side, and announced, "I know honey needs his muesli," to which I'm sure I rolled my eyes and said, "C'mon Kaz, even for you that's too much," but he loved every fucking second of it. And it should have felt embarrassing, but it didn't, and I didn't mind the way the attractive female staff looked at me.

Women loved Kaz.

"I'm gonna get you laid one day," he promised me.

So anyway, I'm losing the thrust of all this. I just, I miss those days, strangely, and I guess I'm trying to paint a scene. Because it was really too much. I mean just for his own job, you know. Like, as much as everyone loved Kaz, there's no way on Earth the management wasn't probably doing some mental math about all the money they were losing on his giveaways.

>< >< ><

It was maybe a few months into our friendship when I first visited his apartment. I mentioned it was in East Harlem, somewhere in the 110s between Third and Second, which is not a gentrified neighborhood by any stretch (despite what the realtors might tell you), but the apartment itself was huge and just as fabulously decorated as you might imagine.

Kaz was a bit of a cinephile, which makes sense since he was an aspiring actor, and we blazed and watched, I'm not sure what, I think *Five Easy Pieces*. Good movie. He blazed all the time, actually. I didn't mention that, but he did. I don't remember him saying anything around that time about things at work, other than that, despite his unbelievably sunny disposition, he didn't like the barista gig because a) retail sucks and b) he's an actor, after all.

Acting was his passion. He said he was immersed in a two-year method acting residency as a chronically blazed, depressed Homo Sprite barista. I think at this time maybe he had the green dye in his hair. I told him he deserved to win an Oscar: I'd never believe he had even the slightest inkling of depression.

I remember he got a loud knock on his door while we were watching the movie. Maybe he'd also been getting a lot of text messages and not responding to them, I don't know, maybe I'm just imagining that now. But I definitely remember the knock on the door, it was more like a solid pounding, and remember, this is East Harlem. You don't just open the door when someone bangs on it. Shit, even I was nervous. But he just paused the movie and got up and I think I said, "do you know who that is?" and he opened the door slightly and said something in hushed but sharp tones in Spanish.

Another note about myself: Missouri actually has far fewer Latinos than the rest of the country. You wouldn't necessarily guess that with St. Louis and Kansas City being large cities and all, but that's the defense I'm sticking to as to why my Spanish is so bad. Also, I suck ass at languages and retained nothing from my three or so years of high school Spanish other than "dónde está baño?" and

"Me llamo Kenny," the diminutive version sounding more appropriate in Spanish with all the vowel-ending sounds. So I had no idea what he was saying, basically. But the conversation was brief and short and I never heard what the other person was saying and he or she never came in.

"Everything all right?"

The usual open-book Kaz didn't exactly blow me off, but he said it was nothing and used some Spanish expression that I gathered meant "nosy neighbor." I tried to inquire a bit more, you know, I'm pushy myself, but he deflected more as if the subject was intensely boring and just encouraged more blazing. I didn't object. We used the pause of the movie to smoke more and then finished the film.

><><><

Around this time period, I think I asked Kaz about some of his acting gigs and everything, and watched a demo reel taken from some off-off-Broadway shows he'd done. I remember there was some web series he was auditioning for that would film in Toronto. I also remember him talking about putting together a one-man show, although he was hesitant to tell me what it would be about. He finally told me "the immigrant experience" which made me mentally roll my eyes, since he was an exceedingly wealthy white guy. I don't think he was really the archetypical immigrant, but whatever.

He mentioned around this time he really needed to get out of New York and maybe it was about this time that I pieced together his excessive marijuana use, his comments about his job and his family, and deduced, using that big brain of mine, that maybe he was seriously depressed and maybe things weren't alright in Casimir-land. I also have the tendency to pathologize other people in the same way I assume people pathologize me. I'm always diagnosing people as having the same problems as me.

We did talk about his depression, here and there. He mentioned that maybe his father's feelings toward him leaned more toward antipathy than he first let on. That was the word he used: antipathy. I asked him how his father would feel if he became a famous, well-respected actor, in a way that suggested he was talented and it was only a matter of time before he'd get his big break. He said something like his father would hate that, because if he got famous, people would know he was his father's son and his father couldn't then disavow him. I asked if his father knew he was an aspiring actor and he said he did, but I wasn't convinced entirely. It seemed more like Kaz told his father in a way that maybe ensured his father didn't understand, like there'd been a miscommunication between him and his father and Kaz did nothing to correct the misperception. I could picture Kaz taking advantage of some technicality like that, not telling his dad exactly what he was up to ensure those stipends kept coming in.

So I know this doesn't sound like much. And really, there isn't going to be much, really, it's just little things I'm trying to connect, you know? Like, you don't see big moments while they're happening. That's not the way things work in the real world.

You can drive yourself crazy by obsessing over these things.

I did notice that he was working less shifts. When I first started hanging out at the coffee shop, he worked every weekday, but then it'd be three days a week, then down to just two. I remember it was down to two before he got the axe. And maybe it was partly my fault he got the axe, because when he was down to two, I'd feel especially inclined to take him out to a lunch or tip him because I felt bad about his increasingly worse work circumstances. Actually, now that I think about it, I asked him about his reduced work schedule around that time and he said he was missing work for some auditions, and that seemed perfectly plausible: a guy like Kaz wasn't going to be a barista forever.

I half didn't want him to get the web series in Canada because he was the only person I hung out with, really.

I remember I hadn't seen him for a week or so when — oh I should add — Kaz could be pretty terrible at responding to Facebook or texts at times, which is just something you had to get used to with him. I mean, something a normal person would have to get used to. I never did, I found it infuriating. Especially when a diva like Kaz could post 10 different changing hairstyle pictures in an hour and neglect to respond to a message, fucking infuriating, but again, you just couldn't really get mad at the guy. The second he responded, those bad tidings would all just melt away.

But I'd noticed he wasn't working and he hadn't responded to the texts I'd sent. I asked that fine Latina coworker who said, with obvious pain, that Kaz wasn't working there anymore.

I was shocked. Apparently, behind the scenes it wasn't as a big a surprise, although all the rank-and-file coworkers loved him. Management, suffice to say: not as big a fan.

I feared that it'd been partially my fault. I'd seen some of the disapproving stares from employees that looked a bit more like authority figures than the average sunny barista. Really, any employee who wasn't farting rainbows and doing handstands was probably management.

I called him soon after, which I'd rarely done before. We both hated phone calls as a matter of principle, but I was genuinely concerned for him. Sure, he didn't need the money and he said how much he hated the job, but I thought he was just saying that. He loved that place, and that placed loved him.

"It's bullshit, man," I told him when I finally got in touch with him and we met at a cafe up in Harlem, and of course he agreed, but nonchalantly. Like, I was madder about it than he was.

"Papi, be serious you're just mad now that you're going to have to pay for all that muesli."

No, fuck them, I resolved, I wasn't going back to that place anymore. Kaz *was* that place.

He tried to pass it off a no big deal and said he wished them nothing but the best, and he wasn't sullen or anything — that just wasn't in his DNA. He'd said other people were getting laid off and he'd had a bad attitude behind the scenes, which I didn't believe for a second. It was just a stupid coffee spot, nothing to get too worked up over. I didn't ask him if he got fired for giving away too many products, which is what I suspected.

I told him I was sorry that I wouldn't see him every day, but that I'd still be around for whenever.

Would I even willingly come up to East Harlem, he asked, knowing that I always preferred to hang out in what we might call safer neighborhoods.

"Yeah Kaz, even East Harlem."

"And will I get a departing hug this time without your squirming to get away?"

"Kaz, like I even have the ability to squirm with how tight you squeeze me."

"That's what I like to hear."

See, I can be a good guy when push comes to shove.

><><><

Despite all the promises, I just didn't see Kaz much in the following weeks. I was applying for other jobs myself and also around that time I think I was going on a couple of MeetUps, maybe because I wanted to avoid a situation where I depended too much on just one friend. That's a situation I've found myself in several times over the years and my time in New York had been no different.

I remember I got a Facebook message from him.

Let me see, I can read it right now. It said: "Hey Papi, can I crash at your place if need be?"

It doesn't look like I responded on Facebook. I guess I responded by text, but I don't have that phone anymore. It's sometimes hard to read Kaz, as I mentioned; he liked being upfront and making things a bit uncomfortable, and I'm sure I brushed that off as Kaz being too forward. You know, the hugs, the making things uncomfortable when it was good for a laugh. I mean, I wouldn't want him to crash with me, and also of course it wasn't my place to do so: I had roommates, and he'd never met any one of them. I'm sure I said something like, "Sure, if necessary" or, "Sure, but the second you blast Scissor Sisters after midnight, you are getting the boot."

><><><

I met him some time after that. I believe it was around June or July, maybe about three or four months since we started hanging out. I remember he wanted to meet up at his apartment but I demurred, that's such a trek for me. So we met downtown, at a place called Cones on Bleecker Street. (By the way, Kaz hated the Big Gay Ice Cream Truck mini-empire that was popular in New York at the time; he claimed they stole his pizazz.)

So, we're getting gelato, and I remember I get a large, which is three scoops, and he gets a small, which is one. I don't know why I remember that. I figured he was on a diet. He looked good. He'd obviously lost a ton of weight since I first met him, and lost weight since the last time I'd seen him, just a couple of weeks ago, but like I mentioned, he was ... zaftig, that's a great word, and the word that I feel best conjures him up. Like, pleasantly plump. Like, if a fat person loses a ton of weight, they aren't skinny yet, you know? And because he didn't look skinny-skinny, or sickly skinny, it was hard for me to really tell if something was wrong, but he was definitely losing weight.

And Kaz, he must have been a good actor: when I had first told him he had a big break just around the corner, I was just saying that to be polite. I mean, it's hard to tell when someone in a terrible off-off-Broadway play is talented, you know? And when I'm talking off-off-Broadway, I'm talking, like, Kaz's plays were the Staten Island equivalent of off-off-Broadway. But either I'm daft or he's a convincing actor because as we ate our gelato I had no idea anything was seriously wrong.

So we ate our gelato outside on the little benches, looking at all the passersby, enjoying the fine summery weather. I remember two European-looking blondes passed by and Kaz waved at them to get their attention and complimented the colors of their dresses, and they smiled at him, and by extension, at me. Who could pull stuff like that off except Kaz? Pretty ladies like them would naturally be standoffish from any unsolicited, street-level compliment, but a big gay fun dandy like Kaz posed no threat. He just radiated love.

I remember that, and I remember after we'd finished up our gelatos, he asked me, "do you ever just want to get away?" It's something I figured might be coming: maybe acting wasn't working out, he was still unemployed but he had money, why not go and try something new somewhere else? Hell, I would.

I'm sure I agreed.

"I can just disappear if I want to," I remember him saying. At this point I'm sure I was just nodding along.

"But I don't want to. I like being me."

"I like you being you, too." I remember saying that because it's so dumb.

"I don't think I'm going to be around much longer."

I guess I wasn't done with my gelato around that time, because I remember having a spoonful in my mouth when he said that. I have a weird habit of chewing on things: I remember chewing on the plastic spoon and taking it out of my mouth to respond.

"Don't say that man, you'll be around as long as you want to be."

"Not if my dad can help it. And he can. Back into the tank with me."

I don't remember what I started saying at that point because then he just started speaking:

"There's really something to it, just merging. Just imagine, merging into another person, just disappearing, all your troubles just disappearing, knowing that you aren't alone anymore." And I remember his eyes were closed as he spoke. And at the time I thought it was nice, we were really connecting. "And it is nice, trust me, it's nice. It's like being in a warm bath."

I'm sure I said, "Hmmm," or something at this point. I don't remember Kaz not seeming lucid or seeming particularly stoned. Plus, from my experience, he could always handle his high.

I frankly, of course, didn't know what the fuck he was talking about.

"The thing is, though, talk about warm baths, it sounds nice, doesn't it? But who wants to take baths? You grow out of that."

And here was my contribution: "Yeah, plus your tub gets all dirty. And you're sitting in your own filth too, if you think about it. I remember taking a bath when I was young and seeing, like, the dirt floating around in the water, and thinking, man that's going to go right back on me."

I remember dispensing that pearl of wisdom.

"Don't ever change, Ken."

"Don't plan to."

"It's just ... my father is going to make me get back into the bath, so to speak. I fucked up now and there's nothing I can do about it."

"You're an adult now, though. You can do what you want. I mean, no offense, but New York definitely beats Venezuela. This is your home now." I just assumed maybe his dad was threatening to stop paying his rent or something.

"It's the worst of both worlds. I don't want to get back into the tub. So he's going to drown me in it, so to speak."

At this point I had no idea what he was talking about or how to respond. I think I gingerly tried to broach the subject. Like, what did he mean? What could his father really do to him? I remember he said other things about this melding and there was some cross-talk where I was just trying to figure out what the hell he was talking about and I missed a bit of what he was saying. When I think about it now, I can hear him saying 'tual,' like "ritual," which might be just my imagination. But I do remember he said, in a real quiet, sad way, and with finality: "he can make it happen and there's nothing I can do about it."

I'd never seen Kaz so undeniably low before. Like, it just did not compute, this gaudy firecracker of a man looking down at the ground like that, like, on the verge of tears. Not literally, I don't remember seeing him about to cry, or I don't *think* I remember seeing him about to burst into waterworks, but just the way he looked, so downcast. It was like seeing a puppy with a set of crutches or a rubber ducky with an eyepatch shaking a paper cup, begging for change on the street. It just ... was wrong.

I think I asked if he wanted to go to a bar and talk about it. You know a bar is a more appropriate venue for these talks than a curbside bench.

I think he said sure, but without looking at me. He didn't move to get up, and maybe I was waiting for him. Neither of us got up.

So, I just started nervously talking.

"Maybe I'll get a shandy at the bar. No one likes shandies but it feels like shandy weather, you know? Everyone hates on shandies. I wonder if there's, like, a type of shandy that the shandy connoisseurs use to get people into liking shandies. You know? Like, try this. 'You think you know shandies? Well, try this, this will blow your fucking mind.' Although I guess that's tough because a shandy can be made with any soft drink, technically, right?

"What do you think, Kaz? Think there are special shandies like that?"

I remember he looked up at me, and it was heartbreaking. He looked at me, then away, wiping away at his face or something, like debating with himself whether he wanted to say it.

"It all started when I lost that job. I fucked up real bad. My father didn't like that. Even though the money was nothing, he didn't like that. He thinks it shows that I'm not, like, fit to exist. On my own, I mean. It was a mistake and now he really thinks *I'm* a mistake. I mean he's always thought that but losing that job cemented that idea in his mind. I didn't even tell him. He just knew.

So I'm a dead man, really. I'm dead. I'm a dead Kaz walking."

And before I could offer any placating words he said something that drove a dagger through my heart:

"It was those giveaways, Ken. It was those giveaways, and you tipping me for them and treating me to lunch for them. They saw it as bribes, they did, they did.

"I shouldn't have given away all that stuff. I've always wanted people to like me, you know? It was those giveaways. I shouldn't have done it."

"Kaz I'm so sorry. I — I said a million times you didn't have to give me that stuff. You know, I can pay for my own coffee, you know?"

"I know, Kenny. It wasn't your fault. I forced you. You know how I can be."

And I'll never forget the look he made after that. It was so fleeting, and it's so easy to read things that weren't there, but he refused to make eye contact. Like he was going back and forth in his mind about what to say.

Then he said: "There's a way you can pay me back."

I don't know how my face looked when I heard that. It might have been a look of shameful indignation. I'm a defensive person. I don't take being attacked very well, or made to feel bad or responsible for something, even if it *is* my fault. But here: was it my fault? He'd just said himself it wasn't. True, I accepted his free food, but I'd told him he didn't need to.

And now it's my fault he lost his job?

"Sure," I said, but rather than really focusing, I was sorting through my own hurt and bruised ego. I'm sure my throat felt sour, my head was swimming and there were evil little butterflies taking flight in my stomach. That's the way I feel when I'm "under attack."

"I need to you shave off all your hair and give it to me."

I think I laughed. He was just fucking with me, I figured. Well-played: his jokes were usually quick one-liners or something. He'd never wound me up like that only to deflate the tension.

But he wasn't laughing. In fact, he looked despondent, the worst I ever saw him. Maybe he saw then that his back was really against the wall.

"Seriously?"

He put his face in his hands and said something like "forget it," but I didn't entirely hear him.

"Seriously? What would you do, wear my hair as a makeshift beard or something? Or you want me to, like, what, embarrass myself in solidarity with you?" I was halfway between being offended but still suspecting he was just fucking with me; fucking with me in an unusually cruel, elaborate un-Kaz-like way, but fucking with me nonetheless.

"It's not that. It's not that. I need help, it's the only thing," he said, but at this point his attitude changed, because maybe he embraced the failure. Kind of like you're backed up against the cliff and you're out of bullets and you see the bull is still charging. Like, what are you going to do except light the cigarette and jump off?

"If you're not going to give me your hair, then you definitely won't give me your blood, or a tooth. Hair was just the baby step. I can't blame you."

I don't remember how I responded to that. I don't think I did, at least not directly. Maybe I joked, saying there had to be other ways to humiliate me to make him feel better. Maybe I offered him my shaved pubes as a penance. Maybe I said blood and hair sacrifices were the first time I saw him really get in touch with his South American roots. I don't know what I said, or if I really said anything. I think I actually just stayed relatively quiet, mumbled half-apologies in confusion. If I recall, I think I did, yeah that's right, I did say I'd shave my hair for him if he really wanted. Of course, I didn't expect him to follow through with that; like, I expected him just to say, "Of course you don't need to do that."

I don't think he responded.

We never got that beer. I think he apologized for himself, said he was just acting crazy and under a lot of stress with his father and had dropped acid recently and was still on a residual bad trip, which isn't how I think acid actually works but who am I to say.

>< >< ><

I reached out to him the next day. I think I called him after work and left a voicemail. Didn't hear back. Texted him a couple more times that week, then maybe messaged him on Facebook. No answer.

Then maybe a week after that phone call, I got a Facebook

message from him. Here, give me a second and I can look it up. I have it in my inbox.

"To My Favorite Kaztomer,

Kenneth. Or, because it's my last message, Kenny-Ken-Ken-adoo.

I appreciate your friendship. I'll tell the girls of Le Bois to have a giant orgy with you but I don't know what sway I have there anymore. And don't worry about not letting me crash with you out there in Coney Island. While I do love the Mermaid Parade, that's only once a year, and I don't think Coney Island would have been able to properly contain all of the fantasia that is Casimir.

I won't lie, Ken. I'm scared. I shouldn't write that in this message since there's nothing we can do about it but I feel the urge to be honest about it.

There's a fabulousness to this world. I would recommend doing mushrooms sometime. While I know they scare you, they are relatively safe way to expand your mental horizons to come to grips, even if just a little bit, to the possibility of wider realities.

That sounds like such pretentious nonsense, I know. Such pretentious caterwauling.

Just know that there is such a thing as true transcendent connectivity. It can be used for good or ill. When it's good, it's a feeling of such bliss. To feel all your problems slip away. Wouldn't it be nice for all your fears, your failures, your self-hatred and loathing, everything you think is wrong about yourself, to just disappear. I know you feel listless and bored and cranky. I know what that feeling is like. I know you feel like life is essentially meaningless and boring and disappointing, and in a sense, it is, at least in the way life is currently lived. But there are other ways. There's a way to get there, too. It's a true connectivity with the universe.

Maybe it's the way we are before we're born.

My father is going to force me back into some kind of inferior version of all that. I'm too much of an original for him. :) It's a strange thing, because as good as that all sounds, I don't WANT to go back to it. But I don't have a choice in this matter.

But I don't want to scare you or let you down. I don't want you to worry about me. I shouldn't have said as much as I did because I don't want any trouble to find you. Just think of me back in Venezuela, but in a happy Venezuela. Just picture people drinking cocktails out of pineapples or melons.

It's a bullshit image, but then again, what isn't?

What a downer to end it on. But you are a downer of a guy, aren't you? Just know that I mean that in the best way possible. :)

Don't ever change, unless it's to become happy."

Of course I called and texted and messaged him. (I never got an email address from him.) Days passed and I didn't hear from him. Then his phone disconnected. Then I stopped by the coffee shop and no one had seen him. I remember calling his number again around that time and someone else answered, like the number had been purchased by someone else who didn't speak any English. I didn't know what language these people were speaking so that was an obvious dead end.

I went up to his apartment in East Harlem. It wasn't hard to follow someone into the building. The first night I went no one answered. The following night I went and a shy, hesitant but ultimately friendly woman answered. It seemed the apartment was now occupied by what I'm guessing was a Dominican family of five, all in Kaz's large one-bedroom. I did my best with my elementary Spanish to ask the woman and her husband about Casimir, but they'd never met him. Their oldest son, who seemed to be in his early teens, spoke English and told me they'd never met the previous occupant, and I agreed that if they'd met Casimir, they'd remember him.

They gave me the live-in super's number and his English wasn't too good, either. But he definitely knew Casimir, and said he moved out a few weeks ago. I asked him how he learned Casimir intended to move out. Like, did Kaz come into his office one day and pay the last month's rent or something and announce he was moving out, or did he just bail? The super understandably wanted to know why I cared, and I told him I just wanted to make sure my friend was all right, he'd been acting weird recently. The super said things like, "you know how things are in buildings like these" and other things which, given the circumstances, left me with a vaguely sinister impression but I don't think that's how he meant it. I think he meant it more like Casimir didn't have an official lease and was probably paying straight cash on a month-to-month basis.

I asked him how Casimir moved out and he said that he hadn't actually seen Casimir himself in quite a while, but he remembers that several weeks ago several men came in and cleared out all of Casimir's stuff. They didn't seem like they were from a typical moving company, you know? He didn't remember any uniform or logos or anything that suggested they were a moving company but he wasn't really paying attention, he just prepared the service elevator for them, you know?

I'd resolved to reach out to some of his other Facebook friends to find out how he was doing. I remember debating about who to reach out to, and was surprised that he had so few Facebook friends for such an outgoing guy. I looked for people who shared any of his last names in his Friends list but didn't find any.

And then I noticed the change to the top of his Facebook page:

Remembering Casimir

I was stunned and horrified, of course. I think that was a Facebook thing: when they learn of someone's death, they automatically convert the page into an "in memoriam" dedication. I couldn't deal with it. I was heartbroken.

The following day and there was a picture uploaded to his profile. It was adorned with a sentence or two of Spanish that I wish I'd saved. I don't know who uploaded it. You know those weird photographs you see at the bottom of web sites or in pop-up ad things, those ads that show like impossible pictures that you know are Photoshopped or something to get you to click. Like those "you won't believe they took this photograph" or "look what they just found at the bottom of this lake!"

I thought it had to be one of those for a second, but there it was on his Facebook page. It was like a bloated, balded, waxen-looking round face. The vantage point was like you were standing by the body's mid-section and looking straight at the face. The skin had the complexion and rubbery texture of a hard-boiled egg. You know that, what is it, roe, those pink fish eggs? There was, like, yellow roe-looking things, but maybe bigger than roe eggs, maybe twice the size. They looked like little sacs. And those sacs were spilling out of his empty eye sockets.

And it was Casimir. I knew it. I could tell in the face, in the nose. It was him.

And the next day it was gone. The whole "in memoriam" page. It makes me think the "in memoriam" was put up automatically when some tidbit of information about Casimir's death floated onto the internet. Maybe some online web crawler picked up a death certificate or something and cross-referenced it to a Facebook page and the changes were made instantaneously, one of those things that even the most airtight operation can't control with the way technology works these days. But then someone caught wind and pulled the Facebook page offline. So if it's some kind of conspiracy, they're good, but not infallible.

I searched online for Casimir with all his surnames and put in searches for New York or Caracas or Venezuela but I never found anything. I looked up the largest aluminum manufacturers in Venezuela but what am I going to do with that?

>< >< ><

So that's it, really. See, I told you that you might be disappointed. I am, I suppose. But that's the way things are, in the real world, and this is nothing if not the real world. I'm proud to say I've been living in the real world my whole life.

I've moved back to Missouri. Kaz's situation didn't cause my departure, but it did hasten it. I had had my big city fun and it wasn't for me, I tell myself.

I tell myself to do something. It's only been a couple of months since Kaz's death has been "confirmed" (and I consider that Facebook mishap a confirmation, albeit a removed confirmation). I still feel indignant about what happened, and the wound is still raw and the memory still fresh. The ardor is still there, not yet dulled by job searches and the churn-and-burn of my Missouri transition and the natural eroding process of time.

But how long is it going to last, and how will it survive the pressures and distractions of daily living? I don't know, but if I'm honest, I'm not hopeful. Because it's a big, wide, scary world out there, and while Kaz spoke about this blissful connectivity, I don't know anything about that. I hope he was telling the truth, or speaking from some kind of experience. But that picture I saw certainly didn't look blissful. It looked terrible. It's the worst thing I've ever seen in my entire life.

Kaz spoke about some altered blissful state, but that's not a state I know anything about. I only know about the real world, where the best you can hope for is to just to manage and maintain.

A DEEP HORROR THAT WAS VERY NEARLY AWE

7099 Brecksville Road, Independence, Ohio

THERE WERE THREE toilet stalls in the men’s room at the Sunoco Gas Station at 7099 Brecksville Road in Independence, Ohio. One of them was occupied.

If you were, say, washing your hands and looking at the stalls for whatever reason, a mistaken glance, perhaps, you'd see in the space below the door a man's feet, his black work boots and dark blue Wrangler jeans. (This was one of those bathrooms that had a distressing amount of clearance room between the stall doors and the floor.) The man's feet flexed a bit, not staying stationary, but not in any unusual way; just in the usual fashion of a man using the toilet, shifting in the usual way a man does as he distributes his weight.

The stall had been occupied all day. Men came in, most used the urinals, less fortunate travelers whose activities required the use of a toilet obviously selected one of the two unoccupied stalls.

If any of those less fortunate travelers accidentally opened the door on the stall occupied by the man with the black work boots and dark blue Wrangler jeans, they'd see that the disguise ended at his waist. From there emerged a man-sized praying mantis of vivid turquoise, each armored eye extended several inches in front of its face, connected by stalks. Each eye came protected by its creator with three cruel-looking scorpion tails that shook with anticipation. The mantis's oversized claws were angular spiders whose legs ended in sharpened chutes. If the claws got to eat, their wastes would excrete through the legs and drip out the chutes.

No one accidentally opened the door, despite the door always being left unlocked just for such an occasion. No one would see what lay inside. A pity. Someday, someone would walk in on one of Ormond's creations.

The mantis creation was his personal favorite and it hadn't had any action for years. He'd been proud of that one, and he placed it in the stalls of truck stops and gas stations that had inspiring names - your Independence, Ohio, your Liberty, Texas, or your Prosperity, South Carolina. That working creation had been one of his proudest moments. A shame. One day, someone would accidentally push one of those bathroom doors open and see what lay in store for him.

><><><

Another gas station, this one in Schenectady, New York. Schenectady, what an evocative name for so routine a town. In the spirit of that evocative name, Ormond tried something different. The legs in that stall wore straight-leg Levi's and steel-toed black Dr. Martens. The body came furnished with Ormond's attempt at a long-sleeve brown athletic shirt, in the style of a Lonsdale, or some other brand a 60's UK street punk might wear. He couldn't get the shirt right, though, and in frustration didn't put much effort into the texture work, telling himself that this subtle sartorial aberration made the monster more singular and otherworldly.

He had a working man's back story in mind for this one. The face was a classic skull, but with blood-capped stalagmites for teeth and pulsating anemones for eyes. The trick here, or so Ormond thought, was that the eyes would pulse, but they would not shift or follow the movements of its prey, giving the creation a detached, almost disinterested mien which, he hoped, would make it seem somehow scarier. But Ormond ended up not liking the creation, and neither did his superiors.

He tried to create works of art, to impress his superiors, even though he didn't have that much time left in his tour of duty. He wanted to inspire, come up with new ideas, to keep the job interesting. Not like it mattered anyway, he thought ruefully, as his creation occupied the stall, undisturbed, for the entire shift.

Ormond would need to talk with the higher-ups about some ways to get some more "intake," opportunities for his creations to interface with the public. They were a wary group, and he knew he would need to mollify their concerns, let them know he would preserve the integrity of their venture. But they had to infuse some new ideas, otherwise their whole operation would be requisitioned off.

><><><

It was 8 p.m. on a Wednesday night in mid-October, and Frank meandered around the surprisingly large Sunoco Gas Station, located at 7099 Brecksville Road in Independence, Ohio. He'd filled up his tank, paid at the pump and then parked, feeling it was as good a time as any to stretch his legs and pick up some road rations. Maybe Red Bulls. He knew they were terrible for you, and Frank, middle-aged and overweight as he was, certainly didn't need to add to the problem. He didn't have diabetes but he looked like he might, and if he was ever so diagnosed, no one would ever feign surprise with a straight face.

Gas stations were a no-judgment zone. They had a kind of working class, metal vibe to them, people passing through, no shits given. Getting some highly sugared and caffeinated drinks when you are on the road was one of the only youthful thrills — if you could call such a thing a thrill - still available to him. Hanging out at night, cruising around, all caffeinated up, *Master of Puppets* or *Among the Living* blasting, pit stops at the mall parking lot, just fucking around. Didn't sound like much, but nights like that had been high school highlights for him. So fuck it. Used to do some drugs and drink too much, now Dunkin' Donuts during the day, Red Bulls at night. Party down.

He stalked the aisles, thinking about grabbing some Fritos, and picked up two KIND bars, too, knowing they were shit for you but pretending to believe otherwise. The gas station clerk, an older white guy maybe in his sixties, gave him the head nod, which Frank returned with gusto. Frank didn't hang out in gas stations much, though he looked like he should; when people met him they often thought he was a trucker or some other blue-collar worker, like a mechanic or plumber or something. Cop-face, was how some people described it.

When you're a white guy who is middle-aged, bigger, bearded, single, gruff and casually profane, people tended to think you can fix their sink or might ticket them for riding their bike on the sidewalk. His look probably got him better-than-average treatment from cops, security guards or other blue-collar sorts. Frank was actually just an account executive at Time Warner Cable. People were inclined to valorize blue-collar types, and he suspected they disliked him a little or were disappointed somehow when they learned he was white-collar, like he was somehow turning his back on some caste they'd prematurely assumed he belonged to.

Or maybe they just understandably hated Time Warner.

Frank took his final bounty of Red Bulls, energy bars, Fritos and a fruit 'n' nut mix up to the counter. The old man greeted Frank and rung him up, working in that belabored, overcompensating way that old people sometimes utilized, perhaps as a way of saying "go easy on me." Ring something up, lean in, make sure it was right, single-finger-peck at the register, lean in, double-check. Really making a show of it: *congratulations old man, I get it, you are still a productive member of society*. Frank wondered when he'd be that way. There was a sensibility, an aesthetics of being old that he still felt estranged from, thankfully. Maybe it was from being single. Domesticity aged you.

"Find everything you need, sir?"

"I certainly did. Wish I didn't find the Fritos, but you know, what are you going to do?" Frank rubbed at his belly, a move he did pretty often, come to think of it. He was quick to self-deprecate, perhaps a way of softening strangers' expectations of him.

"Well, glad to hear it, sir." The old man had a magazine on the countertop, spread open to reveal an advertisement for some local business school: "For those short on excuses and long on ambition," the ad read. Frank motioned to the ad, and when he was sure the man understood what he was motioning toward, said, "Do those kind of people really need the extra help?"

The old man gave a puttering, quizzical look and then chuckled, said "Amen to that, brother, Amen." Frank wasn't entirely convinced the old man connected Frank's satirical comment with the ad, but whatever.

Frank paid and took his bag and shimmy-stepped away. Eh, should he? He should.

"Hey sir, is there a bathroom I could use? I'm a paying customer, remember, I earned it." He lifted his bag.

The old man, amiably, said, "Even if you weren't sir, I'd give it to you." He explained that the men's bathroom was out back, in a separate little building and you had to input a 4-digit code on "one of those door lock things." He gave Frank the code. "Three-Seven-Eight-Seven" Frank repeated it, and then covered his mouth, said, "Oh shit, I don't want to give that out to just anyone," and the old man laughed. There was no else in the gas station. "Oh, that's alright," the old man said, just to speak.

Frank thanked the man and made to leave and then stopped, and asked if he could leave his bag there. "Of course," the old man said, "I should have offered that. We do our best to maintain high standards back there but still, you don't want to be bringing anything you later plan on eating back into the bathroom."

He gave the man his bag, thanked him and added, "Maybe I should bring those Fritos back there then," and when he felt the man didn't understand, added, "Keep me from eating them!" and the man did his old man laugh of questionable understanding and wave-saluted Frank as he left.

Frank turned the slight corner upon opening the bathroom and was glad it was bigger than he would have guessed. It smelled overwhelmingly of ammonia and cleaning product, the sanitary equivalent of spraying on excess cologne when you don't shower, most likely, but hey, better than the alternative. The bathroom was empty, another plus.

Two urinals ran across the right wall. He went over to one of the two urinals and allowed it to serve its function — urinal apotheosis - keeping his stream on the urinal cake. 100% accuracy, he thought. Despite that broad "we" the old man had used, Frank didn't think that the old man was personally coming back here and pitching in to clean up. But the old man wouldn't need to worry about dead-shot Frank. Frank made that urinal cake bleed blue.

He walked over to one of the two sinks, which were tucked into the left corner, perpendicular from the urinals. Behind the sinks were three toilet stalls.

He washed his hands, something he rarely did after just peeing. ("If you have to decontaminate your hands after touching your dick for a couple seconds, then you got major problems," he remembers someone said to him long time ago.) But, eh, gas station.

He checked himself out in the circular mirror above his sink. He didn't look good. He looked like a fat, bearded middle-aged man, which he was. At least he had always been fat, so it didn't hang on him unnaturally, like some of those people whose bodies are clearly processing what to do with the excess weight. Frank's fat was evenly distributed, absorbed into the make-up of who he was, if that made any sense. He didn't have any wrinkles, really. A result of easy living and easy pleasures, he thought, looking forward to some Red Bull and cranked-up *Number of the Beast*.

He groaned, mentally. He should ... he didn't want to, it was a fucking gas station, but better here than some other gas station, or holding it. Better to clean out the system; those Red Bulls and Fritos were going to play havoc on his system anyway.

No one here, too. Good, these were those stalls that had, improbably and ridiculously, those huge bottom gaps (like 20% of the size of the door itself) and those side gaps between stalls that let you kinda see the occupants. Like, yep, there's a big fat guy sitting on a toilet; yep, there's a big fat guy getting up to wipe himself; yep, there's a big fat guy flushing. Stalls should be hermetically sealed, but he guessed that you got to let the gas station crackheads know someone could see what they were doing if their bathroom rituals started involving pipes and tinfoil.

He walked to the stall on the far-left end. Always go to the far stall. There was somebody in the middle stall, he realized; he saw the toes of black work shoes sticking out near the bottom gap. Silent as a mouse, that guy, apparently positioning himself to have as little cheek square footage on the toilet rim as possible while still maintaining balance.

Couple of moments later and he heard someone else come into the bathroom and occupy the farthest stall. Now there were three men shitting in a row, mere feet from each other, a situation which always struck Frank as inherently comical. The bathroom humbled all, although the users of a gas station men's room were likely a humble lot to begin with.

He did his business quickly. He didn't like looking down at his fat folds, having to push his little dick (little by comparison, remember, little by comparison) from under his fat folds to make sure he didn't pee on his leg. Something about doing this in a gas station was depressing, like he felt like he should be doing drugs or something, or like he hit close to some kind of toilet-use rock bottom, like taking a dump in a gas station should be forcing him to re-evaluate his life choices.

He flushed — always flush right after, he might look like a slob but he wasn't an animal — took a swipe of toilet paper and ... fucker. It was a deceptive TP dispenser. There'd been a couple squares visible from inside the metal dispenser, but that was it. One feeble pull and he was left with an empty cardboard roll. What, would the crackheads steal the toilet paper, you needed to lock it up in metal dispensers and have us pecking at it like hamsters for water?

Yeah, probably, realistically. Fucking goddamn America was going to shit.

He groaned again, mentally: fuckkkkkkk. He looked down at the toilet, back at the dispenser, back at the toilet, like the Gods of Lavatories must see the privations of one of their needy acolytes and dive down to remedy this injustice. Fuck. He could just wait it out until the other folks leave and run into their stalls like a fat pilfering raccoon. He pictured himself running over like a ninny, pants down at his ankles. Fucking hilarious, how'd he get into these fucking situations? Oh, that's right, he took a dump in a gas station men's room. Not hard to figure out. This was no backstage bender or blackout bloody nose from his youth, but no fucking picnic either.

So he waited, poking into the metal dispenser, as if maybe some enterprising crackhead balled up toilet paper and stuffed it somewhere, like the prisoner who examines all the corners of his cell for an emergency spoon to dig himself out. Fucking hilarious.

How long has that guy in the middle stall been here? *I mean, he'd been there from before I even got here? I first pissed, then washed my hands, and I haven't heard shit from there (no pun intended), not even a flush.*

He knocked on his side of the wall, perhaps a bit intemperately, like he was fueled partly by the resentments of any poor schmucks who might be waiting to use that middle stall before he got a chance to make use of that precious toilet paper. When you're knocking for toilet paper in a men's room, you got to go all in. Like staring down a bear. No room for fear.

"Hey man, can I borrow some toilet paper in there? This stall is empty, can you believe it?"

He tried to deepen his voice, speak brusquely but unthreatening, as if to accentuate that this was a man-favor, you know, help a guy out? "I've never done this before, believe me, this isn't on my bucket list, asking for toilet paper in a fuckin' gas station."

No answer. He waited a beat to make sure no answer was forthcoming, and tried again. "I know, man, sorry, but can I please get some toilet paper? If you could just, pass it under the gap, lord knows the gaps are big enough. Sorry. Again, I can wait a second, not like I'm going anywhere."

No answer.

"Anyone alive in there?"

Maybe it was a crackhead in there after all. Or a homeless person, would he really want a homeless person handing him toilet paper? *I mean a non-smelly homeless person would be fine, but can I just imagine getting a clump of toilet paper passed to me that smells worse than this ass I'll be wiping? Guy passes me a dead rat, can I imagine that, be hilarious.* Wipe myself and get ass cancer immediately.

What should he do in this situation? Ask for toilet paper from the farthest stall, create a toilet paper courier service, handed-off under each stall until it reached him? If the middle stall wasn't game then it wouldn't work. Fuck it, he'd have to wait until the farthest stall left and use that stall. Hopefully that guy didn't punish his stall too bad.

"Uhhh, I'm almost done," he heard a timorous voice, far enough to know it was coming from the farthest stall. It was the voice of a teenager, or young adult, responding to an authority figure. Frank guessed he'd deepened his voice too much, hah, hoped the kid wasn't expecting him to step out and be Batman.

"Thanks, brother."

Frank flushed again, just for the euphonic optics (there was nothing left there to flush), left the stall and washed his hands. He tucked himself into the corner, away from the farthest stall, since he didn't want to seem like he was hovering over the poor guy. But what about this guy in the middle stall?

He peered under the middle stall as best he could without crouching down. He saw those black shoes, legs in blue jeans doing usual toilet-ministration shuffling. The feet switched positions. The guy was alive in there, at least. Maybe he didn't speak English? No, it was obvious Frank had been addressing him, anyone would have said something, even something like "No English." And anyone in America knew "toilet paper," unless the dude was wiping his ass with his hand in there. And if he was using his hand, all that toilet paper was going to waste!

The farthest stall opened and the kid looked kind of like Frank imagined. Early twenties white guy, 5'7", thin frame, hoodie without the hood-up, scruffy facial hair, something about his chin and nose looked eminently punchable. Not that the kid looked like a bad guy or anything, but there are some people who just have a punchable annoying face for whatever reason.

The kid nodded at Frank as he walked out. Frank nodded back, and the kid went over to the other sink to wash his hands. "There's plenty of paper in there."

"Thanks, man." Frank stayed back, still, planning on waiting for the kid to leave the bathroom entirely. It was a little embarrassing, the whole situation, and he didn't want to go in the stall just yet, imagining the kid might be especially attuned to listening in on him for whatever reason. The kid spoke to him in a kind of deferential way, probably because Frank looked like what that kid probably thought a classic blue-collar guy looked like. That kind of deference happened quite a bit more than you might guess.

"I think this guy might be sick or something in there?" Frank pointed at the middle stall. "Hey, sir, are you okay in there? Do you need help? I mean, not bathroom help I mean ...." Frank laughed gutturally, "but, like, physical help?"

"Like, do you need a hospital or do you need us to call someone for you?" The kid stepped in, eager to supplement Frank.

Frank looked at the kid, gave the kid an incredulous look about the stall occupant, a 'can you believe this guy in there?' look.

"I think we should tell the gas station owner, I guess."

"I'll do that, I got to get gas anyway. You can go do what you need to, I got it man." The kid gave him a lighthearted but reassuring look. Kid wasn't so bad after all, seemed like a cool guy actually.

"Thanks, man, if this gas station had a bar attached, I'd be buying you a drink for sure."

Frank thought of his musky turd-gristle building up inside him, already causing him to itch back there.

Frank closed the stall and started to do what he came to do. Rim of the bowl was clean; the kid had probably swabbed it with toilet paper to make sure there was nothing wet on it. Good kid, that kid. Frank wondered how long he'd spent in the bathroom, if the clerk would say anything about him being gone for so long, and the car trip he still had in store after this little fiasco concluded.

Dimly beneath those thoughts was the kid, addressing the middle stall again, and the presence of the kid moving toward the stall, intuited through truncated light and the close-by pitter-patter of feet. Then a muffled creak of a stall being opened, and nothing cognizable was heard. There was a forward, lunging motion, of something jerked forward. Frank, fat, solitary, and slothful, sometimes thought himself not a real person, half a person, a creature who could only survive in a world brought to heel with modern conveniences, ready-to-eat meals and customer service on command, to the point he sometimes thought he lost whatever instincts were inherent to the human animal. But something stirred, an eruption of spastic fear, bursting through him with the shock of a hand emerging from a grave. Something was happening, something catastrophic, and it was happening right next to him, just behind this feeble wall.

There was a cacophony of competing thoughts, whirling so quickly as to be without substance. *Stupid*, is the thought he tried to substantiate. Stupid, nothing wrong, nothing could be wrong with his pants down, that wasn't allowable, somehow; but he knew he was wrong, because he heard a pitted sound of a body part being invaded, and before he could rationalize that, the sound of rendering, of being torn apart, and a heaving of great force, and splatter of a great hot weight of blood and viscera. It was dripping, this blood, down under this giant gap between the stalls; although not all the blood he saw was flowing into his stall, some of it was pooling around something pink and meaty, something, God, he didn't want to see what it was but it must have been an intestine or liver or something, these organs he knew of but knew nothing about or what they looked like, and he thought crazily about a hernia surgery he'd had, good God, did doctors have to look at this stuff all the time?! How could they do it? And there came an explosion in his mind but as he stared at the blood and the organs underneath the stall, as the blood and organs refused to disappear like a parlor trick or he refused to wake up, then the shock went into a kind of overdrive, where the shock went from overwhelming to unbearable to abstracted.

He fell down on his bare knees, pants around his ankles still, still clutching his clod of foul-smelling toilet paper. His legs engrossed in gore, his body reacted — move! — and he pushed himself forward, floundering onto his stomach, the warmth and musk of slippery viscera impossible, for how could there be so much warmth to the parts of a human body, maybe this wasn't a human body, maybe this was a trick; but, no, the kid had seemed too earnest, no, this was real.

He scrambled up, got between the gap and the door, as big as the gap was Frank was too big to fit, it was all a fraught blur but he retained enough of himself to unlock the door and get out of the stall.

He was saturated with blood, on his legs and briefs and he needed to pull his pants up or he'd trip, there was blood in his mouth, oh God, and there were patches on his shirt that stuck to him, of a texture more solid than blood, bits of muscles or bone on him, dear God, he couldn't contemplate; beneath that was a survival instinct, he was doing everything right, he was getting out, keep a hold of yourself, there's still the ever slight chance that this is a prank of some kind, people just don't explode - and he saw himself in the mirror, he was still in shock and the middle stall was now open ....

A half of the boy's face, in a grimace of perpetual agony; he recognized the boy's face as if he were an artist who'd spent a lifetime studying his muse, the curvature, the eye, the personality - yes, the personality, for in this moment of hell he craved the companionship of the boy and felt a searing torment at his loss, that agonized death-face as bad as the death-face of his mother or best friend.

The face was cleaved in half, on the floor.

Sitting on the toilet, the lower half of a man - that asshole man who wouldn't answer - his black shoes and dark jeans-

His upper body…

Was that of some iridescent turquoise, man-sized insect with the face of a clown. Beneath the heavy caked make-up was clearly some kind of bug, a large triangular beak-like snout, mandibles. The left half of the face was caked royal blue, the right half magma red. There some small splotches of red on the blue side, which Frank recognized as blood.

Gold imbricated sparkles vertically bisected the blue and red sides of the face, reflected back light. Running transverse across the face, as unnaturally cruel as a railroad track across a pristine landscape, appeared barbed metal that lifted at each end like a slight smirk. Two tendrils of antennae hung wispily from its head, so faint they could only be glimpsed when the thing moved, which it did, twitchily. An unexpected four-sided hole opened above the metal barb, exploding Frank's sense of the geometry of the creature, for surely he thought the beak-like snout was where the mouth would be, but he was wrong.

The creature lifted its arm. The arm was nothing but a long protrusion that ended in tri-pointed barbs. Then another arm emerged from its other side. The other hand had, he wasn't sure how many fingers, but more than a human hand, and the fingers were arranged in such a way as to be nothing like a human hand, and no more time to spend examining because the thing was getting up, moving toward him, not with great speed but it was definitely bounding forward, on those simple, unspectacular frumpy man-legs...

The boy was a chunky mess across the bathroom stall.

Frank was stunned, in a frenzied daze, an ambulant catatonic. He flailed his arms as if reacting to a surprise huge explosion, and then turned and ran, unthinkingly. He heard something sliding and fumbling roughly on the bathroom floor. Something passed him on the floor. He glanced at it. Flesh, bone and blood, a segment of arm. No time, he bounded forward and heaved himself onto the bathroom door and thank God it opened outward.

"Damn man, watch it!" complained a dark-skinned man, looking down and then nursing his elbow where the swinging door struck him. From his angle and proximity to the door, Frank surmised this man had been putting in the code when Frank burst out of the door.

"Run," Frank wheezed, already gassing out of breath. He would never make it his car. "R-hun, hun," Frank repeated, to the extent his lungs would allow. Frank ran, and looked back, hoping his urgency had been warning enough.

He couldn't make out what happened. He saw a collision of forms, the man falling down but the shape continuing on, righting itself after the collision. When Frank looked back, he saw the shoes and legs of the creature and part of him still wanted to believe he was just being chased by a man, a regular, non-imposing man - but when he glimpsed what rose above the waist, the turquoise insect shape, the bold colors that bifurcated the face (flattened outside in the dark, but still noticeable if you knew to look for it), the strange reflection of the gold dust and macabre metal-zipper scar, good God.

The creature bounded past the fallen man and then, mid-stride, seemed to course-correct, turn around slightly and beeline for the stranger. Frank looked forward, pumped his body, heard the screams of the fallen man and then real or imagined sounds of brutality, forget it, keep running, keep running. He was getting close to his car, don't look back, don't look back, he knew if he looked back he'd see the creature gaining. Despair would overtake him, hope would deflate out of him painfully, a searing in his gut, he'd be hobbled, give up.

No, just keep running.

He was steps from his car.

Hand on keys. Hand on keys, he thought. *Don't lose it at the last moment. Hand on keys. Have your hand on the keys.*

He got to his driver's side door (*hand on keys, hand on keys*) and hit the unlock button and the car blinked affirmatively. He had his hand on the door and he couldn't help but turn around and the monster was not behind him. It was out of sight. (*Don't be stupid, get in the car, get in the car*) and he got in the car (*key in ignition, key in ignition*) and put the key in the ignition and started the car and peeled off.

The old iPod connected to the radio sprang to automatic life, crunching out Converge's *Fault and Fracture*. He honked the horn like a maniac, propelled by the abrasive screams of bloody murder and gnarled riffs that blasted out of his radio, blasting out of his brain. The exit was in the direction he ran from, he'd have to pass the gas station store and the bathroom and he thought *fuck it*, just ride over the grassy median but that could destroy his car and then where would he be, he'd be a sitting duck.

So he kept his hands on the horn. He wanted to yell to the old man in the station to get out, get out! but he wouldn't roll down the windows or stop the car, that would be suicide. He hoped his horn was warning enough, but what if the old man or others in the station heard the horn and stepped outside to investigate and ran right into their deaths but he couldn't think that, there was no time or point in hypothesizing. He had to get out, just get out of here.

His car brights picked up soupy entrails and abysmal splatter, sights so disgusting and plainly wrathful that they just couldn't have been constituent parts of a human being, just impossible that the human body could awaken such feelings of repulsion and disgust.

Press on. He sped out of the exit, hitting part of the curb so he spun out but thank God there were no cars, no Mack Trucks careening down the road, no crazed monster of impossible dimensions hanging for dear life atop his car, clawing its way in.

Only about half a mile away did he realize to lower the volume on his radio but he immediately turned it back up. The quiet frightened him, he needed the pounding riffs to cancel out the quaking pandemonium that tore through his mind, and he screamed and shook, pulled on the steering wheel, partly out of frayed exhilaration but mainly still out of disbelieving fear.

>< >< ><

It needs to stay in the bathroom. That is the point. The lower half is too unwieldy to give chase. The fat man should have never been able to escape the bathroom. And when he did, the creature should have disappeared immediately.

Ormond fumed, the indignation of the misunderstood, unappreciated. They'd approved it. They'd approved the design, temperament, the whole agenda. And they wouldn't let him transfer now. He'd never get to airplanes now.

But fine. Understood. Whatever you say.

Upon a Path Suddenly Irradiated at Some Halfway Point by Daybeams as Rich as Hers

BARBARA CROMWELL (BIRTH name: Barbara Ploznek) was making coffee in her kitchen and looking at that strange crack in the wall. It wasn't a crack, really, but that's what she called it when she first noticed it a year or so ago, complaining about it on the phone to her senile mother or one of her girlfriends, whichever. She tried to avoid looking at it because what was the point? A crack in the kitchen wall, who ever heard of that? Of course, it just had to be her luck. Harold leaves her and then the house he'd left her crumbles. As if the house itself was aware of their situation, and, following the lead from the dissolution of their marriage, felt the appropriate thing to do was self-destruct.

Stop being so dramatic.

Of course she was exaggerating. It was hardly a crack, more like something behind the wall had shifted or settled weirdly, made an indentation of sorts against the tile. She didn't know anything about home repair, but neither did Harold so if he were still around it's not like they'd be relying on his perspicacity. She wished Harold or their daughter Kendra was here to hear her use the word 'perspicacity.' See how they'd both react to that. She didn't need them here to know how they'd react. She knew. Harold wouldn't acknowledge that she used an impressive word like perspicacity, no, he'd let that glide on by and just continue saying whatever he was already planning on saying. He never acknowledged something he didn't understand. Kendra might mention it, ask what the word means, but the subtext of her asking would be her surprise at her mother using such a word. Maybe she'd make a little face. Kendra acted as if Barbara's self-improvement only served to highlight her existing deficiencies.

Kendra hadn't always acted like that. Barbara remembered a time when Kendra looked up to her. Kendra had been a cosseted child (although of course she'd never admit it to her friends in Austin), and in turn had respected and almost seemed to revere her parents. It wasn't until she went away to college that a gulf began to form between them.

But it's fine, the bulge in the wall and these thoughts about

Harold and Kendra. None of them were a big deal but she liked complaining in certain moods, even if the complaints lived and died only in her own head.

The bulge wasn't worth paying to fix, home repairs were so expensive and her alimony kept her on a fixed income. The Battle of the Bulge, so to speak. She had savings allotted to her from the divorce, but the people at J.P. Morgan handled her savings and they said you were penalized for taking money out early. Her savings weren't nothing, in the low six figures, obtained largely from her cut of the investments that had been liquidated in her divorce several years ago, but if you'd asked her ten years ago if this was all her savings would amount to, some $200,000, she'd be shocked. It was all much less than a 57-year-old middle class woman should have at her age.

She'd been a stay-at-home housewife before that term apparently became a four-letter word. For her devotion, Harold had hid money somehow, she was sure, and while her lawyer had done whatever lawyers do in divorce proceedings to find out the real value of Harold's assets, she had no inside information to help guide the investigation. During their marriage, Harold had deputized her to write the checks to the mortgage company and cable company and everything, but that was the extent of her dealings with the finances.

And so it was while she was making coffee some typical weekday morning and she just happened to be looking at the crack in the wall when it started to move. Her first thought, her first real thought, was, 'oh no, I'll have to get this fixed,' and she thought extreme things about the penalties J.P. Morgan would levy upon her if she had to take money out. She could add it to her credit card but she didn't want more debt. She thought about Kendra, in grad school for social work in Austin, and how she tried to be encouraging but there was no money in social work, you had to be careful about these things, you don't want to end up like this, cash-strapped with a crumbling wall.

Then the crack in the wall became more severe, right in front of her, and the consoling eddy of her plaintive complaints was severed. Oh God, this was serious, she thought for an instant that the wall was giving birth, or like a sewer had burst and sewage, or something thick and foul, was about to spill out. She actually screamed and spilled her coffee.

The dent broke open and something fell out and she screamed again. Was the house about to fall in on her? She saw a macabre image of herself, crushed, in her dowdy robe, her old, ugly upper thighs exposed, her body decaying for days before anyone checked up on her. But the thing, or things, that leaned out of the opening were small and wiry. Cable wires. Cable wires in the kitchen? How'd they fall through? Must have been a beam or ... but she didn't know what she was talking about.

Back to the quotidian concerns, clean-up and expenses and microwave meals for as long as it took before the kitchen was usable again, and a tiny part of her — or what she told herself was a tiny part — maybe just wished the walls had fallen in on her.

The wires descended down to the floor. Most had fallen out entirely and coiled on the floor. Others stretched back, still connected to whatever they were connected to back in the wall, but those were few, maybe two or so strands. They didn't look strong enough to break through the wall. Gray thick filaments or something, some cross between the insubstantial gray cable wires that connected her modem to the internet and that more annoying thick black power cord that she always had trouble disconnecting when she had to restart the modem.

She peeked into the hole and saw in her mind's eye some anchor or something breaking off and cracking her in the face, but she didn't see anything. She didn't see how these stupid wires could summon enough force to visibly cause a shift in her wall, let alone break through it. There had to be some ... support or anchor or something that had broken? She had no choice, she had to call someone. Cable company? Home repair? Oh Lord, who knows, they'll all rip you off.

><><><

"Hello, Mizz Cromwell," Peter Morris said. She'd remembered Peter and thanked her lucky stars he'd agreed to come take a look, although he didn't promise the world. Peter was a handyman from a couple blocks away, who'd done some work for her and Harold on their deck several years back. She liked that he called her "Miss Cromwell" without hesitation or trepidation.

"Nice to see you, you look well, it's been a while."

"It has. Thank you so much for coming by." They hadn't talked money, but she had a $50 bill for his time or any reference he could provide, unless he really couldn't help at all, in which case she hoped he'd be apologetic and not expect anything.

"How are Vanessa and the kids?"

"Vanessa and the kids are doing fine. Andy got a job offer in Dallas, engineering something, something above my pay grade, that's for sure. Went as far away as he could from here and still be in Texas, I reckon. Mitch is working security, he's not happy about it and says he'll try and change jobs but he's been saying that forever so who knows, you know."

"I know, only so much you can do. Kendra is away in Austin in a Master's program, never to return, I'm sure, unless she can't find a job when she graduates. All you can do is be supportive." She was a bit displeased to hear that Peter and Vanessa were doing fine, although of course he would say that. What would he say, things weren't going fine? Peter was a nice-looking, well-muscled, broad-shouldered and big-handed in a classic working-man type of way, in a way that made her think of *Of Mice and Men* even though she couldn't be sure she ever even saw that movie. Peter was probably a bit simple, but simple was good, earnest was good. He had real skills and he could beat up Harold if it came to that. She chuckled to herself.

"But please, come in, come in, I'm so out of it." Peter had been standing in the doorway this whole time. Barbara, get with it! She invited him in and asked him if he wanted anything: tea, soda, anything she could dance around the wires to get for him, ha ha.

"Oh boy, you weren't kidding," he said when he saw the damage, shaking his head. He kneeled down and from behind him she admired the breadth of his upper arms, the muscle tone impressive for a man in his fifties. Had she gotten so old? As a girl, did she ever think she would find herself attracted to an old man? Did she ever think she'd be an old woman? And yes, fifties are old, I don't care what you say. Popular culture, the world, all told her she was old. The world was what it was and didn't exist for her anymore.

"Mizz Cromwell, I don't know how much I can do ...." he said, inspecting the wires.

"What wires could those be? Nothing in the house has gone out,

I mean all the power works, the internet, thank God, still works, the light for the microwave is still on ... though I haven't tried the oven."

"I don't think these are wires. In fact, I'm sure they aren't." He touched them, and the way they looked in his hands, they didn't look like wires. Wires were smooth, but the way he manipulated these, they were something else, that's for sure. Like, the material they were made of was not consistent, not smooth, but jagged. No company would sign off on wires that looked like that. Not user-friendly. Dangerous, even.

"These are not wires, for sure," and he followed them into the hole in the wall and looked deeper than she'd ever dared and came back looking puzzled, which to her portended future frustrations, like bills and weeks of take-out food. The options around here, what would she be eating, greasy Chinese or Mexican or Applebee's for the next month?

"Those two, for lack of a better term, I don't know what to call them, so let's call them these 'wires' even though they aren't. These 'wires' that are still connected to something, they go into the hole and hook left, and keep going, I can't see what they are attached to but it is ... pretty deep behind the wall." He looked again at the "wires" that had fallen out completely, and went down to feeling them, looking for a corporate logo or something to let him know who to call, and there was on the reverse side of them something that gave them both deep pause. It was a ... stain, an ugliness, a blotch that could never have been sanctioned by a corporation. It was like a stained opacity the color and texture of gnarled, poorly-cooked meat.

She'd given Peter the $50 and he demurred, he was such a nice guy. Peter had called in a home renovation specialist to take a look the next day as a favor. Walter, Peter's guy, came the next day. With Peter, actually. Maybe Peter was especially interested in this mystery or maybe he just liked her (of course she knew it was just the former but still she did her best to look good for them when they arrived), and Walter — the famed specialist - was stumped too. Definitely looks organic somehow, Walter said, Peter ceding authority but nodding grimly. And oh God, Barbara got scared, could this be asbestos or fungus, did she have to vacate her home? But no, don't rush to conclusions, Walter exhorted, it certainly wasn't asbestos, and the way Walter said that it came off a bit too pat, too controlling. Don't tell me how to feel, this is my home, I have a right to be scared. Peter would never had said it like that (hah, like she really knew Peter so well).

Things escalated so quickly. Soon the county health department got involved, which made her upset (she didn't want people to think her home was dirty or contaminated), and both Walter and Peter were still involved, and eventually even a biologist from the University of San Antonio. All this happened pretty quickly. She was thankful for that and frankly astonished, with what she knew about government and bureaucracy. Red tape and things taking so long, usually, but this all developed so swiftly, her home must have been a real big deal.

What was she supposed to do while this was all going on, move out? She couldn't do that. If she had to, she hoped maybe someone would cover her expenses. I mean, this certainly wasn't her fault and she was doing them the favor: She just wanted her kitchen fixed. It was only a few days after the incident and she had practically a whole crew in there. All men, she noted only because she thought about how her daughter would comment on that fact, in her annoying, pointless way. Barbara herself liked all these men being courteous to her.

The biologist and the official from the health department explained as the first order of business that all the costs would be covered for the repair to her home. If the health official determined she needed to leave the home during repairs, they would put her up in a hotel — all nice hotels, she noted favorably from the list she was given — and pay all costs up to $150 a night.

She signed documents that she read — she read every word — and they gave her time to consult a lawyer, but the agreement seemed pretty simple. They'd cover all the costs associated with clean-up and repair, salvage and study everything that was discovered. She retained all ownership to her home and mortgage, of course, and she didn't really think that she could be tricked out of her house with an ancillary document like this, but she was always skeptical, you always hear stories about banks or governments pulling out the rug from under people. She'd made a copy of the contract and emailed it to Kendra, who chided her in her passive-aggressive way for not speaking to a lawyer but agreed that it looked pretty simple and straightforward.

She liked that the university was involved, that made all the officials more trustworthy. All the various officials were very circumspect yet patient, despite, she could tell, their obvious anxiety about exploring what exactly was going on. She didn't think they were pulling her leg or anything. The university people and the health department people were, they said in various ways, excited and a bit frightened about this "discovery." And they'd say "discovery" and almost blush, because the word was so hyperbolic, something out of the movies. Real discoveries were never so major, were instead accretive developments, almost always incremental and, honestly, not too exciting. But this was something else.

The whole process of discovery, so to speak, only took a day, really, and she wanted to be there when the men explored behind her wall. It didn't take much. There was no lengthy exploration like she saw in the movies. The house wasn't that big and the walls not too deep. They'd removed everything from the kitchen, sealed everything up, and were very delicate with her heirlooms, like the ceramic goose figurine she'd kept on the counter, and some of the little figurines Kendra had made when she was a kid, and her orange tabby cat clock on the kitchen wall that she'd gotten in a fine arts store. All these materials were encased in protective coating and kept safe.

When the kitchen was cleared, the hole was further opened, large enough for a careful man to enter with a flashlight.

Not more than a couple minutes after one of the men entered the enlarged hole and they found something, something everyone had to see. It was just behind the wall in the corner of the kitchen. The corner of her kitchen, where she kept the blender and other things that tucked well into a corner — who could have thought that just behind the wall in the corner of her kitchen something so exciting was lurking?

He needed another team here, the man had said. People to come in and remove what he'd found. She wanted to be around and see it when it was removed. And part of her was sure she'd be disappointed, they'd point to something she signed to say she couldn't be nearby, some technicality she overlooked, but no, they were all excited, perhaps overly gracious for this opportunity, all fine good-hearted Texas men and she even felt proud in a way that she had given them this opportunity for such excitement.

She saw it when it was removed, although she didn't understand it. They eventually said, in newspaper reports and articles, that when unfurled, the thing was about four feet in height, but to her it looked like a stumpy frog figure. No, not really a frog, but like a big poorly formed figurine, or like a big paperweight that was intended to be in the shape of something squat and roundish but failed. Like when you go to an art museum and there's an exhibit on some ancient art and the description makes it sound so amazing and majestic but it's really just kind of disappointing, doesn't stand up to what artists could do nowadays. Primitive, that's the word. It was grayish and undifferentiated, a general shape that suggested legs and a midsection and a curved part of the upper body and head or something, but you had to be looking for it to discern it. Some of those wire things connected to its front section. Again, she didn't get a good look at it but what she saw wasn't too memorable.

They eventually did examinations on it, and it was organic. Something they'd never seen before on Earth, and just leave it at that, because if she said anything more it would be speculation.

Her home had been entirely cleaned up and exhumed and fumigated and everything behind the wall photographed, inventoried and removed. Behind the wall they'd found photographs of her and Harold — yes, she was one of those people who still went to the CVS to print out photographs — even framed photographs that she thought had been in storage in the basement or lost in the shuffle of divorce. Mementos from her marriage. Some jewelry Harold had bought her that she was sure had been lost but had thought at the time, good, I don't want anything from him anyway, saves me a trip to the pawn shop. An Elvis oven mitt he'd bought for her years ago from a work trip in Memphis that she honestly didn't even know was still in the house, she thought she'd thrown it out in a fit. And a whole host of other knick-knacks.

One that stuck out, that caught her in the throat was a "thinking of you" card they found the following day deep behind the wall. Harold had sent her that card so long ago, back when he was on one of his interminable work trips. One in Atlanta, she remembered.

When they'd brought out all that other stuff from behind the wall, it had been in one bundle. All that stuff bundled together kind of dulled the larger impact of what it represented: her failed marriage, the lifelong death-until-you-part bond that didn't last to old age, let alone death. That card, unadorned and by its lonesome, covered in wall-grime, was starkly embarrassing for some reason. She saw it, remembered it from so long ago, did the math in her head and Kendra had been only five then — God, how time flies. Harold's kind, supportive words, his paeans to his devotion and their shared bond, his appreciation for her hard work parenting while he was forced to be hundreds of miles away from the wife he cherished and the family he prized. How poetic Harold could be in those days.

She said as much in some newspaper interviews that followed the discovery, albeit in more circumspect, emotionally-sanitized form. She didn't like how guileless and naïve the newspaper interviews all made her seem, even though there was nothing in the interviews that she could point to that was objectively untrue. Bits of her backstory colored the articles, like how she'd always dreamed of being a singer, how she'd been a damn good paralegal before she'd given up her career for domesticity, even some dumb factoid about being able to make a mean spicy omelet. That last factoid really had no logical place in an article about a heralded mystery discovery in her house, but it was a humanizing element, she figured.

Even though it was exciting to have all that attention, she didn't like how the stories accentuated her surprise, the whole rube in the right place angle. Especially vexing was the dominance of one quote: "who knew that every time I put yogurt and blueberries in a blender, there was something like this just a few feet away?" That sounded so dumb and clueless.

Her daughter was quoted in some stories, too, for some reason, and Barbara knew it was contradictory to be both upset about her own quotes yet still wish she'd been quoted exclusively. Like that joke about the restaurant, how the food was so bad and the portions were too small. But she was entitled to her opinions. Why should Kendra get a say, Kendra hadn't even lived there for years; what did she have to offer? That she, too, was shocked and surprised? Who wasn't?

The stories only mentioned that "family mementos" had been

found buried behind the wall, nothing about how they all concerned her previous marriage. At the bottom of some of the stories, expressed in various iterations, was a note that a reporter had reached out to Harold but he had failed to comment. The wording was always unclear as to whether the reporter didn't hear back before the story was published or Harold declined to comment.

She clarified that detail on her own, eventually. Harold had never responded to the requests for comment. How could he? What could he have possibly added to such a world-bending discovery? And another point, that he didn't mention but Barbara suspected wasn't far from his mind, was that a husband who leaves never comes off well in any story.

Harold eventually agreed to meet with her, at his home.

>< >< ><

Harold hadn't wanted to meet at his home, and had told her such. She had said it was better than meeting out at a restaurant, where people could see them, avoid unwanted attention. He doubted that almost anyone would know what she looked like — she'd like that, wouldn't she, pretending to be a local celebrity — and gave himself credit for holding his tongue on that observation. Harold filed away that commendable action, put it in a slot for easy mental access if she impugned him on something else and he needed good character evidence to rehabilitate himself, either verbally in his defense or just to himself upon reflection, to remind himself of the type of person he really was. He held his tongue often, even when he had a good point to make. He took the high road.

But, fine, have her over, save him the awkwardness of having to pay for her meal, and maybe she was right, maybe there would be people who recognized her, even though she was only tangentially involved in this discovery of the century. She'd been in news stories, all that was true. She probably had a bunch of suitors coming out of the woodwork, all types of crazies who would do anything to get their share of the fame. God, he hoped he didn't see her on some humiliating dating show in the next couple of years, doing her best to hold onto whatever sliver of the limelight that had been cast upon her. That would be mortifying, for her. That she wouldn't even realize it was mortifying only exacerbated it. He wished there was some attenuated way he could offer a counseling service: take a look at some of the guys reaching out to her for dates, identify the ones who were obviously interested only in her notoriety, who didn't have her best interests at heart. But, no, that was impossible.

It had been a month after the fanfare. Not the discovery itself, he had no idea when that had been, but just a month after it seemed everything had died down, at least as it regarded Barb. He wasn't even sure where she was living these days, if she was still in their old house.

He didn't know what to expect when she showed up at his door. He half-expected her to be dolled up in a way, to be dressed well, smell well, so as not to disappoint the paparazzi she imagined lay in wait for her. But no, she didn't look like that at all, she looked just like Barb, like a late-middle-aged woman who mourned the loss of her figure, overweight, soft in the middle but still respectable blonde-who-dyed-her-roots Barb.

Barbara didn't know what to expect with Harold, bald, curiously tanned, hirsute Harold, 5'7", Harold who wore monogrammed polos and work shirts with his initials. He always said it paid to look good, look original, and she always thought if he'd been born 6'2" he'd be singing a different tune but she never said anything like that, except maybe during occasional light teasing.

His home was a modest two-bedroom but impeccably designed and decorated. It seemed to radiate its newness to Barbara, as if her own home — the home they used to share together — existed under a hazy miasma of dust that only became perceptible upon leaving and seeing something better. The colors here popped, it reminded her of the art deco hotels in the South Beach neighborhood of Miami. There were six pieces of monochromatic artwork in the living room, three on each side — royal blue, sky blue, tangerine, raspberry, canary yellow, sylvan green — the type of stuff that Harold had groused about in many a past modern art museum that somehow found its way in his new domicile. The work of Elle, no doubt. ("What," Barbara had said to her daughter when learning the name of Harold's then-girlfriend, now wife, "can he only be with someone he can call by one syllable?" It hadn't been a witty comment, she had wanted it to sound rakish, what a raconteur might say, something delivered by Cynthia Nixon.)

Barbara was sure Elle wouldn't be here. She'd be out

volunteering, perhaps, or out with friends. Elle didn't work. Or another way of putting it was: she was retired. Elle had married well the first time around, and gotten enough from her divorce to never need to work again. Hah, she was a talent scout of sorts, then. She was a recruiter, she'd recruited a rich husband and then a good divorce lawyer. Little jokes Barbara thought to share with friends or maybe Kendra at the right time.

She'd never met Elle. Kendra had hung out with Elle several times, and reported that she was perfectly nice, friendly, treated Kendra graciously. (Elle had several other attributes that Kendra left out of the telling: she was sharp, curious, and open-minded to a degree Barbara never was, although Kendra knew her encounters with Elle were constrained and, in a sense, stage-managed.)

Barbara knew Elle was younger than she, about ten years younger, but that hadn't made her feel that bad, really. Elle was still middle-aged. It's not like Harold married a pert secretary. And Elle had her own money. More than Harold, in fact. And then she'd seen a picture of Elle and felt ... better? Elle had something of a fat ass, looked dumpy and round, for someone so rich she didn't take much care of herself, although Barbara thought it funny that Elle had dirty blonde hair much like her own. They could have been cousins, really. What she really didn't like was that Elle had two of her own children from her previous marriage, and from what she heard from Kendra, Harold spent much more time with her kids than he ever did with Kendra.

That's what really bothered her, she thought, although she had an uncanny ability to funnel everything that upset her about Harold into one or two categories, so her anger about the nature of their separation, how he'd treated her, how he'd run out, that might come out in overzealous comments about how wrong it was for Harold to go to Italy with his new family when he'd never proposed any such trip with her or Kendra. How she felt about how he'd screwed her over financially got bracketed into its own separate category of grievance, with various expressed permutations.

Decades together and she got seven years of alimony promised to her and then a pittance of a lump sum and 50% of his stock assets. (In another universe, where she and Elle were friends, she would have asked Elle for her divorce attorney.) She was four years into the alimony ... let's see how open-minded Elle is, let's see where Kendra's loyalty lies, when she needed money and indefatigable Harold was being indefatigable Harold.

Harold was such a putzy, asshole name. Never marry a Harold.

>< >< ><

"Come in, come in," Harold said, looking like Harold. She thought of those little paper cut-out dolls that can be matched with any combination of paper shirts and paper pants. How Harold looked now flooded her memory with all the other combination-Harolds, all the Harolds that stretched out from the years of their marriage. She welled up — this was a mistake, her tear ducts, her gut, said — and fortunately he was turning away, gesturing for her to come inside, and he didn't see it and she quashed it, nipped the feeling in the bud.

Harold recognized her outfit, navy blue trousers and a pastel blue blouse. Harold looked a bit more down market, and Barbara was convinced it was a power-play, like he was doing her a favor in granting this meeting and signaling that this didn't mean enough to him to look nice. If she made any little comment about it, broached the subject as roundabout as she could, he'd just say that it was Sunday, deflect it in a whaddya-want jokey way, but he'd be sensitive and incensed, and that would come out a couple minutes later, in his own curt or sarcastic comment, or in a favor not extended.

"Would you like a drink?" Harold offered, standing near the fridge. From the way the living room was set up, she saw that they would be sitting on couches, on opposite sides of a glass table with a gray marble base. She was glad he was smart enough not to have her sit at a dinner table. Couches had that sinking-in feeling that made you feel at ease.

"Yes, that would be great," and Harold opened the fridge, asked if she wanted a white or a red. She always drank white, he must have known that, and she thought, too, he didn't have any unopened wine? He probably was afraid to uncork it, afraid he'd mess it up and look weak. But she said nothing except, "White would be great, thank you ... not much ... I drove here," and he said, "Of course," and came back and poured something. She saw the label from a distance, and the label was riotously bright in an un-Harold way. The wines he used to get were austere, bespeaking of what he thought was venerated tradition.

She recognized the model of wine glasses. She kept all the glasses, cutlery, everything housed in their kitchen. He must have gone out and gotten the same type of wine glasses. She wondered if Elle knew. Or if she cared, or if that was something she should care about. No, it was a nothing point. She could be wrong; when did she last use the wine glasses anyway?

"So, thank you for meeting with me, Harold. It was very nice of you, very nice. I thought maybe it wouldn't happen, you know-"

He put his arms up, in a show of good humor and casual straightforwardness, "No, no, of course it would-"

They spoke over each other a little, Barbara trying to express that she didn't think Harold would be to blame if the meeting had never happened, she was just anxious, but the point was lost in the brittle cross-talk.

"Well, I appreciate you meeting with me, Harold. I really do," she said to turn the page on that bit of initial awkwardness. Harold had a habit of looking cross; he was a master of the self-martyred look, a sharp, hot glance, as if he just needed to express his anger but couldn't let anyone else see it, then became sulky and sullen like he was really enduring a terrible privation, which could quickly fester into something worse, more toxic, unless the guilty party inquired, pleaded, apologized and maybe groveled enough to pull him back into the orbit of conversation. He hadn't done that, yet, but it was something she had to look out for. He seemed in a curiously good mood, actually, and she didn't know how to feel about that. In a black moment of self-doubt, she thought, maybe he feels that way because he knows this is temporary, just a bump in the road of his day, just a morsel of his past to be sampled and spit aside.

"I didn't know what to expect. I'm sure you've read, read all the stories, heard from Kendra about everything that's happened-"

As she spoke he was nodding and saying "yes, yes," sententiously, as if his "yes, yes" conveyed his own implacable self-satisfaction about his knowledge of the situation. She wondered about jibes his co-workers or friends had said to him following the discovery, things like, "bet you wish you would have kept that house now," and that made her feel good. She wondered if anyone said something like, "bet you wish you never divorced that woman now," but no, no one would say that, that's too cutting and personal. After all the hoopla, she half-expected a letter in the mail from his lawyer, demanding a financial re-evaluation of the house. She didn't think that could be possible — she kept the house and took a lower (significantly lower!) payout from the divorce — but still, she expected it, somehow, that'd just be her luck, wouldn't it?

"Yes, it's amazing, Barb. Simply amazing. I mean, wow. I can't pretend to even understand it. You know, a reporter tried to contact me about it ... I mean, I think a couple have, actually. I don't know, maybe it was just one reporter several times. I remember I told one reporter, just, 'I can't talk about it, I have nothing to add.' I mean, wow. Aliens. Little green men, or something. Or not. I mean, they still don't even know it was, is ... I mean, do they?"

"It, it has been a whirlwind," and she heard herself and she sounded like an old lady making herself sound important, inserting herself into something she'd been only an extraneous part of. "It's, I mean, been something, true," she tried to harden the soft edges of her sentences, of her tone. "Just, what are the odds, something like that, in our house, they estimate, for years, maybe, all that time being back there?"

"When you say it like that, God, it sounds so creepy. Do they even know what it is? I've heard they really think it's an entirely new, intelligent species. It has a brain, a brain that's not like anything they've ever seen before. I mean, with what they know, how do they even know it has a brain at all, that's what I'm asking. Could be something completely different."

She tipped her glass in a way as if to say 'Amen to that.'

"But what do we know, those are questions way bigger than we could ever know," Harold continued. He was self-aware, or self-conscious, like that. He was a smart man, good at his job, but his job was only one tiny little job in a whole big, wide world. Growing up he'd wanted to be an accountant, then eventually an actuary but he hadn't been smart enough, he told himself. But that didn't mean he wasn't smart. He was smart in different ways. He was good with money, he thought, he'd done all right. But he deferred to people who really understood and built upon ideas and concepts that he could only sort of hazily parrot back. "But who am I to say, it's not like I'm in the labs doing tests. If they say it's a brain, they have to have a reason, I'm sure."

They spoke around the issue for a bit, him saying it will "give him something to Google later."

Soon after, he placed his drink dead center in front of him and, while making solicitous, open-palm hand gestures, said: "I just have to ask. Just, entirely out of curiosity, one hundred percent curiosity. Did you ever get any offers on the house, or any appraisal on the house," and as she answered, she heard his mumbled placating words, "I'm just asking," and his lower octave gave her a weird thought that his words were a sort of base for what she was about to say, like a foundation. He sounded genuine. She explained that she didn't have it appraised and had gotten a couple of kooky offers but didn't consider them. The value would be passed on to Kendra, and he agreed gamely with that.

"I just had to ask, just had to ask, it was killing me!" And then he laughed in a way that was audible but, she felt, meant only for himself.

Despite their house providing the setting for a world-altering discovery, they found that they had little to talk about comfortably. Harold spoke at a faster, more excited clip then she was used to, his pantomimes and gestures more animated than she remembered. For show, she thought, or borne of nerves.

She smiled rigidly, as if she was on a job interview, politely feinting. So easy to forget the way people acted, the way people had treated you, when you're in front of them in the moment. She felt an uncomfortable pull, a desire to impress him somehow, to smile and take everything in stride as if she skated by, somehow above everything he said, above her memories of their shared past, as if the miracle found in her home cast her above her previous concerns, transformed her, left her breathing rarefied air.

That's not what she came here thinking, but that's how she was acting now, and she didn't like it. That isn't what she came her for: what she came here for took courage, not something to be smothered under false smiles and light titters. She felt like she was subconsciously pivoting from her game plan, perhaps because she recognized things weren't going as she planned, and through her blank words and stolid, slightly happy mien, she was obscuring the reason of why she came.

"So, Harold," she said, him on his second glass of wine, her still on her first, now with raisins and mixed nuts also sharing the table, "I don't mean to keep circling back to the, to the event!" and she said it with the overstated panache with which they'd been speaking about it.

"The event! Yes, the event!" he said, loudly and awkwardly, like he was trying to accentuate a punchline but got the beat wrong. While Barbara was a frowzy middle-aged, unhip white woman — she knew what she was — she still remembered how she thought about old people before she became one, the way they missed cues, got tones wrong, failed to land a joke or turn a phrase. The way they could be embarrassing. That's what she felt about Harold now.

"But, did you ever read about what they found, with the ... thing in the wall?" She was going to say alien but that felt weird, and it wasn't an alien as far as she knew. "The other things they found in the wall, from the house?"

"Uhhhh," he raised his arms, looked around, "ya got me." And then he added, maybe on the realization he wasn't the star of a sketch only he was privy to, "I heard they found all types of cr-, er, stuff back there. Like, oven mitts, all types of stuff." He said "stuff" coarser, accentuating the hard-ending consonant, in an un-Harold-like way, like a 1950s tough guy he shared absolutely no cultural DNA with, but which he sometimes channeled when he was drunk and with company.

"They found, wow, the things they found, Harold, the things they found back there," and she looked at him and took full stock of his face, his 56-year-old face (four months younger than her, she was robbing the cradle they'd used to joke, a stupid, easy joke), his straight white teeth that weren't so straight and white for most of their relationship, his homely face, but homely in a wholesome way, Beagle-homely.

"They found mementos. Cards that you'd sent me. Little knick-knacks of ours. Even jewelry, believe it or not, those green emerald earrings you got me on our fourteenth anniversary, I remember, our fourteenth anniversary. The Elvis oven mitt I thought I'd lost, Elvis oven mitt," and she wanted to repeat Elvis because then maybe he'd overlook that she said fourteenth anniversary, not just an anniversary but very specifically their fourteenth anniversary. Men didn't keep track of things with that level of detail, that was all right, but who knows what he does and doesn't remember about their marriage. "All things, from our marriage. From our life together."

Harold's expression was more constricted and severe, less sentimental than she'd hoped for. "That means — that means that thing was sneaking around the house behind our backs, or at night, somehow, to get those .... My God, I mean, I guess that's not a shock, put two and two together, but to think of it ... slinking around like that."

"Yes, that's true," she acknowledged, a thought that had long since occurred to her, even been explained to her, and that she'd made peace with. "But what is more important, in a way, to me, is that they don't know what it was doing, exactly. There's no way to know. But everything they found in its, its area, whatever you want to call it, had to do with us. Our marriage, specifically. There wasn't anything of Kendra's there. Nothing. Not even anything we all shared. Just us. I mean, the two of us."

He exhaled in a way that meant "huh," or maybe "geez," a nothing-noise fecund with reflection. He didn't speak, looked ponderous. "Gee, that's something."

"Yes, it is. And I don't know. They don't know how long it was there for. They have estimates, though, based on, I'm not sure what. We had the kitchen area back there worked on, what, seven? eight? years ago, so it couldn't have been before that-"

"Unless the thing can go through space and time in ways that are really over our heads-"

"Well, yes, I guess." He was losing the thread of her emerging point. "Anything can be anything, I suppose, but there's no use in talking about that if anything can be anything. From what they think, based on when we had the work done in the kitchen, and something about dampness or oxidization levels behind the walls or something, I'm not sure, they think maybe it was back there five years. *Five years*." But Harold was still on the "geez" mindset of quiet awe, and the timeframe didn't seem of any singular importance to him. It wasn't something he'd thought about like Barbara had for months on end.

"Five years, Harold. When the problems began."

He inhaled deeply, thrust his chest out, a frankly typical Harold move of bitchy discomfort, one of many a move he did when he felt he was about to suffer an indignity.

"Just listen, Harold."

"Barb, I-" and maybe she was wrong, what she took as bluster and impatience could be hurt and trepidation. Kendra had said he felt terribly guilty about everything, but those were words, her interpretation. He had always been an asshole, a moody, woe-is-me, I-didn't-get-what-the-world-owes-me self-pitying asshole. Harold and Kendra had always thought she was too dumb, too self-absorbed — they had always obliquely and not-so-obliquely joked about "Doctor Mom" or "Mom the Lawyer" or "Mom the Architect" or any other sobriquet they'd joke about to insinuate that just because she didn't have a career, she didn't know anything. Like, if Kendra asked for advice on her career, Barbara's suggestion would always seem to be given less credit than Harold's, even though Harold knew just as little as she did about social work. Harold was no medical expert, yet she didn't remember anyone laughing about "Doctor Dad" if he opined on a medical issue. “Mom the Lawyer” was a particularly cruel and ignorant jibe, since she had worked as a paralegal for many years, and had been a damn fine one at that.

"I, Barb, I - I can't talk about these things.” He was red-faced, some combustible mix of indignation and guilt.

"You don't have to feel bad," she said, words she thought she'd never say, and a sentiment she never believed was possible until a couple months ago, when she thought about the full ramifications of the discovery. "You don't have to feel bad, it's okay. I'm not here to make you feel bad. I've come to terms with everything, Harold. I've come to terms with the past.

"But what this means, don't you understand? If it lived with us five years ago, that explains so much, doesn't it, Harold?"

Harold was shaking his head, feebly munching on nuts, wishing he had the big box with him to partially hide behind, realizing now that the wine was a bad idea. An ache in his forehead and sinuses now predominated, his skull rattling as he shook his head.

"It means, you know, the problems we had, the way things worked out, were ...." She didn't know how to word it, and couldn't even believe she'd have to. It was so patently intuitive. A phenomena not subject to rational explanation had made their home its home, about five years ago. And thusly, so had Harold begun to act the way he acted, itself a phenomena not subject to rational explanation.

Of course, on the surface, you could smother the granular details of Harold's bizarre behavior into some accepted pathology — objectify it as depression, as sulking, as an acute mid-life crisis. That's the preprocessed narrative that people accept on the macro level. Harold had always been irritable, defensive, dismissive, seemed to hold this belief that the life he was living was somehow just a placeholder, that he was waiting in the wings for the prepossessing life that was owed to him to finally come to fruition, when Life checked its balance sheet and realized that this ordinary life full of ordinary humiliations was certainly not all that Harold had had to look forward to.

Harold had told her once that, in his youth, he never really thought he'd ever have to work for a living. The thought was knowingly fatuous, of course. Harold wasn't born wealthy by any stretch, and when he graduated from school he'd have to work, just as everyone had to work. But still he grumbled about having to work, as if work wasn't the expected course for all. And you could create a straight line connecting these seemingly innate traits and what eventually transpired, his growing dissatisfaction building and building until it culminated in the dissolution of their marriage by him just running out one day and moving into a hotel. Literally just one day, while she was out, just one Sunday when the reality of their union became too oppressive for Harold, the unsung prince of history, to bear.

But she knew there was more going on. She always knew. There had to be. She remembered his behavior, his irritability without even the veneer of a rational basis, the put-downs that went from passive-aggressive to invidiously acidic ....

>< >< ><

"I said — how many times did I say — that the sheath has to be placed with the blade so I can cover it when I'm done?" He'd been pointing to the carving knife he liked to use.

"It's right-"

"How many fucking times? How many fucking times?"

He'd mentioned in the past that he wanted the sheath to always be with the knife, but that had been a while ago, he didn't mention it often and it didn't happen often, and he never cursed like that.

"It-" she was trying to say that the sheath was in the drawer, where it almost always was. Yes, it wasn't on the knife, like he'd said he wanted, but it was in the drawer, just right next to-

"Fucking forget it, what does it fucking matter what I ask for anyway," and he slammed the drawer shut, the knife placed inside awkwardly. The drawer jammed on the blade, and the blade fell out and toppled violently on the floor.

"Harold!" but he was already storming off in high dudgeon. What's the big deal, big fucking baby he was.

And there had been other incidents around the same time period, like the time she saw him check the expiration date on a carton of whole milk and begin crying, privately, as if he lived among prison guards looking to take advantage of his weaknesses.

Another time, he flagrantly masturbated in bed before she'd fallen asleep. He'd touched himself so wantonly and aggressively that she doubted he could have been feeling any pleasure from it. He was doing it to subvert her, somehow, to flout their domestic etiquette.

"Honey, are you ...." and then he got up and stormed out of the room, then she realized some of the throaty noises she'd heard from him had been him sobbing. She made to go console him, but he got ahold of himself to some degree and told her he needed "time." Then he came to bed and said nothing.

She'd questioned him around that time, never mentioning that she saw his mourning over the milk or identifying the bed incident with any specificity. She questioned, oh so delicately, as she needed to do with a man as sensitive as Harold, but he put up disproportionate resistance to her queries.

Then, soon after, he left. That was it. He left, and there had been attempts at rapprochement, couples therapy, but he was just going through the paces, as if he was going through couples therapy as a pretext so he could tell their daughter, when attacked, that he tried couples therapy but it didn't work.

>< >< ><

"You had to have thought about it? You had to have? It's just ... it explains so much, Harold. It explains so much about your ...

what happened."

"Your," she was going to say. Typical. She was going to say "your problems," wasn't she? And it was his problem, in a way. That he'd let things go on as long as they did, without muttering a peep. He tried explaining to her that he'd fallen out of love, that he couldn't deal with it anymore.

He couldn't go further with this, both out of his own fear of confrontation and his wish to avoid hurting her feelings. What was the point, it was over, he resolved, it was over. But the bitterness and resentment was too deep for him to broach. She never asked what he wanted to do on the weekends (if anything), how he wanted to spend their vacations, or even what he wanted at the grocery or the drug store. Everything was her, what she wanted, what she thought. She could get mad at him but, God forbid he ever got mad at her for anything, that was beyond the pale.

"I haven't been honest. I haven't. I ..." what had he expected from meeting with her? There'd been a life-altering occurrence that she'd been a part of, and something about that had augured ... something. What had he expected? A completely different Barb? He knew all the tensions held in abeyance were still there, could easily emerge when the pleasantries were brushed away.

He wished she had found a new partner. That's what she really needed — a partner, a match. He should have seen this coming; how could he have not? What was he thinking? Just the unreality of the whole incident with her, their old home, cast a penumbra that clouded his senses. What was he thinking?

"Barb, I don't ... I don't-"

"How could it not? It has to be! This thing invaded our home, it was researching us, spying on us, obviously doing something, and just about that time, just as it arrives-"

This was all speculation, hot air and speculation, so full of holes, and what did it matter, he felt the way he felt, the reason why he felt this way didn't even matter anymore. So even assuming she was right, this thing arrived in their home and what, somehow made his emotions change and compelled him to leave? So what? What, was he to leave his new wife, go back to that airless, suffocating life he fled? And it wasn't even verifiable. He was to drop everything because she had a hunch?

"Don't you see, Harold?" How could he not? How could he not! It was incontrovertible. When you see a broken window with a round hole and a baseball lying in the house, you can put two and two together.

"Barbara, I don't - I don't think that's true. This is all, they don't know anything about it, the stuff you are talking about, there's no, I - we had lot of problems, Barb. We had a lot of problems, for a long time."

He dusted off his outfit, ostensibly for peanut crumbs, and then stood up.

She gestured in surprise. "Is that it?"

Harold fidgeted, glanced, made as if he was going to walk to the kitchen, then didn't, said, "I - yeah - I think maybe," and found he was welling up. There was so much history here, not all of it bad. Most of it not bad. They shared a daughter, brought life into this world, a living manifestation of the promises he'd made to Barb, the bonds he had planned to keep. But old age, hormones, stress, his own failures, her own failures, the multifarious unknown impulses that spring up and beget a life of their own: a million reasons why things work out the way they do that can't be consigned to a label or given an easy explanation.

"So that's it? Giving up again? Running out? Going to run out of your own house this time? Or that's what you did last time already, isn't it?!" Her barb lacked grace, lacked the snap she wanted to give it. "Or are you going to push me out this time?"

The implication of physical violence stunned him, he started to say, "Barb, I'd never," but he couldn't let it out. "I'm sorry the way things happened."

"Don't you see, Harold? Don't you see? You could be so stubborn sometimes, Harold, so stubborn. It's not anyone's fault, Harold, that's what I was trying to say before you derailed me. It's not your fault. How could this be your fault? Look at what we were dealing with! This wasn't money problems," and to this Harold grinned a bit, knowing the reference she was alluding to, Steven and Sue Mocher, always having money problems that eventually overcame their marriage's capacity to withstand them. "This was unprecedented. We had aliens, in our wall, doing voodoo on us, God knows what, stealing pieces of our marriage and sticking pins in them!"

To this Harold smiled, his eyes crystallized with the misting of incipient tears.

"We still don't know. The smartest scientists in the world don't know. They have no explanation!"

"Right," he said.

"You can come back, Harold. You can come back. It wasn't your fault. It wasn't our fault. They say things happen for a reason, and of course, this is bigger than us, of course. This is bigger than us. Everyone in the world wants an explanation. They can't wait to find out what all this means. But to me, to us, it's already given us an explanation. An explanation for one of the most important events in our lives."

"Right," he said. It was so tempting to humor her, to carry on with the desire to pin blame elsewhere, to pretend. He felt a knot of gloom in his stomach, the heavy weight of responsibility. He couldn't sanction the charade, the wishful thinking.

"Barb, no. I'm sorry. I, I left and I'm not coming back, Barb. Things had been going badly for a while. I have a new –'ife." She didn't hear if he said "life" or "wife" but they were interchangeable as far as she was concerned.

She sat silently, the gravity of his recalcitrance sinking in. Then, to interrupt his fumbling around: "Don't you remember, waking up from your dreams, crying, wailing like a baby? Like an animal in terror! How you broke down, screamed even? When I asked you, you said you felt something, a monster, hovering over you, all around you. You were convinced there was something, a monster, something terrible, you said you felt something poisoning you, poisoning us, in the house, and I took care of you, I stayed by you, I kissed you and made you better. And then you left. But you were right. We had no idea then, we thought you were going crazy, but you were right. There was a monster."

"Barb," but now it was a keening noise, a blubbery directive to please stop.

"Do you not remember the dreams?"

"Barb, no." He had no idea what she was talking about, and that frightened him on many levels.

"But you can come back now, Harold, you can come back. We

can start over, fresh. Become a family again, a real family."

"Barb ... I'm sorry, I can't do this anymore. I can't do this anymore."

She was lying about the dreams. That never happened. But the gestalt of what she was saying was so self-evident, she needed an ironclad example to bust through the walls of his doubt to let the truth flood through.

"Maybe you don't remember them, we have no idea how that thing works, how it affected you, we have-"

"No, Barb. No."

He spoke, in a circumscribed way, about how she needed to leave. He was sorry. He was glad to see her, but she had to go, it was concluded. And she maintained a bit of a haughty visage, perhaps to suggest without words how crazy he was acting, how delusional he was being. What more could he want, what other evidence could she provide?

It wasn't working, she knew. It wasn't going to work. He was so stubborn that way. This cataclysmic phenomenon and he refused to believe it could have an effect on him. Harold the immovable object.

She thought of their shared life, all she put up with from him, this gulf that existed now between them; how in a just world, she should be able to call upon their life together, the promises they'd made to each other, the sacrifices she made on his behalf, to bridge that ever-yawning chasm between them.

Couldn't he see? Couldn't he see what was right in front of him?

All those nights of wondering why it had gone the way it went, and then this, this discovery, the world agog and aghast and flummoxed, with this unfathomable reality. A mystery to all, but at least a Rosetta Stone to the language of their dissolution.

Couldn't he see?

But she could see. She could see her gambit that she so fervently believed to be true, that she knew to be true, would yield nothing. How she hadn't wanted to acknowledge it, but her whole life depended on this succeeding, on the resolution she desired. The whirlwind excitement that she'd been caught up in — the attention, the feeling of being instrumental, of having a purpose, of being respected — was revealed as its own temporal phenomenon.

For here she was stymied, and all that made itself clear to her was the dreary, creaking, desperate agony of her failure, and the empty, featureless life stretching out before her.

I've Read With Some Interest About ...

JEN SUPPLEE KEPT the apartment lobby door open for the long-haired Italian tenant with the two wheezing English bulldogs. She recognized him; of course, who wouldn't recognize the modern-day Fabio — at least in both build and hair-length, albeit a brunette rather than a blonde — with the thick Italian accent and puttering bulldog duo, whose sloppy-jawled visages reflected how she often felt while leaving for work in the morning.

"Thank you," he replied in his accented English as he walked the few feet to the elevator. It was hard enough getting those dogs to take a walk, let alone get them up the five flights of stairs to his apartment. Those dogs looked so lazy she was surprised he didn't carry them, an arm a piece like two big doggy laundry bags. She baby-waved at the two dogs without acknowledgement, both dogs seemingly wholly preoccupied with sustaining their breathing, as evidenced by their strained, juicy wheezing and heavy panting.

She never learned this guy's name, but he was a building fixture to her. Fabio with the bulldogs. She'd lived here for three years and hardly knew anybody. Sure, she recognized some people, but never exchanged anything other than brief pleasantries. She wasn't sure why that was, really; perhaps this was counter-intuitive thinking, but she never viewed her living space as an avenue for meeting new people, especially since most of the people in this building were older than her. She'd made some effort when she first moved in — attended the first two annual co-op parties — but nothing really stuck.

Let's see, of the people she "knew," there was Fabio with the bulldogs. Then Well-Groomed Co-op Board Member Guy. Based on his titular punctiliousness and fine grooming, she'd assumed stereotypically that he just had to be gay. She'd then gotten excited when she saw him palling romantically with a woman, because that meant he was straight and therefore potentially available at some future point, until she learned that said woman was his wife. Then there was the Sad Korean Guy Who Worked in Computers in Some Capacity who seemed perfectly nice but too blasé to reveal any interesting components to his personality from their brief interactions near the mailboxes. (That she suspected he had a crush on her, even if it was the mildest of crushes, made her feel bad that she didn't at least remember his name. If he was considerate enough to find her dumpy-ass attractive, she should be considerate enough to at least remember his name.) *"Crush" sounds so severe. What is a tiny crush but a verbal oxymoron?* she thought lazily. *A push, a tap?*

A young Asian woman Jen didn't recognize was standing by the side of the lobby wall right next to the panel of tenants' mailboxes. This unknown person was standing with the heedless confidence of a tenant, reading some kind of pamphlet and partially blocking Jen's designated mailbox slot.

Jen walked behind her and shimmied over to her mailbox. She inserted the mailbox key and opened the box delicately, careful not to hit the stranger. She didn't know what these mailboxes were made of, other than something cheap and flimsy. As often happened when attempting to open her mailbox, the entire panel covering all residents' mailboxes came loose, forcing open several boxes adjacent to hers.

This "new person" awoke from her stupor and moved out of the way.

"Sorry," the new person stuttered.

"Oh, don't worry, you weren't in the way," Jen lied, in the way she often did to minimize her perceived imposition upon other people. "I'm Jennifer, I live one floor up, in 2K. Have you lived in the building long?"

"Three year. Sorry, speak not so good," she said with an apologetic, almost deferential laugh. "Three year," she repeated considerately, with three fingers up, as if remedying the confusion. The woman looked Southeast Asian, possibly Filipino, and the pamphlet she was holding was not in English.

"Oh, three years. You definitely beat me. I've not been here as long. I'm only here about two," Jennifer responded.

"Sorry," the lady said again.

She thought of making a joke but knew it would only be pure sound to this woman. "It's okay, have a good day," Jen offered kindly. With her daily bounty of magazines, restaurant menus and junk mail in hand, she closed the panel of mailboxes and started toward the staircase.

The elevator finally came for the Italian guy — this was a pre-war building, with a single elevator that took several beats after arriving to open — and he held his leash-cloaked arm in the door and eye-motioned toward her.

"Oh, thanks, I'm good. I only live one floor up. Thanks, though," Jen said, in the chipper tone of someone appreciative yet unnecessarily apologetic, since she hadn't expected or asked him to wait. He shrugged and disappeared inside the elevator, which closed behind him. He apparently didn't know her name or even what floor she lived on, but she somehow knew he lived on the fifth floor.

She at least knew the neighbors on her own floor. There was, starting from the stairwell: the young yuppie-bro who lived in the corner apartment just to the immediate left of the stairwell who obviously got high a lot, as Jen had often walked through the redolent musk while going to work in the morning; then her apartment, just adjacent to the yuppie pothead and a few feet from the stairs; then the middle-aged Hungarian super, Noel, who seemed perfectly nice but looked too rough-hewn to be named Noel. (She wondered if Noel was his real name.) Noel lived with his mother and wife in what she assumed was only a one-bedroom, which had to be unpleasant. Continuing down the hallway there was the young post-college couple, the woman a realtor whose boasting obviously concealed some insecurities, her boyfriend quasi-employed who did some intermittent gigs in film; and finally the Indian older couple she never saw, but whose apartment emanated fragrant curry vibes. That could sound racist but it was both (1) true and (2) a positive, as she loved all types of curry and strongly preferred the waft of cumin and cardamom to her adjacent neighbor's marijuana.

She walked up one flight to her floor and saw Noel heading toward the elevator, some cardboard boxes in tow. He nodded and smiled at her, which she returned in kind. His hands were full of cardboard and detritus, and she gave a concerned look as if he needed help and made to move down the hallway to open the elevator for him when it arrived on their floor. She did this even though he was much closer to the elevator than she was and it would have been, if anything, inconvenient to let her maneuver around him to open the elevator door, only to have to move out of the way for him to get his detritus into the elevator. He knew she was just being kind and said, in a low voice, “no need, I got it.”

He kept the elevator door open to continue speaking with her. "There is a board meeting tonight in the basement, just so you know, so basement going to be closed tonight again. Why they pick Mondays for these meetings I do not know."

"Again on a Monday? It’s laundry day!"

"They all take laundry to cleaners who do their laundry for them, I'm sure. They must not know Monday is best day for most people to do their laundry. Because, it's nice out, who wants to spend a Sunday doing their laundry?

"You know Noel, you should run for the board, and the first ruling you can make is no meetings on Mondays. Make them on Fridays, when no one is using laundry."

"True. I use laundry on Friday, actually."

"Governance is hard."

That didn’t express the point she’d wanted to make. The comment, even though it came out of her mouth, took her by surprise. Noel, too, apparently, as he paused awkwardly to see if that comment could somehow be reconciled with the rest of the conversation, realized it couldn’t, and continued with his patter of laundry-based small talk.

"Yes. Well, letting you know, it starts at seven and going to be closed for two hours."

"Two hours? That's what keeps us from running for the board, who wants to spend two hours in a laundry room, unpaid?"

"Yes. 'Nother rule to change," he said, heading toward the elevator. "Good night."

"Good night, Noel," she said as the doors closed. She was always glad when a conversation was cut short by the elevator, as she never knew how to finish them. She just realized that she’d never slipped him any holiday money under his door. Were single women expected to do that, or was that more of a married-couple type of thing, giving out holiday bonuses to the super? Fuck.

Jen entered her apartment. Her apartment was a quick study: to the right, within arm’s length, was the master closet, and to the left there was a short corridor (where all her shoes were kept), which led into the living room. The kitchen was a bit beyond that (“a bit” was right: this was a one-bedroom, after all). Then, moving north, there was the bathroom and then the bedroom, a few feet to the right.

Her apartment was spartan, which made her look fastidious and neat, when in reality she just didn't keep a lot of stuff. Her desk at the office — where her workload and inventory was out of her control — was a disorganized mess. Her apartment was bare because she didn’t entertain much and didn’t go out much, didn’t get super wasted or go to cool parties in refurbished warehouses, didn't have a cramped apartment packed to the gills, or even any roommates who shared juicy stories or savvy intel. She was, according to popular culture, doing this whole single-girl-in-the-city thing all wrong.

It was just her, in an unfashionable, cheap-but-well-taken-care-of one-bedroom apartment with about everything you'd expect from a person who basically used an apartment for what it was intended for: cooking, computer browsing, sleeping, and reading or television-accompanied couch-slouching. Her rare bits of festive uniqueness included gothic-looking red and black desk lamps; two small framed pictures of fantasy landscapes composed of geometric shapes; and two posters she knew were ubiquitous, but ubiquitous for good reason: that Le Chat Noir poster with the striking black cat with the coiled tail standing tense against a blazing sunflower-yellow sky, and that poster of Audrey Hepburn in a little black dress, the one where she was sporting a beehive, chewing on an impossibly-thin cigarette with a white cat on her shoulder. Jen had gone on many-a-date at French restaurants that had at least one of these posters. The two posters were right next to each other, and Jen liked to think that the scared-looking white cat in the Hepburn poster and the strict, severe-looking black cat in the garish Le Chat Noir poster, even though appearing as such opposites, must have become best friends through proximity.

She turned on her computer (which took forever to load, it was so old) and put on a music playlist that the almighty algorithm gods deemed suited for cooking. She took chicken out of the fridge and put water on to boil for a pasta side dish. While the water heated up, she looked up some new ideas on what to do with chicken cutlets, reading one listicle that promised to make her chicken cutlets SPARKLE, which sounded like a process that involved glitter and would end in toxic shock but really just involved herbes de provence and truffle butter. She thought it'd be funny if the article suggested throwing the cutlet into a moonlit ocean overtaken by fairies, or maybe let it spend a few months in the dirt at Chernobyl: that'd certainly make it SPARKLE. (Nah, that's mean, the article was actually pretty good.)

She heard an impolite pound on her front door. Not a repeated pounding. Just one pound. She pictured the burly, just-want-to-get-done-with-my-shift FedEx worker who heaved his sore arm against her door, eager to get home.

She got up from the computer, thinking weirdly that she was glad that the FedEx worker wouldn't be able to look into her apartment and see the defrosting chicken cutlet on the kitchen counter.

Jen looked through the peephole. There was nobody there. She didn't think she'd ordered anything, but nowadays it seemed she ordered many commonplace items through the mail, from groceries to bath towels to garbage bags. It was hard to keep track of whatever *Peapod* or *Glam City* or who knows whatever push-promotion she'd sign up for, forget about, and then get in the mail a few days later. One time she'd gotten a delivery of three honeydews, a reusable water bottle, and a *Travel and Leisure* magazine. Who knows what Google algorithm pushed whatever digital levers to put that offer together. To think, all these brilliant logistics that went into sending her all this frivolous stuff.

The goal she'd set for herself after receiving that *Travel and Leisure* magazine: actually start traveling. Still working on that one.

She kind of liked looking out of the fish-eye peephole. Who came up with this? It was pretty impressive to think that someone, so long ago, came up with a way of seeing such a wide range of angles through a small hole in a door. Wheeeeeeeee ... she looked rapidly through different parts of the peephole, making her boring hallway prismatic, beguiling. She imagined a camera click with each shift of her eye.

Camera one: corner.

Camera two: corner.

Camera three: corner.

Camera four: corner.

Camera five: stairs.

Camera six: Noel's door.

Well that was a blast.

Who am I being sarcastic to, myself?

She'd omit this from her nightly journal entry.

No courier, no package.

Jen headed back to her chicken cutlet when she heard another impolite pound. She was still close enough to the door to really *feel* the reverberation. It had a heft that had to be more than just a hand.

Maybe it wasn't her door? Maybe it was the Yuppie Bro's door, which was maybe, at most, a yard from her door (she wasn't good at gauging distances, but she was 5'5", and guesstimated things using herself as the barometer; the Yuppie Bro's door was about "half of her" away). Maybe he was a drug dealer, and this was some antsy buyer looking for a fix. (No, that was ridiculous. The Yuppie Bro smoked pot. No one anxiously pounds on doors for pot, no one has a "pot fix," and no one says "fix," anyway.)

She stayed silent, aware of a growing unease, a twinge in her chest somewhere between impatience and anxiety, of wanting resolution and yet cherishing seclusion, not wanting to move or do anything.

Seconds passed. *Ten*, she found herself counting up to in her head. That was a slow ten, languorous Mississippis between each count. She was goofing on herself more for thinking of "pot fixes," grounding herself with internal chatter, a way of pulling down the mental blinds, letting in no unwanted light.

Fifteen Mississippi.

Another knock.

No, knocking wasn't right, because a knock is using the knuckles to rap on the door. This was more like, again, an indecorous pounding, like someone whipping their arm against the door. (Spaghetti-arming, she thought to herself for some reason. Was that an expression? It should be).

She wouldn't answer. Fifteen seconds for a follow-up knock was poor knocking protocol. FedEx guys usually knock ferociously and impetuously, as if they are always one package away from finishing their shift and you're the meandering asshole who is slowing them down. If it wasn't a FedEx guy, then she wasn't interested. Management had put some fliers underneath their door some time ago, reminding them not to let in anyone they didn't know (although nowadays no one knew anybody, so those fliers might as well have just said "Trust No One").

If it's a delivery guy, let him just leave it by her door.

Still, she stood motionless in her own hallway, halfway between the kitchen and the door. Her breathless stillness added an undeserved importance to all of this. Even the way she was standing, elbows bent, hands slightly outstretched, like she was a stealthy cat burglar. Like she was the one doing something wrong. Who knows, just some stupid kid in the building playing a prank, or maybe somebody in an apartment repeatedly dropping something heavy, maybe unable to put together a bookcase or something (okay, that one was a bit of a stretch).

Next time someone knocked, she should yell out "no one's here!" That would do it. Genius!

She waited several more seconds, far past reasonable. Funny how slow time seems to get when you are standing motionless, without even a phone to distract you. It felt like ages, she could smell the raw chicken left on the counter, the odor probably seeping into every pore of her kitchen, so next time she went to enjoy a late-night chocolate-covered almonds and TV session she'd lose her appetite from the ghost of raw chickens past.

She walked back into her kitchen. Jen heard another loud haymaker knock just as she passed the garbage can. Without saying a word or even thinking, she power-walked straight toward the door, thinking an odd medley of thoughts, voicing sarcastic complaints to her mystery intruder which, for some reason, she didn't conceive of as a real person, or still saw as some hapless delivery man: *I already walked past the garbage can, which means I was in the kitchen, so you made me walk back out of the kitchen, through the living room, to the door, which I know doesn't mean a lot in a one-bedroom apartment.* This wasn't a witty rom-com, she reminded herself, which of course was something she already knew, but she sometimes felt she fried her brain on so much irreverent, banter-filled television that she had to ground herself back into the real world. She stopped herself when she got to the door, just stared at it, really.

She looked at the adjacent coat rack, every prong filled with a hat or jacket. She had more clothing than she thought, apparently. Ladybug ear muffs? She thought, bizarrely, of throwing all the hats and jackets onto the ground and propping the coat rack against the door.

This is stupid, and she swiftly but carefully pushed her face up against the peephole.

She saw a square box. It looked large, like it occupied the entire hallway, and the dimensions didn't look uniform, like a square box should, but she knew the peephole played with perspective. But it was just a large box. She did her eye-camera trick and there was definitely no one else in the hallway.

They're wasting money on packing peanuts, she thought, lazily and absently, as she unlocked the door. She moved ploddingly, her brain filled with so many desultory thoughts that they almost cancelled each other out, background noise, the mental equivalent of a gently babbling brook. The grains of the door. The knob, too loose, needing to be tightened. Her eyes rheumy, faintly itching from allergies. A nonsensical association between the age of the building and her allergies. The box she was going to bring into the apartment ... she thought of the strange perspective through the peephole, replayed in her mind with new accents of alien strangeness. In her mind the color seeped out of the image, stark bone against complete darkness; the dimensions that were understandably off through the peephole, now sinister, the corners sharpened peaks, the central mass lowered as if waiting to pounce. The disquieting shape she envisioned was now, in her mind, no longer a box, and intermixed with that vision seeped sudden ruminations about witness identification and how quickly the memory distorted the etchings of the eyes, how the mind abhorred a vacuum, and how something scarcely glimpsed took on so much personality upon reflection.

These thoughts played out too quickly to be analyzed — all while she was just opening the door, as simple as turning the loose knob and pulling — and concomitantly she didn't take any of these thoughts too seriously, knowing how goofy they were. But alongside the textured grains of the door, the too-loose knob, her watery eyes, now were added the almost-dreamy gliding of the old door and a growing menace that made her halt.

Jesus Fucking Christ, it's just a box. All this mania for paper towels and tampons or something.

She'd opened the door halfway and fit her foot into the opening. She peeked through the crack.

Her eyes widened autonomically before meaning could be processed.

The strange woman outside pinched-pecked at the door with her outstretched fingers, as if sharply clutching for a berry. It was an absurd motion, something you'd do with a child, a swift sudden movement to make at a little boy that could be played for laughs. The child would be startled from the shock, then smile and clap when he realized it was just a lark, just a little shock by a silly adult. "Stork Strike," or some other goofy name you'd give to the pinch-peck, for the benefit of the laughing child, and then that term would become a little inside joke you'd share with the child to make him laugh in the future.

But that wasn't this. This was someone doing that silly motion, but for real.

Jen stepped backward until she hit against the mirror that hung in the hallway.

Jen concluded that it was a woman at her door, somehow, despite the black hair that obscured the face; despite the bewildering style of clothes; despite the sheer sexlessness of the brawny body that was moving forward through her door. Maybe it was the length of the greasy hair that she associated somehow with some aspect of femininity.

Jen's reactions were all awry, cast adrift by that godawful weird hand-peck, what the fuck?

The woman at her door truly pecked at it with her hand, and hard, too. It was like the woman didn't know how doors worked. It was only because the door had been partially-opened that the peck served any function by exerting some force and widening the entrance further.

"Get the fuck out of here! Get the fuck out of here!" Jen finally reoriented herself to what was going on. *How could I think that was a box*, she thought to herself, but if anyone could be confused for an inanimate vessel, it would be this strange intruder.

Was this woman mentally challenged?

Any vestige of concern for this potentially troubled person was pulverized into oblivion when Jen looked upon her face.

Good God, the black hair ran atop her head and, was that, also *through* her face. What Jen had first thought were suture wounds was organic material, the same color and texture of her hair, and how was it Jen still knew this was a "her" when all the features were so roughshod and impossible. What should be her right cheek was a concave knotting of hard tissue that ran jagged with bits of what at first looked like teeth but only in that they were small shapes of sharpened, calcified organic material. Where her eyes should be ran something sloping and knotty and bony. She had a forehead like a calcified dinosaur skull, like something you'd see in a science museum.

No eyes, no eyes.

The woman was about Jen's height and Jen looked above where the eyes should be, above that sloping crest of white bone, to find pits that might be this poor woman's eyes. As if that would make it better, but then at least this person would have eyes, because all people have eyes, even if they are horribly deformed. *This is ridiculous* emanated from the part of her mind that was still sanguine, *this is all just something ridiculous.* Within those pits extruded more mottled dark hair, hair that spilled forward and seemed to move slightly of its own accord, unseemly hair that resembled the unnaturally extended legs of flies, and something about this confirmed absence of eyes in those pits exploded something in Jen's gut.

The woman moved forward and was now in Jen's apartment. Jen made to do two different things at once, to yell at the intruder and reach down to grab a shoe or something tangible, when the intruder made a sound that was harmonious enough to be intelligible to some being, somewhere, as some kind of language, but to Jen was just a modulated sound that held no meaning.

Jen fell backward and the intruder stormed into her hallway, oblivious to the shoes she trampled over. The intruder tripped violently and twitched spasmodically like a frightened wild animal being thrown into a cage. Her spasms made her fall harder and more violently than expected, and she kicked and slashed out as she got back to her feet, knocking over the Japanese-themed room divider

Jen kept where the hallway spilled out into the living room. Now on her feet, the intruder kicked out the legs of a nearby desk, the desk light atop crashing to the floor, bulb shattering everywhere. The intruder fell again and rolled, whether from losing her balance from the kick or something else.

"Get the fuck out of here!" Jen knelt down and threw a heeled shoe at the intruder, who was now on her knees, again getting her balance. The shoe missed, too wide, but came close enough that the intruder should have at least responded somehow. Flinched or something. But she didn't, the intruder seemed to have a difficult enough time just balancing herself. There was a docility in this intruder, a strange, haphazard stupidity. This amateurishness, coupled with the strain in Jen's arm — she didn't work out, and hadn't thrown anything with purpose since her Mom had forced her to play softball in junior high school — seemed to awaken in her the improbability — and stupidity — of fighting this person.

Get the fuck out of here, she thought. *Run past her, out of the apartment!*

The intruder was in the living room, now on her feet. The front door was still open, and Jen ran out, screaming.

"Call the police! Help! Someone call the police! Help! Police!" She yelled so loudly and shrilly that her throat burned. She slowed a second to ensure she didn't lose her balance at the top of the stairs when the world fell out from underneath her. She was tugged back and landed, squat and hard, on her back, the impact of her head against the tile making her eyes reverberate in their sockets. Beneath her subconscious was a thought of a cantaloupe splitting open on a hot summer sidewalk.

She made to get up and thought: *I'm paralyzed. I'm paralyzed.* In the nanoseconds of reflection she panicked beyond register and was sure that her bladder would release. *I'm paralyzed. I'm paralyzed! Please no, no, no,* but, no, she wasn't, she somehow knew, intuiting the slight self-induced motions of her head and shoulders. She just had the senses knocked out of her temporarily. She made to move — moving of her own volition, thank God — but was back into the nightmare of her present situation.

She was being dragged, with bewildering alacrity, back into the apartment. The intruder's coarse digits were tucked painfully and firmly under Jen's armpits.

"HELP ME!" Jen screamed to pierce glass as the apartment door was closed behind her, and while she couldn't see the apartment hallway anymore she felt it charged with the frantic energy of newly-set pandemonium, of doors opening, of people loudly commiserating and assembling. She thought she heard someone yell her apartment number.

She was being launched through her own apartment; she had the crazy thought of being strapped to the front of a plane. She was propelled against her fridge and practically bounced off it. *I'm going to break my nose against the ground*, she thought, and wanted to put out her hands to break her fall but couldn't find the means to do so. She saw herself from a distance, a gallimaufry of terrible sights culled from fictional or recollected violence: news reports of rioters kicking bodies in the streets, *A Clockwork Orange*, bodies strung up by their necks, mass rapes and amputations, *no, concentrate*.

She didn't hit the ground. The intruder caught her and seemed to prop her up on her feet. The whiplash caused her to fall slightly back, and again the intruder caught her and steadied her.

Jen felt for the first time the slime that had been strewn across her face and body, and breathed in the oppressive, dank humidity that now clung to her. The forceful movements, the flooding of her senses, it was all too much; and the intruder was pointing at an area above the refrigerator and again making inexplicable sounds, sounds that were at first clipped and ugly but, as if the intruder was slowing down to gain her bearings, became more euphonious and possessive of some kind of internal rhythm and meter. Jen concentrated, maybe if the sounds could be understood there could be a resolution, a peace offering made. The sounds seemed so deliberate that she feared she'd hit her head and lost the ability to understand spoken language, but no, the sounds were unintelligible noises that began lilting and ended gutturally, an expression of gravelly emphasis.

"I don't understand," Jen finally said softly, and the intruder grabbed Jen's head and spun her around and pointed again, at an area above and seemingly behind the refrigerator. The intruder's arm was now around Jen's neck, but not maliciously. Rather, it seemed, intended only to prevent Jen from averting her sight from whatever area commanded the intruder's attention, as if everything depended on the sight of some event that would begin and end in an inconspicuous, fleeting instant.

"I'm sorry, I'm sorry - food? Do you want food?" Jen said, knowing that wasn't the right answer. Jen kept her eyes on the general area above the fridge, as if meaning would somehow, hope beyond hope, come to her. The intruder was now pointing at the general spot, leaning in and hovering behind her, seemingly too desperate or stupid to realize she'd slackened her grip. Jen was equally fascinated and repulsed by the glimpses of the intruder's face. Good God, she looked like the old urban legends about the girl who falls asleep and wakes up to find that spiders' eggs had hatched in her cheeks. She looked like an even worse version of that urban legend, like a girl who'd suffered that fate hundreds of years ago and had all the sores necrotize and fossilize.

Jen heard knocking and yelling at her door, thought she heard Noel's brusque, consonant-clipped accent.

"I'm in here! Help! The door is open and he's not armed!" It was smarter to say "he": it reconciled with what the neighbors perhaps assumed was happening, domestic abuse or maybe an unsophisticated, standard breaking-and-entering.

The eyeless intruder appeared subtly taken aback and offended, even, and directed her face quickly at the door, as if she was at least cognizant that Jen was calling to others. The creature balled its fists and slammed them against her own knees, and then huddled her hands on the ridge atop her head. It was an expression of frustration, and she yelled and pointed, grabbing Jen by the collar and pressing her forward.

Jen realized for the first time that the intruder was dressed in some kind of long-sleeve, black cotton shirt, smeared with some chalky white substance. It was incredible to think that this thing acquired clothing, dressed itself: everyday clothing should exist in an alternative universe from whatever this intruder represented.

The intruder was now fully behind her again, pushing her flat against the refrigerator, making high-pitched sounds. Jen was afraid the creature would try and shove her into the area behind the refrigerator, crumple her body and fold her into the frame of empty space between the refrigerator and the wall. Jen was resisting, yet her resistance didn't seem to have tangible impact. The intruder shoved and directed, and Jen's body complied. It took the briefest of moments for her to be fully pinioned, and the intruder tapped her on the head harshly — Jen blinked hard, her eyes were burning, the musk of toxicity coming off the intruder becoming too much to stomach — and again made sounds, pointing upward, no doubt again at that infernal, inexplicable spot above the fridge.

Jen heard the door open and people storm in. "Jennifer!" she heard Noel yell, in his heavy, accented baritone. It was the type of yell someone gives when they don't see you, when they want to know if you are downstairs or still in the vicinity.

"Help me!" Jen yelled, her yells muffled, face against the fridge.

Jen felt bodies rush in and heard the collapse of furniture. The intruder let her go and Jen slumped to the floor, had trouble keeping her eyes open, they stung so much. The heavy musk had settled into something else, a scented, binding mucus. Before Jen fell she could see bodies forming a semi-circle around her and the intruder; through the blurred, stinging wetness in her eyes she made out the Indian woman from her hall and saw that Noel carried an aluminum bat.

"The police are coming! The police are coming! You are going to jail!" she heard someone yell, possibly the young female realtor, and heard someone else — she assumed the Indian woman, based on the accent — scream "Killer! Killer!" and heard another person, a man, possibly even the realtor's semi-employed boyfriend, say, "oh my God."

Noel was frozen in his tracks. He'd just spent the weekend with his nine-year-old nephew who was obsessed with dinosaurs and had showed Noel all his dinosaur stickers and took pride in knowing the name of each type. There was a dome-headed dinosaur with an extremely thick skull that his nephew kept calling a "packy-a-saur."

That's all Noel could think of when he looked at the intruder's face.

"What do you want!" Jen heard a man screaming. It was an unhinged scream, a scream of a man who had no pretense of control, the scream of a man who saw a bloated, eyeless creature of abnormal dimensions that still, somehow, impossibly, bore some faint resemblance to an unthreatening human female.

Jen forced her eyes open, and vertiginous bolts of panic flared when she realized that rubbing and blinking didn't do anything, she was *still* seeing unclearly through some kind of chalky haze, a condition her terror-strewn brain was convinced felt less like a temporary annoyance and more like some permanent defect with the operation of her eyes. Leaning against the fridge for support, the fear rising with each passing second; the chalky haze that smeared her vision failed to dissipate, kept everything cloudy and distorted. She hoped she was crying because then she'd at least know her eyes still retained some traditional functions.

She heard, again, those sounds of impossible communication, and bodies shift and congregate when the intruder moved toward them. She heard people yell and scream and the thud of someone farther away, someone closer to her apartment door, fall down. She sense-saw Noel assume a swinging stance but couldn't see the aftermath but heard an insane, "oh my God!" and felt the air charged with concitation. There was the startling fall of the bat and, above the din of several groping bodies, the sound of something mushy and then Noel's cry of anguish.

Jen lurched blindly to her utensils drawer. She was unimpeded, as all the chaos stayed in the hallway and living room.

The carving knife was where it always was, and she grabbed it.

Through the maelstrom of chaos she caught a fleeting recognition of the well-muscled Italian and the narcotized-looking Korean, when suddenly a white middle-aged bald man she didn't recognize fell back discordantly and somewhere beyond the aluminum bat banged again and ricocheted across the ground. The intruder flailed about, making noises, and despite the motion and cacophony and overwhelming numbers of the crowd, no one seemed to be making a move to contain her.

"Get Noel to a hospital!" a woman screamed with such throat-shredding urgency that her words were barely understandable. Jen saw Noel on the ground, clutching at his torn stomach, surrounded by people. The crowd seemed unsure of what to do, whether to contain the threat posed by the intruder or to flee. About half a dozen people were circled around Noel, making threatening gestures at the intruder, a yard away. Others stayed further back in the hallway, pleasing themselves with the fiction that they were waiting to wave down the police, who must be arriving any minute.

Through her exploding, coruscated vision Jen tackled the misbegotten intruder from behind and caught her in a tight chokehold. She was mentally beside herself, removed from herself with the foregone conviction that her eyes were burning out and that she'd soon be blind, and to extirpate her terror she focused only on what was before her and plunged the sharpened blade through what Jen approximated was the intruder's neck.

The intruder's hands went up in what appeared to the assorted onlookers as a type of abdication, a motion that their cultural frames of reference taught them was only performed by the desperate, despondent or dying, and invoked in them a variant of sympathetic pity. The intruder mewled and clicked, blood pouring from her grievous wound, and she rolled forward, the knife still inside her.

As the intruder rolled forward, the group scurried away, no one thinking to drag Noel with them.

The rolling figure stopped short of Noel and made to get up, made a loud, musical cooing noise that made one tenant think of charmed lovebirds and Spanish moss. The intruder then neatly came apart at the waist, her relatively normal lower half collapsing on the ground, her top half shooting straight up, landing back-first against the ceiling. Her upper body, with arms outstretched, glided noiselessly across the ceiling, over to the cabinets above the refrigerator. The round mass of sloping forehead and bony knotting detached itself and rocketed forward, broke through the cabinets above the fridge and bore through whatever infrastructure lay beyond. The group heard the destruction of wood and plaster and the wrenching of metal pipes.

Jen turned toward the crowd of insistent faces, contemplating what to say and how to say it.

Faithfully and Lovingly

BRIAN ALWAYS HAD a hard time getting ready for work in the morning and took advantage of anything he could to distract himself. Something about the morning stripped him of whatever giddy aspirations he had often indulged the night before. Those aspirations often came just on the cusp of sleep, when his mind was foggy and, for whatever emotional or physiological reason, most susceptible to wishful thinking. All those ideas, wonderfully excellent to the half-aroused intelligence, yet hopelessly absurd at the full waking, vague and quaint imaginings haunted him in the moments when his intelligence scintillated like a star, where the world resembled a stanza or melody composed in a dream. But by morning those aspirations were gone, whether they had been as ambitious as starting up the video game podcast he discussed with his coworker or as modest as resolving to go to the gym once a week. Something about waking up and getting ready in the morning — and perhaps the looming obligations that lay ahead — reduced his ambitions to something more of a velleity than an actionable statement of purpose.

His girlfriend Katie always left for work before him, and it was in the morning, alone, in those precious but wasted minutes after he had gotten ready but before he had to leave for work that he was most susceptible to sentimentalism.

On this Wednesday morning, he was making his typical internet rounds, to the same websites that he'd be circling back through over the course of the day, out of the primary power of habit and the secondary hope of new content. One video on YouTube had been really getting him recently. He didn't know much about country music or care to learn much about it, but this random-ass video got to him. It was (he read the description) a 1981 clip of honkytonk country singer Gary Stewart, performing an apparently never-released track named "Silver Cloud." When the video was taken, Gary Stewart looked to be in his late thirties, his frame thin and wiry, his olive skin leathery, tough and cracked. Gary faced the camera, the right side of his body in the primary position, and there was a prominent wrinkle — it was so prominent it could have been a scar — running from his right nostril diagonally, ending about an inch away from the right terminus of his lips. He wore a black leather jacket and a big black hat. Brian could not identify the type of that hat, but it was the type modern-day hipsters would love to wear but could never pull off.

Gary was performing in what appeared to be a public access station, and over his left shoulder was a bare wooden wall and an indistinct painting of what may have been a forest scene that signaled more than anything as chintzy Americana. The video itself was, as befitting a video from the early 1980s that made its way to YouTube, of poor quality. To top it off, there was a horizontal warbled line of video distortion stretched across the entire video that ran about one-fourth of the way from the bottom of the screen, which bisected the screen into two elements, that of Gary above and his acoustic guitar below.

Gary strummed the guitar and started singing his melancholic song. The melody, vocals and distinctive vibrato never failed to move Brian in some immeasurable way. And Brian felt almost bad to think about this, how clichéd and hackneyed it was to romanticize an untimely death, but the facts he had learned about Gary's life and his almost doomed existence — his drug addiction, the suicide of his only son, the death of his wife from pneumonia and, shortly after, his own eventual suicide by a gunshot to the heart — contributed to the gravitas.

Brian listened to the song two more times, turned off the computer, and left to face the day.

>< >< ><

On his slow trek home from work he got off the Metro in the Brookland neighborhood of Washington D.C., at about 7:15 p.m. He had left work at 6 p.m. and only worked 4 miles away, in Dupont Circle, but the Washington D.C. Metro fails on every level other than, perhaps, its consistently reliable level of poor performance. In that category, it's remarkably consistent.

And the Red Line, his train, was agreed to be the worst of the lot. (He doth protest too much, he knew — dealing with a suboptimal Metro was better than staying in the no-need-for-a-metro-fuck-you-go-get-a-car town of Fredericksburg, Virginia, where he originally hailed from. To give a sense of how far removed his hometown had been from a big city, Fredericksburg — a college town that he figured maybe people had heard of but no one ever had visited — was actually just the geographic reference point he provided to others. He actually grew up in Spotsylvania, Virginia, which sounds either like the worst fake town name or the home of the feared chickenpox vampires (if his hometown had any imagination, that's what they would have named the high school football team; think of the jersey sales!)).

It was the same commute every day: a half-mile walk along Michigan Avenue NE and then one block up when it hit 13th Street NE. Brian was happy with the neighborhood, in everything except its name: Brookland was too close of a homonym for Brooklyn and provided ample grist for the D.C. inferiority complex. In addition to the New York connection, that Brookland was a fast-gentrifying neighborhood gave it sort of an obnoxious reputation to the deathly oversensitive residents of D.C. But he enjoyed finely prepared meals and an intimate cocktail lounge as much as the next late-twenties urban professional, so the whiners were free to go live in Anacostia or Congress Heights if they wanted their "real" D.C. experience, i.e. living and ending each day in mortal terror of a stray bullet.

>< >< ><

He got to their building around 7:30, walked up the one flight of stairs to their second-floor apartment, and was glad to see Katie was already home. Katie was a speech pathologist for the learning disabled, and he didn't ask many questions about her work, but she always left earlier and got home before he did. She was sprawled on their couch with the television on. She gave a tip of the invisible hat and patted the empty cushion next to her, an invitation to sit down. He did so, and they resolved to order dinner in and watch *Film Club*.

Katie was about 5'6", with an aquiline nose, cuddly yet searching brown eyes and long brown hair she often wore, as she did now, in a ponytail. She had changed out of her work clothes into sweatpants and a form-fitting purple t-shirt, a shirt she would never wear outside these days because she was concerned about a beer gut and love handles, a concern that used to manifest in self-effacing comments but was now unspoken, evident perhaps in her irritated face if she stood up too fast, exposed her midsection and importunately tucked her shirt over it. He would want to say something when he caught that face of hers. He could not deny that she had gained some weight in the last year, but that was an issue that concerned her, not him.

It pained him for her to feel insecure, he wanted to tell her she was being silly, she was super fine and if she really wanted to they could stop drinking beer, or go on a diet, or join a gym, or say fuck it and adopt complete body acceptance, or whatever she wanted, but he never found the words and didn't know how to broach the subject. He had *always* been about ten to fifteen pounds overweight, he wanted to say; anger, displacement, denial, resignation, then acquiescence: he knew the drill, he was a body acceptance veteran. He wanted to say something like that in a funny, jovial way, and once tried, but she cast one withering, Medusa-like glance and it died on the vine. He had thought of a different tact: she had a sizable bust, and gaining weight would only make them bigger, something he thought he could maybe present in a funny, ingratiating way, but, again, that approach remained only theoretical.

He could see her tattoos on both her inner forearms, expressionistic, engaging tattoos that had first caught his eye back at Stonybrook University, on Long Island, where they'd met as seniors. That he had met her at all was a minor miracle. Stonybrook was a commuter school where the cliques were made fast and remained durable; he, being an out-of-towner on a full scholarship, had been placed in subsidized student housing on campus and spent many a weekend alone there. It had been a chance encounter at the food court of the nearby Smith Haven Mall. There was a cute girl with "Smith Haven Mall" in refined small type on her inner left forearm. After a groan worthy introduction — "are you the official mall ambassador?" — conversation began and rapport was quickly established.

They found out they were both seniors at Stonybrook, and then they were off to the races. (As an added bonus, she was from Hicksville, New York, such a squalid and dunderheaded town name that, by comparison, made Spotsylvania sound less hayseed and more enigmatic). Her reason for the tattoo, he'd thought, was stupid: something about having worked all around the mall in her youth and she liked remembering her roots, even though at the time she still lived and went to school on Long Island. Being an eager male, she could have said it was where she buried the bodies and he would have kept the conversation going, like an improv comic adhering to the "yes, and ..." rule.

He still thought that the tattoo was stupid, actually, but that tattoo was now surrounded by others, perhaps equally ill-thought-out. The color tableau they created was aesthetically pleasing and visually invigorating, however. His favorite was a squat, red-haired mage, holding a gold cane topped with a blue stone, a character from a videogame he had never played called The Secret of Mana, which was catnip that rendered delirious anyone who happened to catch the offhand reference. She had posted a picture of the tattoo on Reddit, to the collective orgasm of a thousand old-school RPG geeks.

At least these were injected doses of personality: he had no such flair. He was just a somewhat overweight, 5’9” white guy graphic designer with auburnish brown hair, a matching beard, a square jaw, bright bluish green eyes, and a 7-inch cock (he’d measured). Not the most exciting thing to be, but not the worst, either.

><><><

There was nothing notable about the following work day. His office was understaffed, he was underpaid and overworked, but that's a complaint expressed, rightly or wrongly (but in his case, rightly), by everyone. At work, while eating his signature salad, he listened to another Gary Stewart song. He kept his headphones on all day during work — they centered him, he felt, and created an additional barrier for people wishing to annoy him — and piped music through the computer throughout the day, either classical or ambient instrumentals to blot out the rest of the office. During lunch, though, he could really listen.

"Sittin' up here in this New York townhouse, decorated in gre-ayyys and blu-ueees and ... everybody knows, love won't grow, for a cactus and a rohhhse," sang the Kentucky-born, Southern-raised Gary, in that inimitable, wavering, heart-rending croon of his. A "New York townhouse" was one of the last places he could ever picture Gary, and he wanted to know the backstory for the song, but his Wikipedia and Google searches had been unavailing. The way Gary elongated "grays" and "blues" sucked him in every time, and the way he spread out "rohhhse," extending the melody but keeping the pitch the same, imparted something melancholic about the nature of love and fidelity. What that was, exactly, Brian didn't know.

"When that ole wild streak beneath my skiiiiin ... sets my crazy spree again, they'll all say" — and here cuts in a higher pitched voice, who he always pictured as one of Katie's friends, a little smugly saying the line — "I told you so,"' and then Gary's voice joins back in, the higher-pitched voice singing the background vocal, "love won't grow, for a cactus and a rose."

>< >< ><

He missed Katie, and was lucky to be with her, and she with him. But, come to think of it, he couldn't remember a single exchange they had shared last night. Had they spoken at all, after ordering food and watching television? He thought of her, in anguish, in a quiet despair — the type of despair that is uniquely personal and private, when you are alone and not using your mood to jockey for affection or favors or anything else, when you are truly saddened and alone. He thought of him pushing her away, or him storming out of the room despite her crying pleas, and her being alone, inconsolable. None of that ever happened, and never would happen, but it was a mental trick of sorts that he'd taught himself, to make him more outwardly affectionate and loving. Thinking of her like that, even for the briefest moment, destroyed him, and made him want to do nothing more than be with her, kiss her and hug her all over. Even if they fought — even if they had fought and he was resolute in being incontrovertibly in the right, like him being upset about her breaking a commitment — he utilized his trick, and before he knew it, he was the one coming back to her, to kiss and love and reconcile, to pledge his fidelity and admiration and affection for her, to feel her arms across his back and her breath upon his face.

They needed to hang out tonight, get out of the apartment, do something fun. They hadn't been to the Brookland Pint recently, that'd be fun, they had a great beer selection and solid southern comfort food. Now would be the time to eat there, anyway, since they had already scattered their diet plans to the winds for the foreseeable future.

"Sometimes fallin' makes more sense, than sitting in the middle of the same old fence," Gary sung loudly and dramatically, after the instrumental section of the bridge, without the high-pitched background vocalist. It was the one part of the song where Gary sang almost from a position of power, as if, after pouring his heart out, this was the part he of the song where he demanded your attention. "Ya gonna lose any way you go, love won't grow, for a cactus and a roooose," he sang the second part of the verse quieter, more restrained, almost as if in defiance of the background singer coming back to add the harmonies.

><><><

"Hey honey," he greeted her at the bar. She'd managed to secure a seat, which came to mean she'd been there for a while. The place was packed; perhaps he underestimated the draw of the after-work happy hour crowd.

"Hey there," she said, and took her jacket off the stool she'd been saving, making sure not to accidentally strike any of the bargoers standing adjacent and practically on top of them. She did this in a somewhat belabored way, as if to draw attention to the fact she'd waited for a while, been boxed in, and had to obviate the many vexing demands for the spot.

"Geez, it's packed," he said, pushing his way into the stool and arching his back to create a little breathing room.

She should have gotten a table, then, if sitting at the bar was such an ordeal, he thought. He almost said it. If he'd been with a guy friend, of course he'd say something to that effect, in an incisive, just-fucking-around way ("not a table man, eh? A man of the people, I see") but that'd be a bad move here. He couldn't do that with her, would just be interpreted as antagonizing, better to avoid the argument.

He made a move to hail down the bartender and, perhaps by the miracle of proximity, got his attention. "I got you the peanut butter stout you liked," she said, and sloshed it forward to him. "Oh," he didn't notice she ordered it, and he did like that beer, but he drank it every time he'd come here and he had wanted to try something else, something less sweet.

"Aww, thanks honey," he said, and now the bartender was soliciting their order and Brian fumbled around, "do you know what you want to eat?" he asked Katie but she said, blankly, "I didn't look at the menu yet, I waited for you," and he went to apologize to the bartender piteously but the bartender had already used his deductive bartender life-skills to move on.

"Sorry man," Brian said with a hand-wave, and in a tone that meant sure-I'm-sorry-but-it-happens, you-know?

He could feel the penumbra of Katie's low-level annoyance creep over the whole interaction.

He pivoted to more grandiose subjectş. "I started on the Moon Project, with Matt, today, at work," he lied. The Moon Project was his placeholder name for the side project he'd been talking about for a while. He and his friend Matt wanted to create an app that, after giving you the weather, displayed particularly evocative depictions of the moon and the general weather conditions, done in a heavily-stylized chiaroscuro. He was the graphic artist, Matt the tech guy. Matt wanted an eye-catching type of magical realism, like a Studio Ghibli film; Brian wanted something more understated and lissome, something with minimal motion and a repeating motif, like an eye blinking in the center of a full moon, or little stars twinkling at the edge of a crescent. Matt was correct that his idea could be a bolder showcase for Brian's work, and Brian agreed, but the designs at the firm he worked for were often big and brash, and working on something more subtle could be a good change of pace.

"Oh," she perked up? "How sneaky, I'm impressed how you always are able to fit in stuff you want to do at work. What did you guys do?" She had always encouraged him to pursue side projects, whereas he was usually satisfied just by thinking about someday doing them.

"Yeah, of course we are still working out how we want to do it, and we mainly talked about the tech side of things," he backpedaled so he wouldn't have to talk about it too much. He mainly brought it up as an escape hatch, a way to wrest the conversation toward something that she knew meant a lot to him, so she would be delicate and forgiving if she happened to be in a bad mood. It was working, she was drinking her beer and liking it.

They ordered food and talked, and soon enough she was laughing and swapping beers with him, as they often did. She had a pilsner with the sunny name of Right Proper Being There, which was a nice reprieve from the heaviness of his stout.

"Aww, I'm happy you're working on that again. You are so talented, it's amazing. I wish I had technical expertise, it's awesome."

"Aww, you have ... auditory and verbal talents."

"Hah, great. I can be the spokesperson for your company someday."

"Spokesperson-in-chief, please."

She clinked their glasses, now on their second beer each.

"You have real talent. And nothing is sadder than wasted talent."

He nodded knowingly. She had ambitions she spoke of: learning German was the only one that immediately came to mind, but he was sure there were others. He never pressed her on those.

"Of course there are things sadder than wasted talent. What about this. A puppy, waiting for his puppy parents to take him to school, only to find out his parents have been abducted, shipped to China and turned into dog food."

"Nooooo, stop!" she said, although smiling. "That's horrible! And racist."

"I know, but it's sadder than wasted talent, right? So much sadder."

"Nooooo, that puppy! I just imagined this so-sad scene, this adorable fluffy fat golden retriever wagging his tail but no one ever comes!"

"Okay, okay, I take it back, the fat fluffy puppy is licking his lips and wagging his tail and both his parents — they are happily dog-married, his parents, and the dog-dad wears glasses because he's a dog-professor — pick him up and bring him to puppy school, where he graduates first in his class and rolls over and always sits on command and gets first dibs at the best biscuits."

"Aww, better. Why can't the dog-mom be a professor?"

"Okay, they are both professors of dogology, at Barkley University in California."

"Better!" She pointed a mock-accusing finger at him and squinted her eyes, and then the food came and she kissed him on the nose.

After dinner and three beers apiece, they started settling up their tab. She was telling him about a family friend of hers, named Mindy, that she wanted him to meet, who she hadn't seen "since forever" and who was going to be in town for only a couple of days.

He agreed, and waited for his turn to talk to tell her about another project of his. He told her he had an idea for a horror-themed porn, where the Devil forced a guy to choose between getting back together with his terrible ex-girlfriend or having to sleep only with men. She looked up at him, nodding slightly and skeptically, as if expecting another bit of information to clarify what she'd just heard.

"It'd be called *The Ex or Dicks*." And she laughed, a big splattering laugh, getting the homonym immediately. Someone next to them laughed, too, repeating the title.

"Get it, Ex or Dicks, Exorcist, pretty good, pretty good, right?" He patted her on the back. "I get it, I get it," she patted him back, much the same way.

He'd had that stored for a little bit and was glad it paid off.

With their tab settled, they went home.

>< >< ><

Brian walked a couple steps behind Katie as they walked the remaining blocks to Raski, the "pricey" (per Yelp) Indian restaurant where they were meeting Mindy. Mindy was the "family friend" Katie had referred to meeting the last couple of days, soft allusions which accreted to an actual definite plan, unfortunately occupying a choice Saturday afternoon.

Mindy was a "family friend," a "couple years older" than them, whom she hadn't seen for a long time, yet seeing her was "important," although he'd never heard of her before in the Katie Pantheon of Important People. When he'd asked yesterday what to expect, Katie said she was her mother's best friend's oldest daughter, but again, Brian didn't think much of it, and didn't really know why Katie seemed somewhat anxious. Not nervous really, but she carried the air of an obligation that needed to be adequately executed, as if this was more formal than a friendly reacquaintance.

As they had gotten dressed that morning, Katie finally gave him the 411. Mindy's husband was a practicing speech pathologist who was a higher-up executive at Johns Hopkins Hospital in Baltimore, Maryland. According to Johns Hopkins' website, there were no current positions in the speech pathology department but, as these things happen, Mindy had told her mother, who told Katie's mother, that a mid-level position was going to soon open up. A salary had been floated but not settled-upon, but either way even the orbit to which the salary hovered was well above what Katie currently made.

Mindy worked as a consultant, mainly in Philadelphia or New York, but happened to be in D.C. on business.

"Baltimore, though?" he'd asked. That's all he needed to say. "Baltimore?" Leaving D.C. for Baltimore, that's like leaving New York for Newark. Plus, it was a far commute. Johns Hopkins wasn't even in downtown Baltimore, it was in some weird northern neighborhood. Really, he thought, his face revealing a hint of sadness as the inference became clearer, not really in commuting distance.

"Do you want to move to Baltimore?" he asked, the trill in his voice putting the emphasis on whether he was part of the plan.

"It's just an option, something to keep in mind. *Please*, I just want to explore this! It's not like I'm in a field where opportunities come along every day!" was her response, and he obliged, nodding and smiling meekly, but in a woebegone way so as to have her comfort him and tell him, of course, it was just in pursuit of something that likely would never happen, just a way of exploring options and maintaining contacts. She didn't, though, and he said, "I'll be on my best behavior," but again, in a too-sweet way, and she said, "that's the spirit!" and gave him a face of forced gaiety as she sped around the house and into the bathroom to get ready.

She'd showered (something not always done on the weekend, truth be told), washed and dried her hair, putting it into an updo with an austere muted navy blue clip. Her earrings, usually something that tried to project a feisty personality, like cute skulls or faux-emeralds in black orbs, were instead demure and proper. Professional. She wore a long-sleeved black blouse — all tattoos covered, he'd noticed — and spent more time than usual primping, clipping, and prepping. He wore a brand-new green sweater and, rather than his usual crumpled, beyond worn-in blue jeans, wore crisp, only-worn-once new black slacks with his black work shoes, the ones that weren't worn in yet or bitten up at the toes.

As they later walked toward the restaurant, he hobbled a step or two behind her, mentally kicking himself for donning shoes he probably needed a few more weeks of continuous wear to break in.

"So, what's the game plan again?" he asked. He wanted to know if there were parameters to follow, anything on or off limits. Intel. This was important for her and he didn't want to fuck it up. Rather, he wanted *her* to fuck it up, so Baltimore wouldn't be an option.

No, that wasn't true, he thought, even though the idea of her fucking up, and him being able to console her, lifted his spirits, gave him an opportunity to feel needed. He saw that play out in his mind's eye, her disappointed but happy to have him as her dependable partner, exorcising that disappointment by pressing her body against his and cuddling on the couch. He wanted it to go well, he corrected himself, but hoped that a position in Baltimore never came to fruition.

"Just, you know, be cool. We're cool, it's all cool, I haven't seen her forever but I remember she was, well, not conservative or anything, just, I don't know. You know, normal."

"She's not cool enough for the tattoos," he said, rubbing a forefinger along her inner arm.

"No one's cool enough for the tattoos," she replied. "You know, just be normal, nothing weird or anything."

Sangfroid was not his strong suit, and comments like that didn't help. Like he was the weird one? He brushed past it.

"I will stick with the safest of subjects. 'Hey, so, that Lincoln Memorial, amiright? Isn't it great that the museums here are free? They should be free everywhere!'"

"Exactly."

"So what does she do again? She's a consultant, right? So what does she do?"

"She ... consults? For ...."

“I can ask her questions on that, if you want, to get information on it, so you don't have to ask, you can just act like you know it."

"Great idea, that's great!"

He could tell she was nervous. She was rubbing her hands together, itching herself a bit on her side, the blouse being a bit too tight. He hugged her and kissed the side of her face. They were a block away.

"It’ll be great," he assured her.

"Thanks honey. Thanks for coming with me, I really appreciate it. Hopefully this won't be too bad for you."

"I'm sure it won't be," he said, and felt a twinge, hoping he wouldn't look back on this in a couple years as a pivotal moment, where she got a job offer and they had to make difficult choices, had to choose between him and Baltimore (God, losing to Baltimore). He'd go with her to Baltimore, he already decided ... assuming she wanted him. His countenance dampened a bit, but he swallowed hard, and followed her in.

They were 10 minutes early, but Mindy was already there, seated. (Thank God, he thought, small talk while waiting for a table was the worst.)

The restaurant was ultra-modern, all glass and shiny surfaces, consisting of one long but narrow space of tables, with booths against the wall and sleek chairs lining the middle of the space. Above and behind the booths was a mirror that ran the length of the restaurant. Silver beaded strings lined the ceiling. A couple of feet away from the chairs was the bar, which ran the full length of the restaurant. Katie and Brian were led down the narrow restaurant aisle to their table, all the way in the back, in the corner, where Mindy occupied the booth against the wall. Water cups had already been set for them.

"Don't get up!" Katie said swiftly and coyly, as Mindy's head moved upward in recognition. "It's so nice to see you!" Katie added as she sat down and reached her hand across the table and shook Mindy's fingertips in what looked like a cross between a handshake and an entreaty.

Mindy laughed as her fingers were lifted up and down and said, "Thanks, you too!" excitedly.

"I'm Katie's boyfriend," he said, realizing he forgot to say "hi" and didn't wait until their handshake had been completed.

"Hi, Katie's boyfriend," Mindy said, still laughing, looking genuinely happy to see them. "Do you have a name?"

"Yes, hah, Brian, sorry about that," and he looked at Katie and held the 'sorry' for too long and Katie looked at him, wide-eyed and a bit sternly, just to say "keep cool."

He looked back at Mindy. She had long black hair and was unattractive. She had large epicanthic folds by her eyes, a flat nose, thin lips, and a maw befitting a tycoon in a clichéd political cartoon, perhaps someone eating cash from a trough emblazoned with a dollar sign. It was hard to pinpoint what it was, exactly, about her face that made him think that. He realized it might be her teeth — her teeth were too large, and combined with her face, she looked a bit like the modern-day anthropomorphic version of Alvin from Alvin and the Chipmunks. It was hard to gauge her height, as she was sitting down, but she looked shorter than average, compact but not fit, and had an extremely large bust. DDs, he thought, and imagined a life history of her cruelly being called "Butterface," guys interested in her throughout her youth only for her chest.

"What do you do?" she asked, with a tone that suggested it was the second time she asked.

"Oh, I'm a graphic designer," he answered, and she looked impressed enough. He wondered if he had missed a bridge in the conversation that led to her asking him what he did for a living.

"Oh—" she started, and the waiter, a dapper, thin, neatly shaved man — according to the law of restaurant authenticity, likely an Indian man — in a suit vest and tie came over to take their drink orders. Both Katie and Brian visually prompted Mindy to order first, and she did with aplomb, getting the most expensive cocktail. Katie went with the second most, and Brian, as was his custom, looked seriously at the drink menu for the first time and ordered the first thing that came to mind. Mindy told the waiter they needed a second to decide on appetizers. Drinks, appetizers, entrees, coffee and tea — this was going to be an ordeal.

Brian continued on with the small talk, not speaking until directly prompted. It was a delicate balancing act: he didn't want to come off as narcotized, but he also didn't want to talk-out all the air in the conversation. He let Katie lead, and she got into a good groove where they talked about the prospective position in Baltimore in a circumspect way. Mindy reacted excitedly and, after hearing about Katie's current job, exclaimed, in an unjaded way, that Katie would be a great fit.

"Though you'd have to move to Baltimore," Mindy said, making a knowing face and putting snarly emphasis on 'Baltimore.' There was a pause. "Job doesn't sound so great anymore, does it?" she said, looking at Brian, again in a knowing way, and he snorted out loud and said "I know, I know." He kept his attention fixed on Mindy, feeling Katie's searing gaze on the back of his neck. He even broke out in a little sweat, as if heat waves were shooting out of Katie's eyes.

The drinks came, and he almost just grabbed his and took a

taste-tester swig (as he called it jokingly, after Katie's repeated attempts to get him to stop in order to "cheers"). Now, what a trained ape he was, he waited for everyone, clinked glasses, and took a delicate sip, lemon and cilantro overpowering the London dry gin, which he didn't object to. He then tried Katie's drink, which was a champagne cocktail of Prosecco, ginger syrup and candied ginger. He offered a sip of his drink to Mindy, which was a gracious, inclusive, and kind of flirty thing they did with female friends. She declined, good-naturedly. Too bad, she'd ordered a chai-gin and he wanted to use his offer as a means of trying her drink.

He took two substantial sips and found himself halfway through his drink. "Got to put on the brakes. So, have you had any time to go to any of the museums?"

This triggered a long monologue about the museums she'd visited and how great they all were.

When she was done, he capped it off: "my favorite thing about D.C. is all the free museums. It's amazing. They should be free everywhere."

"I know!" she exclaimed. And she went on some more about what museums she visited, Katie joining in to ask about certain exhibits and offer other touristy suggestions.

That conversation carried them through the appetizer ordering. He'd finished his drink, about the same time Mindy did, and she ordered another, so he did, and so Katie downed hers a little faster than she'd liked and ordered a second, also. Brian ordered the masala chai-gin.

He had one other conversation thread in his back pocket — a deep dive into what Mindy did for a living. For now, Katie and Mindy were talking nostalgically about their greater hometown region. From the sounds of it, their respective times in Long Island didn't involve a lot of intersecting, unless their mothers had been directly involved.

"Ohhh, Nadeen, I remember her!" Katie said, carrying a high pitch, perhaps excited they'd found a mutual reference point. "I remember her from camping trips we went on, she was so sweet, I remember she made the best s'mores," a comment to which Brian bit his tongue, since making s'mores was pretty easy and didn't leave much room for artistry. "How is she doing?"

Mindy's mouth hovered over the rim of her drink, and it appeared as if she was either investigating something floating in the drink or acting like she could possibly see her reflection.

"She was eaten by a bear."

Brian's inhalation of his drink reversed, and spectacularly so. He blew out a fine spray of chai-flavored gin, whose fragrance seemed to hover in the air, linger almost, as the spray descended back down to Earth, Earth here being the table they all shared. He covered his mouth, but couldn't stifle his laughter, just gave it more of a reverberating bass sound.

"Sorry, sorry," he snort-laughed, still covering his mouth. "You're kidding, right?" She had said it so dryly, so matter of fact.

But he knew the answer before she confirmed it.

"No, seriously," and Mindy made the slightest scoffing noise, the tiniest concession to how incredulous it all sounded, which was not nearly the lifeline he needed right now, "she was eaten by a bear, about four years ago."

Only through a sheer force, an exertion of will, could he stop himself from actively laughing, but he couldn't dispel the smile. He smiled, buckled again and giggled, had to put his hand to his mouth to cover his expression, now almost giddy. "I'm sorry, I'm sorry," he pleaded, "just, just 'eaten by a bear,'" he said, as if the dry comedy in such a line was self-evident to all. "I mean, I'm sorry, you know. I'm really, really, really sorry. That's tragic, that's terrible, that's tragic," but he couldn't do it, just saying "tragic" after hearing "eaten by a bear" was too much. He pictured a bear on stage, wearing a feathered cap, delivering a Shakespearean soliloquy. "Tragedy."

He lost his composure again, had to practically double-over and look down at his knees like a punished boy fearful of his father's belt, try and stay silent and motionless, but that didn't work, the giggles and snorts all the worse given how hard he was trying to control himself. He became frigid, as if he was a yogi trying to gain total mastery over himself, his face beet red, just as the waiter came over, hesitantly, to bring them their appetizers.

><><><

After they'd walked several blocks and she was sure Mindy was not nearby, Katie made sure she stayed several feet in front of Brian. She wouldn't let him touch her, and didn't sit next to him on the

Metro.

The night didn't get any better.

"Katie, please, c'mon, I'm sorry," he tried a couple of times, which only managed to make things worse. Just his voice, these meager ministrations, were prods to her. He would let her cool down, he reasoned. She immediately made for the bedroom, to lock herself inside, away from him, but he said, "no, I'll take the bedroom, you stay in the living room," planning that the opiate of television would hasten her recovery. She wordlessly went onto the couch after seeing him enter and close the bedroom door.

He tried, a couple of hours later, and she wouldn't say anything, except, "no, go away, I don't want to talk to you." He kept pressing, perhaps thinking he could bowl over her defenses. But no, she insisted, and harshly. "Get away from me. Get away. I don't want to talk to you, I am so angry at you, I can't. I can't even look at you!"

"I'm sorry, I'm sorry," he pleaded, and he was sorry. He felt terrible, but she was being overly dramatic. Mindy hadn't been traumatized, she hadn't been unduly offended, once they'd gotten to eating he joked and apologized and parried and things proceeded apace, new topics of conversation arose. Katie even gave him looks of approval, although even then he suspected that was just to keep the illusion of bonhomie while she stirred and rived inside.

He planned on waiting her out. She had been watching The Big Bang Theory, feel-good mindless television comfort food, but still she never came back into the bedroom. He played on his phone, read a bit, even napped, and then it was dinner time. He poked his head out, as passively and mollifying as he could muster, and asked her, oh so delicately and patiently, if she was hungry. "No, and I'm not making any food for you," she said, and he returned to the bedroom.

An hour or so later she entered the bedroom. She had obviously already brushed her teeth and gotten ready for bed. He hadn't eaten, was feeling the onset of mild hunger pangs.

"I'm going to bed."

"Okay," he said. And then, "honey, honey, I'm sorry. Please, please, talk to me. I'm sorry, I couldn't help it. It didn't go that bad other —"

His message was muddled, and he was presenting several lines of argument at once, but it was only when he said "it didn't go that bad" that she reacted. She was flagrantly taken aback, and he saw a face of disgust, as if he'd done nothing but engage in the most obstreperous bleating.

"Don't you even —"

"No I mean, other than that."

"Don't you even! I should have known you couldn't control yourself. I never should have taken you."

"I'm sorry, I'm sorry."

"Is that all you can say, you're sorry? Offering her to drink out of your glass?" she stammered, face writ large with repulsion, as if that wasn't something they'd done frequently with other female friends. "And you never asked about her job, like you said you would, to give me something to talk about." He forgot about that, he realized, but that was different, that was innocuous, he was being held to too high of a standard. "And then, the bear thing," and even at that he wanted to laugh, it still sounded funny to him.

"Please," he said, concealing his urge to smile, despite feeling torn up inside, despite portending a night of disconsolate agony. When she was like this, she wouldn't let him touch her, wouldn't let him cuddle her, wouldn't let him talk to her, and he'd feel so alone, assured she would leave him, and it was the worst feeling on Earth. It was being stricken, exiled, all of her previous exhortations to love and fidelity cast asunder, revealed as fickle, capricious lies, nothing more than blandishments and inducements contingent on what she saw as good behavior. No, he couldn't bear that.

"Please," he pleaded again, "please, I'm sorry," and his worst fears were realized, as she leveled him with imprecations and painful comments about not being trustworthy, about her not being able to rely on him, painful comments that he'd try and submerge and categorize as "said in the heat of the moment," nothing more. The outburst didn't quell her, and she roiled in bed, on her side, not letting him touch her. The night went on, and he cried in his pillow, loudly and somewhat showily, to make sure she heard the sobs.

Brian thought of Gary Stewart, his desperate trill, the pain and isolation he expressed so poetically, and the life he led, as tragic as the art he created. Self-destruction, self-abasement, the sensitive figure striking it out on his own, were all poetic idealizations that fascinated him, a small flame he warmed his hands on while imagining the conflagration of romantic oblivion. He listened to Gary, he knew, to inoculate himself to the concept of being alone and depressed and abandoned, to find the romance and high art in it, but he knew he couldn't do it, when push came to shove. He could sing along to "Single Again" — "Single againnnnnnnnn ... born to lose, dying to win" — and find the beauty in the quavering resignation, but if it came to it, Brian would beg and plead and cry for Katie to take him back.

He couldn't do it. He couldn't be alone.

He tried various tactics — that he was terribly sorry; that he was an idiot and made a mistake; that he couldn't help that he had laughed; that the lunch hadn't gone that badly, that Mindy seemed engaged and enjoyed herself, that Mindy said they should hang out again — all these supplications, different as they were, were rejected all the same.

Katie didn't comfort him, and in fact got madder, knowing what he was up to, trying to deny her self-interest and make this all about him, when she was the one who was embarrassed, she was the one disappointed, she was the one who'd built up these expectations and had them dashed. It was her career, her life, not his.

Time passed, how much he didn't know. Brian tentatively assessed the situation and concluded she had fallen asleep. He felt weak and shaky from hunger, and knew he wouldn't be able to fall asleep. He was of two minds: often times, when they fought, she'd go to sleep, wake up and apologize, and they'd find themselves at equipoise. On the other hand, he feared falling asleep and waking back up into an active fight, into her anger and scorn, and better to enjoy this relative calm, gather his thoughts and prepare for the real possibility he was coursing toward relationship-oblivion.

He put his hand on her side, which was covered with blankets. Katie felt soft and almost-cuddly. He had to remain optimistic. Things will be alright. He had to think this way, for his sanity and conception of his place in the world. He imagined Katie approving of this positive outlook— he often imagined her watching over him, being cuddly and sweet, approving of him when he was doing something considerate and kind. So he crept up in the dark and threw on his jeans and went into the kitchen.

He'd go out and bring her home Ben and Jerry's Chunky

Monkey ice cream, he thought. It was her favorite and she'd finished their stash a while ago and they'd never gotten more. He'd get several pints. There was no limit to the strange and unnecessary penances which he would meekly undertake when in a contrite mood.

He already planned it, the desultory way he'd bring it up, and after she woke up and forgave him, she'd be reminded as to how sweet he was and say "awww baby" and put her hands on his cheeks and kiss him.

He put on his black North Face down jacket, checked that he had his keys and wallet in his pocket and, quiet as a mouse, headed out to the grocery store.

>< >< ><

He was being proactive and doing something about a problem. Katie would be proud and probably tell him so later after she'd calmed down. He walked to the grocery store with determination and even smiled outwardly at his inner thoughts, as if there were people meeting and nodding to him. He smiled with the singularly beautiful irradiation which is seen to spread on hopeful faces at the inception of some glorious idea, as if a supernatural lamp were held inside their transparent natures, giving rise to the flattering fancy that heaven lies about them.

Late night grocery stores were always inviting places. Even in the throes of his romantic troubles everything seemed outsized and poetic, but late night at the grocery store was always a special thing. He remembered in college, stoned and ambling around the grocery store, the freedom to think he could buy whatever he wanted. It was all here, always here, for his exploration: random pickles, random ice creams, Spanish-language sauces he'd never heard of, whatever he wanted. He felt that again now a bit, going to the ice cream section and picking out three Ben and Jerry's Chunky Monkey pints and heading to the cash register. He could get or do whatever he wanted, he told himself. The cashier, a short Hispanic man that could have been a teenager, gave him a knowing smile, just like the cashiers always had done when he'd been a stoned college kid with his motley collection of junk foods.

"This stuff is so good, yeah?"

"Yeah, I know, it's for my girlfriend."

"Hah yeah well make sure you get to eat some, too, you were

the one to go get it. Finders, Keepers, amiright?"

"Hah, yeah. Thanks, man. Have a good night," and he grabbed his green plastic bag and headed out. Brian hadn't checked his eyes, but he wondered if they were red from crying.

He started on the seven blocks back home. He realized he had no idea what time it was, and there was no one else out on the streets. That wasn't entirely surprising; D.C. was a weird place like that. Other than the rare exceptions like Georgetown, street activity was almost all centered by the Metro Stations, so where they lived, several blocks away from the nearest station, was usually quite quiet. It was better if it was quiet, since they lived not too far from Providence Hospital, and he didn't know what it was or why it was, but an unseemly element sometimes hung around there. So "too quiet" was good.

>< >< ><

He headed north on NE 13th Street, his left hand gripping the plastic bag, tight to his body, his right shoulder riding against the brick wall. He was close to home, and, with his right hand still in his pocket, he held onto his keys through the key ring, had them almost-wrapped around the front of his hand like brass knuckles. It helped keep him awake.

As he started turning the corner toward his apartment, two males appeared before him, both roughly his height, if not a little taller. They wore black hoodie jackets, one standing directly in front of him, facing him as his mirror opposite, left shoulder against the brick wall; the other stood to Brian's left, forming a semi-circle around him. Brian wasn't sure what was going on. He just wanted to get home.

"Wallet," the one standing directly in front of him said. The other made a movement in his jacket to reveal something. Brian couldn't see what, but from the context and heft of the item, Brian assumed it was a gun.

All thoughts occurred at once. The two men, he could tell, were both black, perhaps black teenagers or in their early twenties. They wore black hoodies and black gloves, dark pants and dark shoes. Other details came to him — the one forming the semi-circle around him had an unusually wide nose, he could see a glint of an earring in the recess formed by the hoodie. (That's stupid, to wear something reflective; they are young and stupid. He might shoot me impulsively.) He shouldn't look directly at their faces, he thought in a flash, they wouldn't like that, they don't want to be seen, just do what they say, keep calm, stay calm.

"Wallet," the man in front repeated, this time darting his hand out in what landed as a punch, to Brian's midsection, but became a groping, searching hand, investigating the front two pockets of Brian's jacket.

"Here," Brian said. He always kept his wallet in his right front pants pocket, and handed it over to the kid directly in front him, his left hand still holding the plastic grocery bag. "That's all I have, I swear. Please, don't make this worse, don't turn this into anything more than it needs to be."

He wanted to sound composed, resigned and weary, a D.C. veteran, a mugging victim veteran, perhaps, someone who knew how this was supposed to go and wanted to get it over with quickly and painlessly. In reality, Brian was scared shitless, just trying to breathe deeply, stay calm, stay calm, stay calm, they don't want to hurt you. His driver's license, his credit cards, his metro card, his workplace ID, about $100 or so in cash in the wallet, just take it. He even thought, optimistically, about the hassles of cancelling all those or getting replacements, which he felt was a good sign, he would get out of his soon, not a big deal, this happens, stay calm. He debated whether he should lie and say that he worked for Legal Aid or the NAACP, that he was one of the good guys, so they would cut him some slack, grant him some form of mercy, but it was too risky, maybe that would be patronizing, he should just keep his mouth shut.

"Give us the bag," the guy in front said after pocketing the wallet.

"It - it's just ice cream," Brian said, tragicomically he realized, but said nothing else and dropped the bag. As the guy in front of him bent over slightly to pick it up, the one to his left struck him in the midsection, around the left side of his ribcage, for reasons he couldn't fathom.

"I'm sorry, I'm sorry," Brian stammered, unsure of himself. Maybe it was disrespectful to make them pick up the bag? His mind raced.

He saw one of them look around, to make their getaway, he hoped, while the other — the one forming the semicircle, he realized — rasped, "keep yo' fucking mouth shut, bitch, keep yo' fucking mouth shut," and then added, "phone, phone, give us your phone" to which the one directly in front of him added, "yeah, just give us your phone."

"I don't — I don't have a phone on me, seriously, I swear, I don't," and he meant to point in the direction of his apartment building, as if to say, I was just going out for a second, but he caught himself.

"Keys, these your keys," the one in front of him said, and made a quick grabbing motion for his right hand but missed.

"Your keys," the one with the gun then said, "phone and your keys, now" and the one in front of him added, "your keys, which apartment?" Where Brian's nerves had been shot, now they were destroyed; he felt an icy, sinking, almost frenetic panic. It coursed through his whole body, through his chest, down through his stomach, down both legs, electrifying him and pinning him to the spot.

No, he couldn't, he couldn't. Katie.

"No, they aren't," he mumbled incoherently, without a plan. "Please, just take my wallet, I don't have a phone, I don't have a phone," he repeated, as if he didn't acknowledge their request for his keys it never happened, they would drop it and forget it. Stall, stall, why aren't they running, why aren't they are trying to get away?

"Keys," the semicircle one said, and dove his left hand across Brian's belly to wrench the keys from Brian's right hand. The man's right hand still held the gun in line with Brian's midsection. Brian didn't pull his hand back, but tightened his grip around the key ring. He hoped, he didn't know what or why, but he hoped they'd get frustrated, cut their losses and leave; they already had his wallet, he didn't have a phone, please, please, he thought, and he raised his right arm. The semicircle one lost his grip, and Brian flung the keys, far over their heads, aiming for the top of the low-rise apartments across the street, and then there were two firecracker shots and Brian's stomach was on fire. First it was two separate streams of fire, and in a second, before he even hit the ground, the streams converged and spread, and it was his whole stomach, his whole midsection, that was on fire.

He fell backward, and he saw the two figures running away from him, up NE 13th Street. His body had limits before, he thought, crazed, he knew where his stomach ended, he knew what equilibrium felt like, what his body was supposed to feel like, where things ended and where things began, but now he didn't, a floor had opened up in his body and things were spilling downward, inside him, uncontrolled, the usual heft of his stomach roped and pirouetted and was felt in his thighs, in his knees, in his feet, and the fire burned frigid.

He screamed, he knew, he screamed, as the solids in his body either liquefied or released liquids, he didn't know. He couldn't move and his head was smashed, he realized, he felt wetness on the back of his skull where he'd bashed his head at the terminus of his fall, and everything poured out of him as he yelled again, oblique nubilous objects under a crimson smear.

>< >< ><

TWENTY-EIGHT MONTHS LATER

Katie shook the pan rapidly, the broccoli and noodles riding the sides of the pan and soaking up the oil and grease. "Riding the half pipe," they called it. "Oh yeahhhhhh," she said to herself, enjoying the sizzling sound, mimicking the movement actor-chefs did on television. If her boyfriend (ahem, she still needed to correct herself, her fiancé) were around, maybe she'd even try to flip the broccoli and noodles for no reason, like she was making pancakes, just ‘cause. She poured in a little more sesame rice oil and sherry and the flame sparked up a bit, "huh-hooo!" she said, now she was cooking with gas. She then added the last vegetables, the peppers, snow peas and bean sprouts.

Stir fry wasn't much to crow about, but her cooking classes were paying off. She now enjoyed experimenting in the kitchen. She used to always feel nervous cooking, getting the timing of everything right. Years ago, when she cooked, she preferred to be alone, uncomfortable with the pressure of another person watching or waiting on her. That wasn't a problem anymore. If something went wrong, her fiancé didn't make a big deal out of it, he didn't apologize or say he was sorry and over-emote.

The meal came out well, and she and her partner were pleased.

They killed a cheap bottle of red and made love soon after. No, they fucked, actually. Her on all fours, looking back at her fiancé. She enjoyed reaching back and feeling his balls while he thrusted behind her, enjoyed that look of satiety and desire on his face, got turned on even more by his hands around her tight, lithe hips, the ease by which they massaged and stroked her body serving as a continued testament to her diet and exercise regime.

He loved how she looked back at him and matched her gaze, loved her squeals and coos, got especially turned on by her tattoo-dappled body. That was the look he always preferred, the type of porn-girls he always sought out, and now, for the last 20 months, that was the type of lady he fucked. It never got old.

Trevor pressed down on her, and from his breathing and position she knew he was going to cum. She loved the exhilaration of knowing he was trying, and failing, to manage and time the release. She delicately cradled his balls, she wanted to feel his release. He came inside of her.

They laid together for a few moments, their breaths and sweat intermingling. After he rolled back over, she excused herself to pee, came back and cuddled with him. They maintained that position for a while until his arm started to go numb, and then they rolled over onto their respective sides. Fuck brushing their teeth and getting ready for bed, they decided. Live in the moment.

Around 3:00 a.m., when they were both long asleep, one of their two black wooden dining-room chairs tilted, the right front and back legs several inches off the ground. It stayed in this position for over a minute, then the two legs came back down, making only the modest sound one would expect. They slept through it, and even if they hadn't, even if they'd both been in the living room (which, in a one-bedroom apartment, doubled as a dining room), who is to say whether they would even notice it, unless they'd been paying particular attention to that one innocuous black wooden dining chair for that specific, otherwise unremarkable minute.

No one was there to see it, so for all intents and purposes, it never happened at all.

>< >< ><

The next night after work, Katie and Trevor went to Mintwood Place, one of their favorite restaurants in the neighborhood. As much as they enjoyed eating in, Adams Morgan was a culinary treasure trove, and it'd be shortsighted not to take advantage of it. They couldn't afford to buy a home in Adams Morgan and certainly couldn't afford to start a family here (nor would they really want to, given the abysmal reputation of the public schools and the prohibitive cost of their private school alternatives), so it was best to eat out while the gettin' was good.

Katie acted like a proper adult that night and brushed her teeth for bed. Trevor joined her, brushing his teeth while behind her, his arm over and around her shoulder, his groin pressed up against her backside, which was protected only by her cotton panties.

Katie appreciated his embrace and wanted sex. She didn't want to go to bed just yet, she didn't much enjoy the slow drift off into sleep and needed the soporific of sex or other intense physical exertion. She didn't say anything, though; better not to say anything, you can't distract yourself forever, she thought, but instead distracted herself while in bed, in typical desultory fashion, by checking and re-checking the same websites on her phone.

Thirty minutes of reading and Trevor threw in the towel and put on his nighttime eye mask. Katie told him she'd join him in sleepyland soon, but she didn't. She kept playing around on her phone while rubbing his arm. Minutes went by without any reaction from him, so she rubbed his arm harder, a sign of affection and her ploy to try and keep him up. It didn't seem to work and, barring tugging at his cock or sticking her fingers up his nose, he was out for the night.

She closed her eyes, hoping to sleep but being unable to. Time passed. Trevor was still next to her, she thought. She wasn't alone. Their blinds were imperfect, which suffused the small bedroom with an annoying ambient light, a perpetual twilight zone. She could track time passing if she opened her eyes and, if there was no ambient light seeping in, it was dead of night. It hadn't gotten that late yet.

She didn't know whether she feared being awake or falling asleep. She couldn't tell what state she'd been in when she experienced what it was that she feared.

It came that night, only for an instant. The dust that danced in the suffused light fused together, the space between space compacted and there was form. A center could be established, could be felt, two protuberances, shaped so that they must have been arms, something arced above her, the physiology of the shape now breaking down, nonsensical, but what floated above her and looked down at her must have been a head. It looked down on her, she knew, even though her eyes failed her in the dark, but for her crepuscular visitor, who knows what it could see or not. She just felt it, her mind explaining what happened into a narrative she could understand. And a few breathless moments later, and she felt that it had left her, although, alone in the dark, she had no way of verifying that, just as she had no way of verifying it had ever really arrived.

>< >< ><

Katie checked around the bedroom the next morning, and nothing had moved, nothing had changed. Sometimes she woke up and a book had been moved, or clothing or magazines by the foot of the bed had been pushed away, or something above her on the nightstand had been toppled over. She asked Trevor sometimes, and sometimes he'd say yeah, oh sorry, I moved that, but then sometimes she asked and he had no idea what she was talking about. Men aren't perceptive like that.

Nothing in the bedroom had been moved. Nothing in the apartment, that she could tell, had moved or changed. But she'd been visited again. She knew it.

And when these things made themselves known, it was always the moment you'd least expect.

>< >< ><

She was in the bathroom the next morning, brushing her teeth in her routine of getting ready for work, after having taken a shower. The door was slightly ajar to let out the humidity, but the bathroom was still nice and warm.

The liner of the shower curtain ripped and cascaded. Her eyeliner, make-up and bric-a-brac lunged violently in various directions, some items into the bathtub, some into the sink, and even some into the toilet bowl. Katie leapt back, arms up as if someone pulled a gun on her, and her back hit hard against the towel rack behind her.

She saw only her own terrified visage staring back at her in the mirror, herself looking ridiculous, arms still up, toothpaste smeared still at the corners of her lips, but she saw herself reflected back through a nebulous something, a distortion, while there was nothing there — nothing there, nothing there — she couldn't see herself reflected in the mirror just in front of her, just this outline, this outlined container with no volume.

"Katie."

Brian, she thought first, then said aloud, scared, almost too afraid to mouth both potent syllables. "Brian."

"Are you alone?"

"Yes," she said, not capable of thinking. Trevor left for work before her. Her stomach roiled after she spoke, the language of fear, of vulnerability.

"I-need-to-speak-with-you-but-I-can't-be-sure-I-can-now. I-can't-keep-myself-here. I-can't-keep-myself."

She had difficulty understanding him, what he said came out jumbled, his voice swiftly fading.

"It's me. It's Brian. I'll come back. I'll try to come back. I am sorry about the mess."

She kept straining herself to listen, to concentrate, for many moments after she ceased to feel or hear anything. He was gone. For minutes she couldn't move, until the build-up of toothpaste and backwash starting burning the back of her throat and made her sick. She spit and washed her mouth out.

She could see herself in the mirror, her skin pale. The common expression, the hackneyed supernatural explanation for such a look, came into her mind and she immediately destroyed it, saw the expression in her mind — "looks like you've just seen a ghost" — in big block letters and exploded it into a million minute pieces, ground it into dust. It was so stupid.

But what else could it be; her cosmetics were all over the floor, the shower liner was ripped and dangling, half-off. She gathered herself, her equanimity returning through the basic act of retrieving her scattered goods and putting them back in their assigned places. Fishing some of them out of the toilet dented her composure a bit, so jolting, so random and frightening, and determining whether she should salvage them or throw them out took her off this routine-induced auto-pilot (she opted for the latter).

She went back to the bedroom — she would be calling in sick, she thought absentmindedly — and, still in her underwear and the purple shirt she planned on wearing to work, sat on her bed and started to surf the internet on her laptop. For what, she didn't know.

She should go to work, she thought moments later. It wasn't smart to stay here, assuming what she felt had happened had even happened. She should get out of here, be around others, by the end of the day the normal routine will have washed this experience away, rooted her back to reality and convinced her that none of this had actually happened.

"Katie."

She almost lost control of her bowels and if she wasn't bleeding out then she was peeing herself, the center of her panties now soggy and wet, her thighs now damp, the unmistakable, base-level recognition of released urine. She froze and held her breath and just stared ahead, as if she was hiding, hiding while sitting on the bed in her own small bedroom.

"Katie, I came back. I was able to do it."

She didn't respond, her face shaking slightly, but her hands uncontrollably. The laptop fell out of them. *I should grab it as a weapon*, the thought flitted into her mind, but she didn't move, her hands shaking so much. That was the most immediate thing that gripped her mind. I need to stop shaking, I need to stop shaking.

"I have control sometimes, I can come back if I focus, I don't know how, exactly. Sometimes it works and sometimes it doesn't. It hurts so much. Sometimes I can come back and exist here for, a long time, I can't tell time, I can't tell days, but I can tell it's for a long time. Sometimes it's just moments, seconds maybe, and it hurts so much and I can't maintain it and I disappear, I go back. I'm always trying. To come through."

"Brian." She said aloud, something she knows for a fact was said aloud, in this world, in this reality, saying something to hopefully drown out all the things she just heard said inside her own head, to chase it out.

"Yes, Katie," she heard in response, and she wanted to cry, or scream, or both. It wasn't in Brian's voice. It wasn't in any voice, really. "You aren't crazy," she heard, and by God she must be fucking crazy, because that's what a crazy person who hears voices would tell herself to convince herself she wasn't crazy.

"You aren't going crazy. It's me, Katie. I'm sorry if I've scared you. I try to come back but I lose control sometimes. I slip through ... slip back, and I enter this world, your world, and I fall and try to hold on. I'm just as clumsy as I used to be," and if there was something else said immediately after, she didn't hear it, but then heard "but now it hurts more.

"I think I have control now, Katie. I think I have control. I just feel it. I feel centered. It hurts so much. Trying to come here, it hurts so much ... when I fail, it's agonizing. I feel myself disintegrating."

She almost laughed, in his piteous pleading she recognized the man she used to live with, the life she used to share with him. She looked up and it was undeniable, the aphotic image, no longer opaque or murky but the black shape carved out of the fabric of the world and inserted here, in the rough shape of a man.

><><><

Brian, when he found himself able to return to the world he once knew, made sense of his environment in ways he didn't understand. No sagacious figure greeted him in the afterlife to explain how things worked. Colors were flat and extremely muted. It was only his sense memory of what, for example, a lit light bulb looked like that allowed him to discern that the dull color emanating above him was in fact yellowish tinge, or that the socks Katie wore were likely white, that prevented everything from appearing as one amorphous, continuous shade of gray.

He had no sense of smell and no sense of taste. He shouldn't have had a sense of touch, or sight or hearing. He had no organs fit to those tasks, yet he saw, hazily, and touched, indelicately, and heard, not like he used to but just felt a sort of noise that rendered understanding. He had always wondered how animals had experienced senses, how amazingly different the world must have seemed to a dog or a fly. Now he was something that inspired that kind of bemused wonder.

"I have control," he either said or thought. Most times, when he gathered all of his strength and constituted himself, he quickly lost control and scattered again, painfully, lapsing back into the dead space, that sentient agony.

"Please tell me I'm not going crazy," he heard Katie say.

A distributary form emerged from the shape before her and lifted up her laptop a foot above the bed. The laptop moved to the left, then the right, then was dropped onto the top of a dresser. The drop was botched, it must have slipped from his grasp because it landed hard on a bunch of her books and papers. She saw a lip gloss fall off the dresser and hit the ground.

"Sorry, I don't have good control over everything. You must think I have a vendetta against your make-up supplies after what happened in your bathroom. But you saw me lift your computer and move it. It was on the bed, and now it is on the dresser. I did that, not you. I'm real."

That term he used — "your bathroom," not "his bathroom" or "their bathroom" — reached him in a way and, maybe it was just somatic memory, but it made him pained and sick. There was no "him," no "their." The "their" that was didn't refer to him. He didn't have sufficient control over his transmissions for her to hear variations in tones; everything he said to her was processed in her brain as phlegmatic, unemotional.

She couldn't tell he said the following both sadly and urgently, or the halting way he expressed himself, afraid his core would break and he'd be flung from this dimension, forced to reconstitute himself:

"Your boyfriend. You have to leave him. You have to. You have to get far away from him, break off all contact."

"What?" she said.

"You have to leave him, you—" and, a beat, a moment, she sensed a frantic scurrying, almost like a scared animal struggling not to fall off a ledge, and he was gone.

><><><

"Katie, Katie, Katie" Trevor said, looking at her cheek while he sat next to her on the couch, her eyes still on the television. "Katie, Katie, Katie." He pronounced it "Kady." The diminutive version of her name was perfect for her, cute but still feisty. He repeated her name in quick succession like this when he was trying to get her attention or turn himself on. She ignored it, locked her jaw and felt her face get hot. Couldn't he just shut up and let her watch the fucking show in peace?

"K-dog, what's up," he implored, his body movement shifty and interrogative. She'd been very distant the last several days. She'd gone out with friends the last several nights, not inviting him.

Everyone needed their own space. They only hung out tonight when he insisted on spending some quality time together, and she barely spoke to him during dinner, having drunk three beers — a lot for her, given her general no-carbs stance — and been reproachful the whole time.

She'd explained her sour mood a couple days earlier with a disdainful shrug and "work stress," but he couldn't imagine she was telling the whole story. If anything, she always talked openly about work stress as a form of vocational expiation. And her work stress was never that bad. Unless she'd been getting fired (which he asked about, that's how bad her attitude was, and she denied it) or she'd been sexually harassed by her boss behind closed doors or something, he had no idea what it could be. Either way, it wasn't fair for her to treat him like this.

He tactfully moved to take the remote out of her hands. She made an inchoate movement to resist, but didn't, and he took the remote and paused the show.

"Katie ... did I do something wrong?"

Leave me alone! she screamed in her head. *Bothering me about this will only make it worse*, she wanted to say, the very thought of having to express herself about any of this already made her blood boil and her stomach roll. She felt hot in her chest and didn't want to be touched.

"C'mon, nothing can be that bad, my slappy seal, you," he tucked his arm around the small of her back. Slappy seal, that was a new one. She kept looking away but he worked his face into her line of sight, looking hopeful and cheerful, like this was all a misunderstanding, like she was confused about being upset. As if he was saying, *hey, it's me*, like his presence extinguished all sadness. She relented, of course; he had that power, that square-jawed optimism. "This is something we can do," was a common refrain of his whenever she got frustrated at something, and, even if it wasn't true, it usually lifted her spirits.

"It's just, I think, maybe, just, I don't know, I think I've just been thinking about what happened to Brian. You know, Brian. With our engagement, our wedding, coming up, I feel, I don't know, guilty. Guilty that I'm still here and he's dead?"

That wasn't exactly true, of course; it just came out, and at least skirted the curtilage of the truth.

"I understand," he said, and of course he did, and made a brief face to reflect that he did indeed understand. But a moment later and his face was back to its inveigling optimism. "Look, think of it like this. Brian, I mean you know I never met him, but he sounded like a sweet, good person. Someone who loved you," and here he put his hands on her hands, in case saying Brian loved her would make her emotional, which it didn't. "And I think he would want you to be happy, wouldn't he? And you are happy with me, aren't you?"

"Yes, Trevor, I'm happy with you," she said in a dumb, jokey sarcastic way, and then straightened up and repeated, seriously, "yes, Trevor, I love you and I'm happy with you."

He hugged her. "There, then it's settled. You have no reason to be unhappy. In fact, you have every reason to be happy." She hugged him back and kissed him, and then found herself in a bind, because now she had to act like there was nothing left to be upset about, as if he'd diagnosed the problem and implemented the solution.

So for the rest of the night she continued to be in her own little world, interrupting her interior life with little pats and hugs of affection, like a little timetable to show she acknowledged that he was still here, all the while still fixated on all the unknown things that had yet to be unfurled.

>< >< ><

When Brian returned, it was in the morning again, while Katie was getting ready for work and after Trevor had already left. She was sitting on the foot of the bed, fully-dressed, putting her shoes on, when he appeared. She first looked up because the bin of dirty laundry tipped over. Then she saw him, and she was startled, but, surprisingly, not scared. If anything, she was relieved. It had been over two weeks since she'd spoken to him. In the interregnum between her first encounters with Brian she'd been unable to think, unable to comprehend, unable to plan for the future. She'd been in stasis, and she needed answers.

"I'm glad you're back," she said aloud, to no one in particular, just the room, perhaps part of herself still unable to believe anything like this could be happening.

"I take it you are alone," she heard, the Brian-sized shape gliding over from the laundry bin.

"Yes. I've been thinking non-stop about what you said about Trevor. It's killing me."

The voice that rang in her ears still lacked timbre and tonality. It was like re-reading a transcript long after the experience it recorded; the information was there, but the context, the sense-impressions, were absent.

"Why don't you tell me about him?"

"Brian, please. You need to tell me what you meant. This is important to me."

"Why don't you tell me about him? I've been trying to come back, but it's hard. It requires intense concentration, and it's painful being here. I don't belong. It's unnatural. And when I fail and disperse, it's agony."

"I'm sorry. I appreciate it, I really do, appreciate you coming to visit me. It must be important, and I appreciate it. You were always so sweet to me."

There was a pause, and again, the same flat affect.

"He does seem like a nice person. Why don't you tell me about him? I can see you. My, I don't know, vision, or whatever it is, is spotty, and I really need to focus. Since I haven't seen him before, in real life. I-R-L, if people still say that. I don't think I can concentrate enough to see him."

She did, hesitantly, begin to describe him. Just in general details; his age (33), his height (he was tall, 6'3"), she said he was sweet and she loved him. Brian pressed for more details, and Katie provided them, again hesitantly, going into such detail as his skin tone (olive), his hair color and style (dirty blonde, somewhat longish), his eye color (green), even his general build (muscular) and Brian even asked what his most noticeable feature was, and Katie balked, said, "are you kidding me?" but in a flirty, upturned way, as if still in the throes of their early, nascent relationship and he was making a fun request of her, like to reveal a secret talent. "His chin, he has a very nice chin, very square."

"Ahh," he said. "Thanks. Now I might be able to picture him." And, not displayed for Katie on account of Brian's lightless shape, were his glazing eyes, riveting onto her, with the eloquently keen reproach of a creature recognizing the treachery of those who had seemed his only friends.

"Okay. So, you have to tell me. You have to tell me. What did you mean, why did you say I have to get away from him?"

There was a long pause, and, even though his presence was still felt, the "shape," so to speak, was still there, she feared he'd left. She leaned back, up against the pillow, as if to better canvass the room, as his locus had shifted.

"So, you aren't scared?"

She wasn't, anymore. "No, I'm not. You don't scare me, not even as a ghost," she said sweetly.

"I see," he said. Katie bulldozed any fear she had, he felt, through acting coquettish and dainty, the way she did when they first met and the way, he figured, she acted when she first met Trevor and whatever other male suitors she had had in the interim. And he was trying to laugh maniacally, conjuring up as much disdain as he could, intonating with as much malevolence as he could muster, but all for nothing, he realized, because either she didn't pick up on it or, in his condition, it wasn't coming across.

"Do you think this is about you, Katie?"

"Well, I—"

"Do you think I've come back all this way to gossip? I've told you how it hurts to come back, and how much it hurts to try to come back and fail, it's agonizing, and all you do is sit here and think I've come back for you. To hold your hand and help you out and be your best man at your wedding, or to tell you little secrets of your new husband-to-be, about him cheating on you or whatever skeletons he has in his closet."

Even in death he was meek and craven, Brian felt. His lifelong weakness of character, as it may be called, suggested that he was the sort of man born to ache a good deal before the fall of the curtain upon his unnecessary life should signify that all was well with him again, but apparently even the cessation of life hadn't put an end to that. She couldn't hear all the elements in his voice; the malice, the regret, the inversion of the acquiescent piteousness she expected from him, that so stained him that she apparently expected it even in death.

"I died for you. I died for you, do you remember," and if he could cry he'd be doing so. "I died for you because I loved you."

"I loved you, too, Brian."

"No, you didn't, and you don't love me now, and that's the problem. That's why I'm here. I mean that literally, that's why I'm bothering to reach out to you, and in another way. That's why I'm not at rest. That's why I'm stuck here.

You can't be with Trevor. You can't be with anyone, now or ever."

"Brian."

"No!" he shouted, the explosion only heard to him; to her, it was the same milquetoast tone. "No. There's a reason why people visit the graves of people they love, why they light candles and recite prayers. Every culture does this. Every culture, every religion, just feels that urge to respect, to love their dead. You just feel it.

"Desires and impulses like this exist because there is a way to satisfy them, and a purpose to satisfy them, don't you understand? You get hungry because there is such a thing as food. And people of all cultures and religions respect and love their dead because they feel that there is a need to. Instincts exist in a world where those instincts can be satisfied. People who take on new lovers, new partners, when their dedicated partner dies, instinctively feel guilty, feel guilty like they are betraying the dead. And for good reason.

"That's the thing. These impulses exist for a reason. Because where I exist now, love is the only currency. And you don't love me. Maybe you never loved me. But I died, I sacrificed myself for you, and it was the right thing to do. I'm not saying it wasn't the right thing to do. But now you have to do the right thing, by me.

"You cannot take on any other lovers. You have to love me. Your love has to belong to me. Just like when your grandfather died, remember, your grandmother didn't go out and start dating. Her love for her husband never died."

"Brian — Brian, that ... that can't ...."

"No, it is, Katie. To think, you thought I was coming back here, for you, still your lapdog. No. I'm in agony. Spare me. Don't tell me how you think the world should be, how the world should change and exist so you can live the type of life you want to live.

"I'm telling you the how the world is."

"Brian, what do you expect—"

"I told you what I expect. I told you. You can keep asking, but it's not going to change."

"Brian," she said, and made a motion to extend her arm but, not knowing where to place it, retracted it. When she extended her arm he could see the splotches of her tattoos. There were some shapes and configurations he didn't recognize, and a primeval part of himself wanted to inquire, but he refrained.

"Brian, I am so, so, so sorry about what happened to you. I feel terrible about it. I can't ... I can't express it to you enough, how awful I feel. That whole night. That whole day. I'm ... I'm so sorry I was such a bitch. I've changed. I'm sorry. I'm sorry, I'm so sorry."

"Do you think I'm going to smile at you fondly and drift away, Katie? Do you think you can just say words to me and then go about your life, your happy life, while I'm stuck here, in this ... this purgatory."

He didn't want to use that word, it wasn't accurate, but it was something he knew she would understand. "The unloved ones, the abandoned ones, the deserted ones, the ones who deserve better, we're stuck here. Maybe everything you are saying is true. I doubt it. But it doesn't matter. You can say how grateful you are, you can talk your big game, or you can be appreciative and understand something that I learned, something I lived by: being a good person requires some sacrifice. I sacrificed myself for you. I'm not asking nearly as much of you. All I'm asking is for you to sacrifice enough to put me at rest. You still get to exist. I exist now, only in pain. If you love me, or ever loved me, in any way whatsoever, you'd do this for me."

"Brian," she started again, now visibly panicked. "Brian, am I supposed to live alone for the rest of my life? Is that what someone who loved me would want for me?"

"Shut up, Katie. Just shut up. You can't talk your way out of this anymore. I don't give in anymore." He fumed, even in death he was just her inconvenience, a great hitch in the gliding and noiseless current of her life. "You just want me to tell you you're right, you just want me to tell you that the world is the way you want it to be, that you can live the life you want to. But you can't. This is the way the world works. This is the way the real world works. Here I am, in front of you, dead but not yet at rest. It hurts so badly, being here, it hurts so badly, not being at rest, and if you could end this suffering by living alone, by loving me, my memory, being loyal to the man who saved your life and gave up literally everything for you. How could you not do this?"

"I - it's not fair to Trevor."

"Spare me."

"I - I don't love you anymore, Brian. I'm sorry, I love Trevor."

"Love is circumstantial. You will get over it. You love your life, right, you love being alive. Those men, they would have raped you, would have killed you, for all we know. Of course, you don't know, do you, what exactly I did to save you? Think about that. Just think about what I sacrificed to allow you to keep on living. That's where you should find your love.

“And you never loved me, I don't think. You never appreciated me. You took me for granted. If that job had come through, you would have left me, took our little love and brought it to the pound and put it to sleep. I'm not stupid. You only loved yourself. How stupid and pathetic I was. I lived my whole life in ... in thrall to you, only to be kicked around and taken for granted.

“No, not anymore. You do this."

The robotic cadence of his voice was grating in its monotony, if that made any sense. The pitch agitated the inside of her ears, or something inside her mind.

"Leave me alone. I don't want you here anymore. You've upset me."

He wanted to laugh or scream, cause a conflagration and immolate himself, rip out everything about her and himself and turn themselves inside-out.

"You don't get it. Leave him, or we'll find out if you really love him. Maybe he'll join me here."

"Brian what happened to you? This isn't you. This isn't you, this can't be you."

"Oh it's me," and he tried to smile but there was nothing to smile, still a fog whose man-shaped border was delineated, ever so slightly, by a darker, more ashen form of gray. He was working so hard just to keep himself together, the preternatural constituent elements of himself heading toward entropy.

“I’ve seen things you people wouldn’t believe. All those moments, lost in time, like tears ... in ... rain.”

He thought the Blade Runner line would be cute. A bit of levity.

A piece of himself, if any such pieces remained. It hadn't worked, and his moment in her reality was slipping away.

"I'm telling you one more time. Leave him. Leave him and never love another again. And if you don't, if you can be so unconscionable, so wretched and inhumane as to leave me in this state, then you'll see exactly who I've become and what I'm capable of. As I said, and which you were too dumb to pick up on, I've seen things you can't imagine. I lived my life weakly. I won't let that weakness continue.

“The more I see you, the more I hate you. There's no pain I wouldn't inflict to end this agony of mine. If you think I'm not capable of it, then you're wrong. Don't put yourself in a position to find out how wrong you are.”

><><><

Where I am, we don't need roads, he'd thought to himself at one point. He didn't remember when, probably early on, before he'd perhaps understood the gravity of his situation. It was constant nausea, even though he knew he had no mouth with which to heave, no stomach to empty. He drifted through the liminal states of the universe: the material, which was still "the world," to him — reality — and whatever this other state was, this go-between.

It was in this go-between that he learned through other desperate strivers like him exactly what he was, and why he was, and why they were doomed to never rest. The information came to him through means he still didn't understand — a fragment, a wisp of information a suffering soul would pass through him, as if it had always been there, knowledge excavated, not learned. All these wisps and fragments and learning by osmosis revealed to him the sorry state of unloved existence, some of these sufferers having been here for an incalculable period of time, forgotten, unloved, despondent, those that could have loved them now all dead themselves. Their impossible situation left them unable to conjure up whatever exultation of spirit was needed to pass over. And you needed a store of that to make an attempt. Every time his grasp wavered and he disintegrated, every blasted point of him felt sentient, every single point of him a separate accursed entity, facing death with the fresh horror of the first time.

So when he attempted to pass over, it really mattered.

And what mattered more than vengeance?

Theirs was not a world of accumulated wisdom, of learned philosophies and perspectives. Their powers were limited to the observational. In their foreign state, the only activity that approximated happiness was keeping tabs on those in the real world who had spurned them, or, even better, physically harmed them.

One of his fellow wisps had spotted one of the men who had killed him. Brian didn't know who to thank — in their state, they would often bleed over into each other or waft together, impossible to tell where one began and the other ended, a congeries of dandelion spores.

He was able to accumulate himself and pass over into the material world on his twelfth try. His reconstituted parts felt as if they were soldered together, each failed attempt another brand of the iron.

>< >< ><

Charles was the man's name, he'd learned. But he didn't dare express it.

He had followed Charles to the men's room of the Anacostia Burger King. It was a single-stall, a way to prevent drug dealers, thugs and bums from loitering and conducting deals. It had just a toilet and a sink. When Charles closed the door, he didn't notice that it opened again, just so slightly, just so quickly, and for all he could have known it was a catch in the door hinge to prevent it from slamming.

Brian sense-watched the back of the man as he urinated in the toilet. He smelled nothing, heard nothing, really, unless he exerted himself painfully, sensory intake no longer a passive activity but the subject of much straining. He wanted Charles to turn and look at him, create a tableau of sorrow to imprint upon this man, make him understand what he'd done to him; not just killed him, unfairly and unjustly and for nothing, but doomed him to a fate-worse-than-death, the death of the unloved. But he couldn't. What if this didn't work? What if he dissipated? The chance of failure was too insurmountable.

But then something switched. The inward pain expressed outward. He exorcized by doing.

"Charles, turn around," he screamed. Charles adjusted as if he had a crick in his neck and looked over his shoulder casually, and returned to his duty. "Charles, turn around!" he proclaimed again, this time so close to Charles' back that, if he were human, he could stick out his tongue and lick the nape of the man's neck. Brian couldn't see it, but Charles winced for a moment as if overtaken by a flash migraine; Brian saw Charles rub his temple for a moment, nothing more. Charles made movements of zipping himself back up and kicked the toilet valve to flush it (the zipping, the kicking, the flushing; all sounds that Brian should have heard, that he could have filled in from memory, but he didn't hear them, so focused as he was on assembling himself).

Brian propelled himself forward, concentrating on Power, on Force, on Destruction, and as Charles turned around he made a surprised face and slipped backward. He fell over, his ass hitting the side of the toilet. He prevented himself from falling over completely by grabbing onto the nearby sink.

"Motherfucker idiot, shit man," Charles said, his shirt wet, bum piss and whatever else now on the ass of his jeans. He smiled a bit, one of those "I'm lucky, that could have been worse" smiles, and Brian screamed, "It was me! You didn't fall! It was me!" and he shot out an arm and grabbed Charles by the throat, throttling him, and Charles looked out, eyes bulging, at the nothing, the nothing becoming something, before him.

Charles heard screams in his head, scratchy screams that he couldn't make out.

"Are you listening, you nigger? Do you hear me now, nigger? Can you hear that, nigger?" Brian had no racial animus, had even somehow felt guilty — Guilty! Him, guilty, the one robbed and murdered! — that his attackers had been black, as if that sullied his desire for revenge. Expelling the hate felt great. "I bet you hear this now, nigger, don't you! I'm back! I'm back! You thought you could get rid of me, but I'm back!"

Finally, Brian got a discernible response, a look of disorientation and panic, something akin to what he himself must have looked like when two strangers gratuitously blew up his insides.

"Do you hear me now, do you hear me, I bet you can," he said, pressing what he thought should have been hands against Charles' face. Charles stood still, his face and head not moving; whether out of fear or Brian's manipulation, he knew not.

"Charles, is it? It's Charles, what do I look like to you, Charles?"

Charles shook his head, too quickly, in a way you do when you're drunk and trying to get ahold of yourself.

"NO!" Brian yelled, catapulting all his energy forward into what he felt was a slap. Charles reacted, jolted his face back, but stood still.

"You felt that, didn't you Charles! You felt that! See, sometimes things do come back. How do I look like to you?"

"Like, like," Charles said, his gaze flat, his eyes vacant; perhaps he was high and thought this was a bad trip. No, Brian couldn't have that; he needed to leave a lasting impression. "Like," and Charles now giggled, yes, he must definitely be high, "like a static T.V. screen man, like a man-shaped T.V. screen, man," and Charles again giggled, his eyes closed. In the midst of his panic, Charles let his common sense take over; this was nothing, just a bad trip, man, this was crazy, he needed better control over himself.

"Oh, is that right," and Brian felt, again, the anguish of not being taken seriously. He couldn't even inspire fear as a specter. And as Charles subsumed his fear into his exaggerated stoned play-acting, as if degenerating into unthinking would save him, so too could Brian play-act, all that unfettered anguish and rage naturally inclined to go inward, make him feel worthless, no, now this would go outward, he'd be an unthinking vehicle of punishment. Let his rage embody him. Let rage become him.

"Tell me!" he yelled and propelled himself forward, and Charles hung in the air and was gagging, and the laconic cool stoner disappeared, replaced with sheer bewilderment, "tell me, do you even know who I am? Do you remember me, Charles? Do you know exactly who I am? Or have you killed so many other people that you need to take a moment to guess who I am? Northeast D.C., Brookland? I don't even know how long ago. A white guy, carrying ice cream to his girlfriend, carrying ice cream, for fuckssake. You wanted his keys, to rape his girlfriend ...."— on that note, he concentrated all his energy on squeezing whatever he could — "and when he went to take his keys away from you, you shot him in the stomach, and ran. Do you remember that? Is that a dime-a-dozen to you?"

"Nah, man, nah, it's not possible," and Charles' panic deepened somehow, in a way that Brian knew he had his man. He panicked like a guilty man, as if Brian was a potential witness threatening to go to the police, and God how wrong Charles was on that score. What Brian had in store ... the pinpricks of his energy positively dancing, a euphoric delight anticipating the pain he would cause. There was such a freedom, an exhilaration, in not caring about the fate of another, in inflicting violence on a worthy target. This was an exhilaration that spanned the somatic. His whole life he'd been meek, his whole life he'd kowtowed, his whole life he'd thought he was being a good person in putting the needs of others before his, and oh God, how wrong he'd been, oh God or whatever allowed him to come back, let him genuflect before the altar of supreme vengeance and violence and the tearing of the flesh of all who smite him.

"Yes," Brian said, and he felt the release his body memory associated with crying. "Yes, God yes, God yes, this is happening," and he wrenched and tore and little-by-little, his efforts bore material fruit, if just a nick here, a scratch here, a tear there, in his focused frenzy obtaining a mastery of his incorporeal self that he'd never known. He placed himself in the very fibers of this man, occupying the man's throat and resting there, feeling Charles choke on him, gag on him; let him gag on what he created, the man's whole system going into conniptions and collapse, and Brian obtained such a unity of place, performance and purpose that as the man died, Brian almost excused him for his crime, so beautiful and poignant was his satisfaction in killing him.

><><><

There was no point in pretending she'd imagined it. It's amazing how one clings to the illusion of normality, especially when things were going completely, horrifically awry. She was left alone, stunned, a swirling sea in her head. Somehow, she stumbled her way to work and was able, through her fog, to perform at a basic level. Her stomach churned, she felt oddly weightless, and she couldn't stop her fingers from twitching.

She'd have to talk to Trevor, she thought, a way to calm herself down, as if that was a bridge she'd intuitively cross when she got there, as if having a plan of action with one item — talk to Trevor — was sufficient. It was surreal reconciling this dread with the rudimentary requirements of normal life: feeling her coffee to make sure it wasn't scorching hot; looking at traffic lights before entering intersections; answering emails professionally; getting on the Metro; having an unanswered voicemail from her mother and the weird guilt of thinking she needed to call her back, all the while having this unbelievable — say it, Katie, say it — supernatural terror stalking her.

In the modern age, a conversation couldn't just wait until you got home. Before Trevor had even gotten home, he'd already texted her several times, asking what she wanted to do that night, making little jokes, emoticons suggesting twee bafflement at her silence.

"You're here," he said when he arrived home, looking at her as he moved to drop off his work bag at the living room table. She was sitting on the far side of the couch, a glass of water behind her, on the table. That was her side of the couch. A glass of water waited for him on the dresser nearer the wall on his side of the couch.

"So, what do you want to do tonight?"

"Sit down with me," she patted his side of the couch, too cheerfully, she thought. She didn't know how to go about this.

"Okay," he said, and sat down, but in an exaggerated way, making a show of his hands on his knees, to show he didn't know what was up and didn't want to sit down, but rather wanted to get up and get going. He was hungry and wanted to get out of the apartment. He worked all day in an office and he didn't feel like being in another cramped space.

"We need to talk, and it's not about you, it's nothing about you."

"Katie," he said, with a shake of his head, confused but in an annoyed way. If she were breaking up with him, her tone was all off. She was conducting herself so inartfully that he couldn't believe for a second that she was breaking up with him.

"Katie, what's going on? What's up?"

"We need to take a break," she said, but even that wasn't delivered effectively. She scratched her head as she said it, as if even she wasn't sure what she meant.

"What!? Katie, we're engaged, what are you talking about?"

"That's not what I meant, I mean, God, I can't tell you, I don't even know what I'm saying or what I mean. I just wish — I need to be apart from you for a while to figure something out, for your own good."

"Katie, what are you talking about? If this is about your wild cooking, then look, my stomach will adjust." Despite his deflecting, jocular way, and even in the midst of all this confusion and disorder, this lighthearted crack at her cooking stung.

"Hey, what the fuck is that supposed to mean?"

"I'm joking, obviously. I love your cooking. And what is that supposed to mean? What are *you* supposed to mean by all this 'break' stuff? You can't be real! If you're getting cold feet — I mean, aren't I supposed to be the one getting cold feet? Isn't that how that's supposed to work?"

"No, look," and she closed her eyes tightly, "no, look."

"And for my own protection, you said? Or my own good or something? What? Is there like ... is there something I need to know about? C'mon Katie? We're partners, you know? I know this sounds corny and super-cool, with-it Katie wouldn't ever say this, but your problems are my problems, you know? If there's something serious you need to tell me, if there's some, like, real problem, like if someone is bothering you, you can tell me. No, you need to tell me. I mean, I don't —"

"No," she said, and she didn't know what to say or what to do. If she were to do this, it'd have to be a clean break. Just: it's over and don't talk to me again. Or she'd have to move in the dead of night and change her number and quit her job and get a restraining order against him, make him never talk to her again, which was unrealistic and impossible. And unfair. And something she didn't want to do, and which she had no intention of doing, she realized. No, she wasn't going to leave him. That was ridiculous. This was ridiculous.

"It has to do with Brian, again." She made a look as if she was suffering a migraine. In a way, she was. She was talking, thinking, a pressure building in her head, feeling her way through this morass of emotions without a plan. She didn't want to leave Trevor and she shouldn't have to. She loved Trevor, and it would be tragic to have to separate from him. It would be unfair to both of them.

On the other hand, she didn't want to embroil him in something that could harm him. She should be truthful. But underlying all this, as if simmering below her thoughts and influencing them, was just how outwardly ridiculous this all was. Ghosts, ultimatums from beyond the grave. It was impossible, this was ridiculous and — while she didn't doubt that she'd somehow communicated with Brian over the course of several weeks, that she hadn't just gone crazy — the sheer wrongness of it all, the strangeness, inclined her not to be persuaded by his demands.

"Katie," Trevor said, relieved, mistaking the consternation across her face for regret over bringing up this subject again, "this again? Oh, honey," he said and hugged her.

"How crazy would it sound if we should just be apart for—" and she didn't know how to continue without sounding crazy or just outright lying to him, lies she knew he'd catch and lies she didn't want to excuse or explain. "I'm sorry. I just feel like I'm disrespecting him somehow and it's not fair to him. I-really-think-we-should-take-time-apart-just-so-I-have-time-to-think." She said it too quickly, the words all blended together, and God couldn't he just not argue and accept it, please just leave, for your own good.

She couldn't go through with it. She was embarrassed to explain and didn't want to. That was the long-and-short of it: she didn't want to.

She had a right to be happy, too.

"Forgive me. You're going to marry a weirdo, is what I guess I'm trying to say. I'm giving you super advance warning," she said, pulling back from his hug, strange tears on her face. Tears of relief, maybe.

Her exasperation quelled. It was over, Trevor wasn't going anywhere.

They'd deal.

"Trust me," he said, patting and rubbing the area just north of her knee (the spot she liked). "I've known that for a long time. You don't sleep with a girl who has the name of a mall and a magician from a video game tattooed on her arms without being a little crazy yourself."

>< >< ><

Later that night they were reading in bed, the blanket up to their mid-sections. Trevor held Katie's hand, and she squeezed back. He placed her hand atop the blanket near his crotch. "Feel that?" he said.

"Look what I got," and she felt an ever-slight movement beneath the heavy blanket.

"I guess I shouldn't say no, right?"

"Yeah, that's the wrong answer." He threw off the blanket and she felt his semi-hard dick through his gray pajamas. "Feel that now?"

"I do," she said, taking his penis and balls in her open hand and playfully jostling the whole package.

"So, what are you thinking about?" he asked, rolling up the sleeve of her pajama-shirt, revealing some of the color on her arms. "I can reciprocate, too, it's the least I can do," he said, crossing his body with his left hand and rubbing, over her clothes, the area between her legs.

"Well isn't this egalitarian."

"I'm all about equality. I'm still a little stressed out from all that leaving-me talk. It makes me sad. I don't think I can sleep!"

"Oh I'm so, so sorry about that," she said flirtatiously and coquettishly.

"Stop opening your mouth so wide; it only makes me want more what I can't have."

"Oh, I'm so, so sorry about that, so ... soooo ... sorry," she took prime opportunity to over-articulate on each 'o.'

Soon enough, and she was pulling down his pajama pants and putting his cock in her mouth, enjoying the slight chill of it in her wet, warm mouth, enjoying the obvious cues that he liked it, too.

It was only the next morning, getting ready, that she thought about it, and whether that was a turning point. Brian had made his ultimatum, and Katie responded to it by sucking the cock of her new lover.

She wondered if they'd been alone.

>< >< ><

Four days later and she was playing the latest Disgea game on the television, with Trevor sitting alongside her on the couch, watching and commenting on the action and her tactical decisions. Trevor still wasn't sure about the ins-and-outs of all the characters. She was getting in her zone, realizing how much she missed the pleasures of tactical JRPGs, feeling like a nerd expert being able to explain the goings-ons to Trevor. She couldn't indulge him too much, because her video game talk sometimes had the unintended consequence of turning him on.

"Hold on, hold on, hold on," she said with mounting excitement, moving a character in position on the grid for the kill.

"Why — oh, Jesus!" and just like that their Samsung 42-inch television detached from its stand and, vaulting toward them, landed hard on the floor, screen-first, bringing everything else connected to it tumbling down in an uncoordinated, ugly mess.

"Jesus fuck," Trevor said.

They both sat there stunned for a moment.

"You need to go easy on that game," he said.

"Trevor I didn—"

"I know. It was a joke." He stood up and inspected the damage, manipulating the television as best he could to get a look at the screen. "Can you help me lift it up? It's all broken." There was a grooved crack in the screen. "It's like it jumped. Like it committed suicide. Look the stand didn't even snap, it's not like it snapped and the T.V. fell, the whole thing just, like, leapt forward."

>< >< ><

She told herself and felt many things all throughout that night and into the next days, debating about what to do, changing the narrative of what happened subconsciously in her mind, but eventually she settled on it just being, at worst, a recrudescence, a flare-up. It wasn't anything, none of that was real; it was like a cold sore, it came up and you dealt with it and it went away, it was harmless. She told herself an assortment of contradictory and confused things and whatever their truth value, they worked on soothing her frayed nerves and doubts. What was she to do? Tell Trevor that her dead boyfriend was haunting them, a sentiment which became more and more ludicrous as the days went on. Perhaps she had just gone temporarily crazy. Maybe that's what an anxiety attack was? She always heard stories of people blacking out and forgetting things and always dismissed that as excuse-making bullshit, but maybe it was true? Maybe it was real? I mean, what other explanation could there be?

If that was the case, she wondered, the guilt must have been submerged more deeply than she knew and been erupting in ways she couldn't fathom. She'd felt terrible about Brian, of course, as any normal, feeling human being should, but she'd fallen out of love with him months before his tragic death. They weren't a good fit. They had no future. Perhaps her love of being loved had gotten the better of her conscience, and though she had agonized at the thought of treating him cruelly, she'd encouraged him to love her while she didn't love him at all. Then, when she did see him suffering, her remorse set in, and she did what she could, short of breaking up, to repair the wrong.

But it had been trying. She hadn't felt the spark with him and she didn't like the way he made her feel. His constant apologies and penances made being with him feel like a chore, an obligation, and his groveling only made her fits of pique grow and feel more justified. And that's not who she was, or who she thought she was. She'd become soft and lazy and spiteful. If anything, she felt guilty about not breaking up with him much sooner; for if she did, he wouldn't have been out, alone, getting shot en route to bringing her ice cream. Thinking about that — alone, getting shot, getting her ice cream — filled her again with the guilt that had lain dormant. It had to all be in her mind, and all this nothing but manifested guilt. That was the only thing that made sense, was consistent with her feelings and the world as she knew it to be.

They put the television back upright, but it was non-operational. She stayed relatively silent throughout Trevor's grousing, though when she spoke, it was apologetically. He'd said there was no reason for her to apologize, but she insisted here-and-there, just apologetic asides, until he said, somewhat harshly, "Why are you apologizing? The T.V. fell, you didn't do it, it just happened. Stop apologizing," and then she apologized for apologizing and he shook his head and kept futzing with the television. "I mean, I'm just sorry," and her insides spazzed icy-cold, filling her, as if there had been a temporarily inactive world inside her that had just sprung to gelid life.

Why that was, she didn't say, although she had an inkling of an idea of what caused it.

>< >< ><

Should I run away? she thought, several days later, as she walked home from the Woodley Park Metro station. Should I just run away? She could move back to Long Island, tell Trevor it was over when she got home, just beg him, please don't talk to me anymore, tell him she needed space, and then let relationship-entropy take hold. Unless one is proactive, the bonds of affection gradually weaken over time. Realistically, he'd get over it. She'd feel terrible, but she'd get over it, too. Hell, she already felt terrible. Just another thing to add to the list.

People get over things. People are adaptable. That's what she should do. A solitary life isn't the worst thing on Earth. Many people live happy, productive, engaged lives without a partner. She wasn't sure if she'd wanted kids, anyway. That's what she'd do, she resolved, although she didn't do it. Out of a combination of disbelief, reproof against what was expected of her, her native recalcitrance, her love for Trevor and the fear of disrupting her life, she just didn't do it. Even if she should, she wasn't going to, she realized; less a statement of ideology and more a statement of how-the-world-was.

How-the-world-was was them making dinner together, the next night, in their crowded kitchen. She did the cooking and he was the jack-of-all-trades: sous chef, dish cleaner, remover of obstacles and taste-tester guinea pig. The task at hand was homemade pasta sauce. The kitchen was littered with peeled garlic cloves, discarded leaves of basil that didn't make the cut, empty cans of crushed tomatoes (which Trevor was then bringing to their recycling bin), experimental olive oils and organic peppers and all the assorted pots, pans and strainers. They were in the zone, kind-of, which meant that they were always in motion but not too coordinated, bumping into each other, scrambling to make space on the counter when needed and Katie calling audibles ("Add a dash of the pink Himalaya salt!"). Trevor would respond with a "Stat!" and get to it. Katie still felt a bit uncomfortable around the presence of flames and the smell of gas and sharp serrated objects, i.e. the building-blocks of cooking, and was glad Trevor was there; she considered any meal preparation a success as long as they didn't run into each other with a knife and every meal a success if it didn't poison them.

Trevor was heading back toward the kitchen to get the last empty can of crushed tomatoes when he lurched forward, falling face-first onto the kitchen floor with a tumbling thud. Katie screamed and, as he fell, the carefully orchestrated arrangement of food and devices exploded, a farrago of clattering and noises and shapes that lasted a breathless second. She thanked God that Trevor didn't impale himself on a knife and that no pot of boiling water fell atop him.

"Honey!" Katie yelled out and moved to help him up, immediately thinking to instruct him not to wildly grab for things in the kitchen: he could have burnt his hands on the flame or gashed his hand wide-open on a knife. She decided to table that until after the meal was over and she was sure he was alright, no need to rile him up and give off the impression that she was more interested in kitchen rules than his own well-being, even though such flagrant violations of kitchen rules did irk her.

"Honey, are you okay?!" she asked him again as he stood up, her left arm tucked behind his lower back. She looked down at the ground, basil leaves, onion, and cracked pepper spilled on the floor. She turned to look at him. "Honey, are—"

He launched backward and she instinctively retracted her hand, just before his lower back slammed against the counter top. He arched awkwardly, his pelvis thrust forward after the collision. "Trevor!" she yelled, as his body stood, unmoving. As if in response to her call, the back of his head smashed with conviction into the microwave just behind him. The sound of his head against the rigid metal aborted the words she was forming. The effect was unnatural, there was no forward momentum which could have caused that, he'd stopped moving; and she realized she had trouble seeing, the kitchen had gotten so smoky yet she didn't smell anything burning and certainly the fire alarm wasn't going off.

Trevor's head jerked forward slightly and then, again, the back of his head crashed violently with the front of the microwave, and he hung, implausibly, the force pinioning his head against the microwave keeping his feet off the ground. His head rotated slightly to the right, then to the left, as if cradled in an invisible hand, and his head pushed back, harder, as if boring through the metal, and then it ended and he fell, like a disposed rag doll, tumbling down and landing hard on his tailbone.

"I told you, Katie. I told you." Brian emerged in the form of a consistent sweep of smoke. "Do I need to sound scarier for you," he said, and for the first time his intonation changed, a charged sibilance. "Do I need to sound scarier to convince you to listen to me, Katie? Was sacrificing myself not enough for you? What more would I need to do, Katie? Well, this must be it. Isn't it?" The front and back of the shape were impossible to discern, but there was a movement of some kind, a searching presence behind the fog.

Trevor looked up, and weakly punched at the shape from his sitting position. The blow changed from a strike to something else, to perhaps the way a man would cradle a precious stone, for when he passed his fingers through the aphotic shape it sparkled and bloomed like bioluminescence. A memory of Trevor pushing his hands through Biscayne Bay.

"Trevor, isn't it? You don't even know who I am, do you? Thanks to Katie's description, now I can see you." Brian's voice again was robotic and still; if there was emotion there, an explanation for the way the words sounded, then it came only through context.

Trevor took his hand back.

The shape didn't move, and neither did they. After what felt like minutes, Trevor slid up, steadying himself against the kitchen counter.

"Leave here, Trevor. Leave Katie. Leave her permanently, leave her forever. If she won't get you to leave, then maybe I can.

"Did Katie even tell you about me? You have to at least be able to guess who I am. Did Katie tell you how I died? Did Katie tell you about the anguish, about the pain I feel, continuous pain, pain in increments that you cannot even imagine, that you couldn't hope to imagine? Did she tell how much it hurts just to come back to this world? And when I say hurt, I'm not speaking poetically. I'm speaking of pain, the physical pain, of a creature living without an essential component of what it needs to survive. Imagine living without skin, Trevor. That's what it's like. I have no skin."

And he spoke and explained the pain of dislocation, caused by being abandoned and unloved and deserted, and he spoke with an ever-growing vigor, the rapidity of his speech belying the detached speech patterns, the ghost behind the machine.

"So you need to leave, Trevor. If only you could feel this pain, if only I could skin you, cook your organs and then put you back together again, then you could know what I'm feeling and I wouldn't ... I wouldn't have to persuade you like this. How pathetic I guess I am. All this abuse and I'm still wheedling. Begging for something even though I'm in the right.

“The guilt she feels; that feeling of guilt that any normal human would feel after taking another lover after the death of their partner ... there's a reason for that. There's a reason why every culture honors that guilt. So you need to leave, Trevor, and she needs to be alone, to love me, and to love me only, so I can move on. So I can be at rest."

And the fog dissipated.

Just like that, and it was gone.

"Katie!" Trevor yelled and ran toward her. She stood immobilized. Trevor put his arms around her and nudge-walked her to the couch. She sat, catatonic, staring ahead.

"Katie," he said again, this time forcefully, in an intimate whisper.

She felt a surge inside, of turmoil, of panic, coursing through her body and into her digits, her heartbeat accelerated, sweat formed at her brow; no, let her go back to being catatonic. She felt that she was going to lose control of her bladder and bowels; her stomach corkscrewed, a fire in the pit of her.

She shivered, looking around the room. How surreal, they were sitting in their respective spots of the couch, in their apartment, their apartment, a place that existed in the real world, a real place, reality ... and could they just go about their day, sitting on the couch, pretending like none of that happened? The thought was enticing, captivating: she wanted to be sucked up into that fantasy — yes, a fantasy, wake up, concentrate, her subconscious implored — and she just wanted to ignore Trevor's insistent bids for her attention and just turn on the television and forget the world. She even moved for the remote despite Trevor's rising panic and clicked, looking at the television absentmindedly, as she'd done a hundred times before ... and saw that it was still cracked, a nasty disfiguring scar across the face of it.

She broke down, tears pouring out of her, tears so fulsome that she could hardly breathe, her sinuses all clogged. She sputtered and curled her face into Trevor's chest, her excretions smearing his shirt with abandon.

"Katie," he said, putting his hands on her shoulders and pushing her back, but delicately, enough to get some space between so he can look her in the eyes and talk. "Katie! What was that? What, what is going on? Was that ... was that—"

"I'm sorry, I don't know what to say ... I — I don't know what to do! I haven't known what to do! Can you blame me?! It's impossible — this isn't possible ... It's not possible!" she repeated, and he agreed, it's not possible. He wasn't just forced into the microwave by a murky shape, they hadn't just conversed with a belligerent creature from the spirit world; but if it was a hallucination, then it was a shared one, and the deep sting on the back of his head abjured belief in fantasy explanations.

That had happened.

As if reading his thoughts, she cradled the back of his head with her left hand. "Forgive me, Trevor, I'm so sorry I forgot your head, are you okay?" She felt the slight dampness there, the ridge of the cut. "Oh my God, I need to get you a bandage."

"No! We need to speak about this! What are we going to do?"

"I don't know!" she sob-yelled. "I love you! I love you! I don't know what to do! I'm sorry I didn't tell you ...."

"It's okay," he said, overwhelmed with fear. Her panic was infectious. Run, he told himself. *Run, Run, Run, Run, Run, Run.*

"We'll think of something," he said, sotto voce but not meaning to, intending on speaking with authority. "I just ... we just need to think, what can we do, what can we do, what do we know ..." — *Run, Run, Run, Run, Run, Run, Run*, every nerve in his body hollered — "I love you, too. Sorry I didn't say it when you said it, but you know I love you, I'll never leave you." He meant that to sound like an assuring declaration of fidelity but, to him, it came out meekly, as if somewhere deep inside he knew he was signing his death warrant.

"Trevor, you have to leave, you have to get out. You have to leave me, that's the only thing that we can do, realistically," she said, still stuffed up and borderline inaudible. She hiccup-laughed, snorting on snot, thinking that she said "realistically," as if anything here was realistic.

"No. I can leave you temporarily, I can hide out for a time, but, no, I can't leave you. I'd never leave you. We need to figure out something long-term, how to stop this." He felt somehow like he was play-acting at stoicism, like he was performing before an omniscient adjudicator of virtue. *Run, Run, Run, Run, Run ...Run!* his body and senses, apoplectic, seemed to shout. He felt weak, like his own body was narcotizing itself, putting an end to his aspirational bleating. Maybe it was the injury to the back of his head. He felt woozy and dehydrated.

She hugged him, and he hugged her back.

"Ok," he bounded up — *Run, Run, RUN, RUN, RUN, RUUUUN!* — "tell me everything you can about this." He walked to the kitchen to fill two cups of water. He should go get a bandage but he didn't think the cut to his head was that bad, and he needed to think, can't waste time.

"Okay," she began, not knowing really how to start; what was there to say? "Brian had demand—"

Katie shrieked, an ugly, discordant yelp of panic. Her head rocketed into the arm of the couch and she swung wildly. Her face was ensconced, a bubble of tears and mucus. She was pressed into the couch and she felt a sharp force around her throat. "Help!" she managed to get out. "Help!" came another muffled plea.

"Katie!" she heard Trevor yell. She heard him run forward, but couldn't see, her surroundings viewed through an encroaching tenebrous prism. She felt Trevor's rushing momentum abruptly shift, heard a walloping noise and the unmistakable heft of a body colliding and collapsing against the far well.

"Don't worry, he's still alive.

"I've gathered strength. I've gotten more control over myself. It still hurts terribly, but I have more control now. Who knows how long this can last.

"It would never work. You'd never do it. You'd never sacrifice something for me, and if you did, you wouldn't love me. You never did, or if you did, you stopped a long time ago, well before I died."

"I love ... you ..." she gasped, the force pressing upon her too much to bear, she felt like she was sinking into quicksand.

"Don't say that." He couldn't tell if she was saying "love" or "loved" but it didn't matter.

"I love you. I love you," Katie insisted.

"No, you don't, and I'm doomed. I'm doomed to this. Things didn't work out in life, so why should they work out afterward? This is just it, this hell of an existence is it for me. I can't make amends, that ship has sailed, there's nothing I can do, you don't love me and never did, your ... loyalty now would do nothing for me, if it ever could. And I hate you now. I don't want to" — and as he spoke, somehow, he watched superimposed images of their first meeting; them making love for the first time; one of their cuddled conversations in the dark, her saying "I love you" and him holding on to that, storing it deep inside him; her forgiving him after he'd left her unattended at a work party and forgot their work-party battle plan, her holding his hand and promising there was no reason to feel so bad; her kissing his tears away when he felt bad about something, what he couldn't remember; them at a petting zoo in D.C., teasing her when a goat stuck his head in her Fossil Sydney Shopper bag and she freaked out; the two of them making jokes when he got a hemorrhoid for the first time, her making him an Epsom salt bath and sitting on the bathroom floor with him, reading, so he wouldn't be lonely while he sat in the tub; but the image that stuck the most was them hugging together in bed, so tight, forming a circle, an infinity sign, and those moments existed somewhere, never-ending……

"I don't want to but you left me like this. You don't love me and wouldn't sacrifice for me, you get to live your life and I'm doomed to this and you couldn't end my suffering for me, you could have but you didn't!"

"I ... love ... you ..." she pleaded again, her hands grabbing weakly, and he could tell that she was trying in vain to use her hands as pincers, hoping to find a tear in him so she could rip him out of this world.

"You better hope Trevor really loves you," Brian responded, and found a comforting finality in that.

Her throat tore viciously, violent spurts, her trying insanely to catch the copious liquid in her palm, as if to put it back in her neck to salvage herself. I'm dying, her mind exploded, I'm going to die.

Trevor came to during her death throes and rushed toward her. She was dead before he reached her. The moment he realized the face he held in her hands was not her anymore — was her lifeless, dead carcass; carcass, a word for animals in a slaughterhouse — he fell over and vomited. He wished he hadn't seen it — her primal fear, her askance look in his direction, as if he was going to be the last thing she ever saw, no, no, no, noooo, God no, God no — and he'd heard what Brian had said.

Love has its own dark morality and had been, he'd always thought, purely subjective. There were external indicators, he now knew, and, as heartbroken as he was, feared for his future.

Story Title Revealed About Halfway Through

THE OLD MAN had trouble getting up. Ryan Caskey recognized that old man: it was him. Everyone ages. He of course knew this day would eventually come.

Ryan didn't remember why he wanted to get up in the first place. Senescence, forgetfulness and immobility were the rewards at the end of the golden trail. Ryan. He shouldn't refer to himself as Ryan anymore. Did anyone call him Ryan anymore, on the rare occasions he spoke to someone, or was it always "Mr. Caskey" or "Sir?" Ryan was a young person's name. It no longer fit his reality.

He pushed himself up with his shaking, febrile arms. It was a slow process.

>< >< ><

Oh, you are watching him get up? We won't make you wait here until he gets up. Give us a couple of minutes and get back to us. Go make a cup of coffee and come back and he should be up.

>< >< ><

You're back. Now Ryan was up, and he still couldn't remember what the rush was. Did he need to go to the bathroom? No, although in his condition you can never be too sure. He was in his home, alone, no wife, no live-in nurse. Not at an old folks' home. He couldn't afford one of those.

So Ryan, in his most befitting yet still ill-smelling robe, shuffled over to the kitchen. He was up, might as well use this opportunity to make some food for himself. What could he make? No, really, what could he make? He thought of pasta and tomato sauce but even that felt like a Herculean effort. Lifting the pasta sauce was challenge enough. It was an iron dumbbell. What were they filling these bottles with, cement? He tried to unscrew the cap but that was a fool's errand: the lid was cemented with cement. Filled with cement, cemented with cement, his mind so fatigued it couldn't venture through the thicket of his thoughts to come upon any other words. You used to be verbose, try harder, but just thinking of other words was exhausting.

He tried another thought. What did they do, put mud in these sauce cans? But that was no good. And what did it matter, who did he have to talk to, anyway?

So he made a bowl of raisin bran. He used the cleanest dirty bowl in his sink. It's fine, he thought without thinking. He had no fresh milk so he ate it dry, the cereal cardboard for his parched throat. He really only ate the raisins. The whole process — preparing, taking the bowl, sitting, eating — took humiliatingly long. He had no one to be humiliated in front of; he felt humiliated only because there existed the faint memory of a time when he wasn't old and embroiled in the concerns of the aged and dowdy. There was a stink around the apartment that he knew was just the smell of unwashed flesh exacerbated by whatever bacteria flourished on the aged.

>< >< ><

Look, can you come back in a few minutes? Time is relative and he's too old to know any better, just come back whenever, just let him eat in peace. It makes no difference.

>< >< ><

Ryan's bladder was pressing with fluid, and he made to go and relieve himself. Please let me make it this time, he thought, the same plea he thought every day. He was using his walker for support, to his chagrin. He was still prideful and used it sparingly, only when absolutely necessary.

He wouldn't make it. His leg was wet and he was reaching because something else was wrong. Frightening dagger-pins in his lower back, the work of a flying sadistic demon, crazy old people thoughts; no, your thoughts, you are the old person, Ryan. Ryan, you are the old person, and this is just an old person dying, heart attack, kidney failure, who knows, who cares.

>< >< ><

"Emmmnmn!," Ryan grunted. Dr. Henry Grobeau's calming palm cradling the back of his neck. Dr. Grobeau's metal-clamp black desk lamp, usually just obnoxiously bright, was now ferociously so. Ryan hand-swatted to signal Dr. Grobeau to pivot the light away from him. He did so.

Ryan took stock of his surroundings. On his back on Dr. Grobeau's couch. Same office as always, the office he visited twice weekly. His appointments were usually 6-7 p.m. Mondays and Wednesdays, but it felt later than 7. He was famished.

And he could drive to get a burger if he wanted to. Or he could make food at home. He could do whatever he wanted, because he was twenty-four and in good health. The same age he'd been when he arrived for his appointment earlier that night. The same age he'd be when he went back home, watched television, did push-ups, read, jerked off, or did any such thing. He was young: a short word of five letters with a million implications and inferences. To be young was to be at the peak of living. To be young was when goals could be met. To be young was to be alive, for fuckssake.

"I think that sound you just made upon waking was the most excitable I've ever seen or heard you in the three years you've been coming to see me."

"Mmmhmmm. I don't doubt it." And Ryan smiled, too, breathing heavily, so happy to be young and alive. The joyfulness of a rapidly beating heart. The sensual delights of adrenaline. He could get out and run a marathon. When was the last time he felt this way? Ever?

"And you're smiling, too. We've created a monster here, folks. I think that's the first time I've seen you unguarded, Ryan."

"I don't doubt that, either." Week after week, month after month, Ryan came to see Dr. Grobeau, his cognitive therapist, to cogitate his way out of his depression. Because with a cognitive therapist, what else do you do but cogitate? Cogitate was the right word. At times it had been cajole, persuade, argue, plead, inveigle, explicate, articulate, beseech, demand, implead, supplicate. No, those words weren't really accurate, not fully. Sure, there was a core of truth to them. But to describe Ryan's behavior and "method of expression" (a Dr. Grobeau phrase) with such a litany of colorful verbs obscured more than it revealed: for, truthfully, mainly Ryan talked dispassionately. Dispassionately, that was the word.

For Ryan had a problem, that much he knew, and that problem was that he couldn't really be depressed, for how could one be depressed if one's mood never changed. It wasn't a depression: it was a life-long drought. It was a permanent plateau. For he had no passion for life, because he knew that the thrills of life (to the extent such things could be classified as thrills) were temporary and not worth the trouble of the pursuit.

Ryan didn't talk about this with anyone other than Dr. Grobeau. He didn't like talking about it because when you don't care about things, you don't care to express yourself, either. His thoughts weren't important enough to express. There were plenty of insufferable boys and girls around the world who probably shared that same insight, but expressed them as a pretext, with an ulterior motive, to be congratulated for their cleverness or insight. Those were the people who knew such feelings were a passing phase, or maybe even a fad. You know they don't believe it when they talk about it. Oh, how fun it is to be a depressed loudmouth contrarian skeptic, isn't it? All those junior league rhetoricians who couldn't wait to corner you and impress you with their arguments and philosophies. These new atheists, neo-nihilists, anti-natalists, whatever they were, they were all annoying.

Ryan wasn't like that. That gave him a sense of pride.

But really he didn't care. No, really. See, he'd tried in the past talking with other likeminded people, tried finding a kindred community online. There was an infinitesimal ping of "satisfaction" in finding a like-minded person. But he didn't care. See, that was the problem. He just ... didn't ... care. And he suffered because of it. He was a pragmatist, and it's hard to be a pragmatist when you're too lazy to live. It wasn't cool. This handicap wasn't cool. Barely functioning isn't cool.

Nihilism wasn't a cause that inspired you to go out and seek converts.

Not caring is a type of death sentence. A living death.

The end.

But it hadn't always been that way, he had to admit. There'd been some things he'd been passionate about in his youth, weren't there? There were. Being a good person, that had always been important to him, and he had prided himself on his punctuality and manners. And if he was really a nihilist, deep down, why would he care about things like that?

And he believed in medical science, and wasn't entirely opposed to the idea that this nihilism, depression, whatever you want to call it, had some deep-seated, reversible foundation. So in the depths of his torpor, he agreed to the last-ditch effort of Dr. Grobeau's enhanced hypnotism.

"You know, I hate to say it, Dr. Grobeau. I mean, you know I hate to say something worked. It would be devastating to me to say something worked."

"You have a reputation to maintain, after all."

"I know, right? I'm not saying I'm still not a grouch, but I have to hand it to you Dr. Grobeau, that therapy worked. Hypnotism worked. I saw myself as like, an old, dying man. It was terrifying, really."

"Tell me more."

"It's, of course, it's funny. Of course, getting old is something we all know is coming. But, being old, being alone, to sort of, to 'see' that, in a way. I don't know. It ... I feel like it kick-started the battery. It's like, maybe nothing matters on a grand scale, I don't know. But I can be depressed and pathetic when I'm old. Why waste my youth on that? I don't want that life. To be old, alone. I want something better. I have plans, you know, I've had plans. Things I've thought about doing for a long time but never did."

"Painting, I know."

That's not what he was referring to, but sure. He wasn't a half-bad painter but he hadn't tried his hand at it since he was a teenager. "Yeah, things like that. Maybe I don't have the answers, but I have to at least try to do things. Like the things I've always wanted to do in life. This is a step in the right direction. That really was terrifying, Dr. Grobeau. That needs to come with a real trigger warning."

"Hah! Well, sometimes you need to rub those wires together to get the engine beating!"

"I'll say."

>< >< ><

It was almost 8 p.m. The session had run long, but Dr. Grobeau realized quickly that the hypnotism was working. After three years of fairly fruitless therapy sessions, of psychotropic drugs, of two-person book clubs of *Feeling Good* and *Mind Over Mood* and *Feeling Good Together* and *The Mindful Way Through Depression* and *The Will to Meaning*, and, boy could he go on and on, Dr. G would set his medical license aflame before he'd interrupt something that actually appeared to be working. Ryan had been fidgeting in his trance-state, in mild combat with something, and that — detecting a perceptible feeling in the young man — was a breakthrough.

Such an impermeable monotone the boy had. Never smiled.

Seemed to understand humor, could emphasize a punchline, but even when he said something funny or insightful he derived no joy from it, learned nothing from it. He was a boy who didn't suffer from a dearth of self-insight. He knew himself all too well. He was what he was and believed it would never change. He'd been a boy buried under six feet of earth and all their conversations prior had been tantamount to "so you recognize you are six feet underground? How does that make you feel?" At the end of their prior sessions, the weight upon him was still there, immobile.

But this breakthrough was something.

And even better, Ryan looked at him and shook his hand and said, "Thanks, Doctor. I feel, I really feel inspired, seriously. You know I wouldn't say that."

"I know you wouldn't."

"I feel like ... I feel like, again, I might not know exactly what to do, but I need to try now, while I'm young and I can do things. I have to work on my goals. I need to be true to myself."

"I'm so glad to hear that. See you next week?"

"Of course. Thanks Doctor."

>< >< ><

"Y'all coming?" Caroline asked, waiting for Mitch to catch up to her at the entrance of the convenience store. "Y'all coming" wasn't really a question, more like a statement.

"Y'all? There's only one of me. I may be big, but I ain't several different people. You North Carolina people really do talk funny," Mitch responded. Mitch was short for Mitchell but everyone called him Mitch so that's what he went by.

"Puh-lease, my name is Caroline, that's basically Carolina, so take my word for it. I'm the authority and it's you South Carolina people who are all confused. Besides, plenty of people from South Carolina say 'Y'all,' if you haven't noticed. As they should."

"All right, all right, point taken, point taken," and Mitch lowered his head slightly and made a weird upward swing with his hand that was supposed to invoke some Southern-style courtesy.

They made a beeline for the candy. The other people in the convenience store, assuming they were even interested in the mundane conversation of strangers, might just think they were a happy couple, with their general smiling and good spirits. But the more discerning could perhaps pick up the forced notes in their brittle gaiety. For Mitch and Caroline were only on their third date, where minor distinctions and factoids were still being dragooned into duty as the predicates for conversation. See, Caroline was from North Carolina, and only a month ago relocated to South Carolina. Pretty innocuous and unexceptional. A thin reed to hang conversation on.

But if you were Mitch, who was understandably nervous and desperate to keep talking, you'd act as if this was a distinction of some importance, despite neither Caroline nor Mitch caring too much about the merits of their respective home states. But Caroline, also a bit nervous, played along, because Mitch was pleasant and good-looking and, just perhaps, being pleasant and good-looking was enough to merit a third date when you were new in town, and the town itself — the euphonious but not at all Romanesque Florence, South Carolina — didn't appear to have too many options for single women in their mid-30s.

Caroline looked younger, which invidiously made her even less interested in the "newly single" (read: divorced) middle-aged men who seemed to exclusively populate the online dating services. That she was blonde, relatively fit and well-proportioned, and cursed with a coquettishly high-voice rendered an oleaginous inference to everything older men did to court her. That they responded favorably to her, obviously attracted to her, counterintuitively grossed her out. Just imagining that perhaps they thought she's younger than she was, like they "scored" by getting a date with a woman they perhaps thought was half their age, meanwhile knowing they had an ex-wife or, even worse, a young child of their own ... ugh. Cast a pall on the whole thing, and maybe she was entirely wrong, but this was dating, not a criminal trial, and if she was wrong in her assumptions, she owed no one any right of appeal.

So Mitch, being actually a year younger than her, combined with all the other factors, was enough to get her, albeit with mixed feelings, on this third date.

They were in line at the convenience store, buying candy for the movie theater. Caroline turned back to Mitch.

"I'm real country, as you can tell. I know maybe it's a South Carolina custom, you know, all that fancy Charleston money, to go buy candy at the movie theater, you know, after taking out a home loan to afford it, but convincing you to prep ahead and buy the candy at the store, that's country-smarts. I hope you appreciate that."

"Hah, no, I appreciate that country-smarts. I thought it might be a trap, you know, like a lady on the first date slowly reaching for the check. Just let the record show that I was more than happy to buy you candy and drinks at the movie theater. I'd still certainly buy you drinks afterward, though. The day is young, still."

"Oh, drinks, maybe? Let's not get ahead of ourselves now, huh?" She gave him a flirty smile — something he'd appreciate, she knew, the gestures that led to positive reinforcement occurring to her almost automatically, a lifelong tendency coaxed into habit through her career in sales — and thought to herself that she was being misleading, felt bad about being misleading, and then realized, was she being misleading? She hadn't formed an opinion about him yet. She didn't know anything about the language and customs of pre-relationship dating: the whole process had a weird, inscrutable energy.

"Would you really have been happy to have paid crazy prices at the theater?"

"Well, let's be real, I wouldn't be super happy about it, exactly, and I always do appreciate a good bargain, but I'd certainly have done it. I think it's a cool thing. Early movie, convenience store candy: you are a cool, different lady. I don't want to talk too loudly about sneaking candy in. You already got me committing crimes for you. I don't want to get caught. Who knows if you'd still date me after I got out of the clink!?"

As they walked across the parking lot to the theater, he thought how he'd be grateful for when the movie started and he could enjoy the respite of silence, of not having to perform. He wasn't a natural talker.

It was an early showing, only 3:15 p.m. on a Saturday. Caroline liked day movies. Movies were enjoyable but not particularly exciting, and she liked keeping her nights open for the possibility of something enriching or unique, whatever that might be. Also, weekend night showings tended to be populated by loud, chaotic teenagers, who had always annoyed her (even when she herself was a loud, chaotic teenager). Nowadays, teenagers filled her with fearful unease. Especially in boring little cities like Florence, where teenagers didn't seem to have anything to do, and traveled en mass to movies or malls.

Also, most people didn't like matinee showings — especially not suitors — so suggesting them was a good way of weeding out the stubbornly uncool.

So, a matinee showing it was.

Here they were.

><><><

They were seeing *Pretty Deadly*, a comic book adaptation unfamiliar to both of them, but which had gotten pretty good reviews and proved to be a surprising commercial success, given that is was something like a supernatural Western. Mitch didn't know about it. It had been Caroline's choice, and given all of the superhero and comic book movies that dominated the multiplex, this one seemed at least like an interesting one, presented as something like a prestige picture. That was something Mitch liked about her: she made decisions. She could decide anything and he'd be down, as long as he got to be included.

He thought it best to look like a man of action, so he selected their seats. Really a no-brainer: about four rows back from the screen, left center. No one sat in front of them, or even in the same row. He explained his Goldilocks decision making — not too close, not too far, center of vision — and she responded, "We make a good team. You make the responsible decisions, I make the fun ones."

She flash-opened her pocket book, his bright yellow peanut M&M's bags unmistakable. The obvious Pavlovian implications of her impish grin and the stutter-start wrist-twitch act of flashing — even flashing a goddamn pocketbook of candy — shot him through with a surge of excitement, his heart skipping a beat. Oh boy.

He smiled but said nothing. After they settled in, he turned around to assess the theater and also to buy time (with her fond feelings, best for him to let the movie start and shut up, as if those fond feelings would stay preserved throughout the movie as a matter of right). He'd been a bouncer during college, and inculcated some good instincts that were subconsciously linked to preservation and assessment. Exits, weirdos, stuff like that. Pretty small theater, which made sense, as this movie had come out a while ago. Maybe only 15 rows, 8 seats per row, bisected down the middle into equal halves. Closest people were a teenage couple, two rows behind theirs. Some solo old people in the back, enjoying those senior citizen discounts. Biggest group was a group of three, which bode well for any potential noise disturbances.

The lights dimmed and the movie experience began, which nowadays meant the interminable advertisements wholly unrelated to movies, save for maybe a dumb pun. *Do Phones Dream?* One advertisement asked, displaying garish green swirls meant to be trippy. *If they did dream*, he thought, *I hope they'd have more interesting dreams than that.* Didn't look like anyone was going to sit in front of them. As long as no super-tall guy sat in front of them, this should be all good.

This wasn't the type of movie that attracted a late arrival crowd, but you never know.

He unfolded his hand toward her, open palm.

"Want a high-five? Or would that be a middle five?" she asked.

"Scalpel," he said in a low monotone. The way he said it felt like a movie reference or something, but he couldn't even remember what movie or pop culture he was referencing. He opened and closed his fingers greedily.

"I always wanted to be a doctor, when I was young, actually."

"If you only wanted to be a doctor when you were young, then you didn't always want to be a doctor." He'd intended that to be playful, just one smartly delivered line in a flirty joust of repartee, but his hushed tone added a finicky delivery. He also worried what he said didn't actually make sense. What did that even mean? As if to overcompensate for that persnickety tone, he over-pumped his hand, as if to say, 'I didn't mean it like that, I'm really just a silly kid.'

"I meant that in a good way."

"Sure you did," she said, unclear herself of what he meant.

She thought of a stand-up special she'd seen, where the comedian talked about dating in middle age and asking his dates: "So, what did you *want* to be when you grew up?"

She dropped the M&M's in the pulsing Venus flytrap of his hand, which he quickly unwrapped.

"To be continued," he said, as the commercials ended and the first preview began. "You're free to have some of my candy, of course."

"Don't eat all of it before the movie starts, because like hell you aren't getting any of my candy."

"Oh boy," he said, also not sure why, sure she was joking but she was speaking a bit too loud for a movie theater. So much of dating depended on visual cues, he realized, and staring straight ahead in a darkened theater certainly wasn't conducive to that. Why was he being so sensitive? She seemed fine and like she was having a good time. Still, he wanted to gently squeeze her hand, and her to give him a gentle squeeze back, just as a sign that he didn't need to worry for any reason that he’d been acting boorish or stupid, confirmation that his dumb little comment hadn't been interpreted as something insensitive or weird or malicious or whatever. This was stupid, this was just a date, calm down.

But he did like her, he knew. She was pretty and fun and smart. He wanted to know that she liked him. God, he sounded like an overeager kid. It was depressing to think these needful feelings never go away.

She had gotten Swedish Fish, which is a sign of quality, he thought. Of all the candies to get, they were the most grown-up. A refined palate. Them, or maybe Peppermint Patties.

>< >< ><

Ryan sat down, the only person in his row. His plan couldn't be effectuated if there was no one in front of or next to him. There was an older couple, maybe late 30s or early 40s, a couple rows in front of him, and some solo old people behind him toward the back. A pretty sparse attendance, though he expected as much. There was a teenage couple also a row behind him.

His choice of movie and show time had vexed him quite a bit. He had to pick judiciously. Could he go to some big comic book blockbuster or Transformers 4000 or something on a Friday opening and really be angry at idiots talking loudly during the movie? Maybe that was part of the experience? That’s like going to a special ed class and complaining about there being too many retards.

No, the real crucible would be going to a real prestige project like this and having some idiots blather through that. So, the best showing, he figured, would be a critically acclaimed, mid-tier film at an odd time. Ergo, this one.

He had to continually convince himself that this made him feel great, that he was being proactive. Rather than just going through life, subjecting himself to the whims of others, just taking it, he was out, scouting, putting his own plan into action. No longer did he have to suffer in silence at some aggressive, inconsiderate asshole's obliviousness; now, such a person was just setting himself up, unwittingly, as a potential target.

Maybe just thinking of going through with it was enough.

He felt at his right pocket, which held a folded-up Gerber serrated knife, which he'd had since he was in high school. Just push the lever and pull the blade back and, schnict! (he liked to imagine the noise), out comes the 5-inch blade. Only with knives could you brag about packing a 5-incher. And in his left pocket was its buddy, another Gerber-brand, a little shorter — 4 inches — not serrated but having a wicked-looking hooked curve. Stabby and Gutty, he called them, always in that order — Stabby in his left pocket, Gutty in his right — though he'd never used either of them to stab or gut anything, except maybe frustrating plastic packaging.

Maybe he wouldn't go through with this. This was probably a good movie, and he was interested in watching it. People view art in almost moral terms, and this was supposed to be a good movie, so the people who selected this movie to watch couldn't be all bad, right? They had to have some redeeming qualities. This wasn't some big dumb lowest common denominator comedy, some Fat-Man-Fall-Down type of movie. But then again, that group might consist of families, just parents looking to distract their kids for a bit, maybe not really people worthy of an untimely death, exactly.

The calculus of retribution was trickier than he'd first thought.

As the movie started in earnest, he stood up to head toward the back row. He registered a flash of light as he turned, coming from a few rows in front of where he'd previously been sitting. A cell phone. Marked for death, he thought gaily, as if this was all just a joke. What was he doing, what a hypocrite, right, he himself had stood up right as the movie began, certainly a faux paus. Cast no stones, right?

He calmly paced toward the back row. Just him and a very old man, someone he imagined might have just been deposited here by an old folks' homes, or maybe a sad old man movie theater townie, someone who just showed up to whatever was playing. He gave the man a seat-wide breadth and watched alongside him.

>< >< ><

Caroline texted on her phone. It was brief, as texts go. Just one text. But she did it so blithely. Nothing to suggest it was an emergency, or she'd checked her phone in error, no post-text apology-face. Not even a half-cocked phone, an effort to minimize the glare. Nope, just felt the vibration, looked, texted back, put the phone back on her person, still on, and then focused her attention back on the screen.

It'd been a work text and she needed to respond to help close a deal.

>< >< ><

Ryan enjoyed movies, had the utmost respect for them. The goal of art was to present something that got through your defenses. Through all his nihilistic torpor, he always responded strongly to art. That's why he was here, to preserve and defend art, and to strike a blow against the boorish incivility that so infected society that people didn't even notice it anymore.

This movie was proceeding along nicely, well-acted, interesting camera shots and scene composition, one solid action set piece so far. He wasn't riveted, but he was enjoying himself. He looked over at the old man, curious if he could glean an opinion from his body language. He always wondered what the average, casual moviegoer thought about the films. In another life, it'd be cool to have worked in movie polling or something like that.

The old man didn't seem to really be paying attention. *Wouldn't it be funny if this man was dying or something, having a stroke, and I noticed it and saved him? Oh, the irony. That'd be perfect.* Ryan focused more on the old man to see if there was any such thing happening, but no, the man just seemed out of it in that old, desiccated way, that state of being redolent of creeped-out grandchildren on forced family visits, mothballs, ancient sucking candies and deeply-yellow stale urine. He thought of his hypnotism session and shuddered.

Ryan watched as best as he could down toward the front aisle, where the "cellphone-woman" sat. He couldn't see anything far away, but the inability to confirm what he suspected she was doing — texting away, being inconsiderate — only served to anger him further. As luck would have it, the theater wasn't too big and he had a clear line of sight on her, and while he saw no light or anything, he felt she shifted and fidgeted in some tell-tale way. Not in a way that showed she was necessarily texting, but in a way that showed she was indolent, distracted, impatient, all the concomitant personality flaws that lead one to the ultimate sin of movie texting.

And it's not like he was crazy: everyone hated movie-theater texters, everyone knew it was a problem — movie theater attendance has been plummeting precisely because of these awful people — but nobody did anything about it other than grouse. It was like there existed a poisonous fog that only he was susceptible to; people wondered, what's the big deal, get over it, what are you complaining about? No, it was worse than that; it was like there was a poisonous fog that everyone was susceptible to except they all wore gas masks while he refused. Why should he change the way he lived when he was living the right way?

He didn't like that faulty logic and it bothered him. His logic could be unsound at times, but that didn't mean the emotional thrust of his actions was wrong. The specifics could be wrong but the gestalt was correct. He'd have many defenders, he knew.

Ryan concentrated his attention on the old man and invented stories for him. He wanted to speak to him, ask him about his life. Administer him food — soup, he figured, naturally — or even give him a soap bath. The man was probably all alone. The world was so sad. That's really what it was, wasn't it? The world was so sad, and his crusade was one thing that people should be joining in to make the world a better place: respecting others, not ruining the enjoyment that comes with the shared experience of public art, of high spectacle. Standing athwart the rapid degradation of society and yelling *STOP!* That's what he was doing, and this restored mental vigor excited him.

>< >< ><

What was he doing here, really? This was all fun and good but he wasn't going to hurt anybody. He'd never hurt anyone, not even when he'd had credible claims to self-defense in school. Everyone had tussles in high school; not him, he'd skulked away, kept quiet.

The closest he came to violence, let's see, was in high school, when he'd once driven around town while holding Stabby. Just cruising. Calling it cruising makes it sound cool, doesn't it? He'd just been cruising, bored on a school night, until he started following some pretty blonde's car. At least, he remembers her as a pretty blonde. He didn't remember why he followed her, but he just did. Not for that long. She eventually pulled into a house on a cul-de-sac and he drove past her and she remembers she looked at him, that kind of skeptical and judgmental face that pretty blondes have perfected, while maybe some members of her family were coming out of the house to greet her or repel him, and he just drove off, counting it all as a victory.

There was another incident, of course, like he could forget. In college, he snuck into the dorm room of a female student who lived on his floor. *Snuck into* sounds dramatic. He'd knocked on her dorm door, but knowing it was empty and would be empty for a while. Appearances' sake only. He then pushed it open. Kelli, that had been her name. He didn't know her roommate or remember exactly why he knew they wouldn't be around. But anyway, he went into the room and for a couple seconds walked around in that innocent way, that plausibly deniable way. Closing the door behind him was also closing the door on that deniability. He poked around, finding her bras and underwear but doing nothing with them, having no interest in whatever fetishes lead men to want to fool around with undergarments. Knowing he should leave and having no reason not to, he opened her closet, his countenance bemused, as if still appearing innocent for imagined spectators watching his life unfolding on the screen.

He'd gone into the closet and closed the door. It had been the middle of the day and the dorm room windows were open so there was still enough light to see. He had grabbed a loose hanger and made a hook with it in his hand, arching his arm as if waiting to strike, making a demonic face. How crazy would it be if she showed up right now, opened her closet, saw this boy she knew and maybe kinda sorta liked, now with the face of a frenzied baboon, makeshift hook in his hand?

He'd bit the hook of the hanger and threw it on the ground. He'd tucked his hands into this armpits and clucked silently, walking around the small closet like he was a chicken. He was crazy, he'd told himself, right then at that moment. He'd snuck into a girl's room, hid in her closet, and was clucking around like a chicken. This is the end for me, he had thought. Those were the actions of an objectively crazy person. But maybe that was something he was just telling himself to obscure the fact that he wasn't crazy, that there was some reasoning underlying his madness, an unexplored foundation fueling his rage.

He'd stealthily left the girl's apartment and went back to his dorm room, and it was like it never happened at all.

><><><

Mitch looked over at Caroline. Or over her shoulder, at least. She was fidgeting with her phone, he could see the refracted soft glow that slipped through her fingers. She looked back at him quickly, friendly.

"Want any candy?" she asked-offered in a warm-hearted whisper.

"No thanks," he replied.

His glances hadn't signaled anything to her about the propriety of texting, and he resumed his focus on the film, his deep nasal exhale the circumspect version of a groan.

STABBING PEOPLE WHO TALK OR TEXT IN MOVIE THEATERS TO FUCKING DEATH

Ryan thought that maybe he should make a movie about his crusade for movie theater etiquette. That's a nonviolent way to get his message across, a possibility which carried the improbable but not impossible chance of acclaim and celebrity. Eh, he had no film experience, nor time nor money to invest in a project. He was like that, a hundred unpursued fancies that he nursed for years until they turned sour, reminders of his reneging on himself.

So the movie went on and Ryan watched, keeping an eye, as best he could, on his fellow moviegoers. Nothing jumped out at him and he didn't want to jostle or be a distraction, oh, the irony there. He went to the bathroom and looked at himself in the mirror. Yup, that was him. The mirror was smeared somehow, and he saw himself abstractly, the smearing playing weird tricks of perspective on his face. Too cliché. He often thought in cinematic terms, in camera angles and mise–en–scène. He read somewhere that people who wish to create art, but don't, end up making art out of their own lives.

He looked at himself in another mirror, one unblemished and directly under the light. There was no one else in the bathroom with him so he smiled, a big chomping smile that, accentuated by the lighting, could land him in a toothpaste commercial. He expected a canine tooth to twinkle.

What a wily guy he was.

He returned to the theater, edging back to his latest seat selection. The old man didn't look back up at him. To think, before that experiment with Dr. Grobeau he had bottled himself up completely, convinced himself that nothing mattered. But that wasn't true: that was just what he'd told himself because he'd felt so forlornly ineffectual. He had a tune in his head that he called the hero's homecoming.

That feeling was ephemeral, as short-lived as the scene in the movie he was watching. He experienced such an entangled combination of thoughts and emotions. His emotions were like fingers intertwined together, or kudzu overtaking a tree, such a mess he couldn't even begin to sort. He felt silly, deep down knowing that he was fooling himself, that he wasn't going to do anything, he was just going to go home and rue, just like he always did.

It was better to not care, to be numb. That realization plunged himself deeper somewhere, not deeper into anger, really, but one of anger's cousins, pride. Some emotion that scorched his throat. Meshed with all these emotions, somehow, was a deep-love and affection for the world. He knew it was a contradiction. Despite the bile in his throat and the shame and aggrievement that inhabited his body, he thought of taking care of that old man, volunteering, working at a soup kitchen, doing *something* of value. Losing himself, somehow, submerging his eddying emotions into productive, beneficial activities, something that would lift his spirits and make him feel connected to something larger, either humanity at large or whatever psychological fulfillment that came from working steadily on a labor of love.

Perhaps as a way to obfuscate these feelings, or re-direct them through physical action, or choke off what he feared was the flowering of "weak" feelings, he wrapped his left arm around the old man's face. Maybe he was doing this to be irresponsible, to get caught, to end this; the equivalent of being atop the bridge, feeling vertigo, and jumping to end the psychological anticipation and dislocation.

He moved his arm surreptitiously, but securely enough to prevent the old man from yelling.

It was a cruel joke that he was playing on no one but himself. Still he felt those feelings of love, communion, the wish to help this old man while he squeezed, as if watching the scene from afar as an observer sadly shaking his head.

This would lock him in. Maybe that was his motivation: end his infernal doubting, his chronic inanition. If he killed this old man, he had to carry out his plan. He couldn't back out, let this old man die in vain.

See, if you'd stopped dicking around, if you'd taken action against those who truly deserved it, the self-absorbed pricks and cunts who cut people off, who talk too loud, who expect everything and give nothing back, then you wouldn't be here now, torturing this old man now, would you? God, he wanted someone to stop him. He almost laughed: he wanted to stand up and yell "somebody stop him!" as he continued squeezing the air out of this old man's lungs. It was true, he didn't want to be doing this, but once he started, he couldn't stop. What purpose would be served by killing a harmless old man? Why wasn't anyone noticing him? But no one was, because no one ever knows or cares about anything other than themselves. The old man pushed on Ryan's knee, only at the very end, maybe serving as his version of an exclamation mark on this whole sad affair.

He couldn't look at the body, resting permanently in its seat .... The man was surely dead. Ryan's left hand stayed python-gripped around the old man's neck for minutes after the man had stopped breathing. He didn't know what the man looked like and he couldn't bear to graft a physiognomy onto his shame.

>< >< ><

And why did this old man die? Because those fucking uncivil assholes, those talkers, those texters, those line cutters, those abrasive, self-absorbed art-ruiners the world over had been allowed to flourish unabated. This was Ryan's tragic beginning, the tragedy he'd never get over.

His penitence would come from the death of the deserving.

He looked down at the bitch near the front row and her asshole male enabler. No version of justice would sanction the murder of that innocent old man yet allow the pardon of those guilty parties. If he were to go to the gallows, he had to make sure some feeble version of justice was imposed. He thought of that poor innocent old man, who died in a sense for their sins, for the sins of everyone who acted with careless impunity and went unpunished, in this society of tech-enhanced narcissists and their craven enablers. The emotion bubbled inside him, his shame dissolving like an Alka-Seltzer tablet in the coursing, mounting bile of his rage.

>< >< ><

Ryan stood up and moved down the aisle, sitting directly behind the man. The texting woman — she wasn't texting at that moment, but to him, she would always be "the texting woman" — sat beside the man. Ryan sat in silent, steaming judgment of what the woman did. The man, too, was to blame, for it's fair to judge a person by the company he keeps, and the man had failed to intervene and remind her about the proper etiquette expected by non-barbarians experiencing art in a paid, public setting.

Ryan made an extended chute of his right sleeve and furtively took hold of Gutty. Swathed by his sleeve, he clicked the knife open. He opened Stabby carefully, while keeping it in his left pocket, and positioned it so the blade poked upward. Easy grabbing. Gutty, he kept in his right hand, underneath the protective cloak of his sleeve-encased hand. He rocked back and forth: silently, of course, so as not to cause a distraction to the other theatergoers. He could plan murder and still be respectful of other people's viewing experience.

>< >< ><

The movie was pretty good, Caroline concluded. It was fun, serious enough to be engaging but not without a sense of humor and panache. The violence was a little more than she expected, though. "Good God!" she said at one point, when one character took a shotgun blast to the face. "Can you believe that?"

"Yeah," Mitch responded.

Other times when she blurted something he'd not respond, just nod or something.

Movies were a weird date, she realized. They were a good date for hanging out with someone you didn't really want to engage with. They should be reserved for first dates, last dates, or parental obligations. They should have gone to a wine bar, there was a good one in town. She felt like she didn't have the patience anymore to watch movies. She barely watched movies at home without doing something else such as surfing the internet, folding laundry or chatting with friends.

The camera stayed on the lead actress's bare back as she bathed herself with a bucket. What was that actress’s name, Teresa something? Right as the scene ended, she turned around almost completely, both of her heavy breasts — especially heavy for her slender frame — exposed.

"Whoa there, hello there boobies, no wonder you picked this movie, eh?"

Mitch quietly snort-laughed, only loud enough to signal he heard her.

Ryan sat behind them, listening, his gut, throat, nerve endings and all the other parts of him that alighted at the wrongs of others, all the place where his vengeance emanated, all quaking in righteous ecstasy. He was eagle-eyed to her slouching, bat-eared to all her insufferable, asinine comments. All he needed was the ideal moment to strike. He needed to do it while his temper flared beyond the point of misgivings. If he lost his resolve, he’d just think of the old man.

The man in front of him leaned toward his mate, said something softly, stood up and made his way toward the back. Going to the bathroom, most likely. This could be his chance. Imagine the beau, coming back to the theater, his girlfriend dead. Finally quiet. Would he even notice? Maybe he'd wonder why she wasn't being intrusive and obnoxious. Maybe he'd think, thank God, she got the message.

No, that wasn't realistic. Maybe the man was walking out on his own, fed up with her behavior? No, talk about unrealistic. He was almost certainly using the bathroom. This could be his chance! But if the man was only peeing, he'd surely be back in a minute or so. Or maybe ... he could go the bathroom and stealthily kill the man, stow the body somewhere. That would give him the time he needed to kill the girl unmolested. For if he attacked the lady while the man was sitting next to her, the man could overpower him, stop him even, before the deed was done.

Ryan got up and made his way to the bathroom. He saw the man washing his hands. Ryan froze, silently envisioning flinging Stabby effortlessly into the man's thick throat. The man was bigger and broader than him, and had the mien of a man who knew how to fight, or at least a man who engaged in stereotypically manly activities. A UFC-looking lunkhead type. The man finished washing his hands, dried them off on his hands, nodded at Ryan — who was still by the doorway — and left the bathroom, no doubt going back to the theater.

"Man, your girl is a talker, isn't she?" Ryan wished he could say, and the man would make an eye-rolley face to show that he knew, say something like, "Yeah man, I know, I can't take her anywhere" or something, and then all of Ryan's anger would probably dissipate. An acknowledgement, a meager form of atonement. That's all he wanted, really.

Ryan peed at the urinal, staring blankly ahead. Who could see the thoughts in his head? If only they knew. As he washed his hands — something he almost never did when he peed, but he did now to be dilatory — he thought how cool it was that no one knew what he was thinking.

He went back inside the movie theater, hands around the knives in his pockets.

He took mental note of the two teenagers who had their feet up on the seats in front of them. No one was sitting directly in front of them, true, but rather a couple seats in front and over. Maybe the people in the row in front of the teenagers wanted to sit in front of the teenagers, but chose otherwise because of that rude imposition? People who put their feet up in movies were another type of consistent vermin. Policing the ethics of moviegoers was exhausting.

Ryan sat, waiting. He tried to focus only on the ambient sound of the theater, the blood pumping in his ears. If you assume that human life is important and has moral value, then the decision to take another life was an important decision imbued with value. Contemplating these weighty decisions was much more exciting than anything else he'd be doing; when his mind was locked into this task, all the doldrums and middling depressions that otherwise had free reign throughout his mind were locked out.

Who to strike? Which would be the better subversion of expectations ... to kill the texting woman, or her complicit beau, or switch gears entirely and go after the foot-resting teenage couple? He couldn't dither for the whole film.

Where before his decisions would be limited to the best way to distract himself from the creeping futilities of the day, now his decisions directly impacted the lives of others. Plotting murder was freighted with responsibility, and he took those responsibilities seriously. As Dix Steele put it, there was no sacrifice too great for a chance at immortality.

>< >< ><

An on-screen explosion sounded. Mitch winced slightly, moving his eyes to keep time with the arcing camera shot, although his attention had lapsed at some point (was it hot in here?) and he wasn't sure about the significance of why that girl shot that guy. Maybe that was something that'd be explained later? But the movie was almost over.

"Why'd she do that?" Caroline leaned in to ask.

He leaned toward her. "I think—"

Caroline turned her box of Swedish Fish toward Mitch, offering up some of the last fishes in the box.

"No I'm—"

"Don't worry there's still some down there, just got a slide your finger all the way down."

"No I'm good, have to save room for dessert, you know, with wine?"

"Oh we're getting dessert now, too? But we just had candy."

"That doesn't count. Always room for dessert."

"You're speaking my language."

"So I think she told him earlier in the movie—"

"Mhmm," Caroline was checking her phone as Mitch explained what was going on. Caroline listened to what he said and responded, "Ohhhh I get it ..."

"And that's why you get dessert, so you avoid ending up like that gal," Mitchell said, pointing upward at the screen at a disappointed female character. Caroline registered that as a low-key misogynist comment and thought about responding but didn't. She didn’t respond and Mitch continued: "If you catch my dri-"

The dark of the theater crushed Mitch’s head. That's what it looked like. A shape snatched closed. It happened so quick, first Mitch was talking and then he was gurgling, and it wasn't the shadows — of course it wasn't — it was someone using the full force of their body to seize his head. Caroline moved to punch, ineffectively, and the space moved and she saw blood, she saw blood before she could have possibly seen blood, because first she saw the knife go out and back in and then she saw the blood, and it was on her and in her mouth. Mitch had been stabbed, straight into and through the right side of this throat, and it was still happening. It hadn’t stopped. Mitch was still being stabbed, dead, she thought, no one looks like that and is still alive, his neck a pit of escalating gore....

"Hey, sit down there, man!” someone yelled, a comment that Ryan recognized has pretty funny, given all that happened before, all the talking. I’m the one keeping the peace at the movie theater, you fuckwit, and you yell at me?!

"Are you happy now?” he hissed at her, leaning over Mitch’s seat, Mitch’s body now crumpled over the shared cup holder. “Here you go. Take a fucking picture. It can’t wait until the end of the movie, can it?”

"Shut up!" someone yelled from the back of the theater, and a sympathetic chorus joined in. They must not have realized what he’d just done. Even in murder no one paid much attention to him.

Caroline screamed, and as Ryan stood up he pictured himself artfully strewn with gore, blocking the projection, the aesthetic of the image sexy enough to win untold converts to his cause. He gripped the butts of both knives with his middle and index finger because he bet it looked cool — this could be his signature pose — and then readjusted because that wasn't practical. Caroline ran down her aisle, toward the side exit and Ryan gave chase.

The theater was now in full pandemonium. The strategic moviegoers who’d been previously wondering if they could complain about the disturbance and weasel out a full refund for a movie they’d already seen 95% of were now scrambling to leave with their lives. There’d been no gunfire from what they could see, only a strange, obscenity- and scream-filled encounter, but in this day and age this could only be prelude to a mass shooting or an "Allahu Akbar" encounter.

"Think you're getting away with all this! This is your fault! Stop her, stop her!" Ryan yelled as he chased after her. A middle-aged man fecklessly got in front of him. Ryan could picture the spiel the man intended to give before the man even had a chance to speak. ("Calm down, son," the middle-aged man would have undoubtedly begun...) A flurry of slashes and stabs dispatched the obstacle quickly.

Ryan believed his own hype; he barely slowed a beat, as if suffused with the holy force of aesthetically-divined vengeance. Behind him floated the furor of Hitchcock, Bergman, Kubrick, Scorsese, Allen, Malick, Kurosawa, Altman, Herzog, every artist who ever suffered the ignominy of the insufferably ignorant, the callously inconsiderate. Even the fucking Lumiere Brothers who invented film must have at one point screamed "Shut up!" in French to some shifting asshole who couldn't sit still to watch a few seconds of blurry footage of a train pulling into a station. Ryan saw the "texting woman" run into the deep shadows that led behind the screen itself, into the employees-only hallway next to the screen.

He entered the hall, hot on her heels. It was poorly-lighted, long and narrow. There was nowhere for her to hide, unless any of these side doors were unlocked. He could see her running away, now halfway down the hallway, about 15 yards in front of him; in another 10 yards, the hallway turned right. There was no one else here.

"Justice is coming!" he yelled. He didn't know what he was doing. He'd expected to be caught by now, or to have been shot by the police. They must be on their way.

All he had in him was that initial assault at the seats. He should have killed her, not her male partner, who only really seemed to be in the awkward position of responding to her, not actually initiating the conversation. This was, ironically, beginning to drag for him; somewhere, in a future film adaptation, an audience member was checking his phone or whispering to a colleague, and Ryan wished he could be reborn and burst out of that movie screen to machete-hack that asshole to death.

She screamed, supernaturally high-pitched, the shriek echoing down the halls and maybe even through the walls, a shriek of panic, a madcap attempt to get help. She turned the corner and he didn't like not being able to see her, so he picked up the pace of his sprinting. For all he knew, the corner turned into the lobby or something.

He rocketed around the corner, both arms pumping furiously, feeling the sting of lactic acid accumulation in his muscles. He didn't see her but kept running. There was the subtlest reverberation, a sense-impression in his legs and muscles, some sonic ripple he detected coming from the wall to his left. That door in front of him had just been closed. He barged forward and forced it open. He was right, because the force twisted her arm and blew her off the door: she'd been trying to figure out how to lock it. Fortunately for him, the door didn't lock from the inside, but required a concessionaire's key.

This was apparently some small storage room. He saw industrial-sized bags of popcorn kernels, IV fluid-looking bags of soda syrup, large brown boxes emblazoned with *Mars Corp.* He thought it'd be funny to open one of those *Mars Corp* boxes and grab a Snickers. Maybe he's in a Snickers commercial right now? Maybe he was *just* hungry/angry. Getting Hangry? He'd bite into a Snickers Bar and be in zen peace. Wouldn't that be funny?

There was someone else in here. A movie theater worker, a butch-looking white teenage girl, in the purple-and-black shirt and hat foisted upon her by movie theater company policy. She stood paralyzed. From what he could tell, it looked like she'd been maneuvering behind some boxes to get some of that IV Coke fluid when this whole scene exploded before her. This storage room was well-lit and he could read the name tag on her chest. Shelby.

Shelby looked at him and his right hand. He felt it now, too. He was bleeding, a puncture wound in his right palm. Must have stabbed himself with one of his knives while forcing open the door.

The woman he was chasing was just now getting off the ground, which seemed absurd, she hadn't even fallen that hard. She must be milking it for sympathy, some automatic stimuli from her usual life, he figured, always looking for sympathy or attention.

His zeal for cosmic vengeance was returning.

"Shelby, is it?"

She didn't answer intelligently but of course that had to be her name.

"You can leave, Shelby, just leave, I won't hurt you. You are just doing your job, Shelby, and you don't want to risk your future for defending a terrible person. That's a terrible human being." He pointed at the texter and finally got a good look at her. Her face was obviously stricken and haggard with the grime and sweat of panic, but he could see beyond that to her normally attractive, entitled, texting self. Even with the blood on her clothes, the blood of her beau.

"Shoot him!" the texter yelled at Shelby, which just added more layers of confusion. Shelby felt at herself as if she did in fact have a gun, but of course she didn't. Was there something else she had, pepper spray? No, nothing, just a set of larger than average keys, keys that someone had once told her could be rolled into a fist and pressed between your fingers to form a type of claw, but of course that'd been said at a normal time and hypothetically, not in actual contemplation of a crazy maniac barging in on you with knives drawn. Shelby was positioning the keys through her fingers and wanted to cry, how stupid and ineffectual that would be.

"She was talking, texting, carrying on during the whole movie. I'm a paying customer. We are all paying customers. This is why movie theaters are dying! Don't you understand! Your job, your ... I know you're just a kid, but your livelihood will be gone if people like her keep coming to your theaters and ruining the experience for everyone!"

Ryan blinked hard and in between blinks saw Shelby moved to action by the ineluctable force of his logic, just as briskly and automatically as a dropped apple moves to the ground by the force of gravity. He saw Shelby produce the infidel to him, her neck exposed, for the killing stroke, Shelby looking up at him the way Aztecs must have looked up to the shaman that conducted the ritual sacrifices for the harmony and preservation of their tribes.

After a few more blinks and after wiping the sweat from his brow, he was back to the prosaic reality. Shelby's emotionally overcome face promised no resolution.

Shelby put her palms up in a show of appeasement and said, "Sir. Sir. Please calm down, sir. Please. We can ban her for life from the theater. That's enough punishment, sir. Isn't that true, ma'am?"

The woman nodded vigorously. "I accept that. I'm sorry, I'm truly, truly sorry. Do you understand me? I'm truly sorry if I ruined your experience."

Ryan saw both the fear and the newfound, steely determination in Shelby's face to take control of the situation. She was good. He caught himself hoping things worked out for her, as if he himself wasn't the one causing the problems for her. He imagined personally praising her to the manager. He felt the sickly sting in his hand again and looked, then looked at his chest and saw the stains darker than red cherries, and smelled the hot stench of his sweat and the iron and salt of various people's blood.

He must have looked like a lunatic. No wonder she wasn't listening.

"It's lies. It's a lie to apologize when you've already been caught." Then, appealing to Shelby again, "If she cared, she wouldn't have done it to begin with."

And with nothing more needing to be said, he proceeded upon the texter. First he glimpsed the horrified visage of Shelby, then she was out of his peripheral vision and then, for the duration of his sacred act, it was like she never existed. Then there were screams and the texter toppling backward in fright as he made his intentions clear. The texter put up a shockingly pitiful defense. Maybe this was due to fatigue, resignation, because she still couldn't believe this was really happening, or because of that ultra-modern ailment, where one believes one truly must be the leading character in the universe's movie. She put up her hands to make a show of resisting but Stabby in her midsection and Gutty stuck into the crook of her armpit and that was that, and on her face was the boom of realization, a look more piercing than any sound. He had her stuck, he thought, like a marionette, he could make her dance if he chose to. But he took no pleasure in this anymore; he performed his tasks now only out of obligation, like the slaughterhouse worker who made some strange connection with a slaughtered-cow-to-be but deals death swiftly only because he has quotas to make and orders to fill. So, both still standing, he brought her close and leveraged his position atop hers, and the knives came to her throat in powerful arching strokes but his body held her up so she didn't fall. The ferocity of the blows were no longer delivered with malice, but instead to fight inertia, to move Ryan beyond the act of thinking and to trick his brain into continued action. He let her go when it became obvious that there was no longer a point to his assault.

He didn't even know her name. Her body no longer even looked human. A mutant, that's what her corpse looked like. Her head was still attached to her body only by unseen ligaments pulling miracle duty. He turned to Shelby and she looked like she was staring at Satan himself.

The doors kicked in and there stood four uniformed police officers. The storage room was small enough that when they entered, even tentatively, they were essentially upon him, maybe only two yards away. Shelby was still on the other side of the small room, still standing in the midst of the boxes. They were yelling at him to drop his weapons, to put his hands up.

This was stupid, he thought. His hands were already up, palms exposed. Weapons? He brought his attention to his hands and he wasn't even carrying any weapons anymore. He didn't have any more weapons and he wasn't holding anyone hostage. There were four cops, why didn't they just tackle him? Shelby should run toward and seek protection from the police officers, that'd be the smart thing to do, why was she still standing there?

He put his hands together to signal that he would allow them to arrest him and at first it felt like when he'd accidentally sprayed Binaca in his eyes. Then that quickly became a thousand times worse, a fresh sickly hell. His sinuses were drowning in horseradish, he thought. The mucous membranes in his eyes, nose and lungs seemed to swell and shut down and he was blind.

He didn't care about living anymore but reacted only by instinct and groped about for support and heard one loud crack and his hip detonated. He distinctly felt the exploded bone fragments rocket around inside his groin, imagined all the blood vessels that ran to his genitals puncturing and the blood hissing out of them like steam from a pipe.

He fell backward and descended into darkness.

>< >< ><

He was convicted of two counts of murder in the first degree for the movie theater couple and two counts of murder in the second degree for the middle-aged man and the old man. He was sentenced to die. That was appropriate, he felt. He had a separate lawsuit against the police for excessive force, for macing and shooting him in the groin even though he was unarmed. He didn't want to bring the lawsuit, he obviously had no use for the money, but his criminal defense attorney insisted upon it, part of the overall strategy of intimidation. He was sure his criminal defense attorney was receiving a referral fee from any proceeds from the civil suit.

What seemed to incense the commentariat the most was that his civil lawsuit was meritorious and would certainly result in a favorable settlement. It turned out the officer who shot him had three previously substantiated internal affairs complaints for excessive force, one of those force complaints being an improper discharge of his firearm. Even Shelby eventually testified that Ryan didn't have any knives in his hand when he was shot. It was all stupid and he felt it was a distraction, but he became convinced that he could will any money he recovered to funding independent filmmakers or support online personalities he liked.

He lived for several years afterward, the gears of justice grinding as slowly as they do. He refused to appeal his conviction, but used the ongoing civil lawsuit — and the commentariat it attracted — to voice his reasons for his "crusade," as other people called it. Civility. Civility was missing, he propounded to anyone who would listen.

He took solace in some of the Facebook groups he saw in his support, most in jest but some not. The memes and the shitposts. The calls to release him as a "Political Prisoner Against the Continuing Dumbassery of Our Culture," as one petition went. He didn't like some of the mean commentary he read about his victims. He cared not a whit about their personal lives and was concerned with them only for how they acted in the movie theater, and felt it was sad that their families had to read additionally terrible things about them. It was bad enough for their family that they must have learned that their loved ones were exposed as shallow and disrespectful moviegoers.

He also didn't like the love letters he received. Well, he liked them, of course, in brief instances, when their existence confirmed that at least someone out there thought of him; and he liked the feelings of affection they instilled in him; and he liked the sheer reprieve from his loneliness. But he didn't want them, not really. They ascribed a viciousness to him that just wasn't there; he wasn't the bloody-minded animal they thought he was. He was smart and well-reasoned, and it was ill-reasoned to send love letters to a convicted murderer. Where was their common sense? He wanted to re-direct their attentions onto something more worthwhile, like his philosophy of living each day with respect for one another. Part of that respect had a natural contrapositive: that when people acted disrespectfully, there needed to be ramifications for that. Otherwise, people would act as they wanted, and it would always be the brute, powerful and callous steamrolling over the meek and considerate.

If he had to select any part of the attention he was proudest of, it had to be the transformation of his surname into a verb. Like when someone "Caskey'd" a loud, inconsiderate patron at the Baltimore Museum of Art by shoving the offending patron down the stairs, or "Caskey'd" a texting theater-goer at the Guthrie in Minneapolis by kicking him hard in the back of the head.

He'd never have accomplished anything like that if he hadn't taken a stand, and the people understood that. If he'd just gone along with his normal, boring life, who would he be? A nobody. Another person steamrolled over, left to vent only in his mind. Better to be notorious than disappeared; and he was only notorious to some people. To others he was an inspiration. That's why he had to keep getting his message out. Because people were taking a stand, and their minor acts of defiance were all the more effective with the bloody seriousness of his acts continually afresh in the collective imagination.

A Gob of Minty Spit in the Sink

I SOMETIMES WISH you people would talk to me, and I know there are many people who'd want to do so. Who wouldn't want to talk to me, really? There are so many questions you should be asking me. You half-suspect that there exist things like me, but you're wrong. Those half-suspicions are an evolutionary holdover for when we feared saber-toothed tiger attacks. Ancient instincts for an advanced threat. There's nothing like me you could expect.

I'm being flip, I know. It's like I'm trying to impress you. I used to be like that in real life, always wanting the upper hand.

I could talk to you, if I wanted to, but I don't. I have an interesting story to tell, too, a story that could get a laugh.

I choked to death. No, that's not the funny part (not to you, hypothetical person, though I've had some funny incidents with other people choking. I've had people inadvertently choke before I had anything to do with them, and even though it was inconveniencing, I could see the gallows humor in it).

Anyway, back to the story of my choking. I woke up one night, panicked about forgetting to take my pill — Luvox, I think it was called — which is an anti-OCD medicine that also helped me sleep. Oh, the irony there is double-layered. First, I was already sleeping! I didn't need the pill! Second, if it hadn't been for my OCD, I wouldn't have burst up with a start about forgetting to take my OCD medication. Well, maybe that's not irony. Okay then, smart aleck, then how about: if the OCD medication had actually been doing its job, this all could have been avoided.

Anyway, being a good husband and not wanting to awaken my wife, I felt around in the dark for my pill bottle, which was just above the bed, on the headboard. I'd found it, opened the bottle, fished around, retrieved a pill with my ring finger, downed it with the half-cup of water that I'd left by the bed and then ... guh ... guh ... guh ... I was choking.

See, there are these synthetic tabs they put in pill bottles, and I don't even really know what their purpose is. I think they do something to keep the pills fresh or something. I'd noticed this tab before, always thought maybe I should take it out or something, but then what did I know, I'm not a pharmacist. It was larger than the pills itself, and large enough for me to choke on.

I maybe spent too much time deluding myself, but then panic set in and I woke my wife and raved and tried to do something and I remember her fear and confusion and anguish and then, my death. That was the worst moment of my life. That might not be surprising — it's me dying, after all — but what it did to my wife, how helpless it made her feel, just her look. It's devastating, and that's a lot coming from me.

And how embarrassing. A smart guy like me, a geothermal engineer, felled by a freshness packet.

The figures in the beyond thought so, too. I won't get into semantics and, remember, I'm not even really talking to you, and I'm tired so I'm not getting into all that. You only get one story tonight. I'll just say that the vast majority of people just die and that's it, nothing else. Consciousness is lost, that's the whole shebang. A blank screen. But some others are different.

I get to see my wife at times, communicate with her, in my subtle and sweet way, if I help them. I get to check up on her. So that's why I do what I do. For them. For her.

>< >< ><

I'm on another job now, actually, but I can't even call it a job because there's no effort in it, really. I wish my real-life job had been so easy. And it's not even a job because I serve no function that they couldn't do on their own. Maybe they just liked the idea of striking a deal with me, I don't know why. It caused me no moral anguish. Time flows differently there, of course, but I surmise my decision to help them took the real-world equivalent of about a second. Sure, sounds good to me, what do I have to lose?

I guess my job involves some discretion, but not really. The secret is I just sort of pick randomly. They think there's some method to the madness, but no, not really. I do generally select younger people because I'm spiteful. I was always one of those people who was very sweet, loving and loyal to people who I cared about, but could never give a shit about strangers. That was my life, and that's sort of my life now. Maybe I died and went to heaven!

Anyway the shift's almost over and you're washing your face in the sink. I wouldn't be explaining this story to you, anyway, you don't look interesting. If you looked interesting, I wouldn't be doing this. Or maybe I would anyway, got to make quota and can't control when I'm conscious and able.

You're washing your face and you don't see me. You don't see me until I choose to be seen. Appearing when you're lifting your head from the sink, either after washing your face or spitting after brushing your teeth or whatever — just lifting your head from your sink, that's my M.O. Maybe because that's a position I always felt vulnerable in. Well, it seems to work so I'm onto something.

You lift your head up from the sink and I'll be there.

>< >< ><

"Old friend, ho-ooo-ld on," you hear sung inside your head, a friendly baritone, as if from headphones keyed straight to your brain.

"Cause you toss and turn every night because you just know something ain't right but it's getting better, I promise," chimes in a spunky female, in the same key.

"Olllllldddddd friend ... stay strong ... take what you need and move on," the baritone ends in key, with rousing finality.

That's just some fucked up positive shit I add for no reason from a couple of bands I used to like when I was alive. Music in the wrong context can be quite terrifying. I don't know. I can't explain the process, but you're panicking now anyway so it worked.

You turn around or maybe you see me in the mirror, the flayed flesh and the faces upon faces. The layer-cake trick, I call it. There's flecked, reflective skin, deposited all about you like you've been in a den of giant snakes. You see me and among the panic there's a kind of sadness about how much there is to the world you don't know about, what a magical unexplored world, because you see me and the way I gleam and prance and you know you've never seen anything like me before. I'm another world.

"I'm burning my time now ... some things, can't be said aloud ... from my lips to your ears!" yells an anthemic chain gang of male vocals, a raucous basement party performance that exists nowhere but inside your mind, for only as long as I let you hear those words.

You're alive and as you draw in a breath I implant in you the sensational pain of being disemboweled. Being specific, really, the sensation of your upper torso launching off, looking down at the smelly coils of your innards, at your lower half kicking upright as beasts — wolves, tigers, bears — consume you as you watch, and I like to add something exotic, like a griffin, just in case I'm dealing with someone educated, just so I can wonder if that detail got noticed in the scrum of chaos.

That implanted sensation is enough to do the job. Your brain and heart give way and you fall to the ground, dead, your bowels and bladder emptying, the blood and mucus from your nose running. Again, time runs differently for me here, but if I had to guess, it's only been maybe five seconds from when you looked up from the sink. Longer than it took me to sign on the proverbial dotted line.

That connects well enough to how I started. That's a reference to something earlier, and that's a good way to end a story, I remember. You're dead anyway, actually, so there's that, too.

That's been enough from me. I have quotas to fill, and in the process of talking to myself I've already started on another job. Remember, time works differently, here, as I've said. So here I am, apparently, another job.

It's time to get ready for bed. You're walking to the bathroom.

I Will Soon Be Home and Never Need Anyone Ever Again

THE LANDSCAPE WAS flat and uninviting, the cold, artichoke-colored ground ingrown with roots and branches to trip over, and the final destination, to the extent there was one, was unexciting. That was all the woods around his house had to offer. He walked around in them, "got lost" there, but got lost in a harmless way, secure in the knowledge that a sustained five-minute walk in any direction would find him back among the semi-rural tract homes that made up his development.

These woods were really just a stretch of undeveloped land near his house. To get there, he walked through the cul-de-sac at the end of his block, through the yard of one of the houses at the roundabout (always making sure to keep a fair distance from the house itself, as he didn't know the people who lived there) and, soon enough, he'd be surrounded by whatever trees these were, these tall, thin trees with white bark.

He'd tried to look up what kind of trees these were. Birch, Sycamore, White Poplar, Quaking Aspen and Ghost Gum were all tall, thin trees with white bark. It'd be awesome if these were Quaking Aspen or Ghost Gum, but the latter were native to Australia, and he didn't think they could even grow here in western Wisconsin, let alone would someone be cool enough to actively plant them. Australia sounded like it got all the cool stuff: Tasmanian devils, kangaroos, jumping spiders. Quaking Aspen was a possibility, and that evocative name felt thematically appropriate for how he acted while walking out in the woods, pretending to be venturing somewhere important, mystical even, when it was just the same rinky-dink woods. He knew that in reality these were likely just birch trees, but he liked to pretend otherwise sometimes, as if these woods held enthralling mysteries.

Are you really lost if you know there's no chance you'll stay lost, Thomas Egeland, aged fourteen, thought to himself as he crunched through the dead brown leaves. No, he decided, he wasn't really lost. Whenever he left the woods, he'd either emerge onto some street he recognized, or, if not the street itself, the street sign would ring a bell and he'd know how to get back home.

He knelt around a pile of dead leaves, feeling clammy mud

sticking to the knees of his jeans. *Dammit*, he thought, but not really. He'd sort of intended on getting mud on his jeans. He thought it was cool to have dirty clothes, if it was done artfully, casually. Like, reminders of adventures, or mementos from yard football or something. Not that he played yard football. One kid at school, Patrick Mahon, often wore ripped jeans and made it work for him. It helped that Patrick was tall and good-looking, had residual popularity from elementary school, skateboarded and listened to punk music.

Thomas didn't play sports but he wished he did. Unlike some of the other kids in junior high, who came up with ex post facto reasons for not playing sports and partly built their identities around those stances, like complaining that sports were stupid or pointless or encouraged group-think. Those kids complained about sports but had other things going on. Thomas admired, in a sense, how confident those kids were, even if he didn't really understand why anyone should care about what they said. While he was out, alone, wasting time in the woods, they were all hanging out, drinking and smoking and maybe fucking. They were together and he was alone, so maybe they were doing something right.

He delicately pushed some of the gathered leaves aside, hoping maybe a frog or something would hop out. No such luck. He'd never seen a frog in these woods but it'd be cool if he did. He looked up at a sparrow on a thin branch. The sparrow did nothing, just hopped once or twice and tweeted. It was a cute, pudgy-looking bird. Thomas looked up at it, staying quiet. A passerby would think he was looking up at it reverentially, and that's what he was going for. It was just a bird, he knew, probably even the most common type of bird, but he was trying to look reverentially up at it like this was something important, some transcendent thought about the beauty and splendor of all earthly things, something to sustain him and provide solace through the rest of his boring day.

It wasn't taking. It was just a bird, albeit a cute one. He was just walking in the woods with nothing to do.

He traipsed around the woods for another twenty minutes or so until he decided he should get going. It must have been around 4:45 p.m. and, as it was late autumn, it was getting dark. He had homework to do. Leaving the woods, he saw brightly-lit homes and pretended like he was coming back to civilization. He found himself on a familiar street, and became instantly nostalgic for his time in the woods for reasons he didn't understand. Maybe because he knew his homework would be boring and frustrating and somehow beneath him, and futile wanderings around the woods in the cold was still better than that.

He'd been right. His redundant English assignment required him to summarize and editorialize on three chapters of *The Red Badge of Courage*. This assignment was just a retread of material they'd already discussed in class. In fact, he'd been the one who initially volunteered in class to summarize two of the chapters just a few days ago. Teachers were so dumb and lazy. He wished he could just write "please refer to my class contributions on this very topic" but of course he couldn't do that. He was one of the "good kids" because he did what was asked of him. He didn't go above and beyond: just tried hard to do what was asked of him and do it well.

It nagged at him if he didn't do what was expected of him; it didn't even matter if he disliked the teacher or the subject, he just couldn't let the teacher or anyone else think he was stupid or didn't understand something. He knew school was essentially an idiot daycare center, but he still didn't want to let any teachers down, as if they really cared either way. He saw his schoolwork as somehow a moral reflection of himself, and he often (favorably) contrasted himself morally with the vapid morons in his classes, who either couldn't or wouldn't exert themselves, and made a virtue of his obedience and respect, no matter how much he disliked a teacher or their class. His good grades reflected his moral worth, and the practicality of his approach. You do well, you get good grades, and then you move on in life.

He suspected that, if he wasn't already smarter than his teachers, he'd grow up to be. If he asked a pointed question that went beyond the four corners of the classroom discussion, the teacher would crowd-source the question to the listless classroom — "and what does everyone else think?" — and let the disinterest or ignorance of the class pass for a verdict or buy the teacher time to change the subject. Thomas was cognizant of the tricks and tactics utilized by the stumped educator. Other kids might not see it, but he did.

Whatever. Homework was all stupid anyway. Homework was

part of the system, and systems existed to continue themselves. So do what was asked, and try to do it well. He performed his work diligently, and then went back to punch up certain sections with fancy vocabulary words or shades of nuance to show that he'd given even some iota of thought to the material.

When it was time for dinner, he set the table with the cutlery and dinnerware, as he always did. He ate dinner with his parents, everyone in the same chairs around the table as always. The seat next to his was empty, as his sister, Monica, was away at college, a junior at the University of Wisconsin-Milwaukee. She had transferred there only recently, at the beginning of this school year after finishing a two-year stint at community college.

Monica's departure saddened their mother, Thomas could tell, but not because of anything obvious. More in a slight wistful way, like the look his mother might give when walking past Monica's room or in the way she'd recount some boring memory they'd shared as if it were somehow telling, or maybe in the way she still kept the fridge stocked with some of the foods Monica liked even though, as far as Thomas knew, Monica wasn't expected back home anytime soon. His mother seemed sad for typical clichéd reasons, like that stupid *Fleetwood Mac* song where she sings about times changing and people getting older, real basic stuff which maybe seems really profound when you're middle-aged. It seemed to Thomas that his mother was trying to spend more time with him now that Monica was gone, despite her knowing that he preferred to be alone. In that sense, Monica was annoying him even while she was away.

Thomas could never tell what his father was thinking. He was probably happy he could slot his daughter in the mental category of "doing a respectable thing: away at college." He probably was happy he didn't have to hear her coming home late from bars or have to make any more small talk with her loser friends or analyze the predatory motives of the scumbag men in her life. Out of sight, out of mind, Thomas guessed.

It was hard to know what his dad thought about anything, as late as he worked. If Mom ever got Dad talking at dinner, his responses would always be curt and clipped, and any moments of levity would come from Dad talking badly about an incompetent employee of his at the auto yard, which made Thomas feel bad, as Thomas always felt bad for the person who earnestly tried but still failed. Thomas hated the kids at school because they didn't try, but to try and still fail was sad.

His father often acted prepossessed with other concerns — impending workplace or personal disasters — and having to interact with his family at all left him temperamental. So, his regaling his family with a story of workplace incompetence was the most they could expect. These types of stories made Thomas anxious. As much as Thomas hated school work, he was confident in the tools and tricks he'd honed that so far had gotten him his steady stream of A's. He'd never worried about doing well academically. But the real world wasn't like that, Thomas knew. An impressive memory couldn't get you through real-world work like it did school work. Real-world work couldn't always be completed given ample time, at your own pace and in isolation, like homework could. You could fail in the real world despite your best efforts.

Back to his room afterwards, where he stayed up too late and, even when he tried, couldn't fall asleep. This was *his* time, alone at night, when he was safe, away from the bullies and tormentors that made each school day a living hell. This was precious time, to be savored. As well as he did in school, he wondered sometimes how well he'd be doing academically if he didn't have the handicap of endless anxiety and the fear of what fresh, embarrassing horrors the following day might bring.

Life was so short, he knew, even at fourteen, and free time so precious, that it was a crime to waste it with sleep. He jerked off three times, letting the cum settle on his T-shirt and stomach while lying flat on his back in bed until the delirium of continued consciousness got him thinking he was a dissolute bum in the alley surrounded by a pool of booze. Eventually his consciousness surrendered to the unwanted transition into tomorrow.

>< >< ><

"With the death penalty, it's like, you know, it's almost like survival of the fittest in a way. So, yeah, there are issues with cost or things with the justice system but it's natural in its way because it's, like, the survival of the fittest to weed out people who shouldn't be alive," explained Brynne Connor during Mrs. Gordon's Social

Studies class. Brynne was a straight-A's student like Thomas, which enraged him. She attended all of her classes, did her homework, and circled the correct bubbles.

She is a fucking moron, Thomas screamed inside his head. It devalued his own hard work that someone like Brynne also got all A's: in fact, most of the people who got all straight-A's weren't genuinely smart, critical thinkers, or even intellectually curious, just well-trained bootlickers. Thomas strained his hand harder to get Mrs. Gordon's attention so he could respond to what Brynne had just said. Brynne was a nice girl (ostensibly; they didn't socialize at all but he never had a problem with her), but seriously, did a conscious human being just say aloud what she had just said? Did she hear herself speak? Why didn't any teacher ever call any student out for saying dumb, flabby nonsense? What she said was absolutely retarded, and the teacher, of course, like all teachers, wasn't calling her out for her rambling incoherence but instead was just nodding along. Brynne's comment couldn't go unremarked, no matter how well-behaved she might be. Thomas strained his hand harder, doubtful he'd get called on since he'd been called on earlier.

The classroom's desks were all arranged in a horseshoe shape. He pivoted as he raised his hand and Larry Mullens, who sat across the aisle on the other "spoke" of the horseshoe, locked eyes with him. Thomas noticed Larry's gaze and a cold bucket of water splashed in his innards. So it begins today: Thomas had forgotten, he wasn't allowed to draw attention to himself.

When Larry realized Thomas was meeting his glare, he aggressively leaned in and twisted his body, like someone about to throw a punch. Larry sneer-laughed, then signaled to Edward Vroc, his burly, Cro-Magnon friend sitting beside him. Larry head-nodded in Thomas's direction to clue the Cro-Magnon to the frame of reference for his forthcoming taunts, and then flailed his arm in a mock imitation of Thomas's earnest hand-raising. Larry was savvy enough to keep his pantomime low-key so as to not accidentally get called on by Mrs. Gordon. Dumb fucking idiot teacher was so naïve that she might actually think Larry was genuinely raising his hand.

Mrs. Gordon actually did see Larry's outstretched arm, but then when she saw who the arm was attached to, she must have just assumed Larry was only mocking a fellow classmate and not actually volunteering, so she went back to canvassing for a student until she picked Debra Rauterberg. With Debra speaking and no chance of being called on, Larry, making sure Ed was watching, did another crude impersonation of Thomas's earnestness by daintily batting his wrists.

Larry always went back to that: allusions to Thomas's supposed homosexuality. The charge was so off-base as to not even bother Thomas, at least not as to its substance. Larry might as well call him a dinosaur or any stupid fucking thing, but, God, it still made Thomas all hot and angry to be the target of abuse. It wasn't the substance of what Larry said, but that he was consistently saying or doing things to mock him. It made his adrenaline kick in and his stomach churn. It drained him. For some reason other students thought it was funny, probably because Larry was better-looking and generally better liked. Thomas hated the unwanted attention, the commiserating smiles of other classmates — classmates who knew better, who Thomas knew didn't really have any beef with him, but just joined in out of habit, or boredom, or to ingratiate themselves with Larry, or to just belong, for the fun of being included in a joke, maybe just grateful *they* weren't the butt of it.

What added an inexplicable, acidic tinge to this state of affairs was that up until about sixth grade, Larry and Thomas had been pretty friendly. Thomas had even gone to Larry's birthday parties and had played hockey with him and some other kids back when Thomas's mother was still forcing him to do things like that. But at some point during the sixth grade a memo must have gone around declaring Thomas a persona non grata (or worse, "persona fagitus": That was the type of stupid, mean unfunny joke Larry would have made. One of the terrible things about being the target of bullies is it gets you thinking like they do).

The bullying was at its worst when there were girls paying attention. Thomas remembered, and would always remember, the first time Larry unmistakably insulted him. It had been so weird and sudden. The first unmistakable insult he remembered coming from Larry happened in Spanish class toward the end of sixth grade. Their Spanish teacher had made everyone switch seats every quarter, and, in the last quarter, Larry had been assigned to sit next to Thomas. They sat next to each other largely without incident. (Come to think of it, before Larry had been assigned to sit next to Thomas, he had been assigned to sit next to Amanda Schroeder, one of the prettiest girls in their grade. Maybe Larry was upset he had to leave Amanda's side and took it out on Thomas.)

Lara and Charlene, two other pretty girls, sat behind them in class during that last quarter. Lara, it turned out, was just a mean person, whereas Charlene was quiet and unassuming but essentially a follower. Fortunately, since Lara and Charlene sat behind them, Thomas didn't have much occasion to interact with them. But the four of them had been assigned some group project one day, and out of nowhere Lara just said to Thomas, "you look like a fag." He remembered Charlene breathing in quickly and covering her mouth but obviously laughing, and Larry smiling sort of sheepishly, not sure how to respond or if he should say anything. (And yes, Lara's attack was completely unprovoked, Thomas was sure of it. A consequence of becoming so emotionally distraught over being bullied was that Thomas kept fastidious mental records of each bullying incident, as a way — he hoped — to learn to avoid or defuse future situations. That incident he chalked up to being unavoidable, as sometimes you just get stuck with bitches and assholes.)

Larry then said: "No, trust me, Thomas is as straight as a line. A really curvy line," and Lara belly-laughed as if Larry really sized him up, like Larry should drop out of school immediately and become a professional comic. Thomas remembers internally rolling his eyes, more offended at how dull-witted Larry was and how stupid these people were: at least come up with something incisive and clever. Later during that same class period, Larry went to pick something up off the floor, and in full earshot of all three of them, said: "Thomas, I'm not picking this up so you can stare at my asshole, okay?" Again, Lara laughed, and so did Charlene. Thomas was left red-faced and silent. He remembered thinking, at least Larry put more thought into that joke. He hadn't realized at the time that Larry's picking on him — and inviting others to join in — would quickly escalate into what seemed like a permanent tradition.

The comments would become meaner and meaner. Thomas's assumed gayness, his physical weakness, any time he had a pimple, or a bad haircut, or wore something that someone took issue with, his family, his dad's business, his sister's supposed sluttiness. It would escalate and escalate. Thinking about it — the fact that he had to deal with this, to worry about it — psychologically unmoored him. *I'm supposed to be protected, safe, this was school, for fuckssake*. Thomas was always just minding his own business and he had to deal with this, this kind of civic death, this character assassination. Larry and his cohort's jokes were lame and stupid, but still, the torment and the memory of torments past all hung over Thomas like a regnant cloud. He pictured a life meter, slowly draining.

Larry was acknowledged to be a good-looking kid. He had a symmetrical face, unusually dark-olive skin and dark black hair, was tall and generally thin without being scrawny and had a "butt" chin that was recognized as an asset rather than a liability. (Thomas knew that if he'd had a butt chin, he'd get endless grief for it; unique characteristics were ex post facto targets for ridicule rather than the cause of such ridicule.) Thomas compared unfavorably, but for reasons that somewhat eluded him. Thomas was average height, willowy and undeveloped in his upper body, and had flaxen hair so light it bordered on white. Worse, Thomas's pale complexion seemed to accentuate the red grotesquerie of any pimples, which he sometimes accumulated around his chin and lip area.

But Thomas certainly wasn't awful-looking. Wasn't blonde a desirable color? His skin blemishes were terrible when they occurred, but they were (thankfully) somewhat rare: there were kids in class who had far worse acne than Thomas. There were kids going through all types of gawky, awkward phases who somehow eluded the bullies' attention (and, of course, some who didn't). But it just seemed somewhat capricious and random. Half the time he'd be mentally screaming, like Winston at the end of *1984*, for Larry to torment someone else.

In the 5th or 6th grade, he remembered, mothers (including his own) would say how nice and handsome Larry was, and he vaguely remembered suggestions to befriend Larry because he was well-liked and popular. Larry used to be a basketball starter but Thomas didn't know if that was true anymore. Thomas didn't know the comings-and-goings of popularity, and knew there had been a kind of seismic re-ordering of things in the jump from elementary school (which ended in 5th grade) to junior high. But he comprehended that

Larry was still at least loosely associated with popularity and was friends with other popular kids.

The bullying with Larry had never become violent or physical, not really. Maybe this had something to do with Larry still wanting to be broadly liked and not perceived as déclassé. The popular girls Larry feted would tolerate alpha male one-upmanship, but probably not outright violence. Or maybe Larry didn't want to compromise his grades and get in trouble. Maybe he even retained residual warm feelings toward Thomas from their previous sorta-friendship. Who knew?

But while Larry didn't get directly physical, when he recruited Ed Vroc to join in, the bullying definitely became suffused with the threat of incipient violence. Vroc enjoyed being big and stout, and savored the tension of tormenting somebody who he knew couldn't or wouldn't fight back. Thomas also had no amicable past with Ed that served as a safety valve against violence: Ed had gone to a different elementary school and they'd only met this year.

A couple weeks ago, Thomas had walked past Larry's locker, where Larry, Ed and some other kids were hanging out. In past situations when he'd accidentally found himself in the wild with Larry and his cabal, Thomas would do his best to keep his distance, essentially hug the opposite wall, but for some reason on that occasion he'd allowed himself to be in lunging distance of the group. He did his best to avoid eye contact. (Although it was a paradox: looking scared and mousey would embolden his tormentors, but faking confidence could also provoke them to reestablish their dominance. With them, you just couldn't win.)

Whatever look he was attempting at that time, it didn't work. Ed had lunged out and said something like "watch-out-timber-faggot-fall" and smashed downward on Thomas's stack of books, pushing him off balance and slamming all his books onto the floor. If there was any bright spot to this, it was that everything fell in a fairly uniformed clump, so Thomas could pick his books up quickly and discreetly to minimize his shame and embarrassment.

But people saw. People heard.

He remembered, quite vividly, seeing Larry's face as Ed lunged at him. Larry's eyebrows raised and his head bolted back a bit, and he didn't look happy or like he was even enjoying the spectacle.

Larry looked, if anything, a bit shocked. When Ed turned back to him, Larry put his hand on Ed's shoulder and mouthed something, maybe like, "c'mon, man," or "you're crazy, man," or something short and mildly reproachful, but in a jovial way like he was saying this in Ed's best interest. Whatever it was, it wasn't castigating. Some of the other kids they were hanging out with laughed or rolled their eyes; one kid said, "dammmmn son," in that exaggerated way they do in urban movies.

No one protested; no one stood up for Thomas; no one helped him.

He blamed Larry. Larry had been his friend. Ed was a dolt, a go-nowhere moron and, as repellent as Ed was, he was a roach, a big dumb barking dog on Larry's leash. Of course Thomas still wanted to tie Ed up to a post and beat him to death with a baseball bat. Obviously. But a part of Thomas felt that Ed was too dumb to morally condemn. It was Larry that enraged him, because Larry was the instigator, and he was smart enough to know better.

The gay mincing was the only bullying event Thomas endured over the course of the school day. Which made it, relatively, a good day. But like the other episodes, it left its psychic imprint upon him. He wasn't safe from bullying even during an active class lesson. Maybe this was his fault. He let things fester. He couldn't forget or forgive. The substance of the attacks themselves was silly garbage but what they reaffirmed was that he was actively disliked; that his education could be compromised and that he was unable to defend himself and those in authority were unable, unwilling or uninterested in defending him. Teachers would excuse anyone from anything as long as they didn't have to get involved.

To the extent Thomas ever got in trouble, it was for mild insubordination or attitude problems, which was against Thomas's very nature, as he was, if anything, deferential to authority. But sometimes ... how could he respect these teachers, really? Thomas, so obedient to authority, even *he* couldn't always suppress his true feelings. This dumbed-down pablum these teachers foisted upon them. These teachers, giving all these idiots who didn't understand the material, or even attempt to, a "good job" or a gold star, meanwhile doing nothing to protect the engaged kids, the kids who might actually accomplish something in life.

And to think that Larry's bullying had this effect on him, fostering resentments, causing him to further disengage, thereby compromising his grades and, ergo, his ability to get into a good college and perhaps affecting even the course of his whole life, and that NO one was doing anything to stop this just made him angrier and angrier and angrier, until all the sounds and experiences and events of the school day were drowned out by the pounding heartbreak of his intractable situation.

>< >< ><

His mom made him spaghetti and meatballs that night for dinner, which the two of them ate as they watched a movie at home. She offered to watch whatever he wanted to watch, and while he had some ideas about what he'd like to watch — maybe an action or horror movie on some of the trashier channels, he was in that sort of mood — he claimed to not have a preference and deferred to her choices. She insisted he pick something and he demurred, so she chose the news, thinking that was a good pick since he was smart and liked to stay informed. But Thomas didn't much care to watch the news. He didn't care to listen to other people's opinions, and he always bristled about the way a fact or story was presented, thinking about the motivations of all the true players behind the scenes.

"What do you think about that? Do you think it's a good idea they're reducing the money to that program? I don't know how I feel about that," his mother said. Thomas hadn't been paying attention to the news, just staring at the meatball he was pushing over a little hill of pasta, enjoying how it was coming apart with each twist of his fork.

"I don't know. It's an interesting issue, though. I'm trying to know more about the world, actually, so thanks for putting on the news. It's good to hear about this stuff," he said, as convincingly as he could without actually knowing what issues were being discussed. "No problem," she responded.

He knew what Mom was trying to do. To make a connection with him, she'd sometimes ask him what he thought about something current, and he usually responded curtly and then immediately felt bad about it. He just didn't like expressing personal opinions. He didn't want to be judged, and especially avoided saying anything controversial or conspiratorial. The only time he ever really wanted to join the fray of conversation was in limited occasions at school, when he needed to correct someone else's stupidity or arrogance.

Even though he was, to be honest, quite depressed from the day's relatively minor bullying event, he knew it wouldn't be fair to take his bad feelings out on his mother, so he faked a sort of distracted equanimity. *She must think I'm so boring*, he thought. He had preferences: there were things he liked, directors and artists and musicians he followed, sometimes which he talked about with her (like when she would ask him about a certain book she saw him reading, or about the music she heard him listening to in his room). He felt bad about keeping everything bottled up inside. His mother was none-too-bright, content with mainstream television and *US Weekly* and evinced no interest in scratching below the surface of anything. *God, what a pretentious prick*, he thought about himself, dismissing this woman who cared for him like that, who cooked his meals and drove him to the mall and tried playing chess with him and defended and hid him from the furies of his father.

Sometimes she'd plan a day for them to watch a movie together, and put him in charge of the selection. The local library had a surprisingly deep collection of films, albeit not too much in the way of new releases. While he hated sharing his opinions with others, there was no escape in those situations. He always hated suggesting things because he took personal responsibility if someone didn't enjoy something he recommended, like it was an extension of himself that was being rejected. If he knew he'd have to express a preference, he'd put enough thought into the assignment to make sure he'd pick an appropriate good-quality movie they'd both enjoy. He'd picked some good movies for her recently: smart, mature films about love like Wim Wenders's *Wings of Desire* and Steve Buscemi's *Trees Lounge* (plus, the former had a performance scene featuring Nick Cave, who Thomas really liked, although he didn't mention this to Mom so as to avoid having to explain the appeal).

And at those times, after a successful selection, he'd indulge himself and think, *What other fourteen-year-olds were choosing movies like this*?

><><><

His masturbatory fantasies that night were unusually baroque.

Usually, they were just small-scale fantasies about approachable girls in his class who were nice to him. They were often innocent, maybe just a girl he liked kissing him, placing his hand on her chest, and then arranging a later "date." That's all: just confirmation of being desired.

When he was particularly depressed or distraught, his fantasies became correspondingly over-the-top. Tonight, he beat up a slew of maniacs that invaded his school, impressing everybody with his unknown kickboxing skills that had just been waiting idly for an opportunity to be displayed. Every girl in his class happily flashed him as his reward. The flashing had been their idea, all of them so caught up in the exhilaration of the day's events. He saw Andrea, Alisa, Rachel, Katie, Jana, Amy, Bernadette, all happy, all topless. Bernadette and Katie weren't conventionally attractive but he encouraged their participation: he wanted everyone to get along, to join in, and they too were getting off on the devilish thrill of it, this liminal zone where everyone encouraged, no one judged. Even Brynne, why not, she could be there too, and when she flashed she joked about it as penance for her stupid comments in class. First they all flashed him separately, and then in unison, laughing and giggling, and touching each other, too, delighting in the sight of each other's breasts, the freedom of acting free of judgement, and then they all led him into a backroom, to express all of their mutual joy with him physically.

He came and as he transitioned into sleep, he was joined by his topless classmates, all together in luxurious repose.

"Help me," Thomas heard. He knew he was asleep and dreaming, and the lack of urgency allowed him to drift through the dream, as if on a soft, safe current of air. He was in a field of some kind, and it was chilly but he didn't feel cold for whatever reason. More like, the temperament of the world was chilly.

This world around him was a striking, deep azure. As if to balance out the intensity of color, the trees were intuited white shapes existing in negative; colorless bubbles in space where trees should be.

"Help me," said the pale young girl crouched before him. She was appealing in a doleful, non-threatening way, with a symmetrical face and softly pleasing features. While her voice was plangent with need, her pose — crouched, knees bent, hands on the ground by her ankles — suggested something else, like she was going to flee, or pounce.

"How?" he heard himself ask.

The girl flew straight up, up toward the negative space of the trees.

"How can I help you?!" Thomas yelled at the accelerating shape.

Once she cleared the highest tree of negative space, she glided backward in a straight line, until she floated out of view.

"I'm stuck and can't be freed," she told him. Even though she had disappeared, her voice registered at the same volume.

Thomas stared up out of a deep dark well, looking out impossibly high onto the night sky, which was now backlit by the gentle, almost humble radiance of her pleasing face.

>< >< ><

Like a gunshot in the night, his alarm popped the bubble of his sleep. *God, no*, he didn't want to get up, he wanted instead to drift back into the stasis of sleep. He was monopolized with an almost preternatural, pre-conscious dread and anxiety. *No, I don't want to get up*. Does the mouse look forward to the maze? Especially after it learns: here there will be cats? He held onto whatever sense of quaking awe and grandeur that had passed over from the dream, which only illumined the hard-edged misery of having to get up and face another school day.

"So, let's hear the names of some Latino Americans you were able to come up with," Ms. Young asked the American History class for the latest asinine waste of everyone's time. Today, they were each given a handout that required them to attempt to list 10 American celebrities in each racial and ethnic category: White Americans, Latino Americans, Female Americans, African Americans, Native Americans, Jewish Americans, Asian Americans, Muslim Americans, and so on. What he wanted to do, just to be a troublemaker, was to rudely investigate the selection of the groups: why no Hindu Americans? And wasn't "Asian" Americans insensitive, in that it conflated South Asians and East Asians and Persians as if they were one in the same? And why was the order selected, didn't that unconsciously reflect the perceived importance of each group? Why were Whites first? He could play these sophistic parlor tricks all day, and was building up his resentment to sufficient levels to get up the nerve to throw a monkey wrench in her lesson plan.

"Salma Hayek," one student offered.

"I think she's actually Mexican, as in from Mexico. I don't think she's American," another student responded.

"Ahhh," Ms. Young said with that smug shit-eating grin, "note I didn't define 'American?' Mexico is part of the Americas. What does it mean when we say 'America?'" As if she expected the class's collective mind to be blown, as if it wasn't perfectly natural to refer to "Americans" as people who lived in the United States of America in an American classroom. Ms. Young was also, at worst, hypocritical and, at best, forgetful, because at the beginning of the class she had specifically said "American citizens," which, under any normal phraseology, would refer to the United States of America, not, say, Ecuadorians.

He kept his mouth shut, of course. He didn't want to attract any attention to himself. For some reason, that relatively mild mockery he'd experienced yesterday was a tipping point that'd prevent him from raising his hand unless absolutely necessary. Neither Larry nor Ed were in this class, fortunately, but there were others in this class who, while not progressing yet to bullying, had made it known they didn't like him. He could tell.

Ms. Young was later smugly satisfied when the class wasn't able to come up with a list of 10 famous Muslim Americans. *White Christian Americans outnumbered Muslims, like, fifty to one in this country. Of course it would be easier to think of famous white celebrities! God, this was so stupid.* The class was easily able to come up with famous Jews and African-Americans, no doubt to Ms. Young's pedantic chagrin.

Then onto Native Americans, and one student said, "Michael Jackson," in all seriousness, and Ms. Young responded, again in all seriousness, in a veritable back-and-forth of po-faced idiocy, "Oh, did Michael Jackson claim Native American blood," in that exact pretentious phraseology, and the student, a moron named Bradley, continued on in his ignorance. "You said Native American. Michael Jackson, he was born in America, he from here," and Ms. Young said "ahh," and wrote ‘Michael Jackson’ on the board as if that was an acceptable response. Bradley was obviously not paying attention to what was going on, or was he so dumb to think that Native American meant anyone who had been born in America? *No, that wasn't possible. Shouldn't Ms. Young correct him? Shouldn't students be held accountable for these things?! What the fuck was the point of all this!?!?*

He couldn’t tolerate this anymore. He raised his hand and, when called on, said: "I think it's weird that ‘Asian’ is one group. It makes it seem like Chinese people or Indian people or, like, Afghani people are all the same. Why is that one grouping?"

And Ms. Young didn't respond, probably using the class commotion as plausible deniability, and when he asked the question again, she just responded with, "interesting observation, what does the class think?"

"No, I'm asking *you*, why'd you group them all together? This lesson is supposedly about racism, right? Isn't the question itself racist?"

"Let's see what the class thinks," she fielded, as if this was her intent all along.

"What is wrong with you, bro, what's your problem," said Darren, a classmate. There was commotion again with students all chiming in and soon the class ended, nothing resolved, his incisive question punted as always, just another fracas in another worthless day.

>< >< ><

He sat with Anthony, Jim, and Jay during lunch period and ate his school-bought pizza. They never hung out outside of school, so Thomas guessed that just made them all acquaintances, at best. Thomas wasn't opposed to hanging out, it just never came up, and by the time Thomas got home from school, he was too exhausted, depressed or upset to deal with other people. These guys were more like co-workers in an interminable job, and when they could punch the clock they just needed to get away from everything that reminded them of their burden and decompress in their own private ways.

The seventh and eighth graders all had the same lunch period (the sixth graders had it one class earlier). Most kids stayed in the cafeteria. Some ate lunch in certain classrooms if they wanted to hang with a particular teacher for whatever reason, while some snuck off campus to go to the Starbucks in the nearby shopping center.

Thomas always stayed in the cafeteria, as he really had nowhere else to go. Larry was usually in the cafeteria, too, although sometimes he wasn't. Thomas had once walked past the gym at lunchtime and saw Larry palling around with Mr. Robinson, a gym teacher and basketball coach, and some other kids who Thomas assumed also played sports or something, so maybe that's where Larry was on the days he wasn't in the cafeteria. Ed was rarely in the cafeteria at lunch; who knew where the fuck he went. Thomas was grateful for Ed's complete absence and Larry's sporadic absences, and reminded himself that things could always be worse.

Larry was in the cafeteria today, though. Thomas could see him several yards away talking with three other boys near the little concessionaire stand by the entrance to the hallway. He ignored their presence, and they seemed to ignore his. He wished they'd just go walk somewhere else. He hated himself for caring, for devoting any attention to these people, but he couldn't help himself. He realized that the group, while still being preoccupied with other things, with their candy or drinks, was ambling toward him. He sensed that he was being talked about, or that Larry was looking in his direction.

He did his best not to stare but took stock of who Larry was hanging out with. There was Dan, a big blonde kid in his math class. Dan didn't speak much and Thomas never had any problems with him. He knew Dan played basketball and that's probably how he knew Larry. There was Billy, who he didn't know too well as he didn't have any classes with him this year. He'd had classes with him last year and didn't have any problems.

And then (and here Thomas's heart sank): Darren, the kid who had confronted him rather rudely in Young's class. He was sure they were talking about him, the way they were looking at him. Then, perhaps just as the very act of studying something might change the results, the quiet, frightened-rabbit tension of his eavesdropping drew the group to him.

"Afghani," he heard Darren say, too-loudly and with a strange, dunderheaded intonation. His heart sank and his stomach exploded in fireworks, a Pavlovian response to what he knew would be another emotional trial. For a minute, he deluded himself into thinking that the comment was too strange to have anything to do with him, he was just picking out one word and running with it. But, no, he knew that Darren was referring to their shared American History class, no doubt mocking him as if using the proper term for someone from Afghanistan was self-evidently worthy of scorn.

Darren was looking at him, and made a dismissive face when he met Thomas's gaze. Darren made a series of head nods, to which Larry responded, looked at Thomas, smirked and laughed. Dan and Billy looked a little confused, looked at Thomas as if that would aid their understanding, and then Larry leaned in and said something to them, likely spreading the contagion of Thomas-hate.

Larry separated from the group and paced over to Thomas. He stood over Thomas's table, too close. Larry's group, which had been dallying around hesitantly, followed a few steps behind.

"When's your sister coming back?" Larry asked. The tone wasn't lecherous, just passively interested, someone just making conversation. He wanted to tell Larry to fuck off, but he could see how that would play out. Larry would turn to his group and play dumb about Thomas being so defensive. He could imagine it now, Larry turning to his friends with a mock-shocked look and asking, "Thomas, Thomas, what's with the attitude? Temper, temper," which Larry knew would invoke laughter from his pals, who by then must have figured out what was going on.

"Is she coming back for the winter break? She's a sophomore at Milwaukee, right?"

"Junior," Thomas responded, hesitantly. "I don't know, though." Larry's casual tone, the way he established that he knew Thomas enough to know that his sister was in college at Milwaukee, but that his knowledge wasn't current enough to know what grade she was in ... Thomas knew what Larry was doing. He felt like he was watching his own snare being set. Or maybe not, maybe Larry was just toying with him, or doing reconnaissance for future bullying behavior. Larry could be like that sometimes. He could be a vicious, cruel bully when he was with others; but when he was by himself, he could be completely blasé. But Larry was in a group so…

The look on the rest of the group's face was difficult to read. Perhaps ignorant of Thomas's emotional baggage, they looked at him almost like a potential equal, as if, sure, they'd joked a little about that spaz Thomas, but maybe Larry had some actual relationship with him and was asking question in earnest.

"Think she'll go back to working at Hallmark during the summer?" Monica had worked there while attending community college the last two years.

"I don't know. I doubt it."

"Nice," Larry replied. "Well she needs to come home soon. She needs to bring that fine ass back here," he said, too quickly, like he was getting away with something.

"Right, yo!" Darren said, slapping Larry on the shoulder as if it was uniquely liberating to hear another publicly express the objectifying comments he too had thought. He expected that Darren would soon end up being another convert to the bullying church of Larry. Thomas turned his head and heard someone, maybe Larry, saying, "she got those big-ass titties, too" while the others in the group laughed.

"Yo, be honest," Larry started, "you ever get a good view of those titties? Like, see her come out the shower?"

"Oh hell yeah, I wish I could see those," Darren added. Dan and Billy were both somewhere between laughing and being embarrassed. Billy said “Yo, Larry, that’s fucked up,” but quietly and continued laughing.

Larry continued. "I heard my boy Benneton said she has those big fat nips, like those big, not the nipple itself, but the area around it."

"Areola," Dan clarified.

"Yea, air-ee-ole-uhs. That's what I heard Benneton said. He fucked her all last year before her dumb ass left community college and he said she had the fattest areolas, and her nips were the same color as her tits, so they blended together like ghost nips." Thomas wasn't sure who this "Benneton" referred to and didn't want to know.

“Word?” Dan said, potentially interrupting Larry’s flow to determine the veracity of his horrible comments. “That sounds pretty hot.”

“I can’t believe you are putting up with this,” Billy said, in a tone of conflicted comraderies. He was laughing at all this, though, perhaps not realizing that Larry was actually intending to hurt Thomas. *Poor innocent Billy, maybe he thinks Larry and I are actually buddies and he's just busting my balls.*

"Of course Thomas is going to put up with it. If he tried anything he knows I'd beat his ass worse than Benneton did to his sister, no homo."

"Hah double no homo on that one," Darren added.

Larry kicked the leg of Thomas's cafeteria chair. Not hard, but hard enough to make the chintzy silver-chrome plastic buckle. "You wouldn't do shit," Larry added, a verbal kick to go alongside the physical one. And the palimpsest of Larry's faux-joviality was gone. There was the glimpse of ruthless delight, the creature that kills not to eat, but for the domination inherent in the act.

Thomas had been silent the whole time, his face and neck hot, fuming. None of his lunchmates said or did anything and Thomas wouldn't dare to turn to look at their mortified faces.

"Yo, let me ask you something, and be honest. You can admit that your sister is hot, right? Like, I know she's your sister, but you have to admit, she is fucking hot. I mean, that blonde hair, that dancer body, how stacked she is, you can admit, she's hot, right? Like, if you weren't her brother, you'd think she's hot, right?" Thomas found his head swirling in so many directions he couldn't move, couldn't respond, felt the burning of acidic upchuck in his throat, all that fury and shame and rage practically choking him.

"Man, you are retarded," said Billy, punching Larry playfully on the shoulder. Billy had that transfixed quality, like he knew he was doing something wrong and stupid but still wanted to hear Thomas's answer. Dan was now just covering his mouth and laughing sheepishly but looking side-to-side like he was waiting for an excuse to depart.

"No one could deny those titties," Darren added, giddy, as if this was his first dabble in the freeing world of bullying. Thomas doubted it would be his last, no doubt he was intoxicated watching Larry the Maestro.

Now he'd have Darren to worry about the in the future, too. Larry made bullying so effortless and almost-charming, in his way. There was an undeniable fascination that was obvious even to

Thomas; he couldn't guarantee that, were he in someone like Dan's or Billy's position, that he'd look away. He'd like to think that he would, but he understood it must be such a bewildering, mesmerizing thing to watch. Although he was bearing the brunt, he understood the fascination of the cocked trigger.

"Well, alright, I know this isn't something you want to talk about. She's fine, don't get me wrong, we all know she's fine, but I get why you wouldn't want to talk about it." Larry made a gesture, putting his arm out and tilting his wrist as if expecting Thomas to extend his hand for some kind of shake, even though Larry was several feet away and surrounded by his friends. Maybe that was some new, popular gesture Thomas wasn't familiar with.

"Oh, so that's how it is? I get it then, I get it. No daps? I see the real you," and the group laughed again, as if this nonsense made sense. He didn't know how to react; he just maintained his look of confused destructiveness, staring hot daggers.

"It's cool, don't worry about it. Just don't come and shoot up the school."

Darren mumbled something that Thomas didn't hear clearly, but he mentally reconstructed as, "nah, faggot don't have the balls to do that."

The pain was slow-motion: the stewing, lingering, the way it seemed set, lodged inside him, slowly expanding in heat and intensity throughout his body, contaminating him. Meanwhile, his thoughts were sped-up, too jumbled to articulate. Somewhere, he thought it best to say nothing, as if to somehow shame Larry in the court of public opinion through the obvious discrepancy in their temperament, as if Thomas could win people over through stoicism. That was stupid, he knew. This wasn't fair.

"Awww, little Thomas gonna explode? Look at him, he looks like he's gonna burst. Probably going to run home and jerk off into his sister's underwear drawer. Nah actually, I bet that slut doesn't wear underwear. Okay, be like that, don't sweat it. Just, when she comes back into town, give her my number, okay?"

Another Larry trick, always ending on a little tag or joke. Then Larry trotted off with a confident step, his crew a couple of paces behind. Billy was shaking his head a little, something like "damn": the tension was too much for him. He shared a look with Dan.

Darren enjoyed it, and was talking to Dan in seeming obliviousness of his discomfort.

>< >< ><

After school, Thomas wandered alone in the sparse woods around his house. He'd felt nauseous for the rest of the day, and didn't look forward to explaining his low appetite to his mother. He wished he could tell her, but he felt ashamed on so many levels. That she'd produced and raised a son defective enough to attract bullies (bullying wasn't randomly distributed, after all); that he wasn't able to handle his own problems; that if he told her about it, he'd be worrying her and making her feel helpless.

Worse than the bullying (okay, not worse than the bullying, but pretty bad, on a deeper existential level) was how Larry monopolized his thoughts long after the event. He imagined authority figures confronting Larry, and Larry, perhaps genuinely, dismissing all of it as just a lark, nothing to get so worked up about it. "I didn't mean any of it, I was just joking around," the Larry in his imagination said. God, he shouldn't even have to be thinking about any of this, but he had no choice. He had to strategize, think of a way to minimize his encounters with Larry.

If Thomas had tried to fight back, he'd lose. Larry was considered a good kid, meaning he did well enough in school, didn't get into trouble, and didn't get into fights. It's not like Larry was some seasoned fighter. But he was certainly bigger and stronger than Thomas. And Larry was smart enough to needle, be a little physical but nothing dramatic, and if Thomas swung first, Larry would knock him out and Thomas would be the one expelled. Even if Thomas could prove whatever Larry had said to instigate the fight, words never rationalized violence in the skewed bully-favoring logic of willfully-blind appeasement that was junior high.

It didn't seem to matter to any of their classmates that Larry's whole performance was a transparent attempt to look cool, to curry favor with others by tearing down a weak target. Didn't anyone remember that Larry and Thomas had been friendly just a few years ago? Didn't anyone question Larry's purported motives for any of this? Of course, no one probably gave any of this a moment's thought, just enjoyed the spectacle. That Larry's comments were stupid, simple, lacking in any snap or wit ... didn't that even matter?

And how pathetic was *he*, judging the performance of his abuser? No wonder he was the target.

Thomas knew he was defective, in a sense. He couldn't function, couldn't relate to people, was scrawny and craven and yet, counterintuitively, narcissistic and brash. Above all, he was smart, and knew his problems and limitations. Maybe that's why he didn't want to confide in his mother. She must be aware that he had no real friends, that he spent almost all his time alone. She probably had her doubts about him, about his life and his mental and emotional health, and he didn't want to confirm her worries.

Things will get better, he told himself, despite every instinct and fiber of his being and what he knew about the arc of the universe. Teenagers are unusually stupid, cruel and petty, popular culture told him. But maybe he'd keep his head down, go to a good college, get a good job, lead a good life, and all this would be behind him, nothing but a memory. Adolescence is the worst time in everyone's life, he told himself, despite the fact that it actually appeared that many adolescents were living great lives, had great friends, and were creating great memories.

Like Larry, for instance.

"I think that branch has had enough."

Thomas looked down, and his hands were silty with bark and debris. The twig he'd forgotten he was carrying was shorn, gnarly and jagged where he'd stripped it.

"Heh, so it is," he said, casually throwing the tree piece onto the ground. He brushed his hands together and wiped them on his jeans. He instinctively wanted the man to think he was cool, even if he didn't know when the man had appeared, why he'd stopped, or why he was even talking to him.

"Sorry about that," Thomas said.

"No need to apologize to me." And then a beat. "That branch, maybe, but not me."

That was another thing Thomas did: apologized if he did something poorly. Like if he missed a free throw in gym class, he'd apologize to his teammates or, even more lamely, the gym teacher, who couldn't care less and would sometimes give a shrug that was meant to be friendly and say, “Thomas, why are you apologizing to me?” Sometimes it wouldn't even be if he did something poorly; just if he got called out on doing something differently or strangely. He'd once apologized to a teacher who'd observed him holding his pen in a unique way. His instinct was just to apologize, and each time, he'd be asked why he was apologizing, and even though he had no cognizable answer, he did it, each time.

"Hah, yeah, I guess so." The man in front of him was Caucasian, looked fit and healthy but not overbearingly so, had short brown hair, a smooth face and black-rimmed, round glasses that looked like they could be designer. Thomas wasn't good at identifying designer things. More like his glasses framed his face well. The man looked to be in his early- to-mid-20s, wore blue jeans and a dark blue patterned sweater. Thomas wondered strangely if he'd picked them out himself, or if he had someone, like a girlfriend, to help him, as women were generally more attuned to those sorts of things.

"So, what are you doing out here?" the man asked.

"Nothing much. Do you-do you live around here?" Human interaction made Thomas inherently uneasy. Other people were capricious. A terrifying thought came to him: maybe this guy was trouble? That'd just be his luck, as if he emitted a persuasive pull attuned to the wavelength of the world's predators.

"Live here? It's the woods. Well, not really the woods. It's woods where you can still see people's houses in the distance so I don't know if that counts as the woods. But no, I don't live in any of these houses around here. I'm just chilling out here, doing nothing, I guess you could say, just like you."

"Oh, cool. I come out here a lot, sometimes to look at birds." (*Gay!* Thomas thought. Although it was true, he did like to look at and hear the birds; he liked the way they hopped about.) "But anyway, I come out here a bit — a lot — and I've never seen you before."

For some reason Thomas's mind discarded the possibility of danger. This guy didn't seem dangerous. Maybe he was high or something? It seemed like almost everyone in their early 20s around here smoked pot. But no, the man seemed remarkably sober. He felt like he could give the guy a pop quiz on any random subject and the guy would know all the answers.

'Never seen you before,' Thomas had said? *Did that sound accusatory? Like he was the sheriff of these parts keeping score of*

comers and goers?

"You the sheriff of these here parts?" the man asked, looking at the ground in the near distance.

Thomas froze. Had Thomas articulated that thought, and was the guy repeating it to make fun of him?

"I'm just kidding, man. Yeah, I'm out here, sometimes. I try and go a lot of places. This is the best time to be out here, when the air is crisp and clean and uncluttered, you know, before it gets too cold, before the snow covers everything. I like to watch the animals, the squirrels, make their wintertime preparations. It's relaxing. You observe the sky and the birds, I get the ground and the squirrels. Together, we got 'the woods' covered."

"And what happens if a squirrel runs from the ground up into a tree, who claims that? Also, we have to find someone to observe the insides of the trees or under the ground and then we'd really have the whole woods covered."

"Yeah. You have any woodpecker friends or worm friends?"

"Not yet." Hearing the word "pecker" aloud was enough to make Thomas uncomfortable, as if the conversation was now redolent with sexual innuendo, and his initial skepticism came back to him. Why exactly, would a seemingly better-than-normal guy in his mid-20s be talking to a scrubby, scared-of-his-own-shadow twerpy fourteen-year-old? *"Worm" friends ... was that a threat? Like, buried with the worms? Worm food?*

Thomas was getting scared. "Well, nice to meet you. I probably have to get going home."

"Hey man, what's your name?"

He made a weird fumbled breathing sound, almost like a burp, and said "Thomas." He'd been saying something else, halfway toward giving a fake name, but he was undone by his base habit of submitting to authority figures.

"Thomas. Didn't mean to scare you, Thomas. You looked spooked there for a second. I'm Brandon. Is everything okay, Thomas? I mean, I know I just met you, and it's not really my business at all, but, is everything okay? I noticed you for a couple of minutes before I said anything. You looked upset, or like you were going through some things. If you want to continue hanging out here alone, I can go, I don't want you to have to leave on my account."

"Uhh ...." Thomas didn't know what to say. He kept silent for a second, and knew that if he tried to speak, his voice would be cracked or hoarse. He felt sweat dampening under his armpits and wet pressure building behind his eyes. Thomas was moved, unexpectedly. Thomas was someone who kept to himself in part because, to make it through the day, he needed to calibrate his emotions. The capricious element was something to be avoided, and, while this seemingly good-natured exchange existed on the opposite side of the spectrum from the day's earlier bullying, they were both unexpected and dramatic, both popped different-sized holes in the emotional armor he wore to keep the world at a necessary distance.

"I'm okay," Thomas said, clearly not. He imagined Brandon saying goodbye and heading off, never to be seen again, Thomas wondering for the rest of his life what became of him, returning to this spot again and again in hopes of running into him. Thomas fled from emotional engagement out of self-preservation, but then obsessed and cherished those rare moments when someone had expressed genuine kindness. Thomas still remembered fondly an experience at this place called The Rusty Pelican, somewhere in Florida, where he went with his family for dinner while on a vacation maybe three years ago. They had a waiter named Tracy. While that sounds like a female name, he was a male waiter, and Tracy had been so nice to him. Thomas didn't even remember the details of Tracy's fondly-reminisced kindness, and maybe his memory distorted things, or maybe Thomas had just been really sad that day and attached disproportionate generosity to Tracy's behavior. Tracy had been a waiter, after all, and waiters work for tips. But however Tracy had acted, Thomas remembered his aura of general kindness quite fondly. It was sad, Thomas thought, his primary reference point for non-familial human kindness was a waiter from years ago.

"Yeah, I'm okay," the act of repeating the phrase obvious evidence to the contrary. Thomas looked away and tried to turn as if he was looking at something, just to break eye contact. "You know, school sucks and all, but other than that, I'm good. I don't even know why I'm telling you that school sucks. School sucks for everybody, I bet, no big deal," although that was something he wasn't sure about. The impression he got from movies was that, while adolescence was awkward, that's when the most cherished friendships were formed and the most intense emotions experienced, and sometime after college people started really pining for their misbegotten youth. Who knows, maybe in thirty years, his memory will have faded and distorted to such a degree that he'd be nostalgic about his times spent wandering out in the woods alone with precious time to think, even if in reality he spent these times fretting about the next day's dangers.

Brandon would surely take Thomas's desultory comments as a reason to depart. And maybe Brandon was about to, he gave that look-around that people do, as if viewing a clock that only they could see, reminding them of their obligations elsewhere. But the look Brandon gave Thomas radiated such kindness, as if something glowed within him that was poorly served by the canvas available for its expression, the sensitive eyes and understanding smile only hinted at the depths of sympathy that lay within.

><><><

How stupid I am, Thomas thought that night in bed. It was out of pity, perhaps, that Brandon eventually broke off the conversation, allowing Thomas to keep his dignity before he became too overcome with the desire to bleat out all his fears and depressions on this well-meaning stranger. *Man, that guy dodged a bullet.*

Or maybe it wasn't that simple. Maybe I dodged the bullet. Or worse. Brandon was probably a sex offender, Thomas thought, perhaps stupidly. Why else would he be out in the woods talking to young teenage boys? He thought that for no one, as no part of him even believed it, but still he heard his mind repeat it. That was a stupid youthful imbecility, and he needed to purge himself of such sentiments.

He rested in his bed, fighting against nature to stay awake, to stretch out the night, his essential alone-time. Better to exist in the half-roused state he was in and occupy his mind with other things than dedicate himself to sleep and end up in tomorrow and its troubles. So he jerked off twice and went on for a third, his penis strained and scorched until he gave up, unable to conjure the necessary alluring fantasies.

He dreamt again of the girl in the well. Upon seeing her, he thought how smart he must be, how much subconscious brain processing power he was capable of, as she was rendered in this dream exactly like she had been before. She carried a note written in immaculate gold print, which was legible both to his in-dream-avatar and to his dreaming "real" self, and he thought, again, how impressive this was, that he could render print so ornate yet legible and prose so crisp and flowing, all in a dream. The prose meant something to him at the time, but he knew that when he woke the specifics of the dream would become wobbly and imprecise, whatever plaintive poignancy experienced within the dream would seem like juvenile nonsense upon the waking. And maybe it was a self-fulfilling prophecy, but that's indeed how he felt when he awoke the following morning.

The prickly anxiety and hopelessness of having to survive another day at school greeted him. Such wonders he could dream up when his imagination was free, and then, gone. He lay on his back, passively stone-faced, while he felt what only could be described as noiseless, motionless crying.

He wished to be a baby again, to be rocked back to sleep in huge, understanding arms, cooed and cosseted and secured. No one without security ever seriously debated the tension between liberty and security. That was a parlor game, for those lucky enough and comfortable enough to spend leisure time weighing the relative benefits of privilege.

It was a cold day. The crisp air invigorated his lungs, snapped him a bit from his early morning stupor. His bundled clothes again brought to mind the desire to escape into sleep. A temporary suicide, a comedian had once called sleeping, and it was true. Sometimes he wished the bus would explode before arriving; well, not really explode, he just wanted any miracle to avoid going to school. Which was a shame, because he loved reading, he loved learning; it was absurd, really, that he was in this situation. Absurd. The teachers at school do nothing, lazy spoiled fucking assholes with their summers off and pensions. They enjoyed seeing him put in his place. They knew he was more astute than most of them, sharper. His indignation burned him, made his head hurt a bit.

"Hey, Thomas?" It was Brandon, walking toward him, just a bit to the side. How did Thomas not see him; Brandon was practically staring right at him. Thomas could be spacey like that sometimes. ("I can see the lights are on there but no one seems to be home," his father had once said to him at dinner, which drew a sharp rebuke from his mother, to which his father grumbled and played innocent about how his comment had been interpreted. Thomas would never forget that, or his father's self-serving suggestions to "turn the page" when Thomas stewed.)

"Hey, Brandon," Thomas responded as Brandon extended a confident hand. Thomas took it and clenched weakly, then tried to toughen it up, then loosened it when he worried he was being pinchy instead of firm.

Brandon smiled. "You're a funny guy, you know that, man."

"Thanks," Thomas said unsurely. Thomas *was* a funny guy, he read a lot and always came up with bon mots and zingers and cutting comments but never had anyone to tell them to. He read an article once about people selling used underwear, and later saw a movie that had a scene with a bunch of attractive men and women in a club dancing with sweaty abandon in a club. After that scene, he wanted to lean over to someone and say "now *that's* the type of underwear that would sell," but he had no one to say it to.

"Hey Thomas, we should hang out sometime. You like video games and good movies." Thomas made to reply but then realized there was no question there. He was excited and flattered but those feelings were fleeting because he wasn't an idiot. Why would an older, normal, seemingly-cool young man like Brandon want to hang out with him, unless he planned on a) exploiting him or b) raping him. Oh God, Thomas begged for just simple exploitation, the classic "give me your lunch money" idea that, in all his years of being bullied, had never actually occurred. Bullying was much more psychologically invasive than something as simple as a proto-mugging.

He waited for Brandon to make his threatening entreaty. Would he be someone who slowly lords over his power and savors Thomas's squirming, or was he more of the direct, brutish sort? With these last few years of experience, Thomas could make tree diagrams of all the different bullying tactics.

"No, I mean it. You're a good dude." Brandon looked around and put his hand to his temple, smiling, and Thomas feared the jig was up, the veil was going to drop and Brandon's sinister designs would be made clear. But no, the smile was self-deprecating, not aggressive. "This is always the hard part here and I imagine you're not just walking out at seven in the morning for your own health. You got to get to school, right?

"Well, okay. So I'll just cut to the chase. Let's hang out and I'll explain more. But I'm going to be your new friend. And all this shit you deal with at school, give me the word and all that grief is over with. I mean it. I know how it is. Larry, Ed, Darren, Billy, all of them."

Billy? The Billy who'd joined in with Larry recently or ... Billy Gilligan? Wow. That brought him back. Billy Gilligan bullied him and some of his then-friends (and basically, everyone) back in elementary school. Gilligan's behavior was less like bullying and more like out-and-out flaming sociopathy. Rumor was his stepfather used to beat the ever-living shit out of him. Who knows what happened to Billy Gilligan, rumor was he got sent to some rehabilitation center, probably the youngest kid there. All Brandon remembered about Billy Gilligan was his 5th grade yearbook photo. Billy had missed his original yearbook photo and the school made him submit his own to replace it. The picture Gilligan submitted was an unintentionally hilarious spook show. If Gilligan had any degree of self-awareness, it would have been a funny prank, but knowing Gilligan, it was just intensely weird. It was a photo of Gilligan's face in black-and-white, the austerity accentuating his raccoon eyes, which appeared only as dark pits, and his blonde locks appeared ghostly white, swooped across his face so he looked like a battered Dust Bowl orphan.

How'd Brandon know about Billy Gilligan?

"How do you know about Billy Gilligan?" The border separating Thomas's mind and his mouth could be dangerously porous.

"I know a lot of things. Pretty exciting, isn't it? Check this out." Brandon flexed the fingers of his right hand, retracted them as if he wanted to throw a palm strike, then extended them again. "Blam!" he said, and the word, B-L-A-M, emerged out from some invisible passage inside his palm, in big, cloud-bracketed letters. The word measured maybe six inches across and six inches wide. *Good dimensions*, Thomas thought bizarrely. *A good size to be visible but not attract attention. Could be passed off as just a puff of smoke to a passerby*. Why Thomas thought about the aesthetics of this trick, he had no idea.

"Cool. That's cool. You'll have to show me how you did that later." He wasn't really into magic tricks but he wanted to be nice and let Brandon know that he did want to chill with him sometime. Any topic can be interesting if explained by an adept, enthusiastic practitioner.

"You aren't suitably impressed. I low-balled that. I tried to do something that shows you I mean business, but not something that would make your head explode and turn you into a babbling idiot. I low-balled that. Shit. Here, let me try something else."

Thomas was about a block away from his bus stop. He strained his neck to look down the block to see if his bus might be coming, but he was at a bad angle.

"I should really get to the bus stop. Not that I like school, but I wouldn't want to go back to my mom and get her to drive me if I missed the bus."

"I hear you. Just check this out. Well, let me think, actually, I don't want to blow up your world here or anything, I understand you got to get to school and such." Brandon put his hand to his chin for a moment, thoughtfully. "Okay, how about this."

He indicated toward some of the light brown and orange leaves covering the yard in front of where they stood on the street. The crackly leaves rose up, perhaps a foot off the ground. The leaves swirled in a wide circle, sensually, like they were stretching out, enjoying a kind of lazy indolence. There was no question that the leaves were tracking the wide motions of Brandon's fingers. Thomas imagined that *Flight of the Plum*s song, or whatever ditty played when Bugs Bunny did his tricks.

Following the flume motion of Brandon's fingers, the leaves flew up further, almost zestfully, like they wanted nothing more than to fly straight up and had finally been given the opportunity. The brittle leaves soared and then popped into crispy dust with an audible "poof." The leaf-powder came back down in a straight line, as if siphoned through a funnel, to rest atop Brandon's outstretched hand, which lay flat like he'd just thrown 'paper' in *Rock, Paper, Scissors*. He quickly pulled back his hand, and the leaf-dust stayed aloft a beat behind. Then, looking like orange-tinged glitter, it wafted harmlessly onto the cold roadway.

"For the record, the hand motions mean nothing. They were just there for flair and to let you know that I was controlling all that."

"I figured you were."

"But, you know, you weren't impressed with my 'word' magic so I really had to hammer my skills into your head."

"I appreciate the efforts."

"So, still want to hang out later?"

"Sure."

And Thomas gave Brandon his cell phone number and pointed indistinctly up to where he lived, at the top of the street's incline. Brandon didn't need that information but he didn't say anything. Flexible plans were made to hang out for later that day and Thomas went to his bus stop with whatever special effects he'd just seen operating only in the background of his mind. That was incredible yet somehow unmoving, like all tricks of prestidigitation. Thomas had previously thought about learning little visual coin or card tricks, back when he'd thought about burnishing his reputation at school and getting a "thing," like the punks or the jocks or the hip-hip kids. But that'd been a dumb idea and ever since he held a low opinion of magic tricks. What predominated in his mind now was how cool it was that he'd made a new friend, but he didn't want to hold onto the certainty of that too strongly because you never know.

He worried that his mom might think it was weird that Brandon was so much older than him.

>< >< ><

It was 2:30 p.m. and Thomas was back home from school. His mom was out somewhere and obviously his dad would be home much later. He checked his snacks supply. Double Stuffed Oreos, Whoopie Pies, Swiss Cake Rolls, ice cream, potato chips, Tostitos, pretzels, various salsas and cheese dips. He ate about four Oreos a day and an occasional Whoopie Pie or Swiss Cake Roll. (In his mind, the two dessert cakes were rivals, so he always had to pick one or the other, as if the two wouldn't mix in his stomach.) He knew he was at a blessed age where his metabolism could burn through the junk food.

Thomas heard the knocking at the front door, loud but polite, and looked out the blinds to see Brandon, still wearing the same outfit. Brandon gave him an imperfect devil horns, as his thumb was also sticking out. *Triceratops horns*, Thomas thought.

Thomas opened the door.

"Hey man."

"Hey Thomas. You have to formally let me in before I can enter."

"Shut up, man."

"Hah yeah, I know, you called my bluff." Brandon came in and Thomas gave him the tour. Thomas offered him anything from his fine selection of quality junk food, and Brandon took a Whoopie Pie and ate it and seemed to like it, but Thomas got the unverifiable impression that Brandon was eating only to be nice. But then again, Thomas knew he was a veritable weirdo who obsessed over the smallest things. Some of Brandon's bites seemed too small, and some were too big; there was no flow to his eating, and whether he took a big or small bite the masticating was seamlessly efficient in an unnatural way. And toward the end it seemed that Brandon noticed that Thomas was noticing it, and only then made more of a show of chewing.

"Good Whoopie Pie," he said once the treat was fully eaten, rubbing a bit of the extant cream from the wrapper onto his thumb.

"No one says that. They're all the same, you know. Spit out by a machine."

"Wait, you're telling me that wasn't handmade?" and then a giggle. "I know, man. I'm just being weird."

Thomas continued showing him around the house, but the whole time Thomas had the soft feeling that this was somehow all perfunctory. As if Brandon knew all this already, or that this was all somehow just a prologue to something blessedly unforced and inevitable.

They assembled an enviable collection of future snacks and played video games. Brandon was pretty good at *Smash Brothers*. After they had an equal amount of 1 vs. 1 wins, it seemed appropriate to move to a co-op game, as if a grudging truce had emerged. They chose *Grabgonders*.

They skirted around the paramount topic, which was what exactly inspired Brandon to befriend the cranky lost little lamb that was Thomas. They talked about the Oakwood mall, girls, video games, computer tech, and cool films. Brandon made references to some niche films and music, and to a cool music venue in the greater area that Thomas vaguely knew about.

Brandon did most of the talking. Thomas didn't want to reveal too much of himself just yet. Film and music tastes were personal somehow, constituted a greater sort of admission about oneself than video game tastes, where the critical consensus on what games were good was fairly unanimous. Thomas was caught between wanting to impress Brandon with his film knowledge but feared critical reprisal for expressing appreciation for something that Brandon thought was stupid or lame. So Thomas joined in enough to let Brandon know that he was at least minimally well-versed on the subject, but didn't articulate anything that would lock himself into any position on the subject.

"You're a squirrelly dude," Brandon eventually said, and then looked over at Thomas with an anticipatory smirk. Thomas looked at Brandon, looked back at the television screen, then looked again at him while narrowing his eyes, looked back at the screen, and then looked back at Brandon, narrowing his eyes into a studied exaggeration of vengeance.

Brandon laughed. "So, here's the thing, man."

Thomas figured whatever Brandon was about to say would address that magic show from before.

"So, Thomas, I'm going to be your friend."

"Yeah, you said that already. You already are."

"No, I mean ... look, you ever read *Calvin and Hobbes*?"

"Of course. *Calvin and Hobbes* is the best." Thomas had cut-outs from *Calvin and Hobbes* on the interior of his bedroom door. (He'd only shown Brandon where his room was, but hadn't shown him inside). His love for *Calvin and Hobbes* was an admission he'd never make at school. Sure, it was universally cherished in the larger world, especially among the critics who mattered. But at school, you never know what opinion might be considered "gay" or stupid or too revealing. Sharing things was a first step into people exposing you. All people needed was a hook into you.

"Well, I'm like Hobbes, then, although I don't want to stroke your ego too much in saying that makes you Calvin, because that would mean you'd be a child savant. No kid, certainly no six-year-old, would have a vocabulary that extensive. That ... grandiloquent. Dare I say it, that magniloquent?"

Thomas turned to him.

"See what I'm doing?"

"Indubitably. Did you study all the words ending in 'quent?"

"Study 'em? I live 'em! Why do you think I'm such a delinquent?"

Thomas snorted and rolled his eyes on that one.

"Well-played."

"I'll take that as an acknowledged doth of the cap," and Brandon mock-did so with his right hand, still able to admirably use Kingvekl's triple-six shooter skill to blast the charging Bull Grabgonders into pixelated red mush.

"I don't remember Hobbes having magic powers, though," Thomas said.

"Well, that's where the comparison ends, I suppose. What I mean is, look ..." and Brandon again made a face of consternation: explaining this uniqueness of his seemed to be the only time his façade of control ever slipped. "I could, if I wanted to, just explain it to you subconsciously, like, the metaphorical snap-my-fingers-and-it's-there type thing. You've seen *The Matrix*, right? I know it came out recently and you're more of a classics guy. But where Neo wakes up and—"

"I know kung fu." That'd been the rare movie Thomas saw in the theaters. Given all the hype, he had gotten his mother to take him to see it. Thomas lacked a personality unwound enough to try a real Keanu Reeves impression, so he didn't. He did say "I know kung fu" slower than he would otherwise have, assuming a situation could be devised where Thomas really knew kung fu and wanted to convey that information.

"Exactly. I could just implant the explanation in your head. But I respect you too much to do that. I think you can just get it if I explain it."

"Well, out with it then. Try me already." Thomas wondered how their friendship might proceed. Everyone had their weird peccadillos that were ignored for the greater good of camaraderie: someone being hot-headed, or sensitive to certain touchy subjects. Thomas fancied himself a logical person, and if someone had some aversion to a topic for some purely emotional or irrational reason, Thomas would have trouble resisting it. If someone was wrong, they needed to be convinced, shown the error of their ways. Was Brandon's irrationality going to be this strange-sounding messiah fixation? That might be a bridge too far to cross, Thomas knew, but he pushed the thought away, an issue for another time. For now, it was nice just to have a friend over. And Brandon seemed so sharp, so put-together, that Thomas still held out hope that he was just misapprehending whatever point Brandon was straining to get across to him.

"Just, look man, here, let me try this." Brandon paused the game and looked around.

"Aww dude, I'm going to get killed when you un-pause it." Pausing the game stopped the animation, and he'd been actively strafing a spread-bomb raven pellet. The herky-jerky resumption of the moving animation would end up with him in the crossfire. When you were in the zone, you didn't interrupt the game. Funny, Brandon pausing the game abruptly was a bigger annoyance than his messiah complex. *Give me a thousand weirdos as long as they only rocked the unimportant boats.*

"Eh, whatever. Not a big deal though," Thomas added despite himself because he wanted be cool. It was a big deal: he had one more life than Brandon and now, after the unfair death that was bound to happen when the game was un-paused, they'd be equal. Thomas liked being the stronger partner.

The keep case for *Grabgonders* floated away from the television and hovered, as if in patient abeyance, before them. The case opened, and the game manual (which Thomas always kept in the designated internal pocket on the left-hand side of the keep case) floated out. All the pages opened in neat, successive order, then the book floated back into the case, and Thomas even heard the appropriate (and still, even under these circumstances, satisfying) clasp of the pocket's hard plastic securing the manual. Then the case rotated a full 360 degrees, floated down to the ground and stood tall, as if held on display at Electronics Boutique.

The case then skidded around. *Impossible*, Thomas thought, as if this was the impossible part, because the ground was carpet and no way the case wouldn't catch on the carpet and tip over. It skidded all the way around them in a circumferential journey until it returned to its original stop. It then floated back up again to its original position by the television.

Thomas said nothing, felt nothing. Somehow he wasn't stunned, as if he'd convinced himself a while ago that Brandon had been telling the truth and the demonstration was almost redundant confirmation. Like a bored security guard not needing to see I.D., *I know who you are*, waving the well-known faces on by.

Thomas flexed his head and ear muscles, felt the tension it caused in his head, a slight strain. There was a jumble of thoughts. Maybe the strain would shake his brain out of a stupor. *Or maybe Brandon said he wouldn't implant thoughts into my head, but he did anyway. He implanted acceptance into my brain, and that's why I'm accepting this so passively?* If that was the case, though, ear flexing wouldn't do anything. It just caused discomfort and made the back of his head feel tense.

"I don't know what to say."

"We'll have plenty of time to talk, man. I don't want to dwell on it. I mean, I know I just did all that. I just wanted to get that out of the way, sort of. Just prove what I was saying was legit, and move on. If you didn't want to be friends, it's not like I'd make you. I just wanted to show you that, you know, we're friends and I can help you. The stuff I'm saying isn't bullshit. That was all, like, a demonstration of services. I can be of use to you, man. You don't have to put up with the shit you put up with in school."

"I want to be friends. Just don't use it any of that stuff to cheat at video games."

"Oh, I wouldn't dream of it, brotha." Thomas had never heard anyone say "brotha," other than in the movies. He never imagined a situation where it wouldn't sound forced, but from Brandon, it didn't.

They continued playing, and Thomas felt subconscious about speaking less. *You don't have to put up with that shit in school*. He knew what Brandon had been talking about. His own recollection of his recent bullying — and the confirmation that Brandon knew about it — made his face feel hot. It made Thomas feel lesser, like he was reduced in some way.

He wanted to say that it was odd that Brandon was to break this out so soon in their relationship. *Maybe it also worked on another level to explain why this normal young guy in his twenties who looks like he should have a bunch of friends his own age would want to hang out with me? Maybe it's like if people start dating and one of them has herpes and needs to let the other person know as soon as possible to be fair to them? Like, just get it out of the way, make sure we're all on the same page. Haha that's a gross way of looking at things, right?*

"Well, I believe you. I don't know what else to say. You've proven it. I mean, I can't explain away what I saw, I guess. So, if this is like *Calvin and Hobbes*, does that mean you're imaginary?"

"You well know that Bill Watterson never resolved the issue of whether Hobbes was real or not."

"You know what I mean."

"I know. No, I'm definitely real, don't worry about that. You aren't tied up in some insane asylum pooping yourself." For some reason "pooping yourself" sounded more vulgar than saying "shitting yourself." More of an affront to Thomas's sentiments; Thomas resented the verb change because pooping was a kiddy euphemism.

"Just that, you know, it's not like I go showing these powers or having these conversations with just about anybody. I meant, like, we're close buds, is all."

There were common sense protestations to make, namely that they'd just met, but again, Thomas didn't. He didn't really even think it, other than noting that it would be a plausible objection to make. If Thomas wanted to make it extra weird, he could say that Brandon might technically be his best friend, since Brandon was over to his house and Thomas hadn't had a friend over in, who knows how long, a couple years? But everything was clicking well, kind of shifting into a natural rhythm between them. They'd be — were — fast-friends, and any objection just felt premature, something that would be thrown back in his face after their inevitable future marathon hanging-out sessions.

Thomas heard the garage door opening. Shit, his mom was home. Not that he was doing anything wrong, but he liked being able to fastidiously plan for all encounters. He'd wanted to mention Brandon in passing a few times to his mother before they ever met, just so when they did meet, she wouldn't be surprised or have any weird suspicions about him hanging out with an older friend.

She came home, saw some kind of video games being played on the T.V. and sighed internally. *Again with the video games, always with the video games.*

"Hi hun, how was your day," she said, putting her car keys back in her pocketbook as she walked through the downstairs living room toward the stairs. She did a slight double-take after she realized there was another boy sprawled on his back, playing the game alongside Thomas.

"Oh, hello, I didn't see you there."

Thomas paused the game (noting to himself that he paused it at an appropriate time, with neither character likely to die when the game resumed) and Brandon stood up to introduce himself.

"This is Brandon," Thomas said by way of sparse introduction.

"Well hello, Brandon," his mom responded. Thomas thought she said that in such a way to poke fun at the brevity of his introduction. No, he was wrong, she seemed happy he had a friend over, which made him feel a bit ashamed at how pathetic he was that his mother gave perceptible signs of satisfaction that her loser son maybe, just maybe, had a friend.

Nothing on his mother's face suggested there was anything out of the ordinary about Brandon or his age. She just asked if he lived in the neighborhood, maybe as a way of fishing out if he was new in town or new to Brandon's school or something. He could tell his mother wanted to ask how they'd met, but she refrained and said she'd leave them to their games: "don't want to interrupt game time."

"Yes, because that's what we call it. We call it game time," Thomas dead-panned.

"That's what I call life. Game time," Brandon added.

She invited Brandon to stay for dinner but he declined, saying he had to eat at home but would certainly take her up on the offer some other time.

An hour later and Brandon told Thomas he had to get going.

"Someone picking you up?"

"What do you think?"

"I think no."

"Yeah, that's ... that means we both know no one is picking me up."

"I know. But, like, you don't need a ride anywhere or something?"

"No. I get around. If I was a djinn I'd have a magic carpet."

"But you aren't, so what do you have?"

"Whatever I want, brotha, whatever I want. K, see you man. I got your numbers, we'll be in touch."

"Me thinks you don't need my numbers to get in touch with me."

"Look at the big brain on Thomas over here, he's catching on. You won't be needing me soon."

"Big brains don't get you dead bullies though, am I right?"

"Oh shit, I like that, my man really *is* catching on."

"Alright, man," and they shook hands. Thomas had only made that comment about dead bullies as a way of maintaining the rhythm of the repartee, nothing more. He also liked ending on a triumphant note, a "hell yeah" type of moment. He regretted it immediately, though. He didn't want Brandon to get the wrong idea, and frankly he never wanted the topic of his bullying to ever come up between them.

"So Brandon, if you see any car with one of those Calvin Pissing on Something bumper stickers, promise me you'll blow that car up real good. I hate those things. You know those are all unlicensed. Bill Watterson refused to commercialize the comic. I think that's cool of him."

"You got it, brotha."

Thomas opened the front door after Brandon put his shoes on and assembled himself within his jacket.

"You know I'm just kidding about the dead bully thing, right?"

Brandon, enfolding the lapel of his jacket around his neck, pointed a finger at him. He waited a beat, and then said, with an ingratiating smirk:

"Are you sure about that?"

Thomas gave an amicably disdainful half-eye feint and said: "Alright man, get out of here."

"Peace, brotha," Brandon gave as his parting comment as he walked out the door.

>< >< ><

At dinner that night his mother brought up Brandon. His father perked up and seemed to listen for a bit but that proved ephemeral. His mother's eventual conclusion was that Brandon seemed like a nice boy. She inquired laconically around the circumstances of how they'd met. Then, again casually, using as few words as possible, about how long they'd known each other.

Thomas knew what she was doing, fishing out details in her roundabout way, because she knew he hated talking about himself. It was admirable, really, that she didn't push, but it still bothered him only because he knew what she was doing, and she knew what she was doing, too. He felt like the subtext was her ascertaining how exactly he'd gotten a friend. Like it was such a big deal. He disliked allusion and this whole tittering subtlety, too. It was like an inside-joke, and he hated inside-jokes. He was a populist in that way. *Just, c'mon, out with it! You want to know how Thomas made a friend*!

Thomas said he met Brandon through Chris Newby, a guy who worked at the Gamestop at the mall. ("Y'know Chris Newby? The guy who works at Gamestop? The guy I hang out with sometimes when he's working." He clarified when they didn't know who he was talking about. She still wasn't sure.)

He remembers vividly the embarrassment he'd once felt when he asked his mom and dad if one of them could drop him off at the mall so he could hang out with Newby while he worked. They'd spoken in low voices to each other about one of them dropping Thomas off at the mall, and one of them said to the other something about Thomas getting to the age where he'd no longer want to spend every weekend night in the house. Thomas heard that and was mortified.

Newby was an older guy, maybe in his mid-20s, who worked at Gamestop, shared the same opinions about games and movies, and often had funny anecdotes about drinking too much, passing out in fun places, scrounging for last-call one-night-stands at Popeye's Pub, and almost crashing his car while getting "slobby" road head. Thomas always listened with pity, disbelief, and envy. There was a real sort of scrappy romance to Newby's picayune stories. Sometimes Newby's other friends stopped by, like the cashier at the pizza shop with the "cherry" Corvette, the Persian dude from the

Sunglass Hut, the muscular guy who hung around when he wasn't working drywall jobs: all bickering, arguing, and fucking around with each other. It was like Thomas's version of the barber shop. He was probably ten years younger than the youngest person he'd ever met while hanging out with Newby, but he could still hold his own with the jokes or the video game analysis.

Newby said something that scared him once. Thomas had been circumspectly asking what Newby's future plans were: you know, Newby was a pretty smart guy, and while he wasn't college-educated, he couldn't want to work at this Gamestop forever. Newby agreed, but added, "you'll see, you have no idea how many people who went to high school with me, went off to college, and then ended up right back here. You graduate from college, get a dumb degree, economy is bad, you come back home, think it will just be a year until you save up money to move out. But you like living rent-free, your friends are all back, too, so you stick around, and then one year turns into a few more." Which turned into an anecdote about running into a cheerleader he always wanted to hook up with in high school, now working as a hostess at Houligans Steak and Seafood Pub.

Not me, Thomas had thought. Hearing about people who left for college and were forced to come back was like hearing about a tragic accident: processed as something that happens to someone else, as a result of circumstances totally different from your own. Another way Thomas's situation was different, he thought wryly, was that he didn't have friends to pal around with here if he came back.

>< >< ><

Thomas realized something while fielding questions from his mother about Brandon. There was a connective thread to all her questions. She thought Brandon was his age. There was a jolt, of reality snapping around him and aligning with what he'd suspected but hadn't definitively known. But that confirmed it. That Brandon could somehow appear to his mother as just a teen boy confirmed, even more than all of his legerdemain, the truth of everything Brandon had said earlier.

>< >< ><

He lay again in bed that night and thought strange thoughts. He was still both tired and energized from bouncing around the room, "fluttering," as his bitch aunt had once called it. When he was younger, he'd traipse around a room imagining himself in various fantastical circumstances, something purely from his imagination or maybe inserting himself into a video game or movie. He wouldn't, like, jump around or anything, just walk around as he imagined the scenario, sometimes make a scene-appropriate sound with his mouth, a bang or boom, and strafe or head-feint or whatever when the impulses in his mind poured through and manifested into the real world. Nowadays, he did that while listening to rock or punk music. He only really did it anymore when he was alone, but he'd let himself go behind his closed door tonight, jumping around a bit and kept enthusiastic time to the music with his head, woodpecker-heading especially during the fast drum parts.

So, where was he? *Right*, thinking about being both tired and energized. This was the closest thing he got to working out. Then he thought about how his mom used to pressure him to play sports, work out, the underlying message being that maybe he should try and get in shape, fill out some. *Geez Mom*, he'd think, *I'm just a kid*. Even he knew as a young kid that what his mom was doing was fucked up, she shouldn't be making him feel bad about what he did and the way he looked.

He couldn't fall asleep and he didn't really try. He put his socked feet on the walls, following the blurred shapes as best he could in the dark. Brandon, what about him? Didn't he present an interesting situation? He didn't want to put much stock in what Brandon said. He half-feared that, like when a girl seems to express interest but then goes back to ignoring you, this whole Brandon thing was just some momentary miscue in perception. He had a tendency to quickly buy into something as a panacea, whether it be a misbegotten belief some girl liked him and that would lead to love and romance and all those good things, or that there'd be some inexplicable ending to his bullying.

Best not to get ahead of himself. Really, the best those flights of wishful fancy had gotten him were sleepless nights like this, where he, against his better judgment, played out the ideal scenarios in his head. He could stay up all night because things were different here, the consequences of the following day wouldn't matter. Stupid, he knew. He wanted so badly for things to be good. He wished he could freeze this night, return to it if things didn't go as he wanted. Tonight, he allowed himself to luxuriate in the perfumed waters of hope.

>< >< ><

Brandon and Thomas became as inseparable as two kids who didn't go to the same school could. Brandon was Thomas's first sleepover guest since grade school, when sleepovers were just a matter of hanging out and watching movies before all this junior high realpolitik came into play, with all this "who's more popular" and "who's dating who" and "who is throwing what party." Thomas had developed a real psychic hurdle to having a sleepover — or really, having anyone over — after an incident with Devon about two years ago. Devon had been a friend of his since he was little, largely as a result of play dates set up by their parents, who were themselves longtime friends. He and Devon had gotten along fine, though, in that period where personalities were less-defined and all one needed to be "friends" was to be the same age and amicable.

But, two years ago Devon got heavily into playing guitar, prima donna 70s freak-out rock: The Mothers of Invention, Pink Floyd, Hendrix, and a whole bunch of others. And, as if required, Devon also got obsessed with smoking marijuana. He started subtly at first, but soon it defined him: his affected demeanor, long hair, new friends, their choice of slang, their resistance to their "corporatizing" schoolwork, their endless proselytizing about the amazing health benefits of marijuana, and their dark warnings about the far-reaching, decades-spanning conspiracy to hide the glories of marijuana from the public.

At first Thomas thought he could find common cause with Devon's subversive views on education and schooling, but found Devon's philosophies were too malnourished with cliché and too formless to be intellectually interesting. As if smoking marijuana and "cultivating inner consciousness" or whatever was a pragmatic solution to anything. Thomas didn't associate with Devon's new clique or his abiding interest, but the two of them had stayed friends, albeit somewhat reduced friends.

But one time Devon came over and the entire time they were hanging out — eating chips, talking and watching television — Devon just kept asking Thomas what he wanted to do, as if they weren't already doing what they'd planned to. They took a walk around the neighborhood and came back to Thomas's house and Devon said he was bored and that he was going to walk home. Thomas had been crushed but played it blasé, just, "okay, whatever, see you later man" and never hung out with Devon outside of school ever again. Fuck Devon, he was a boring, incoherent prick. Thomas didn't smoke pot or care to, but he knew there were plenty of smart, impassioned creators and artists who did smoke pot but didn't make it their whole fucking lives. Devon gave pot a bad name, even Thomas knew that.

That's what kids were doing now. People were smoking pot, going to parties, and boys were feeling tits and fingering pussies and getting hand jobs and Thomas wasn't and he sort of didn't care. That was several degrees beyond what he wanted. He was sure the parties were stupid and lame, the same boring, functionally retarded people he despised would still be there, espousing the same lazy beliefs, discussing the same inane whatever it was that they discussed. He didn't even know what it was enough to even satirize it.

But still, he wanted the invitation.

He didn't delude himself into thinking that hanging out with Brandon was a suitable replacement. Thomas was still a weird loner, except now he had constant company.

>< >< ><

An incident, one of many. An unnerving one, but still, one of many. Thomas was changing in the gym locker room, rigid-backed and close to the privacy of a corner, when Larry hit him several times over the head with a rolled up newspaper and then tried to get him in a single-knee takedown. Larry was largely successful, if graceless.

As Thomas instinctively backed up, he fell, his head barely missing the water fountain. Other students said things like "Oh shit" at that point, either possibly playing out in their minds what would have happened if Thomas had cracked his head on the water fountain and fell in a terminal heap onto the floor, with a pool of red slowly expanding beneath his broken-melon head; or perhaps they were responding to the loud bang noise of Thomas falling on his back.

I'm going to die, Thomas thought incredibly, *this is really it*. He thought of his mom, her happy loving face and all the possibilities she envisioned for him. And he felt searing shame. Wow, his memory would forever be inextricably linked with Larry, and people would debate if it'd just been a prank gone too far, or if Thomas somehow deserved it by dint of his abrasive personality, and everyone would talk about Thomas, the boy who was beaten to death because he couldn't fight back.

Larry thwapped him several more times on the head, and weirdly, the blows became almost taps, like he was keeping fast time on a drum.

"Twenty-five!" And Larry got off him and darted away, tongue-out animatedly, pumped his arms and legs like he was running for his life. But he wasn't really, of course, he was showboating. He hopped and kicked-tapped a foot on a locker room bench, almost like he was playing tag with it. Then he slowed down. Some people were laughing, but most just looked confused, everything happened so fast and inexplicably.

Of all the classes that had the potential to be the worst, gym was obviously one of them. But he'd generally lucked out. He only had it twice a week, and each class was with a different group of kids, so he was only with Larry once a week. Plus, gym class was out in the open, and in front of Mr. Apfelmann, not Mr. Robinson, who probably would have given Larry more leeway.

For all those reasons, Larry generally behaved during gym. Maybe he was too focused on the games to be a dick, who knew. The worst Thomas heard during gym class were grumbled curses from Larry (or others) about his poor or listless performance in whatever stupid game they were forced to play. Or maybe Thomas's lack of athleticism would later be incorporated into some other bullying tactic taken up by Larry at lunch time. But Thomas had usually been safe, even in the locker rooms, where no one wanted to start any trouble while undressing and because Mr. Apfelmann was in the adjoining little office by the front door.

But Larry tackled him, and no one stopped him. It happened so quickly. Maybe Larry's hamming it up was to obfuscate that he very well could have seriously hurt Thomas if the angle of his fall had been a little off. With the attention on Larry, maybe people weren't paying attention to how hard Thomas had fallen. The weirdest thing, Thomas thought as he got up, nursing his sore back — it really hurt, he'd fallen hard — was that Larry didn't even seem malicious. It was as if Larry was the designated cowboy and Thomas the assigned rodeo clown, forced to take the fall while the star strutted. Larry, all red-faced, sped out of the room, perhaps embarrassed that his ploy didn't get the reception he was after.

><><><

It was the dead of winter now, late January. It'd snowed several days before. Thomas and Brandon walked below the treetops and branches encased with snow. There was a kind of majestic beauty, the snow staggered atop groaning branches. Throughout their walk, Thomas enjoyed those chance angles that highlighted the best of winter, the lovely crystalline shapes created by that strange interplay of water, tree, branch, and leaf. The snow gave nature an almost metallic-sheen, an angular precision in the arrow ends of icicles, the muted, wizened silver of once-green foliage, the curious throwing-star shapes left after his mother scraped ice off the windshield.

They were walking through the woods near Thomas's house. He had no idea what this particular area they were in was, maybe some remnant of when this was all farmland. They came to what might have been a clearing and looked around.

Brandon was wearing black boots and a scarf, which he often did. Thomas always wanted to ask if that was just for show. Did Brandon get cold? He didn't have a home, not in the way that Thomas conceived of one. He didn't have a family; or again, at least not in the way that Thomas thought of one.

He came from nowhere, for all intents and purposes. Brandon was purposefully vague but he wasn't human, which Thomas both accepted as a reality and yet also didn't. Cognitive dissonance, it was called. Or Brandon wasn't a human, but his non-humanness so far made no difference to their relationship, except Brandon always came over and had no home to invite Thomas to check out.

Brandon always said Thomas didn't have to believe him on any of that, despite all the magic tricks and impossible feats that should prove that Brandon was otherworldly. All that Thomas needed to understand, Brandon would emphasize, was that Brandon could make his problems go away if Thomas so desired. That's it. Just understand that and forget the rest if you want.

Brandon had oft-repeated that Thomas was a good dude, and

that Brandon had introduced himself so they could become friends and help Thomas out of this bullying situation, which was proving to be tenacious, inextricable ... and worsening.

"Hey Brandon, maybe you can help me at school after all?"

Brandon bit eagerly into a Granny Smith apple and smiled mischievously, or as mischievously as one could with a face full of apple. "Oh, really now? Now we are getting somewhere."

Weird, Brandon hadn't been eating an apple a moment ago. Maybe it played into a kind of roguishness that Brandon was going for, who knows.

"Eh, don't get too excited. I just mean, like, maybe, I don't know, aren't there some self-defense techniques you can teach me?"

Brandon had been taking a galloping portion of apple when Thomas asked that, and he immediately bellowed laughter in the way no normal person could, lest they choke on a heaping helping of chewed apple meat. He slapped his stomach once, so hard was he laughing.

"Alright, asshole, forget it."

"Self-defense? Aren't you a black belt in karate?"

Ugh. Yes, technically Thomas was a black belt in karate. His mom had signed him up when he was seven for weekly classes, and by the age of eleven he'd been awarded a black belt, despite never sparring or proving his relative karate-worth in any way, other than axe-kicking through the occasional worked-over wooden plank. His mom had paid the monthly dues and done her part to fill the coffers of Kiddie Karate Scam Incorporated and that had been enough to get his black belt. He quit immediately after, less the master who has nothing left to prove than just someone becoming dimly aware of the nature of the scam. The fact that he had been awarded a "black belt" somehow became known at school, and, oh God, maybe that had been the Patient Zero of his eventual bullying. Knowing he was technically a black belt made him want to beat himself up.

"Well, c'mon man, I'm just asking real quick. I'm not asking you to like, auto-load that stuff in my brain or anything," which of course is precisely what Thomas was asking.

Brandon shook his head. "I couldn't do that, ya know?"

Thomas wanted to challenge him on that ambiguity. "Couldn't do that" meaning Brandon was literally incapable of doing so, or "couldn't do that" meaning he chose not to? Thomas reckoned there were many, many things that Brandon could do, if he wanted to. Brandon's "ya know" was also quintessentially "Wisconsin-y," and Thomas had never heard Brandon speak with any trace of an accent before. Thomas felt self-conscious about using the term "real quick" when asking Brandon for the favor, "real quick" being one of those Wisconsin expressions that his mother and other old people often said.

Brandon quickly seemed remorseful. "Look, it's just not like that. I can't just train you on something like that. What did you think, we'd be doing martial arts out here in the frozen woods?

"And let's be realistic. Let's talk about the way the world is. First, Larry or Ed or whoever would beat the shit out of you if you tried something. Let's be honest." Thomas's body contracted from the emasculating sting, even though the truth of the assertion was undeniable.

"Don't take it personally, that's just the truth. Do you want to risk getting hurt? It's called a one-punch kill. You get hit hard enough, or in just a funny enough way, and next thing you know your head is cracked on the ground and you're dead. It happens. Remember when Larry took you down in the gym? You got lucky you didn't crack your head open. They are bigger, stronger, and there is a 'them' and only a 'you.'

"Second, even imagine you defend yourself somehow at school and beat them up. Then what? You get suspended, or worse, arrested? And yeah, they've been bullying you for quite some time, tormenting you, putting you under a kind of psychic torture. Making you second-guess yourself, doubt yourself, limit yourself, hate yourself: really, quite insidious what they've done to you. All something the bureaucrats and mouth-breathers who run the school system would never understand.

"You think they are interested in empathizing with you? Forget it. Kids fighting? Suspend both. That's the easy answer and that's what'll happen. Shit, maybe just suspend *you*, because you are creepy and weird and maybe any teacher or other student who witnesses it is biased against you, you never know. People generally like Larry. They'll vouch for him. He does well in school, doesn't cause trouble for others, is on the important school teams.

"And that's how you want to cap it off? Not only do they torture you, they get you kicked out of school, maybe arrested? Certainly derailed on your life path, regardless. You're young, maybe you can't see it, but one misstep like that can have major consequences. You don't get into the school you want, maybe miss some scholarships you would otherwise get, because of that you get a worse job down the line, or maybe you blow your chance to leave this town altogether. You'll be stuck at these stop 'n' go lights for the rest of your life."

Brandon swung his arm around, in a global arc that presented this quiet Wisconsin town as the outer limits of Thomas's world.

"I never should have taught you Wisconsin slang about stop 'n' go lights," Thomas said dryly. The implication gleaned from what Brandon had said — being stuck in this town, working some Joe-job because he'd limited his options by doing something really stupid, something he could never take back — centered him real quick. Imagine trying to explain to some intransigent school administrator about the pain Larry had caused him. To argue against some notation in his record, argue against an administrator who'd repeat, as if with a heavy heart but not really, obscuring platitudes like 'rules are rules' or 'there's nothing I can do.' Thomas's stomach tightened envisioning his attempt to explain to that brick wall in human form. 'So you punched Larry, so you admit you punched him?' the brick wall would repeat.

"Let me tell you a story, Thomas. Sit down, it's story time."

They both looked around for something to rest on. It was snowy and cold, all the way around.

"Well, screw sitting, standing is better for your circulation anyway." Thomas wondered if that was a universal 'your.' Did Brandon have blood that circulated?

"There was this friend of mine, James Holden, lived up in Washington State. High school student. A good guy, respectful to people, smart although not necessarily book smart, but knew right from wrong and had a kind heart, which are really the things that matter.

"So you think I'm going to tell you he was some smaller kid who got bullied by some popular kids or something, right? Not really. James was actually pretty huge. Six-four or something, thick and muscular, could have been on the football team if he wanted to. Had a chin piercing and studs in his ears, into metal and dressed the part, although he didn't overdo it or anything. He looked like an intimidating guy if you didn't know he was harmless.

"And there was this kid, Danny, whose father ran the gym program at the school. Danny was a piece of shit. I don't know if it was because Danny thought his father could protect him at school, or because he had popular older brothers playing college baseball, or whatever it was, but Danny, while not scrawny or anything, adopted this proto-gangster image and would bully people. He had a crew of like-minded assholes, although none really took it as far as Danny did. And he'd bully James, make fun of him, even though, in a fair fight, James would render him asunder if it came to it. That's a cool expression, right? 'Render him asunder.'"

"Indeed," Thomas answered, attuned to the direction the tale was taking.

"Well, James had enough one day, and while Danny was giving him shit for something during lunch — I think Danny was insulting one of James's friends — James got so frustrated he punched a window in the cafeteria and cracked it. He got expelled for destruction of school property. He could have punched Danny's face and knocked his head off, but he didn't.

"He never went back to school. He's not doing terribly. Still lives in Washington. Has a job installing locks for some company. Some of the teachers grumbled to themselves, you know, 'not fair, James was a good kid.' They all knew Danny was a cocky shit.

"James had their sympathy. Think that resulted in anything tangible for James? Nope."

Hmmm.

"Yeah. Maybe his life is better off now, who can be sure? Maybe he wasn't fit for college, he avoided debt, maybe, who knows. The point is the choice was taken away from him for a minor, extremely understandable mistake.

"And what happened to Danny? Nothing. He was fine."

"Nothing, huh?" Thomas stared at Brandon, expecting the addendum to the story any second, Brandon to add "until I stepped in," but none came.

Thomas broke the stare.

"I see what you're saying."

Thomas began to pace desultorily around the clearing, kicked some of the ice that curlicued on top of a log, looking like soft-serve ice cream straight out of the machine.

"Though of course, I could do something about it," Brandon said casually.

Thomas continued kicking around, head down, while Brandon walked behind him at a respectful distance.

"Yeah? What could you do about it?" Thomas asked, as if challenging the premise.

"I could do a variety of things."

"You speak broadly."

"I could make them all go away. Larry especially."

"How do you make someone go away 'especially?' Is that like being just a little bit pregnant?"

Ignoring the joke, Brandon responded, "I could make his disappearance the most glorious of them all." He spoke in a measured, obeisant tone, the way one might when reading aloud favored passages from a beloved book, pausing at the end to let the meaning sink in.

"What does that mean, exactly?"

"I could kill them for you, Thomas. Obviously. That's obviously what I'm talking about. That's what I've said before, too."

Tomas nodded his head, a mild burn in his throat from the weather, the dry cold air.

"I have a secret for you, Brandon. I hate to say it, but I'm wearing a wire. You're screwed."

"Funny. Go tell the M'waukee cops. Wouldn't matter, you know that."

Thomas crouched down and packed some snow in his hands, just for something to fix his mind on. Was a stupid thing to do, the snow was cold and dirty and now he was stuck holding it in his right hand until he could toss it. He needed to wait a couple seconds so his hasty antics wouldn't look obvious.

"I don't know what you are, really."

"Yes, you do. You know what I am."

"Mhmm, I guess so. I guess I won't get any more answers than that." Brandon just was whatever Brandon was. It was just as prosaic as that, and Thomas worried sometimes that Brandon really had done some mental trickery on him to keep him curiously sedate on the still-unclear nature of exactly what Brandon was, where he came from, and the extent of his powers. A variety of people had dismissed Thomas — his arguments, opinions, insights, attitudes — based just on his youth, that he didn't "understand" something just on account of his age. But he wasn't stupid. He was either a precocious child wise beyond his years, or his daily duress had sapped whatever joy was inherent to youth and left him prematurely aged. Whether it was some remnant of his youth that kept him so open to accepting Brandon, or whether it was his loneliness, or some unfathomable combination, he didn't know, and his lack of curiosity or fear regarding Brandon's alienage worried him sometimes.

Maybe it was all too abstract or weird to really think about. He already knew Brandon had powers: *that* was undeniable. The other stuff, the 'weirder' stuff, what good would thinking about that do, really?

"You are going to have to take me up on this offer someday, Thomas. You know, you'll just have to. I'm hoping you'll see the light."

"Yeah, I don't know. Don't get your hopes up, is all."

"Mhmm." Brandon seemed deflated, and, to Thomas, the idea that he'd left a transcendent creature dispirited on account of his stubbornness was queerly satisfying. That he'd left an otherworldly figure disappointed by doing something *good* — by NOT sentencing a kid to God-knows-what punishment — added another layer of weirdness. Especially when Thomas's own private fantasies were filled with all sorts of unholy gruesome vengeance. And to be tempting the wrath of his unworldly friend by forbidding such vengeance ... what a whirlwind these last few months had been.

Thomas putzed around and watched his pal making lines in the snow with his feet.

"Hey Brandon," he called after his perambulating friend. Brandon had taken to staring vacantly at distinct snow formations in trees or cool knots in their hollows. "Sorry if I disappointed you."

He wanted to hug Brandon. Guilt welled up in Thomas so easily, even though he didn't really believe he did anything wrong. He was like that: he'd get so worked up over an issue, argue something so emphatically and bombastically, and then feel a twinge of a guilt hangover, even when he was arguing with his mother, who was almost always on the wrong side of the issue. That he hadn't argued something vociferously, that he hadn't let his ego get the better of him, that he'd been civil: none of that seemed to matter. It was enough that Brandon, who was intelligent and whom he respected, was disappointed in him.

"It's alright, man. I just hate knowing you have to deal with this shit. I take it personally, too. It just burns me up."

"'Burns me up?' You expect me to take you seriously when you say 'burns me up?' I will never take the advice of someone who says 'burns me up.'"

"I only said something so lame so you'd feel better about your own faggotry."

That was a funny word and made Thomas laugh despite himself. It was also unexpected from Brandon. The ensuing repartee defused any lingering tension and let Thomas know they were all good again. Brandon was cool like that; he didn't hold any kind of grudge at all and things got resolved so quickly with him. He truly was 'good people.'

They hung out for several more hours, which included Thomas's bedroom later that night. Brandon apparently made it so no one else could see him, a trick he could — according to him — deploy at whim.

Around bedtime, Brandon bid his adieu.

Thomas had something he needed to ask before Brandon left. He'd wanted to ask for months now, but he feared the answer.

"Hey Brandon. For some time now, I've had these extremely vivid dreams of this girl near a well." And he explained the dreams as best as he could. "Do you, are those dreams related to you at all? Do you know anything about them? They seem so real." And after navigating through Brandon's jesty questions about how cute the girl was, Brandon gave his answer, which seemed truthful:

"No, I really have nothing to do with those. You're a special kid, Thomas. You don't know how special you are. And I don't mean that in some sappy way. I mean, I don't know. The world is a larger place than you'd know. You are a very smart, very special kid, in a rough place. And I know other kids have it rougher, that's for sure, but, I don't know, you're a perceptive kid in a bad spot. I don't want to make your ego go haywire — that is your fatal flaw, let's be honest, you can be an impatient know-it-all sometimes — but your smarts give you access to the wider world, maybe. Maybe I'm not the only special thing out there beamed into your frequency. Or shit, maybe not, maybe you really are just having some really vivid dreams. That's all I got."

"Hmmm. Well, thanks, I guess."

He didn't know whether that answer was comforting or not.

><><><

There was an incident at school with Larry. There'd been many incidents at school, of course, with Larry, or some combination of Larry, Eric, and Darren. Most were trivial, in the grand scheme of things. This one wasn't.

Larry and Darren. Thomas had thought it would be a good idea to sit alone in the little outside courtyard at lunch; most everyone else sat inside at the lunch tables, so he figured this would be a good way to avoid Larry. It generally worked. Larry often stayed inside, occupied with whatever occupied him. For some reason, not today.

There was only one other person outside, Allen Thotkiss, on the far side of the courtyard, back turned. Funny, Allen Thotkiss — pale, poor, mousy, short, underdeveloped, and with exceedingly nerdy tastes — was also a bullying victim, although his abuse was more widespread but perhaps less focused than Thomas's.

It started with comments about Thomas's sister, and Larry's repeated clapping whenever she was mentioned, and his encouragement of others to clap, too. Thomas didn't get it, but intuited it was some kind of sexual reference. And there was mention of Thomas's mother, too, what her tits looked like now, how they must have looked when she was younger. Larry's claim that he used to hang out with Thomas just to look at his mom's and Monica's tits, and how they both flirted with him and obviously needed "the D." Thomas's mom, Larry said, was probably jealous these days of all the cum coming Monica's way.

Larry told a crude rape narrative involving Thomas's mother and Monica without anyone calling it as such. Darren laughed but didn't add much, other than saying "word" at key moments. It was strange: Larry had usually bullied Thomas as a way to generate comedy or excitement for the amusement of other friends. But for Darren, wasn't this old to him by now?

Thomas stewed silently with an intense white heat that he wanted to be interpreted as psychopathic, a look of you've-been-warned potential school shooter rage. His efforts were rewarded by being told to calm the fuck down, and then called various forms of faggot.

Larry sped over, kicked at Thomas's leg, and yelled something. It was only in retrospect that Thomas figured out what it must have been: "Nut shot!"

Based on Larry's movement and kick, Thomas saw that Larry had aimed low, maybe hoping only to kick-stomp the bench, scare Thomas and run off. He liked ending things with a run-off, tongue out, like a mischievous scamp. But he must have mis-estimated because he connected. A sour feeling jolted through Thomas's groin, made his whole lower body feel sick, diseased. Thomas gave a low-groan audible only to himself.

"Oh, shit, dude! Oh my God, I think you hit him! Run, run, run," Darren laugh-yelled, pushing Larry forward as they ran. They bolted back inside, both turning back to look out at the courtyard, faces red, giddily panting, Larry with his tongue out.

Thomas kept his eyes clenched for several minutes until the nausea passed.

>< >< ><

"We cannot let him get away with this, Thomas. You know that. We cannot let him get away with this."

Thomas lay face down on his bed. He didn't think about why he was doing this, lying prostrate on his stomach after school, although if he'd given it any thought he'd know the answer. He was defeated. When he came home, he didn't think at all. He just went up to his room, threw his stuff on the ground, jumped on his bed, and buried his face in his pillow. No thinking. Blackness. Pushing his face against the pillow caused little sparkles and bright shapes to appear behind his eyes.

It was only when Brandon appeared in his ear that the emotion swelled in him, and he wanted to push back at Brandon, as if it was his fault for removing the finger that stymied the emotional dyke.

"I don't want to talk about it now."

"He hit you in the balls. This is fucking ridiculous, Thomas. This is fucking ridiculous. That can lead to serious damage."

"Please," and the way Thomas said it was so wheedling and pathetic that Brandon granted him his wish.

"Okay, brother, I'll let you rest. Don't worry, we'll take care of this. I'll be back in an hour. No, half an hour. I don't want you to dwell on this too much. I know it's terrible, but don't worry. I'm here for you, brotha."

"Thanks, Brandon," Thomas got out through tears and snot. He closed his eyes and his head felt hot and disgusting, like he'd developed an instant fever. The darkness behind his eyes was violent and sick-inducing.

The weird thing about getting hit hard in the balls is it makes your whole body feel almost hollow; your body vibrates in some kind of sublimely demonic timbre. It's like God hits your personal gong and you fall down in terror. And Larry did that to him, and he got away with it.

Thomas never thought about having kids but what if he was sterile now, all because of smirking, smiling, self-satisfied Larry? What would he do in fifteen years if he tried to start a family and the doctor tells him he couldn't, something's wrong with his sperm? What would he say, fifteen years ago some bully kicked me in the nuts? What would be done? Nothing. Nothing would be done, nothing could be done, because nothing can ever be done. He'd have sympathies and consoling and that's it.

Brandon was right. You had to stand up for yourself. His lower back hurt in a pinched way. He imagined kidney failure and easily connected it to his swollen balls.

Brandon shook his shoulder tenderly. "Hey man, you up?"

"I am now." Thomas turned to him, his face red, rheumy and puffy. He gave a weak smile. He guessed that thirty minutes had passed. Brandon was nothing if not punctual.

Thomas's eyes were still slit-closed. He hated showing weakness, especially in front of his friend. It reminded him of his weakness earlier that day, and his sadness redoubled. It was so nice to be in the pressed darkness of his pillow, removed from the troubles of his overwhelming realities.

"Have any good dreams while you were out? Your mystery girl

come back? If your balls don't work in real life, maybe she'll only let you finger her in the dreams." Thomas huffed and turned his head and scratched-pushed at Brandon, but in the affective way of a young, hurt boy who needed the guidance and support of his older best friend.

That's how Brandon was: he comforted elliptically, making jokes around a subject, and soon the distance between you and the hurt widened. The locus of the grief could still be detected but eventually you left the ambit of its gravity.

An hour passed, with Brandon just talking to him about a variety of things, with the bullying spoken about only peripherally. Telling him just to stay the course, things will get better. Don't worry, you won't end up working at the Nelson Cheese Factory. Thomas laughed, said "their cheese is good" softly, and Brandon kept talking.

"You're smart, and no matter how bad things are right now, there's privilege in intelligence. A whole world of nuance and meaning is available only to people like you. People of suboptimal intelligence should be hated, they are beneath contempt. Larry might have good grades but that's through grunt work, it means nothing. Larry only knows how to play the game. He's nothing special. There's no sparkle behind the eyes, no questing in the mind, no yearning in the soul."

Thomas, Brandon explained, should never forget that he was one of the blessed ones, to whom beauty and truth made themselves evident. Thomas didn't know if he believed it.

"You have the wrong idea about me, Brandon. I love your company but I think you have the wrong idea," Thomas said at one point. Whether Brandon was right or not, it was flattering to be differentiated and exalted.

"Brandon, be honest, you don't believe what you said about it getting better. Things don't just 'get better.'" How terrible, Thomas thought, must his situation be if a brilliant being like Brandon was reduced to lying to make him feel better.

"I know. You're right. It's complicated. Things get better when you make things get better. Here's what we do know. Larry is the worst person in your life right now. I think he's a narcissistic sociopath, but he's not reckless. He has his own goals and ambitions.

This is like a hobby for him. He's not a complete degenerate like some of the other fuck-ups, you know the sort, who take things too far and totally fuck up their lives in one fell swoop."

Thomas wasn't sure what Brandon was saying.

Thomas's mom knocked on his bedroom door to check up on him. Thomas said through the door that he had a headache and was tired. *Young boys who don't do much shouldn't be so tired,* she thought. "Dinner in thirty minutes," she told him through the door.

He didn't realize how much time had passed. It was nighttime. He felt fatigued, hungry and parched.

With that thirty-minute limitation, Brandon seemed to shift his tone, becoming more urgent, almost as if he were the bullied, pleading to his tormenter to show mercy.

"Thomas, now's the time. We've talked about making things better for some time now. Nothing is going to stop Larry until he chooses to stop himself, and why should he be the decider of your fate, that little arrogant shit? You're the decider of your fate. Just give me the word.

"Please, God, Thomas, look at me, Thomas, see what you're doing to me? There's no God and I'm still saying, 'please, God.' That's how badly I need you to just" — and here he lightly punch-tapped Thomas on the shoulder with each word — "'give' (tap) 'me' (tap) 'the' (tap) 'word.'"

Thomas groaned, but not unhappily. Yes, he was smiling a bit at this reminder that he could make all his problems disappear if he wanted to, if he would just take the plunge.

"Don't make me beg you with a really long, drawn-out sentence. You'd get a dead-arm by the time I was done. I got one picked out. A really long sentence, a lot of words that could use a punch in between them!"

Thomas almost giggled and was glad he didn't. He felt strangely giddy, a byproduct of his emotional and physical exhaustion. He remembered, of all things, years ago when his father play-wrestled with him outside in the backyard. Thomas's sides tightened with a weird vision of Brandon lifting him off the bed and tickling him.

"No, brotha. It's still no, unfortunately. Still no." Thomas said that pretentiously, the stoic hero.

"Okay man, I respect your decision, I do." Brandon sat beside Thomas and put his hand on Thomas's head. "I don't like it, but I respect it."

Thomas turned to face the near wall. He expected the call from his mother any minute now. The room had gotten dusky, the sun setting early this time of year, in this part of the world. The cold tundra, Thomas called it.

"So, Thomas, let me just say this, and then I won't bring it up anymore, okay? I respect your decision, but you're wrong, and by that, I mean you're viewing this all wrong.

"I get it. You are a good kid. You feel like you are a good kid, whatever a 'good kid' is, and that gives you some iota of meaning. It doesn't help you when you're being bullied, but afterwards, you tell yourself you're a 'good kid,' and because you're a 'good kid,' you still just think things will work out for you in the end. Like, Larry will get his comeuppance and you'll persevere because that's how things are.

"What you are doing is treating yourself as the hero of your own movie. And when I present you this option, of making all your troubles go away, you imagine that there is an audience that's watching you. What would the audience think of Thomas our hero, who decides to use his magic friend to kill Larry? And you think, quite naturally, that our audience wouldn't like that.

"You think, I'll be stoic, I'll get through this and make the good choice and persevere and be the good boy and things will just work out for me because I'm the good boy and I mean well and I'm smart and that's just the way life works, isn't it?

"I'm here to tell you it doesn't. In some sense you know this already, but you still frame your life as some hero's quest that gets a hero's reward. But it doesn't work that way, my friend. It just doesn't work that way. No audience is going to throw their popcorn at the screen for the choices you make. No one would even know. And if you think being good means allowing cruelty to go unchecked, then that's a whole 'nother conversation.

"I'll leave you with that, my man. Enjoy your dinner."

And Brandon left. Thomas was sure his eyes were still a bit puffy and red during dinner despite his best efforts to compress them with a cold, wet towel. His mother asked him once during dinner if everything was okay, which he deflected with an assured nod.

><><><

The weeks passed, and Brandon didn't bring any of it up again. The duo hung out when they could, much the same as always: video games, walks, movies, occasionally hanging out with Newby at Gamestop. (Newby thought Brandon was cool, too. It seemed that Brandon appeared the same age to Newby as he did to Thomas.)

Some other incidents occurred at school, none as cataclysmic as the locker room episode or the "nut shot." All verbal incidents. Thomas did his best to feign disinterest at whatever Larry said, come off as aloof. Maybe Larry had figured he'd taken the physical abuse too far and, while he hadn't gotten caught or in trouble, he knew that his luck could run out just by overlooking the presence of a teacher or hurting Thomas badly enough that the bullying couldn't stay hidden. Thomas had no idea if that was the case, though: he wasn't a mind reader.

Thomas's classwork and homework did suffer, as if feigning disinterest about his bullying situation seeped over into feigning disinterest in the content of his school work. All part of the same big dumb bullshit system. *Like an employer*, he thought. *If the employer doesn't create a good work environment, then the employer can't expect the best work, right?* Thomas knew intuitively that this thinking was counter-productive, but couldn't entirely disabuse himself of the notion.

His hangouts with Brandon became less about his predicament and more about pure escapism, even sometimes approaching outright silliness. If Brandon objected to this new focus, he didn't say anything. Maybe Brandon understood something on a deeper level, the commensurate balance between stress and release.

><><><

Only once did Brandon arguably lose his cool. It happened after Thomas, anticipating that Brandon was about to bring up the Larry-situation, tried to curtly change the subject.

"Methinks you depend on me a little too much," Brandon had said. "I mean, just knowing I'm here, like you can just use my services when you're good and ready. What if I disappear and you wake up and it's another day of school and you don't have me in your back pocket, huh?"

He didn't say it with an ounce of cruelty, could be mistaken just as more of his loopy teasing.

Thomas always remembered the comment but not how he responded.

><><><

A few weeks after that exchange, Brandon announced his departure matter-of-factly. He even said it while staring out the window, nonchalantly, almost absentmindedly.

"What?"

"I've just realized I got to hit the road, my man. I can't be around here forever."

"How long are you going to be gone for?"

If Brandon had been wearing sunglasses, this was the moment when he'd tip them down to the end of his nose: "For good, man. It's time."

"Oh." An explosion of sickly hot fear erupted within Thomas. A conflagration lit up all the internal edifices under which he'd, unbeknownst to him, buried his worst anxieties, and now they spilled out, sharp and nauseating. Chief among those edifices, he realized, was the primacy of Brandon, always there, the pivot point by which his emotional world gravitated.

Now Thomas would again be alone.

"Could I still ask you for advice?"

He knew the answer: he'd only ever communicated with Brandon directly, face-to-face. And if Brandon wasn't around ....

"I'm sorry man, I don't think so. I have to go, you know. You don't need me here. I mean, we are still friends. We'll be friends forever. But I'm needed elsewhere."

"Okay." So many objections and counter-arguments to raise, but he knew Brandon wouldn't be outsmarted like his mother, or throw up his hands and cede frustrated defeat like his father. Could Brandon hang out with him, mentally somehow, like, by telekinesis? He was tempted to ask but somehow knew the result. Brandon had a way of softly sashaying around a direct answer when he didn't want to give one.

"Do you want to leave? Like, you like hanging out with me, right?"

"Of course I like hanging out, man. It's not that simple, you know. We're brothers, man, for life. But I'm just needed elsewhere, is all. The call has gone out, so to speak."

"Okay." Thomas didn't really even know what that meant or alluded to, but he'd long since learned not to query too strenuously into Brandon's explanations. Even now, Thomas felt himself shrinking, his voice softening, his spirit receding. Regressing back to the shy boy he was, already missing the latitude afforded by Brandon's assurances. Foreseeing the lassitude of being forever alone, groveling before a hostile, snapping world, just hoping the powers-that-be let him pass through unscathed.

"Is it because I didn't have you kill Larry?"

Brandon snickered, but not inimically. "It's complicated, man. Complicated. If I'd done that, I would have probably had to leave earlier, really."

"Okay. Well, I'm sorry if I let you down."

"You didn't let me down, man." Brandon switched from cool, dangerous friend to avuncular like no other; or maybe the two operated simultaneously, and Thomas caught the difference the way one catches a different shade of color depending on the perception of streaming light.

Brandon didn't just disappear. They continued to hang out for a couple more weeks, talked about issues with some of their old intensity. Thomas figured that maybe Brandon forgot about his stated departure, or decided to stick around after all.

But no, Brandon didn't forget or decide otherwise. And here Thomas has trouble remembering because he was, after all, only fourteen, but he remembers shaking hands and hugging. Maybe there was another meeting subsequent, maybe even the following day, where Brandon again said his good-byes and they walked out in the snowy fields that he remembered behind his house.

That doesn't make much sense ... no, that can't be right. Thomas remembers Brandon telling him he was leaving while they were inside Thomas's bedroom — Brandon was definitely looking out a window when he first said it — and then he remembers immediately walking outside in the cold with Brandon, where Brandon again shook his hand and they talked about life, the world, and the places between.

Regardless of when it happened, whenever it did, Thomas was

crying, or if not crying, then rubbing his face a lot to hide his bleary eyes and his stuffed nose.

"If you ever really need me, brotha, this is what you do. And this is only if you really, really need me. I mean, *seriously* need me. You go out into a group of people about your age. When I say a group of people, I'm talking at least five people. I want at least five people. And they have to be around your age, and by your age I mean the age you're at when you are calling for me to return. So if it's in five years, it has to be a group of nineteen-year-olds, and so on—"

"I can do math."

"I'm ignoring that rude interjection into my beautiful goodbye speech. Anyway, you yell out, at the top of your lungs, as if your life depended on it, you yell, 'Liber Samekh!' You got that?"

"What?"

"Lie-bor Sam-Ek. Yell that out. Then, after a dramatic pause, you yell 'Oh Father, oh Satan, oh Sun.' If you do that, I'll come."

"Wait, do I say 'Oh Father, oh Satan, oh Sun,' *and,* 'If you do that, I'll come?'"

"No, just the 'Oh Father, oh Satan, oh Sun' part. That next part wasn't part of it, it was just me finishing the sentence. Sorry if I didn't make that clear.

"What, you think I'd have a rhyming chant? I'm ashamed you'd think I'm that fucking lame. I'm also embarrassed for you that you'd think that. *Jesus.*"

"Get out of here." Thomas didn't know whether to be hurt or charmed. "And is that 'son,' like, son to a father, or 'sun,' as in the star in the sky that warms the Earth."

"What does it matter? They are pronounced the same. Goddamn you ask a lot of questions. Because I don't want you up at night, riddled with anxiety, I'll tell you it refers to the star. And thanks for specifying the star that warms the Earth, otherwise I wouldn't know what the 'sun' could possibly be."

Even while leaving, even while giving this deranged promissory note, Brandon had that engaging twinkle in his eye. Brandon tilted his head forward and sideways as he spoke, as he often did, creating the illusion of being an attentive listener. It was a twinkle which seemed to say that although he might occasionally not appear to be of your opinion, there was still a secret understanding between him and you, an endurable bond, and that you might trust him for it.

"So you're Satan now?"

"No, I just want to imagine you saying that at age forty or whatever and you can tell me about all the crazy looks you got from everyone. Hah."

"I'm never going to remember that shit, man."

And to this Brandon shrugged. "If you don't, then you don't. Write it down if you want, because that's the code. If you don't remember, well, then it just wasn't meant to be."

"What if I just did it tomorrow, then you'd stick around?"

"Nope, doesn't work like that. You got to really need my services."

"Okay." Was it some expansive characteristic of his youth that allowed him to accept such pronouncements without challenge? Was it his fealty to Brandon's charms and friendship? He wondered to himself why he didn't retort or rebel when, if this had been anyone else, he'd have to get some last word in, edgewise.

"'Lie-bor Sam-ek, oh Father, oh Satan, oh Sun. You're going to regret telling me that, I'm going to yell it out one day while I'm at a sauna, surrounded by the fattest, sweatiest men on Earth." Despite being abandoned, he still wanted to leave Brandon with a laugh.

"Well, I didn't say I'd appear immediately. I'd wait until you left the room and the smell all cleared. The heavy man smell."

"Heh, whatever."

"And don't use it if the condom breaks or something. It has to be something important."

"Okay."

"Tell that girl in your dreams I said 'hi.'"

"Heh, I will."

If Brandon didn't just leave, just disappear, Thomas could have conjured up an endless series of one-second-before-you-go questions to keep him around. He didn't even ask him how some stupid nonsense incantation could make Brandon actually just appear.

It was all a jumble, really. Thomas remembers they shook hands again, and there's a memory of Brandon looking him in his eyes and nodding solemnly in the way of proud fathers, but that, too, was something barely half-remembered.

>< >< ><

Life went on, as life does. By the age of sixteen, the dreams of the mystery girl had ended; by seventeen, he only vaguely remembered the dreams at all; and by eighteen, it was like they'd never occurred.

His high school life was never good, never what he wanted for himself, but by junior year things had settled into an acceptable, if boring, groove. Larry (and some other "Larry"-types, although none made as lasting an impression) entered and left his world. For whatever reason, tormenting know-it-all weaklings like Thomas lost its appeal for them, or at least enough of its appeal to continue the tormenting.

Thomas graduated high school. Then college, with a degree in mechanical engineering. Then he found himself working for three years in a local company based in a suburb of Milwaukee that designed and manufactured window air conditioners. Then he worked for two years for AECOM, a bigger company, in their satellite office in Milwaukee, helping design central air conditioning systems for office parks. Then he transferred to their main office in Chicago, where he's been working for the last two years. He's now 29.

Monica now lives in San Diego. She's married, and soon after the birth of her first child she stopped working entirely. Thomas suspected behind-the-scenes tension with her husband would eventually get her to work at least part-time. The existence of his nephew compelled Thomas to feign caring about family matters, send cards and messages and wave emphatically in occasional Skype sessions, but he forever resented his sister and how her reputation had tarred him throughout junior high and, to a lesser extent, in high school. He wondered if her husband knew anything of her local reputation. He resented Monica without being conscious of it, his feelings losing their sharp edge until it was a brooding fuzzy feeling of weary obligation, rather than intense feelings of antipathy.

If his parents sent Monica and her burgeoning family any money to help them out, he wanted to request 50% of the market value to keep things even. It should be more, as he was the better child, never causing them any of the grief that she did, never had her bout of lapsed grades or truancy or too-much drinking or bad boyfriends or the general impression of dithering she had until she had gotten married and the watchful eyes of family and friends shifted their focus from her to her children.

His parents maintained whatever it was they maintained back in Wisconsin, spoke of downsizing their home but never pulled the trigger.

Chris Newby met a lady, married, had a couple of children and, from what Thomas gleaned, managed a used car lot owned by his wife's family. Newby was just an avatar now on a social media page that was rarely updated anymore (his avatar was *The Hulk* for some reason). But that's what happens. Nothing dramatic, just people drift apart.

There were countless others: friends, enemies, acquaintances, colleagues, lovers and girls-he-wished-had-been-lovers, who all drifted through his life, playing their part and then disappearing, or maintaining some slight connective thread in the greater digital world that he could tug upon for some slight online reunion.

Just as they could say the same for him.

So now he was 29, and Newby had been wrong: Thomas never ended up back at his parents' home, doing nothing, killing time. Certainly he was killing time in the larger sense that all people were killing time, but he was killing his time with activities he recognized as fruitful, maybe not always in the day-to-day nitty-gritty but in the larger sense. He had gone to a good college, obtained a difficult degree, and proven himself at work. He was, if not exactly swiftly rising up the company ladder, then at least maintaining a respectable pace. There had been a couple of layoffs over the years but, as far as he knew, his name wasn't considered. They liked him enough to accommodate his transfer to Chicago, that ridiculous city of contrasts, of the pampered north and the hellish south and the west that was a dotted mix of the two.

He thought often of how he could appeal to the caliber of woman that he'd always wanted. Engineering jobs were fairly rare in Chicago, as most engineers wanted to go to the Bay Area, Austin, or the East Coast. In addition to its rarity, his job was high-paying and fairly prestigious. He wore stylish clothing and stayed well-groomed. He had an interest in the arts and was knowledgeable about the local scene, had a membership to the Art Institute and the LookingGlass Theater. He knew that membership at the LookingGlass was pretty rare for a 29-year-old; and whenever he dropped that fact upon any of the women he dated (dressed up in some way so as to hopefully not come off as smug), they usually seemed suitably impressed and curious.

Growing up, he'd been ravenous for intellectually satiating content, books and music and film to turn himself onto different planes of thought. He remembered feeling that it was like mental exercise, gym for the mind, cultivating a better version of himself. That's what he told himself, anyway, but he knew that memory could be deceptively flattering.

He still sought out culture and art, when he had the time or energy, but the advantages of keeping abreast with the theater scene, local music scene, the cocktail scene, and the fine dining scene were more immediately felt in the dating sphere, where women prioritized discriminating men with knowledge and foresight. His interest in the arts was genuine, but became professed more than practiced. He even kept abreast of the improv scene, which he didn't really enjoy, but improv had a storied history in Chicago and his knowledge reflected well upon him and impressed others. He'd stomached a couple bouts of improv on dates and even once slept with an aspiring improv-ist.

His knowledge and interests took on an obviously utilitarian, less aspirational dimension. This type of mechanical, practical thinking had always come naturally to him. In the realm of dating, it had helped him to overcome his timorousness to reduce concepts to their baser elements, to read books and articles that brought the underlying equations to the surface. What women wanted and how he could provide that. He had just needed an explanation of how things worked.

Through high school and early college, he'd rejected any advice to improve his appeal to women or to others as bourgeois bullshit, instead pursuing some half-baked aping of the indolent life of the mind. Caring about clothes, the right cologne, working out, all superficial trivialities, business-bro frat boy bullshit, he thought. He'd been concerned with greater things, and had through college

— like he did through high school and junior high — made his elevated feelings known if pressed to.

But he eventually grew out of that way of thinking when he realized it wasn't working for him. It made him even more resentful; what he'd really wanted with all of his rebarbative defiance was, counterintuitively, love and attention. He'd always thought somehow that by being smart but defensive, people would just come to him: just as danger invites rescue or the set traps attract the brave adventurer, so, too, would people be inherently attracted to this mysterious, prickly genius. It worked in movies and television shows. But being an abrasive "genius"-type, he eventually realized, didn't work for him.

He understood that looking good would present an outward expression of his inner beatification. It would make him feel better, too, and give him more confidence. So while he still resented having to do so, he ate well, exercised consistently, and donned the appropriate accoutrements of a successful, educated young professional. A fair chunk of guys who populated these dating apps looked the part but had nothing going on inside, so his numinous sensitivities — paired with his now-fit physique and proper grooming — only made him stand out greater against the dullard-blankness of his competitors.

><><><

He is on a date now, actually, this very moment, with Marissa, a 25-year-old from Iowa who moved to Chicago only six months ago. This is their fourth date. She is sweet and pretty in a leporine way, two buckteeth that did the heavy-lifting to make her seem perpetually eager and chipper. (He didn't know why he thought of this, but at sixteen he'd fallen into ridiculous sexual obsessions with Lola Bunny and Jessica Rabbit. Since at sixteen you have all the time in the night to stare and fantasize and perfect the release, this meant that some of the best orgasms of his life were to crude fantasies about a cartoon rabbit and the animated femme-fatale wife of one of his favorite movie protagonists.)

He didn't see a future with this girl but you never know. He had a first date scheduled with a sexy-looking redhead in two days, and then a fifth date with Anne this weekend, an executive assistant he'd slept with twice. (He knew it was moronic to think like this, but he felt Anne was happy that he set up another date after they'd slept together; he bet a lot of caddish guys never called back after they get laid. That concept seemed so ridiculous to him: why not see someone again who clearly likes you? It made him feel morally virtuous to do so.)

He kept things casual with all the women he dated, although he wouldn't be opposed to something more serious if he met the right woman, whoever that might be. He'd never gotten good at breaking up with women, so some he saw even if he didn't want to, until they sort of got the hint and drifted off on their own, or paired up permanently with some other guy they were dating. His relationships never ended explosively because he never really took any firm stances. Maybe the relationships never solidified into something more meaningful, he thought, because once the point was made — that an attractive, desirable woman found him equally attractive — then there was nowhere else for him to go.

It was as if the cosmos somehow could still pull out a giant magnifying glass and see through his disguises to his essence: the damaged, needy boy. Serving as the cosmos's ambassadors were larger or more naturally boisterous or outgoing men, who would sometimes size Thomas up, maybe to glean what it was that made Thomas attractive to women. These ambassadors would remind Thomas — just by virtue of their existence — of the hostile world that circled about him, that threatened to put him in his place and take away what he'd worked for, remind him that at his core he would always be the wheedling child, privy to the caprice of crueler, more boorish man. He hated the way they looked at him; he knew when it came to desiring, jealous men, there were no innocuous looks, only judgmental glares. He'd known those looks well.

And for some reason he quietly resented the women he dated. So much of his childhood had been spent waiting, begging for someone to reach out and save him. So now, reaching out to these women on dating apps, he couldn't help but resent that they were the objects of *his* affection. He resented that the world was, by degrees, just a bit warmer for them; he sometimes thought he didn't want to be with them, he wanted to *be* them, to know what it was like to have people message you, want to spend time with you, to be kind to you for nothing other than configuration of your face and form, for the subconscious way a presence can lift spirits. If he was reading things that weren't there, so be it, so did the rest of the world, and for once he wanted to be the tabula rasa that meaning was read into.

>< >< ><

The date with Marissa went well. She didn't invite him to come upstairs with her but they made out for a bit by her building and she gave him a lecherous, slow-satisfied dismount at the end of their kiss. She said she wanted to make sure she would see him again and took the initiative to give him another deep kiss, and he noticed her subtle inward biting motions with her lower lip, which he guessed was supposed to be enticing but just struck him as unusual and practiced. He wondered if she read an article about doing such techniques to elicit interest and excitement in men.

He didn't feel like having sex that night anyway, and her questing for another date was enough of a seal of approval for him, although her tact — this kind of flustery come-on followed by restraint — was odd, but not odd enough for him to care or think too deeply about it. He just figured she was trying out some strategy to retain his interest, and it was moderately successful enough to work. He wasn't losing any sleep over it.

He went back to his well-appointed two-bedroom apartment in Lincoln Park. He lived alone and used one bedroom as an office for his occasional weekend work and his more common work-from-home days. His head was a bit foggy from alcohol and the heavy meal — only on dates did he eat desserts — so his push-ups and sit-ups were half-assed and more for the sake of making the mental checkmark than for their effectiveness. He'd have egg whites for breakfast tomorrow and a salad for lunch, for sure, to even out tonight's calories.

He bungled around the internet for some time, digesting jumbles of articles ranging from Latvian port systems to high-speed internet in Finland to why he should invest more in water purification stocks to why Polish women made the best partners. There was porn half-observed and scrolling about on social media profiles and some desultory messages back and forth with a friend, some other messages with a co-worker. Out of the corner of his eye he saw a picture of what could be Cuddly Cartoon Jesus flanked by white puffy clouds labeled as a "Person You Might Know." Cuddly Jesus — or maybe it was more anthropomorphic Cuddly God — an idyll cartoon with a bulbous cream-colored nose and a big bushy white beard, made warm and inviting by the broad swooping strokes used to draw him.

Thomas clicked unthinkingly on the picture and it was Larry's profile.

He stopped in his digital tracks. He maintained friendship with only a select few from back home. He'd cyber-stalked Larry many years ago, back in college, and had then stewed at Larry's typical photos, his typical thoughts, his typical sentiments, his typical opinions, his typical friends, his typical tailgate parties, his typical everything. There'd been no posts from Larry rueing the day he'd been paralyzed from a stray bullet, no accompanying photos of a struggling-wheelchair Larry; no posts from his family consecrating this day or that as a reminder of when Larry had a cocaine overdose and choked to death on his own vomit. There'd never been anything fun like that on Larry's social media profiles. So Thomas, eventually following the self-improvement edicts that had become so persuasive, took control of himself and had curtailed his Larry-stalking.

This came out of the blue. This bit of cyber-stalking wouldn't count, wouldn't be a lapse in discipline because it'd been an unexpected mistake.

But he didn't stop himself.

The cartoon God avatar was thematically appropriate, because from what Thomas gathered, Larry now taught history and social studies at a Catholic high school in Wisconsin. It seemed he was involved in the athletics program and, while social media accounts are far from representative of true life, Larry had enough comments and pictures to suggest he had both a successful professional life and an involved social life. Worse, there were paeans to family, photos with his healthy-looking wife and his two young sons, the wife looking pretty despite her exasperation and being clearly well into her third pregnancy. Soon he'd have a baby girl, it seemed.

What else did they have, a fucking Dalmatian puppy with one dark-ringed eye that they named Spot?

Unbelievable. But what had he expected? Nothing, he'd

expected nothing. There'd been no reason to expect some abrupt descent from the middle-class life that was Larry's effective birthright, outside of some freak accident. The errant bullet and the paralysis, that's the life path Thomas had always hoped for Larry.

Thomas now had a sour feeling in his stomach and felt curiously enervated, as if some emotional lubricant he'd previously been unaware of had seeped out of him. As if there'd been some weird exchange rate triggered by this knowledge, he now felt somehow diminished, less than he had before.

From all his studies and reading, he'd come to the conclusion that the best mindset would be one where ego didn't exist. And on the page — in the world presented in self-help books — that was an idea that he could nod along and ascribe to. But that word — ego — wasn't just some three-letter word on a page. The best world would be an egoless one, but he didn't live in that world. He lived in this world. And whoever tells you happiness isn't a relative, positional good doesn't understand that everything in this world is a relative, positional good.

>< >< ><

He couldn't sleep for reasons he damn well knew but didn't internally articulate. He squelched the articulation at the root. So instead he thought of other stressful things: work, his unknown future, he even rustled up a lurking, abandoned fear of being the random victim of a sidewalk slasher, as if his subconscious was poking around at all the snarling dogs in his mind and asking, "whatcha got?" Anything to pivot away from the true cause.

The night stretched on before him. Half-delirious with fatigue, his eventual dreams were layered and chaotic in a way they hadn't been for years. Ideas scattering angrily like wasps throughout his mind. Now with a sour stomach and damp with sweat, the presence of both infecting his dreams, a running-rabbit dread of looming creatures that grant no quarter, the flaming searchlight waiting to turn its gaze upon him, malicious hooks upon hooks shooting out to drag him before a slavering crowd that yelled out instructions on which portions of his flesh to rip off and render before them.

>< >< ><

The evolution of an inkling into an act is a difficult one to map. There are peaks and valleys and disappearances and sudden white hot revivals. In the following days he struck up an online conversation with Lisa, an acquaintance from high school who wasn't familiar with his sordid history with Larry. Lisa blandly corroborated Thomas's queries. Yeah, Larry was indeed a history teacher, did something with the football team and also maybe the debate team, too. He might run the whole athletics department, actually. Yeah, Larry was married with two sons, and, yeah, his wife was awesome; Lisa knew her from somewhere and knew they were expecting a third child and something-something-something ....

And Thomas let it rest and didn't bring it up with anyone again. He reined himself in, refused to check Larry's social media, but the satisfaction usually brought by discipline wasn't there. He knew that if he indulged in obsession, the way he easily could, it would wreck him. Best to keep himself in check and the feelings of righteous indignation would go away, which turned out not to be entirely true. As sayeth the pop-psychologists and memes, holding onto anger is like drinking a poison and expecting the other person to die, right? The sentiment was so easily dismantlable but don't think about it, let it go, let it go, don't get yourself too worked up…

>< >< ><

A few months passed and the initial feelings of outrage did weaken. Gone was the active discontent, curdled anger and poignant sadness. Time heals. He couldn't get so worked up about something so stupid; what did he expect, really?

He still felt an unsettled feeling of being misaligned somehow, that manifested most often in a sour stomach and sweats if he thought about Larry and his enviable position. Thomas dealt with this with an indolent daydreaming wistfulness, but dreaming of what, he wasn't certain. He just thought blankly of distant things. An image sometimes came to mind, of the pensiveness of a hungry man on a dock looking out at ships going out to sea beyond a horizon line, knowing he's late for dinner but not feeling like doing much about it.

Thomas wanted to be twinkling somewhere, out there, in the blue smear world of seas, ships, and horizon lines.

He dwelled more and more in that peculiar twilight world where present distress merged imperceptibly into memories of fashioned past glories, and as a result was often bored, distracted, and a bit irritable, mentally working overtime to reassert the equilibrium he'd once obtained for himself.

That's how it was until he found himself back in Wisconsin, visiting his parents over Easter weekend. He'd already phased through all the nostalgia there was to feel about the place. He knew that the older you get, the more rose-colored becomes the past, so if you have an unhappy childhood, you pine for that, because the operative word is childhood. A time of more vivid experiences, and a time that was survived, safely put in the past, so it's something the over-anxious brain treats as a halcyon respite.

He knew the science behind nostalgia. He'd previously put nostalgia away, bracketed it in the segment of his mind reserved for enjoyable trifles, but this trip back home brought something else back in him. All the trees and the woods and the paths he used to hoof around his house; when it'd been just him, alone, with time to kill.

On the first Saturday of his return visit, he drove to a nearby Walmart on an errand for his parents and to bring home some of the foods he liked that they never had. While waiting on a four-person-deep line with his cart of dried figs, pistachios and other sundries, he saw the ice-white pallor and prominent long nose of a familiar face behind the register. Allen Thotkiss.

Allen's weak chin appeared to be actively receding, his hair was thinner, and he still seemed undeniably mouse-like. It couldn't be said that time had been unkind, exactly, given how Allen had always looked, unless any changes that come with age are inherently a type of unkindness. Allen probably had been bullied even worse than Thomas had; certainly, he'd had more bullies than Thomas had.

"Hey Allen, how's it going?" If Thomas had forgotten his name, not to worry, Allen had a name tag. Thomas didn't know how to act. He wanted to act blandly, like he was meeting a coequal, just saying hi, and isn't that what he was doing?

"Hi," Allen said, sounding somehow optimistically bedraggled. His voice had cracked weirdly, and he cleared his throat and said, "Let me try that again. Hello there. Find everything you needed?"

"I did, I did, I found everything I needed," Thomas responded cheerfully, as if satirizing the upbeat Walmart training video that he imagined he was participating in.

Wait, did Allen not recognize him?

"How've you been, Allen? Do you remember, I, we went to school together." They went to both middle and high school together, in fact, but he just left it as "school."

"I thought I recognized you. Ms. Gordon's class in the eighth grade, right? She retired a couple years ago. I still see her around sometimes. Go to the high school reunion?"

"Hah, no way. Missed that one. Going to miss the next one, too."

"Yeah, I didn't go either." Come to think of it, he and Allen might have been Facebook friends. Thomas remembered a profile picture of Allen in a lab coat, wearing goggles and mock-yelling while staring at a beaker. Some kind of convention maybe, or a Halloween costume or something.

Thomas had paid for his goods, and now Allen was bagging up his stuff.

"What've you been up to?" Thomas asked.

"Not much, still bowling when I can. When I get any time off from this place. "

"Huh, cool. I'm just in town for the weekend. I live in Chicago now."

"Oh whoa, cool, I heard about this place called Timber Lanes that's supposed to be a great classic lane in Chicago. It's on the bucket list."

"Oh, cool, man. Timber Lanes, eh? I'll check it out."

What facet of his personality required him to add that he didn't live in this dump town anymore, that he'd made it out? And what facet of Allen's personality was there that allowed him to be completely nonplussed, to maybe even be fine with just living here, working at a fucking Walmart, no doubt serving some of the same people who made his early life miserable? How'd that not haunt him? Maybe it did. What was Allen supposed to do about it, spill his guts to Thomas, who was essentially a stranger, both back in school and now even more so? Thomas half-thought to say that they should keep in touch but thought better of it.

He wanted, strangely, confirmation from Allen about how bad their situation had been. This was like both having survived a war together, a war that produced no veterans, no shared pride, no stories. A war that maybe wasn't even remembered. Or maybe just not dwelled upon.

Hell, Allen had probably (certainly) had it worse: Thomas's situation improved during high school, but if memory served, Allen's didn't. In fact, Thomas remembered, Allen had been expelled from high school for some time for stabbing Norman Welmien in the eye with a pen. Suspended for half a year, actually. Thomas hadn't witnessed it, but it'd surely been in self-defense. Norman used to rough Allen up, push him against lockers, break his shit, just your typical alpha-male bullying. One day while Norman was pushing Allen up against the wall, maybe pushing his forearm into Allen's chest and neck (as Thomas now sorta remembers Norman doing), Allen must have given him a quick jab in the eye with the pen. He wanted to tell Allen that he was glad he'd stabbed Norman in the eye. That asshole had it coming. But he didn't.

He looked at Allen and saw a nice, hapless dork. He wondered if they'd been similar back in school. Thomas had had his problems; he was arrogant and pushy, but was he this bad? Allen's countenance belonged to a pestilent plague rat. He looked like a victim. That they'd been comparably treated in the eyes of the bullies was an insult, another subtle, long-lasting way to make Thomas second-guess himself. He didn't really want to associate with Allen, whether due to Allen's rodent-like appearance, the aura of weakness surrounding him, or just that Thomas doubted they had anything in common. Or some combination of the above.

So Thomas just left.

>< >< ><

Later in bed he thought endlessly, as he was prone to do. In bed his mental defenses came down and he felt ashamed of himself and upset on Allen's behalf. Ashamed, because he was so eager to invidiously demonstrate how much better he was than others, wasn't he, now that he had some measure of status? He might not like Allen, might not be able to have any meaningful conversation with him, but they were kindred spirits of a sort, both damaged survivors of some battle they'd both been thrust into.

How many of Thomas's unpleasant traits were just vestigial defensive mechanisms from his youth that had outgrown their usefulness and now hampered his adult life, prevented him from connecting with others? He was so quick to judge and dismiss. And Allen, kicked down and insulted all his life. Where was his happy ending? He might be content with his lot in life, maybe resigned to his fate, but he shouldn't be.

He'd been wronged and the wrong hadn't been avenged. Allen should be stewing, too.

><><><

A week later and Thomas was back in Chicago, a normal work week. Thomas was eating at a little corporate park several blocks from his office. He had never been to this little park before because of its distance from his office. He'd actually passed several equally suitable parks to get here. This park was one of those triangular infills that the City mandates big office developers provide adjacent to corporate towers to create some illusion of green space.

The day was a bit gray and overcast. There were about twelve or so people in this park, other white-collar workers no doubt seeking a respite from the office, either eating lunch, checking their phones, smoking cigarettes, drinking iced coffees, or doing all of the above. On a nice spring day at lunch time, there'd surely be more. On a dreary day, well, this.

He tried to guesstimate their ages. It was easier with women than men. There were two attractive women talking together, a blonde and a brunette, and they wore outfits that suggested they worked together at the same service job. They appeared to be in their mid- to late-twenties. There was another woman, a young Asian woman, clicking with alacrity on her phone. Three men in dress shirts sat around a table, who spoke with the casual pomposity and assurance of young men in power positions. They appeared to be in their late twenties. That's six people around his age right there.

He glanced around at the other parkgoers. A black man with glasses and a beard was circling the edge of the park, smoking, reading something on his phone. He had a John Marshall Law School tote bag. Probably a law student, and at the youngest (assuming he'd went straight from undergrad) he'd be at least twenty-five. Was that close enough in age? How exact did this have to be? What, did Thomas require fucking birth certificates? And what was a peer, anyway? Did that go by education, work status, or personal interests? The law student was also hovering around the periphery of the park. Did the law student have to be in earshot to count?

Don't overthink.

In fact, don't think at all.

Thomas strategized. He looked at his sandwich wrapper quizzically. He thought of saying what he needed to say aloud but slowly, like he was reading it off the sandwich wrapper, a secret message he'd just discovered and was himself probing for its meaning. *Why would I be reading it off a sandwich wrapper, that's fucking stupid. What was it, like an old Snapple cap? Like the local sandwich shop would have fun secret messages about Satan on the wrapper?*

Stupid.

He looked at his phone and maybe he'd act like he'd just gotten a deranged email. Maybe show it to someone, say 'can you believe this?' and then repeat the message, that was technically saying it aloud, right?

No, he had to yell it out, remember? How would he pull that off?

Was there a deaf person around here? Was there someone he could pretend was deaf, like he was trying to yell and convey this important message to them?

No, don't overthink it.

He walked into the middle of the small park, just adjacent to the three power-bros. Two of them were looking intently at the two pretty hostess-types several feet away.

"Lie-bor Sam-Ek!" Thomas yelled. The nearest bro twitched in his chair, startled. Without turning around, Thomas strained his eyes in the opposite direction, yelled it again, this time with a touch of the interrogative. "Lie-bor Sam-Ek!" he yelled, but hoped it came out like, 'Lie-bor Sam-Ek, is that really you!?'

Thomas felt the locus of several strangers' attention placed upon him. He had to commit. He closed his eyes and, elbows bent at ninety-degree angles, palms up as if in rapt supplication, yelled with the conviction of the determined street preacher: "Oh Father, oh Satan, oh Sun!"

He hoped he yelled it loud enough for his purposes, but not loud enough to hurt one of the bro's ear drums and cause a confrontation.

He heard shocked laugher from the bros, felt them slide away. The black law student near the edge of the park looked at him angrily. The Asian woman looked up at him, seemed to quickly determine he was far away enough and not violent-crazy, and returned to her typing. He didn't look but he was sure the pretty hostess women were making faces of disgust and dismissal.

"Oh Father, oh Satan, oh Sun!" he yelled again, but this time with less conviction, as he had the intuitive sense of vacancy, of people moving away from him. He power-walked out of the park, this time speed-yelling "Lie-bor Sam-Ek!" which sounded like gibberish even if you knew what he was saying. He capped it off with another yelled "Oh Father, oh Satan, oh Sun," and then ran a couple of blocks until he was sure none of the parkgoers could see him anymore.

He threw out his sandwich wrapper and trekked back to his office.

>< >< ><

He headed home from work in the rain. It was a close walk to the train, both from his office to the station and from the station to his apartment. It wasn't raining hard, and he disliked umbrellas unless the situation really called for it. People with umbrellas acted, under their black mushrooms, like they owned the sidewalk.

Thomas opened the front entrance to his apartment building and got out his keys to open the locked inner door, where sometimes delivery men waited to be buzzed in. Out of the rain, he swooped his damp hair back into place, checked his phone with the same hand that held his keys, quickly finished an article he'd been reading and made to open the door.

"It wasn't as embarrassing as I'd wanted. When I said peers, I meant friends, so there'd be actual consequences for your crazy outburst. I wanted you to do something you'd have to explain away."

Standing adjacent to the inner door, facing him, was Brandon. He still looked fit and healthy without being overwhelmingly so, still had short brown hair, which looked stylishly ruffled and disarrayed from the rain. His face was still smooth and hairless, but there was some weathering around the mouth and eyes, some slight but noticeable creasing that one would say came naturally with age.

He looked like a healthy Caucasian man in his late thirties or maybe early forties, but if you didn't know him, and he said he was in his early forties, you'd say something like "oh really, you look younger," and it'd be true, but you could see it if you studied him. He wore a dark blue patterned sweater and dark blue jeans and black wire-rimmed, round-shaped glasses.

"I notice you don't have an umbrella. I remember you once saying you didn't like them. Some things don't change. Notice I don't have one, either? I stayed true," and here Brandon made a fist and gave himself a light chest-pound.

"I noticed," Thomas squeaked out. His voice didn't actually squeak, or suggest in any way his conflicting seizure of emotions. Excitement, anxiety, elation, fear: a great big conflagration of them all, the blaze rising higher and higher. First he thought he'd been mistaken, no way was it Brandon. It was that feeling of *déjà vu*, but confirmed, undeniably, irrevocably confirmed. Brandon had been a memory, a feeling; surely a durable and complicated one, but nothing but a memory with nothing empirical to show for it. He'd become a glimpsed angle of something once special from childhood, the signifier that, once mentioned, elicits a strange flooding feeling somewhere between sadness and fondness. That he was back, that he existed at all, was so many things, many of them destabilizing. It was the reaffirmation of a wondrous, terrifying world without answers.

Maybe he'd inserted false memories. Maybe Brandon had just been an older friend, someone Thomas looked up to, and Thomas had just imagined the powers, the abilities, the promises.

No, he knew that it was a lie. How else would Brandon just appear, like he promised, after the silly incantation?

"Not going to invite me up? I mean, I do go down on the first date and all."

"Only go down? You've got to get with the times."

Thomas was speaking nonsense, talking only to maintain a verbal volley he thought was expected of him. He'd never actually hooked up on the first date. No woman he ever dated ever did anything like that, and he'd be wary of a woman who did. He wasn't like that at all.

"Look at you, man, taking care of yourself, I see. Nice

apartment building, looks like you're working out. What would the fourteen-year-old Thomas say?"

"Probably call me a sellout."

"Well, I wish we could go back to fourteen-year-old you and let him know that in the future girls might give him the time of day."

"I'll make sure he gets the message." Thomas was disappointed for some reason. He hoped Brandon didn't think that because he could get dates, things were all hunky-dory.

"I know it's more complicated than that, though."

"It always is."

"So, can I come up?"

"Couldn't you have just appeared in my apartment if you wanted to?"

"You know I could. But you know, decorum and all that."

"Naturally."

>< >< ><

Thomas gave him the tour, with Brandon nodding, slowly and approvingly, the whole time.

"It's nice, it's nice."

"Did you need to come up to know what it looked like?"

"Heh, there you go again. Always prying, trying to know. Is that why you summoned me, to show off your fancy digs?"

"Heh, not exactly." There were still so many feelings competing for attention, but now self-consciousness was the one that surfaced. "Summoned? That's a strange way of putting it. I'm not your master, you were free to not show up."

Brandon smiled, the cagey bastard.

"Well, master," and Brandon bowed slightly and extended his up-faced palm with a flourish, "you rang."

"I did, I did." Thomas asked if Brandon wanted water or anything, another dilatory tactic. Brandon thanked him but declined. Thomas wanted to go get water from the fridge so he could turn his back to Brandon; that way, Brandon wouldn't see him getting red, sweating.

"It's nice to see you again, Thomas. I'm glad you called."

"Thanks, it's nice to see you, too." How silly this seemed, some combustible mix of envy, nostalgia, spite and abandonment. He felt like a jilted lover.

Thomas continued. "I missed you, if that sounds strange. You really were my best friend. I don't think I've ever had a better friend, or someone I felt so connected with, really. I mean, I know that, like, youth is the strongest time for friendships like that, but you know, looking back, it still means a lot to me. I'm glad to see you again."

Beneath his admission he felt the presence of all the abdicated surrogate father figures: his emotionally-absentee actual father, and all the older male friends he'd leaned on for support and looked up to for advice, all the Newbies he'd known and ever quasi-idolized.

Brandon came to him, gripped his hand and looked him square in the face.

"I missed you too, brotha. It's nice to see you again. I'm happy you rang. Something been getting at you?"

If this was feigned earnestness, then it was a trick too subtle for human discrimination. Thomas looked at him and believed him. He abruptly broke the handshake to hug Brandon, and then, saying nothing yet still smiling, resumed the handshake.

"Woah there brotha, don't knock me over, we got work to do, right?"

"Hah, maybe. Maybe I just wanted to see if you were real."

"Me? Why not that girl from your dreams, remember that, the strange girl?"

"Oh, shit." Thomas felt a surge of charged excitement, the onslaught of returning knowledge. So much came back to him, those dreams from his youth, the prospects, the wonderment of childhood romance and fantasy.

But as Brandon showed, it wasn't all fantasy, was it?

"Eh, bringing stuff back, isn't it?"

"Yeah." Rarely has one word hid so much behind it. He felt ecstatically-manic, the sugar rush of childhood ambitions and schemes.

"What's been getting you down?"

"Do I even need to say it?"

"In some aspects, no, you don't. A young man named Larry, I take it."

"Yeah. It's more complicated than that, though."

"I know." And Brandon did know. He knew Thomas's stoic, self-satisfied, rose-scented imagined future didn't prove to be the balm to soothe the scars. No one congratulated him for taking his lumps. There hadn't been closure, no post-credits scene on the agony of his youth.

"You didn't get the extra credit for being a good boy after all, did you?"

"I guess not."

"Larry, seems like he's doing pretty well for himself. He must have reformed himself."

"I bet."

"But people don't really reform, do they?"

"No."

Larry was the same bully he'd always been, Thomas could tell. Even through Larry's well-manicured social media account, Thomas could tell he was fundamentally the same. And even if he wasn't, where was the justice? All the possibilities that existed within himself had been dragooned and diverted by Larry's cruelty. Thomas was lesser than he would have been had Larry never entered his life. The past hovered above Thomas: in his stunted emotional responses, his lingering self-doubts.

But Larry was surely not responsible for *all* of it.

That the nature of the damage could not be calculated with precision didn't mean it wasn't real.

"But, Thomas, I thought living well was the best revenge?"

Thomas just nodded, full speed ahead on his own train of thought, then sniffed a sardonic appreciation at Brandon's wry point.

"Maybe you've come to realize that, in fact, revenge is the best revenge."

"I like that."

"So, are you tired of waiting for things to just work out, naturally, on their own?"

Thomas was smart enough to know where this was heading but enjoyed the mounting speed in which he was being swept along, as if it all proceeded quickly enough there'd be no way to stop it, and then what was he to do? Couldn't be blamed if things just got out of hand…

He'd tried to forgive and forget. Despite himself he'd believed that things would just work out because he'd been a good kid and tried to forgive and forget; hell, he could just tell himself that he had in fact forgiven and forgotten, and then excuse the curdled burning dissatisfaction he felt as something other than what it was ....

"I want to kill his children too, Thomas. I'd do it quickly."

"No, you can't do that, Brandon. I won't let you do that. No compromises on that." Thomas was speaking in a husky whisper, an instinctive fear of being overheard.

"You don't have to be afraid, Thomas. You didn't need to be afraid fifteen years ago, either. I respect the decision you made back then, even if it was the wrong one. You don't need to be afraid anymore. No more scurrying for you."

Thomas smiled and shook his head, retaining his throaty whisper. "You always know just what to say, it's like you know what I'm thinking."

"Incredible, isn't it. So sympatico."

"Indeed."

And there was a miniscule yelp of a worry that he'd just gone crazy, and he was staring at a mirror making bold plans to himself. Brandon maintained impeccable eye contact while items from Thomas's kitchen ascended in unison, by row, then returned safely back to solid ground, then counter and tabletop. One item, a butter knife, floated on over and hovered by Thomas's right shoulder.

"See that, Thomas?"

"I do," he said, his face not moving, eyes warmly fixated upon Brandon.

"Take a picture of it."

Thomas gave a smirk of curious derring-do, uncertainty mixed with excitement. He took out his phone and took a picture.

"See it?"

Thomas looked at the screen. "Not the best, but, yeah, I see it. I'll call it 'butter knife takes flight.'"

"You see that. The knife in the air. No one holding it. This is real. That's proof, see that. That picture won't go away."

"I suppose."

"If Larry was killed as he should have been a long time ago, he wouldn't have had his kids. Why should he be allowed to pass on his genes? I'd kill them quickly."

"I'm not budging on that, Brandon. Not his kids. Just him."

"Okay. Funny, me agreeing to kill his children quickly and painlessly was my version of a compromise. I was actually planning on curling them up into balls and making them eat their own genitals. They still have baby teeth so I was curious to see how long it'd take. But if you don't want them dead, fine. You're wrong, again, just so you know. So sentimental. But last time you were wrong, you still had the excuse of only being fourteen."

"Who doesn't think they know everything when they're fourteen?"

"I knew a hell of a lot when I was fourteen."

"I think time works differently for whatever you are."

"Indeed. If you woke up and found yourself fourteen again, another big day of school tomorrow, with Larry and all the hungry, vicious boys waiting for you, I think you'd come back and beg me to kill his children."

"Maybe. But no children, okay?"

"I know. I was just saying."

"You promise?"

"I promise. I should get going. I have a job to do for you."

Brandon extended his hand and they shook.

"I have to ask, Brandon. If I resisted more just now, said I didn't want you to kill Larry, would we have spent more time hanging out? If so, then I regret giving in so easily. I missed you. I want to know how you've been. I want to know if things would be different, you know, what it'd be like hanging out now, you know? I still think about the stuff we talked about. Obviously, I mean, because here you are after all. But you know, you meant a lot to me. You were the first person, I'll just say person because I don't know what else to call you, but the first person who I felt really cared about me."

"I appreciate that. Everything I said about you before, you being a smart, worthwhile guy, I meant, and I still believe it. You're a good guy. You're a smart guy. You're better than most people. If it weren't for Larry, you'd be even better. And you'd be happier. You would have been. Things have consequences. Not everyone gets this opportunity. I'm glad you're taking it. I'll come back to you soon, after it's done. We'll hang out a bit. You can show me around town."

"Hah. Across the stars to land in Chicago, huh? Something makes me feel you've seen better places than this."

Brandon smiled. “Wherever you are with a good friend, that’s the place to be.”

They were shaking hands; maybe they’d been shaking hands this entire time.

“So, I’ll see you again?”

“Very soon, brotha. Very soon. I don’t want to give you an exact date because I don’t want you doing the equivalent of checking your phone at a specific time, you know what I mean? Try and live your life like normal, no big deal. But very soon, I’ll make things right.”

>< >< ><

Thomas felt hot, woke up and didn’t recognize his surroundings. He was in bed. The sun was up, streaming through the uneven slots in his blinds. As a kid, his blinds had always been uneven, he and his Mom and Dad always said they’d fix them but no one ever did.

He looked first at his top sheet, then the wall next to his bed. He could see cut-outs and shapes on the interior of his closed bedroom door. Comic panels that he’d pasted up from *Calvin and Hobbes*.

This was his childhood room.

Which was fitting, because he was a child again. He looked at his hands, felt his fourteen-year-old face. He suctioned his mouth and bit on his lower lip, his tongue feeling the raised little hematoma that had blossomed the day before when he chewed on his lower lip in blind frustration, to divert his attention, if only slightly, from Larry’s whispered comments in class.

The chronology of reality set in. Was about two weeks ago when Larry tackled him in the gym locker room. Brandon was an evanescent dream already losing form and distinction, like the visions of the girl in the well.

No. No. No. It can’t be.

Please, God, no, please, no, not like this.

>< >< ><

Lawrence Mullens — Mr. Mullens to most students, “Mr. M” to some students, Larry to his friends, and sometimes “Larz” to his football team — was home from work, home being his four-bedroom, three-bathroom house in Sun Prairie, Wisconsin.

He was sick with a cold. Nothing terrible, nothing he couldn’t power through if he wanted or needed to. He easily could have gone to school and played a movie for the class, maybe two days showing *Glory*. He loved that movie and showed it every year anyway. His American History class hadn't concluded their Civil War lessons (he usually showed it at the end of the lesson as a reward), but he could have pushed it up just to teach some classes without having to think while sick.

No matter, better to take the day off. Just a breather day.

His "vacation" day was spent reading an old James Patterson potboiler called *Kiss the Girls* that he'd picked up recently while at a yard sale. It looked like violent trash but he could enjoy such stuff from a certain type of passive distance as long as it predictably buzzed along, hit the right notes and clicked into place at all the appropriate times. He feared that, boys being boys, his sons would eventually go through a phase where the entertainment they consumed would consist mainly of violence and lurid sex. He knew there was nothing he could do for that except try and be an appropriate guide and lead by example.

He'd suggested Holly take the day off, too. She was pregnant, after all. With the boys at daycare, it'd be just the two of them. When's the last time that happened? Last year she'd worked part-time, but once they'd planned on having another child, she started working full-time again to get her salary up so when she got pregnant again she could take prime advantage of her maternity leave benefits with a max salary. She would almost certainly not return to work after giving birth this third time. (He said he wanted her to stay home, and she agreed but expressed mealy-mouthed worry about being bored at home. He knew she was leaning toward his view. Regardless of her currently expressed opinion, they had long ago agreed that she needed to stay at home for the kids and he knew that's how it would shake out eventually, just give her time to come to the conclusion on her own.)

Come to think of it, he was glad he was home alone, actually. It was relaxing. He'd sent Holly a bunch of lovey-dovey texts, which she'd reciprocated in kind. It was nice to unwind, stretch out. Leftover chicken marsala and angel hair to look forward to for lunch, alongside last night's saved football recaps on ESPN. For now, Honey Nut Crunch swimming in whole milk (not that weak skim his wife preferred for whatever reason), a nice Red Delicious apple, and a cup of dank Folgers coffee.

He'd taken a break from the Patterson potboiler and sat at his kitchen table, right hand working the spoon, index and middle finger of his left hand scrolling through the day's stories on his tablet. It was strange being home alone: he couldn't really remember the last time he'd spent a day at home alone, just admiring the place he lived sans noise and bustle. It was a nice house, he thought, taking it all in. It would have been outside their budget had his father not paid the twenty percent down payment as — what had he called it? — a combination wedding and first-child present. The remodeling on the kitchen was particularly tip-top: he'd gotten a good deal, his uncle had hooked him up with a good contractor. It was a fine home to be in, a fine place to raise a family. He was proud of himself for seeing the potential in it, assessing the good schools and the proximity to all the amenities nearby Madison had to offer.

He heard a knock on the front door.

Larry was in a gray *Under Armour* hoodie sweatshirt and blue jeans. For a moment he had an irrational concern that he was in sweatpants and needed to change before being seen by a potential stranger or neighbor. He just *felt* like he was wearing sweatpants; that's the mindset of being indolent.

Larry went to the front door and peered through the peep hole. He saw a stranger, a young man who looked to be in his early twenties, maybe even so young as to be eighteen or nineteen. He had shaggy dirty-blonde hair and a lip piercing, wore a casually distressed gray and black striped flannel sweater and what appeared to be tight-fitting black pants. This stranger was probably too young to know about Kurt Cobain, but if he did, that might be the template for his style. He didn't scan as any of the neighbor's kids or anything — none of the people he knew around here had kids that old — and anyway, even if they did, this kid looked college-aged and colleges were all in session. Unless he was some community college kid, maybe.

"Who is it?" Larry asked through the door.

"It's open door," came the response from the kid. The kid had a deeper, stronger voice than expected. Larry hadn't given it much thought, but he'd expected something whispier or mumblier.

He almost said "open door who?" like he was setting up the kid's joke when Larry distinctly heard the bolt in the door turn. It then opened.

Larry's hand dropped from the door like it was aflame. The kid waltzed in and turned to the partially open door, his back to Larry, his voice speaking over the snatch of outside noise and the errant chirping bird.

"There it is. There's open door." And then, without being touched, the door closed decisively. Not dramatically, not loudly, but with a steady firmness of finality. The kid turned to face him.

"Get out of here," Larry ordered without inflection. Then his fears caught up with his brain and he felt the snatch-jolt live-wire explosion of panic, what a rabbit must feel when the hawk plucks it from off the ground. Larry stepped back, and in the process, took stock of this young man who had come into his home. He was of average height, not particularly tough-looking, not well-muscled, did not appear to be armed or even have any obvious motive for what he was doing. Larry could take this kid in a fight if it came to that. He imagined the one-leg tackle and chokehold he could employ.

"You can call me Brandon. It's what our mutual friend calls me."

"I'm telling you, Brandon, you can't just come into someone's house like this." His faith flashed to mind and provided an instantly charitable interpretation of events, one that his instincts compelled against but his faith interceded on behalf of. This odd kid, perhaps he was not all there in the head. Maybe he was just slow and meant no harm, needed to be guided back to his house. Maybe he was lost?

"Rest assured, I'm at the right place. You can continue being hateful again."

Larry's eyes narrowed and then relaxed. "Brandon, Brandon," and Larry put forward his palms like he was soothing a barking dog. "You need to leave. I don't know what you want, but I don't have anything here, and I'm armed. You need to get out of here right now before I call the cops."

"So many threats to unpack there."

They were facing each other, perhaps two yards away.

There seemed to exist two timelines, one where they faced each for a few moments; another parallel timeline where the front door emanated a slimy, foamy skin of barren black sky, which rose as suddenly as bread rising in a flash forward scene in a commercial. The foam pulled slightly away from the door itself, then separated with a pop, like how a bubble could disembark separately from a soapy solution. This midnight simulacra of the front door went between them, blocking Brandon from Larry's view.

The door then opened, revealing Brandon standing impassively, just as he had moments before this door passed between them. The door closed, then opened simultaneously, letting out a sonic blast of a scream as a universe of spikes and shapes and twirling forms that recalled both swirling galaxies and germs under a microscope rocketed to and fro between the inner frames of this phantom door. This all appeared for an iota of a moment, and all of it — the black door, the swirling galaxies within the door — vanished, to again reveal an impassive Brandon.

Now it was just the two of them, collapsed back into the normal timeline, back to reality.

"Now do you get me? I hate to be dramatic. But I know you like simple things, right? See, black gooey things like that are scary. They are bad things. I showed you a bad thing. So, are you scared now?"

"I, I, I don't know what you want. I don't know who you are. I have a family."

Brandon smiled and took a step forward, which caused a ramming conflict inside Larry's brain. *Run, run, run* mixed with *don't upset him, you won't get away*, and these two sentiments plowed into each other to produce nothing but an inchoate runner's stance, a slight bend in Larry's right leg.

"Well, you have a family? Oh, okay. Hold on, let me head out for a second and go kill your entire family, and then I can come back, okay? What would you say then? 'Don't hurt me, I used to have a family?' Maybe, 'take pity on me, I'm grieving here!'" Brandon laughed, a normal, human laugh, the laugh of a young man finding something genuinely amusing and delightful.

"I'll give you the liberty of asking me one question. Go ahead, whatever you ask and I'll answer it."

Larry arched his back with a pause. He was scanning the

immediate area. Nothing weapon-worthy within his grasp.

"Who are you?"

"Brandon. I already said that. Our mutual friend calls me Brandon and that's good enough for you. Really, you should have asked me 'what are you?' That would have been such a better answer. Even our mutual friend doesn't know that.

"What the hell, I'll give you a not-entirely-accurate-but-better-than-nothing answer to that question. I'm the patron saint of bullied kids. You know all about the saints, don't you, Larry, with your Christian Studies minor.

"Do you remember a boy you went to middle school and high school with named Thomas Egeland?"

Larry was doing his best to maintain eye contact, size up his opponent, and take stock of the best moment to make a move. He thought of the black ink door and his resolve vanished. He knew deep down that tackling this kid wouldn't do the trick.

"I asked you a question, Larry."

"I remember the name. Is that why you're here?"

"You remember the name? That all?"

"I remember him. I haven't spoken to him in years."

"And why would you? Still in the bully business?"

Larry made a face and shook his head, both side-to-side and a bit diagonally, as if not only to convey "no," but that the premise was absurd.

"You tormented him. You tormented him, and what makes it fascinating to me is that you knew better and still did it. You did it quite effectively, I must add. You brutalized him so badly that his discovery that you were doing quite well for yourself really threw him for a loop. We got him yelling out nonsense incantations in a park in Chicago like a crazy person, that's how bad we got him."

"Does he live in Chicago now? I'm glad for him. He must be doing well, he was a smart guy. I know I can't defend whatever it is I did that angered you so badly. But, it's, I was young, I was just a kid. We both were. You know how kids are. I mean, you're almost a kid yourself. How old are you?"

"I'm both older and younger than you think. You see, when you watch movies and there's something with the abilities that I have, they're always ancient. So I can say I'm ancient and you'd believe me. I could make you believe me. But I'm not. I'm actually pretty young. Maybe that's why I identify so well with the young and the tormented. This is just a hobby of mine, really, but it's a hobby I'm really committed to.

"When I make sure all the important things are in order, I console the smart and tormented of the world. I offer them a friendly ear and let them feel assured that I can make their problems go away. And spectacularly so, if they want. And only some say yes right away, most don't, but eventually, they always come around.

"So, yes, it's Thomas Egeland that brings me here."

Brandon took a step forward and there was almost another parallel world blossoming. Larry saw through Brandon as translucent, a perfect white form against a pitch-black world, and saw the outlines of the impossibly dimensioned fish and organs that swam inside him. It was a nonsense illusion, but one that served a purpose, as it quelled whatever part of Larry that still had faith that he could overpower Brandon by conventional means.

"We can work it out. Is Thomas here? We can work this out."

"We are working it out."

Brandon was now tenderly embracing him, both his hands meeting within each other at the small of Larry's back.

"We are working it out Larry. I don't know what you had in mind, but we are."

Brandon breathed into his ear, the sound of a cherished intimate divulging that which is vitally important.

"I don't know what you think you are, or how you think about yourself, but we both know that you haven't really changed. People don't change. You were an opportunistic bully back then, and to the extent you aren't now, it is only because there'd be repercussions that you aren't comfortable with. But you are still fundamentally a terrible person. We both know that.

"You have your faith, and that's great. But we both know who you are. Let's just skip the denials and get on with it."

"Okay," Larry said back, lower than a normal speaking voice but nowhere as breathy as Brandon's sotto voce.

"I like the way your voice sounds. So quiet. Try it again, even quieter."

"Okay." Larry's voice was tiny and soft.

"I like that," Brandon whispered back huskily. "So, okay Larry, I want you to think of all the people you disappointed by being such a bully. Does your wife know? Did your parents know? What would your children think of you? Do they suspect it, in the way you act, that maybe Daddy's a monster? That Daddy likes feeling powerful at the expense of the weak?"

"I'm sorry, sir. Brandon. I'm sorry ... I'm sorry to Thomas. If we are being honest, there, there were others I've bullied in my life, too, taken advantage of. Not only Thomas. I'm just being honest, sir."

"Oh, I appreciate your honesty so much. I'm sure you work hard on it. You are a teacher now. You have children in your charge."

"Yes, sir. I do."

"That's very good, Larry." Brandon's voice was so piercingly soft, the feather-bed exhalations of his breath titillated Larry's inner ear and he found the whole exchange strangely euphoric.

"You can understand by now that I have the ability to watch people over a long period of time. I've been friends with Thomas ever since he was fourteen. So why did you do it? Teenage popularity? Attention? Just the thrill of dominating?

"I told Thomas I'd hurt you very badly. In fact, I told him I'd kill you."

The talk of violence put an end to the strange delight of Brandon's mouthy breathing, their euphonious exchange.

"But don't worry, I'm not going to. Don't worry, be calm, be calm, be calm. Can you do that for me, just be calm and listen. I'm not going to hurt you. I swear. I swear on a higher power than you know, trust me. Okay. Just let me explain.

"See, I needed to earn his trust and get his permission to hurt you. I have my own plans, you know? My own motives. It's a bit ironic, isn't it? I'm not a bully like you, but we all have our own plans and our own uses for people. Don't you agree?"

"Yes, I agree."

"I might have lied to him, but he's my friend, after all. That part was true. I didn't fake that. So I still need something from you. I need to hear you apologize. You apologize, and do it meaningfully, and that will be that. I'll have gotten what I needed, and before I leave my friend for good, I'll be able to tell him honestly that you were sorry, and that you plunged the depths of yourself and came to grips with the real person you are, and pledged to make every promise to change, okay?"

"Yes. I understand. And I really am sorry."

"Thomas wasn't perfect, either. He has to reflect upon the way he was at fourteen, and do his own soul-searching, do you understand? This will benefit everyone."

"Yes, I understand, of course. That makes a lot of sense."

"Now think of your wife, Larry. Your loving wife. What's her name?"

"Holly."

"Holly what? It's Holly Mullens, right? Give yourself some credit."

"Yes, Holly Mullens."

"She has to have seen something in you, right? There had to been something good in you, right? Refine that for me, will you?"

"Yes-"

"And think of your children, both the two you have and the one on the way. See, I can't have a wife, I can't have children. That's not the world I come from. If we were friends and in a different situation, boy, could I tell you some stories. But you have this incredible gift, to love and marry and reproduce, that I don't. I often think, if I wasn't stuck to this life, what I could do if I was so blessed."

Larry swallowed hard and nodded. "It's a struggle. It's a struggle, it truly is sir. Light and darkness exist inside all of us, and I'm really, I'm really trying to move myself closer to the light."

"I know, Larry."

"Thank you."

"So, think of them. Your family. And when you hug them later tonight, when you cradle the belly of your pregnant wife, I want you to hug them with the vigor of a man who is morally and spiritually reborn. Can you do that for me?"

"Yes." Larry's face was dewy with trickling tears.

"Good. And first you must expiate your sorrow, your remorse."

"I do, sir, I do. I am so, so, so sorry. I - I promise you, sir. I promise you."

"I know, my son. This is a way for things to work for all of us.

I'm freed of my responsibility, you get to express remorse, and Thomas gets the apology long owed to him."

Brandon's head rested now on Larry's shoulder. Larry felt the moisture of Brandon's rheumy, relieved eyes. Brandon was crying. Larry placed an affectionate hand on his back.

"I'm so happy, Larry. I feel the love you have for your family. This might not mean anything to you, but I'm happy, too. These are tears of happiness, Larry. Or exemplars for tears. I don't really cry that way, but you get the point. I'm so happy.

"See, I've been lying to you. That family you are thinking about, that family that you associate with those misplaced feelings you have, they are never going to see you again, Larry. Do you think I'd betray my friend like that?

"You won't even get the dignity of understanding how you're dying."

Whatever wells inside someone to let them know they are experiencing discomfort, Larry felt that. It was a sour feeling, with things shifting until they ruptured, all carefully calibrated, a pinhole of pain opening up until the geyser was uncontrollable. But the sources and sequences of the pain were behind the gaze of the mind. His insides were a mass of bridges and highways with backed-up traffic, inscrutable signs with arrows pointing in all directions and leaking infrastructure.

His nose filled with the putrid, pathetic smell of sulfur, and his stomach was heavy with a blocked fullness.

He saw in his mind the rosette of a pineapple, with waxy, needle-tipped, upcurved spines, extending and then snapping off. As if awaking from a narcotic, Larry looked down as he saw all ten of his fingers break off at the knuckles. Then his brain exploded and the pain surged and he was ensorcelled behind a wall of stupor, thinking bewitching thoughts of nothing; then he was a crate of provisions about to be air-dropped off a plane. He heard the crew talk idly about the mission. He was screaming, "No, there's been a mistake! There's been a mistake!" and then he was descending beyond the speed of light, his body aflame, anticipating the horrendous impact, but it wouldn't come;

And there'd be an eagle spearing a fish with its talon and soaring upward and there he was, too, pinioned in place by both scythe and wind while being disemboweled;

And a hundred times he'd be restored again, waking up back next to his wife, the details so comfortably punctilious it just had to be real life — the smells, the sounds, the expressions, the angles — only each time ripped away to the ever-expanding present;

Now his half tongue intertwined with barbed marionette wires;

No sight out of his left eye, only a pressure, what a sentient tree must feel as it experienced growth from its roots;

With his right eye, he saw the nerves and brambles of his left eye extend and curve like a race track, the orb that was his eye appearing like an exploded mushroom at the end of a kebab.

No, make it stop! and there'd be the voice beneath it all, whispering the way out at a register just a drop too low to be understood.

>< >< ><

Twenty-nine-year-old Thomas Egeland heard a knock at his door.

"Thanks for giving me the dignity of knocking on the door."

"I said I'd knock first."

"I know, I know, I'm just playing, come in. Thanks for coming back so quickly. I have a difficult time concentrating on anything when something really important is weighing over me. Like sometimes in college, my stomach would hurt sometimes from stress and I'd be convinced it was, like, stomach cancer or something, so then I'd think, why bother showering or doing anything if I have stomach cancer, you know? I can get worked up like that. That's why I had to get into rituals, you know, they help kind of box myself in mentally, keep me on track. Like, shower every day no matter what, you know."

Thomas knew why he'd gotten stomach pains from stress: post-traumatic stress disorder. He could pretend otherwise, but that's what it was.

"It's done, Thomas. I just wanted to let you know that. It's done. What was coming, came. Justice has been served. I just wanted you to hear it from me."

Antsy, Thomas meant to say, "where else would I hear it from?" but then thought better of it. Then he thought about probing, to test the limits of what details he could endure.

"You know, I had a dream that I was fourteen again. I woke up in my childhood bed and everything. The details were exact. The *Calvin and Hobbes* cut-outs on the door and everything. I thought this had all been a dream and I'd woken up to face another day of school, of Larry. I was sure of it."

"Sounds terrifying."

"It was. You were right, at that moment I would have done anything to come back to reality. You have anything to do with that?"

"Nope."

"Are you sure?"

Brandon smiled, a smile that no one could deny. "I'm sure."

"I'm trusting you."

"While dreaming you were fourteen again, you should have tried sleeping *inside* your dream and dreaming *as* a fourteen-year-old. Maybe you could have conjured up that young girl you used to dream about, and hold onto her, maybe you could have dragged her out of your dreams and into the real world."

"Creepy."

Brandon shrugged.

"So," Thomas asked. "How'd it go with Larry?"

"Justice has been served."

Thomas didn't probe. He nodded solemnly.

Brandon curled both hands around Thomas's shoulders.

"You've done the right thing, Thomas. Just know that. You might have your doubts. Doubts are the natural corollary of the moral mind, because the moral mind investigates and interrogates. A moral mind is a thinking mind, and a component of a thinking mind is its restlessness. Even when a moral, thinking mind reaches a sound conclusion, it still re-investigates, re-interrogates. And during that process, when you have your doubts, you feel a kind of psychic pain. And I hope you continue to realize you've done the right thing. You have. From all my collected wisdom, please trust me.

"It's an uncaring universe. You know that. But that means things can go either way. Your mind dwells on the bad. But sometimes, something can come out of the universe and do something good for you. It's not all terrible."

And Brandon hugged his friend and Thomas hugged him back. Thomas started closing his eyes, and for the time between when his eyes began to contract and their closure he was fourteen again, waking up for another day of school, another day as scurrying prey for the sadists, and a sense-fear quaked inside him, so he fastened his eyes shut so the tears would be choked out of being.

Thomas hugged his friend tighter, to expatiate the residue of fear and terror that seemed to fill his nerves with that passing sense-memory.

The fear dissipated. Thomas was free, and whirling about him like faerie dust was the fullness of life, which was, he realized, only the feeling of being free from terror, of knowing security. But it was the best feeling in the world. To know security was the highest form of enlightenment.

"You were my best friend, Brandon. And you still are. I can never thank you enough."

And he tightened his hug and smiled, with a feeling of joyfulness he'd never felt before, that he'd never even known was possible, now knowing that there really were bonds that didn't break, friends that didn't abandon or forget about you, and, indeed, things approaching miracles existing in this world.

52842413R00219

Made in the USA
San Bernardino, CA
10 September 2019